S0-CFE-209

Also by Graham Greene

THE COMEDIANS

THE
COMEDIANS

Graham Greene

THE VIKING PRESS · NEW YORK

Copyright © 1965, 1966 by Graham Greene
All rights reserved

Viking Compass Edition

Issued in 1970 by The Viking Press, Inc.
625 Madison Avenue, New York, N.Y. 10022

SBN 670-23208-4 (hardbound)
SBN 670-00287-9 (paperbound)

Library of Congress catalog card number: 66-12636

Printed in U.S.A.

. . . aspects are within us, and who seems
Most kingly is the King.

—THOMAS HARDY

To A. S. Frere

Dear Frere,

When you were the head of a great London publishing firm I was one of your most devoted authors, and, when you ceased to be a publisher, I, like many other writers on your list, felt it was time to find another home. This is the first novel I have written since then, and I want to offer it to you in memory of more than thirty years of association—a cold word to represent all the advice (which you never expected me to take), all the encouragement (which you never realized I needed), all the affection and fun of the ·years we shared.

A word about the characters in *The Comedians*. I am unlikely to bring an action for libel against myself with any success, yet I want to make it clear that the narrator of this tale, though his name is Brown, is not Greene. Many readers assume—I know it from experience—that an "I" is always the author. So in my time I have been considered the murderer of a friend, the jealous lover of a civil servant's wife, and an obsessive player at roulette. I don't wish to add to my chameleon nature the characteristics belonging to the cuckolder of a South American diplomat, a possibly illegitimate birth and an education by the Jesuits. Ah, it may be said, Brown is a Catholic and so, we know, is Greene. . . . It is often forgotten that, even in the case of a novel laid in England, the story, when it contains more than ten characters, would lack verisimilitude if at least one of them were not a

Catholic. Ignorance of this fact of social statistics sometimes gives the English novel a provincial air.

"I" is not the only imaginary character: none of the others, from such minor players as the British chargé to the principals, has ever existed. A physical trait taken here, a habit of speech, an anecdote—they are boiled up in the kitchen of the unconscious and emerge unrecognizable even to the cook in most cases.

Poor Haiti itself and the character of Doctor Duvalier's rule are not invented, the latter not even blackened for dramatic effect. Impossible to deepen that night. The Tontons Macoute are full of men more evil than Concasseur; the interrupted funeral is drawn from fact; many a Joseph limps the streets of Port-au-Prince after his spell of torture, and, though I have never met the young Philipot, I have met guerrillas as courageous and as ill-trained in that former lunatic asylum near Santo Domingo. Only in Santo Domingo have things changed since I began this book—for the worse.

Affectionately,

GRAHAM GREENE

Part One

Chapter One

1

When I think of all the grey memorials erected in London to equestrian generals, the heroes of old colonial wars, and to frock-coated politicians who are even more deeply forgotten, I can find no reason to mock the modest stone that commemorates Jones on the far side of the international road which he failed to cross in a country far from home, though I am not to this day absolutely sure of where, geographically speaking, Jones's home lay. At least he paid for the monument—however unwillingly—with his life, while the generals as a rule came home safe and paid, if at all, with the blood of their men, and as for the politicians—who cares for dead politicians sufficiently to remember with what issues they were identified? Free Trade is less interesting than an Ashanti war, though the London pigeons do not distinguish between the two. *Exegi monumentum.* Whenever my rather bizarre business takes me north to Monte Cristi and I pass the stone, I feel a certain pride that my action helped to raise it.

There is a point of no return unremarked at the time in most lives. Neither Jones nor I knew of it when it came, although like the pilots of the old pre-jet air-liners, we should have been trained by the nature of our two careers to better observance. Certainly I was quite unaware of the moment when it receded one sullen August morning on the Atlantic in the wake of the *Medea*, a cargo-ship of the Royal Netherlands Steamship Company, bound for Haiti and Port-au-Prince from Philadelphia and

3

New York. At that period of my life I still regarded my future seriously—even the future of my empty hotel and of a love-affair which was almost as empty. I was not involved, so far as I could tell, with either Jones or Smith, they were fellow passengers, that was all, and I had no idea of the *pompes funèbres* they were preparing for me in the parlours of Mr. Fernandez. If I had been told I would have laughed, as I laugh now on my better days.

The level of the pink gin in my glass shifted with the movement of the boat, as though the glass were an instrument made to record the shock of the waves, as Mr. Smith said firmly in reply to Jones, "I've never suffered from *mal de mer*, no sir. It's the effect of acidity. Eating meat gives you acidity, drinking alcohol does the same." He was one of the Smiths of Wisconsin, but I had thought of him from the very first as the Presidential Candidate because, before I even knew his surname, his wife had so referred to him, as we leant over the rail our first hour at sea. She made a jerking movement with her strong chin as she spoke which seemed to indicate that, if there were another Presidential candidate on board, he was not the one she intended. She said, "I mean my husband there, Mr. Smith—he was Presidential candidate in 1948. He's an idealist. Of course, for that very reason, he stood no chance." What could we have been talking about to lead her to that statement? We were idly watching the flat grey sea, which seemed to lie within the three-mile limit like an animal passive and ominous in a cage waiting to show what it can do outside. I may have spoken to her of an acquaintance who played the piano and perhaps her mind leapt to Truman and thus to politics—she was far more politically conscious than her husband. I think she believed that as a candidate she would have stood a better chance than he, and, following the pointer of her protruding chin, I could well imagine it possible. Mr. Smith, who wore a shabby raincoat turned up to guard his large, innocent, hairy ears, was pacing the deck behind us, one lock of white hair standing up like a television aerial in the wind, and

4

a travelling-rug carried over his arm. I could imagine him a homespun poet or perhaps the president of an obscure college, but never a politician. I tried to remember who Truman's opponent had been in that election year—surely it had been Dewey, not Smith, while the wind from the Atlantic took away her next sentence. I thought she said something about vegetables, but the word seemed an unlikely one to me then.

Jones I met a little later under embarrassing circumstances, for he was engaged in trying to bribe the bedroom-steward to swop our cabins. He stood in the doorway of mine with a suitcase in one hand and two five-dollar bills in the other. He was saying, "He hasn't been down yet. He won't make a fuss. He's not that kind of a chap. Even if he notices the difference." He spoke as if he knew me.

"But Mr. Jones . . ." the steward began to argue.

Jones was a small man very tidily dressed in a pale grey suit with a double-breasted waistcoat which somehow looked out of place away from elevators, office-crowds, the clatter of typewriters—it was the only one of its kind in our scrubby cargo-ship peddling the sullen sea. He never changed it, I noticed later, not even on the night of the ship's concert, and I began to wonder whether perhaps his suitcases contained no other clothes at all. I thought of him as someone who, having packed in a hurry, had brought the wrong uniform, for he certainly did not mean to be conspicuous. With the little black moustache and the dark Pekinese eyes I would have taken him for a Frenchman— perhaps someone on the Bourse—and it was quite a surprise to me when I learnt that his name was Jones.

"Major Jones," he replied to the steward with a note of reproof.

I was almost as embarrassed as he was. On a cargo-steamer there are few passengers and it is uncomfortable to nourish a resentment. The steward with his hands folded said to him righteously, "There's really nothing I can do, sir. The cabin was reserved for this gentleman. For Mr. Brown." Smith, Jones, and Brown—the situation was improbable. I had a half-right to my

5

drab name, but had he? I smiled at his predicament, but Jones's sense of humour, as I was to find, was of a simpler order. He looked at me with grave attention and said, "This is really your cabin, sir?"

"I have an idea it is."

"Someone told me it was unoccupied." He shifted slightly so that his back was turned to my too obvious cabin-trunk standing just inside. The bills had disappeared, perhaps up his sleeve, for I had seen no movement towards his pocket.

"Have they given you a bad cabin?" I asked.

"Oh, it's only that I prefer the starboard side."

"Yes, so do I, on this particular run. One can leave the port-hole open," and as though to emphasize the truth of what I said the boat began a slow roll as it moved further into the open sea.

"Time for a pink gin," Jones said promptly, and we went upstairs together to find the small saloon and the black steward, who took the first opportunity as he added water to my gin to whisper in my ear, "I'm a British subject, sah." I noticed that he made no such claim to Jones.

The door of the saloon swung open and the Presidential Candidate appeared, an impressive figure in spite of the innocent ears: he had to lower his head in the doorway. Then he looked all round the saloon before he stood aside so that his wife could enter under the arch of his arm, like a bride under a sword. It was as though he wanted to satisfy himself first that there was no unsuitable company present. His eyes were of clear washed blue and he had homely sprouts of grey hair from his nose and ears. He was a genuine article, if ever there was one, a complete contrast to Mr. Jones. If I had troubled to think of them then at all, I would have thought that they could mix together no better than oil and water.

"Come in," Mr. Jones said (I somehow couldn't bring myself to think of him as Major Jones), "come in and take a snifter." His slang, I was to find, was always a little out of date, as though he had studied it in a dictionary of popular usage, but not in the latest edition.

"You must forgive me," Mr. Smith replied with courtesy, "but I don't touch alcohol."

"I don't touch it myself," Jones said. "I drink it." And he suited the action to the words. "The name is Jones," he added. "Major Jones."

"Pleased to meet you, Major. My name's Smith. William Abel Smith. My wife, Major Jones." He looked at me enquiringly, and I realized that somehow I had lagged behind in the introductions.

"Brown," I said shyly. I felt as though I were making a bad joke, but neither of them saw the point.

"Ring the bell again," Jones said, "there's a good chap." I had already graduated into the position of the old friend, and although Mr. Smith was nearer the bell, I crossed the saloon to touch it; in any case he was busy wrapping the travelling-rug around his wife's knees, though the saloon was well enough warmed (perhaps it was a marital habit). It was then, in reply to Jones's affirmation that there was nothing like a pink gin to keep away sea-sickness, Mr. Smith made his statement of faith. "I've never suffered from *mal de mer*, no sir. . . . I've been a vegetarian all my life," and his wife capped it. "We campaigned on that issue."

"Campaigned?" Jones asked sharply, as though the word had woken the major within him.

"In the Presidential election of 1948."

"You were a candidate?"

"I'm afraid," Mr. Smith said with a gentle smile, "that I stood very little chance. The two great parties . . ."

"It was a gesture," his wife interrupted fiercely. "We showed our flag."

Jones was silent. Perhaps he was impressed, or perhaps like myself he was trying to recall who the main contestants had been. Then he tried the phrase over on his tongue as though he liked the taste of it: "Presidential candidate in '48." He added, "I'm very proud to meet you."

"We had no organization," Mrs. Smith said. "We couldn't afford it. But all the same we polled more than ten thousand votes."

"I never anticipated so much support," the Presidential Candidate said.

"We were not at the bottom of the poll. There was a candidate—something to do with agriculture, dear?"

"Yes, I have forgotten the exact name of his party. He was a disciple of Henry George, I think."

"I must admit," I said, "that I thought the only candidates were Republican and Democrat—oh, and there was a Socialist too, wasn't there?"

"The conventions attract all the publicity," Mrs. Smith said, "vulgar rodeos though they are. Can you see Mr. Smith with a lot of drum majorettes?"

"Anyone can run for President," the Candidate explained with gentleness and humility. "That is the pride of our democracy. I can tell you, it was a great experience for me. A great experience. One that I shall never forget."

2

Ours was a very small boat. I believe that a full complement of passengers would have numbered only fourteen, and the *Medea* was by no means full. This was not the tourist season, and in any case the island to which we were bound was no longer an attraction for tourists.

There was a spick-and-span Negro with a very high white collar and starched cuffs and gold-rimmed glasses who was bound for Santo Domingo; he kept very much to himself, and at table he answered politely and ambiguously in monosyllables. For instance when I asked him what was the principal cargo that the captain was likely to take aboard in Trujillo—I corrected myself, "I'm sorry. I mean Santo Domingo," he nodded gravely and said, "Yes." He never himself asked a question and his discretion seemed to rebuke our own idle curiosity. There was also a traveller for a firm of pharmaceutical manufacturers —I have forgotten the reason he gave for not travelling by air. I felt sure that it was not the correct reason, and that he suffered from a heart-trouble which he kept to himself. His face had a tight papery look, above a body too big for the head, and he lay long hours in his berth.

My own reason for taking the boat—and I sometimes suspected that it might be Jones's too—was prudence. In an airport one is so swiftly separated on the tarmac from the crew of the plane; in a harbour one feels the safety of foreign boards under the feet—I counted as a citizen of Holland so long as I stayed on the *Medea*. I had booked my passage through to Santo Domingo and I told myself, however unconvincingly, that I had no intention of leaving the ship before I received certain assurances from the British consul—or from Martha. The hotel which I owned on the hills above the capital had done without me for three months; it would certainly be void of clients, and I valued my life more highly than an empty bar and a corridor of empty bedrooms and a future empty of promise. As for the Smiths, I really think it was love of the sea which had brought them on board, but it was quite a while before I learnt why they had chosen to visit the republic of Haiti.

The captain was a thin unapproachable Hollander, scrubbed clean like a piece of his own brass rail, who only appeared once at table, and in contrast the purser was untidy and ebulliently gay with a great liking for Bols gin and Haitian rum. On the second day at sea he invited us to drink with him in his cabin. We all squashed in except for the traveller in pharmaceutical products, who said that he must always be in bed by nine. Even the gentleman from Santo Domingo joined us and answered, "No," when the purser asked him how he found the weather.

The purser had a jovial habit of exaggerating everything, and his natural gaiety was only a little damped when the Smiths demanded bitter lemon, and when that was unavailable, Coca-

9

Cola. "You're drinking your own deaths," he told them and began to explain his own theory of how the secret ingredients were manufactured. The Smiths were unimpressed and drank the Coca-Cola with evident pleasure. "You will need something stronger than that where you are going," the purser said.

"My husband and I have never taken anything stronger," Mrs. Smith replied.

"The water is not to be trusted, and you will find no Coca-Cola now that the Americans have moved out. At night when you hear the shooting in the streets you will think perhaps that a strong glass of rum . . ."

"Not rum," Mrs. Smith said.

"Shooting?" Mr. Smith enquired. "Is there shooting?" He looked at his wife where she sat crouched under the travelling-rug (she was not warm enough even in the stuffy cabin) with a trace of anxiety. "Why shooting?"

"Ask Mr. Brown. He lives there."

I said, "I've not often heard shooting. They act more silently as a rule."

"Who are *they*?" Mr. Smith asked.

"The Tontons Macoute," the purser broke in with wicked glee. "The President's bogey-men. They wear dark glasses and they call on their victims after dark."

Mr. Smith laid his hand on his wife's knee. "The gentleman is trying to scare us, my dear," he said. "They told us nothing about this at the tourist-bureau."

"He little knows," Mrs. Smith said, "that we don't scare easily," and somehow I believed her.

"You understand what we're talking about, Mr. Fernandez?" the purser called across the cabin in the high voice some people employ towards anyone of an alien race.

Mr. Fernandez had the glazed look of a man approaching sleep. "Yes," he said, but I think it had been an equal chance whether he replied yes or no. Jones, who had been sitting on the edge of the purser's bunk, nursing a glass of rum, spoke for the first time. "Give me fifty commandos," he said, "and I'd go through the country like a dose of salts."

"Were you in the commandos?" I asked with some surprise.

He said ambiguously, "A different branch of the same outfit."

The Presidential Candidate said, "We have a personal introduction to the Minister for Social Welfare."

"Minister for what?" the purser said. "Welfare? You won't find any Welfare there. You should see the rats, big as terriers . . ."

"I was told at the tourist-bureau that there were some very good hotels."

"I own one," I said. I took out my pocketbook and showed him three postcards. Although printed in bright vulgar colours they had the dignity of history, for they were relics of an epoch over forever. On one a blue tiled bathing-pool was crowded with girls in bikinis; on the second a drummer famous throughout the Caribbean was playing under the thatched roof of the Creole bar; and on the third—a general view of the hotel—there were gables and balconies and towers, the fantastic nineteenth-century architecture of Port-au-Prince. They at least had not changed.

"We had thought of something a little quieter," Mr. Smith said.

"We are quiet enough now."

"It would certainly be pleasant, wouldn't it, dear, to be with a friend. If you have a room vacant with a bath or a shower."

"Every room has a bath. Don't be afraid of noise. The drummer's fled to New York, and all the bikini girls stay in Miami now. You'll probably be the only guests I have."

These two clients, it had occurred to me, might be worth a good deal more than the money they paid. A Presidential candidate surely had status; he would be under the protection of his embassy or what was left of it. (When I had left Port-au-Prince the embassy staff had already been reduced to a chargé, a secretary, and two Marine guards, who were all that remained of the military mission.) Perhaps the same thought occurred to Jones. "I might join you too," he said, "if no other arrangements have been made for me. It would be a bit like staying on shipboard if we stuck together."

"Safety in numbers," the purser agreed.

"With three guests I shall be the most envied *hôtelier* in Port-au-Prince."

"It's not very safe to be envied," the purser said. "You would do much better, all three of you, if you continued with us. Myself I don't care to go fifty yards from the waterfront. There is a fine hotel in Santo Domingo. A luxurious hotel. I can show you picture postcards as good as his." He opened the drawer and I caught a brief glimpse of a dozen little square packets— French letters which he would sell at a profit to the crew when they went on shore to Mère Catherine's or one of the cheaper establishments. (His sales-talk, I felt certain, would consist of some grisly statistics.) "What have I done with them?" he de- manded uselessly of Mr. Fernandez, who smiled and said "Yes," and he began to search the desk littered with printed forms and paper-clips and bottles of red, green, and blue ink, and some old-fashioned wooden pen-holders and nibs, before he dis- covered a few limp postcards of a bathing-pool exactly like mine and a Creole bar which was only distinguishable because it had a different drummer.

"My husband is not on a vacation," Mrs. Smith said with disdain.

"I'd like to keep one if you don't mind," Jones said, choosing the bathing-pool and the bikinis. "One never knows . . ." That phrase represented, I think, his deepest research into the mean- ing of life.

3

Next day I sat in a deck-chair on the sheltered starboard side and let myself roll languidly in and out of the sun with the motions of the mauve-green sea. I tried to read a novel, but the heavy foreseeable progress of its characters down the uninteresting corridors of power made me drowsy, and when the book fell upon the deck, I did not bother to retrieve it. My eyes opened only when the traveller in pharmaceutical products passed by; he clung to the rail with two hands and seemed to climb along it as though it were a ladder. He was panting heavily and he had an expression of desperate purpose as though he knew to what the climb led and knew that it was worth his effort, but knew too that he would never have the strength to reach the end. Again I drowsed and found myself alone in a blacked-out room and someone touched me with a cold hand. I woke and it was Mr. Fernandez, who had, I suppose, been surprised by the steep roll of the boat and had steadied himself against me. I had the impression of a shower of gold dropping from a black sky as his spectacles caught the fitful sun. "Yes," he said, "yes," smiling an apology as he lurched upon his way.

It seemed as though a sudden desire for exercise had struck everyone except myself on the second day out. For next it was Mr. Jones—I still couldn't bring myself to call him Major—who passed steadily up the centre of the deck adjusting his gait to the movement of the ship. "Squally," he called to me as he went by, and again I had the impression that English was a language he had learnt from books—perhaps on this occasion from the works of Dickens. Then, unexpectedly, back came Mr. Fernandez, skidding in a wild way, and after him, painfully, the pharmacist on his laborious climb. He had lost his place, but he stuck the race out stubbornly. I began to wonder when the Presidential Candidate would appear, he must have had a heavy handicap, and at that moment he emerged from the saloon beside me. He was alone and looked unnaturally detached, like one of the figures in a weather-house without the other. "Breezy," he said, as though he were correcting Mr. Jones's English style, and sat down in the next chair.

"I hope Mrs. Smith is well."

"She's fine," he said, "fine. She's down there in the cabin getting up her French grammar. She said she couldn't concentrate with me around."

"French grammar?"

"They tell me that's the language spoken where we are going. Mrs. Smith is a wonderful linguist. Give her a few hours with a grammar and she'll know everything except the pronunciation."

"French hasn't come her way before?"

"That's no problem for Mrs. Smith. Once we had a German girl staying in the house—it wasn't half a day before Mrs. Smith was telling her to keep her room tidy in her own language. Another time we had a Finn. It took Mrs. Smith nearly a week before she could get her hands on a Finnish grammar, but then there was no stopping her." He paused and said with a smile that touched his absurdity with a strange dignity, "I've been married for thirty-five years and I've never ceased to admire that woman."

"Do you often," I asked disingenuously, "take holidays in these parts?"

"We try to combine a vacation," he said, "with our mission. Neither Mrs. Smith nor I are ones for undiluted pleasure."

"I see, and your mission this time is bringing you . . . ?"

"Once," he said, "we took our vacation in Tennessee. It was an unforgettable experience. You see we went as Freedom Riders. There was an occasion in Nashville on the way down when I feared for Mrs. Smith."

"It was a courageous way to spend a holiday."

He said, "We have a great love for coloured people." He seemed to think it was the only explanation needed.

"I'm afraid they'll prove a disappointment to you where you are going now."

"Most things disappoint till you look deeper."

"Coloured people can be as violent as the whites in Nashville."

"We have our troubles in the U.S.A. All the same I thought—perhaps—the purser was pulling my leg."

14

"He intended to. The joke's against him. The reality's worse than anything he can have seen from the waterfront. I doubt if he goes far into the town."

"You would advise us like he did—to go on to Santo Domingo?"

"Yes."

His eyes looked sadly out over the monotonous repetitive scape of sea. I thought I had made an impression. I said, "Let me give you an example of what life is like there."

I told Mr. Smith of a man who was suspected of being concerned in an attempt to kidnap the President's children on their way home from school. I don't think there was any evidence against him, but he had been the prize sharp-shooter of the republic at some international gathering in Panama, and perhaps they thought it needed a prize marksman to pick off the Presidential guard. So the Tontons Macoute surrounded his house—he wasn't there—and set it on fire with petrol and then they machine-gunned anyone who tried to escape. They allowed the fire-brigade to keep the flames from spreading, and now you could see the gap in the street like a drawn tooth.

Mr. Smith listened with attention. He said, "Hitler did worse, didn't he? and he was a white man. You can't blame it on their colour."

"I don't. The victim was coloured too."

"When you look properly at things, they are pretty bad everywhere. Mrs. Smith wouldn't like us to turn back just because . . ."

"I'm not trying to persuade you. You asked me a question."

"Then why is it—if you'll excuse another—that *you* are going back?"

"Because the only thing I own is there. My hotel."

"I guess the only thing we own—Mrs. Smith and me—is our mission." He sat staring at the sea, and at that moment Jones passed. He called at us over his shoulder, "Four times round," and went on.

"He's not afraid either," Mr. Smith said, as though he had to

15

apologize for showing courage, as a man might apologize for a rather loud tie which his wife had given him by pointing out that others wore the same.

"I wonder if it's courage in his case. Perhaps he's like me and he hasn't anywhere else to go."

"He's been very friendly to us both," Mr. Smith said firmly. It was obvious that he wished to change the subject.

When I knew Mr. Smith better I recognized that particular tone of voice. He was acutely uneasy if I spoke ill of anyone—even of a stranger or of an enemy. He would back away from the conversation like a horse from water. It amused me sometimes to draw him unsuspectingly to the very edge of the ditch and then suddenly urge him on, as it were, with whip and spurs. But I never managed to teach him how to jump. I think he soon began to divine what I was at, but he never spoke his displeasure aloud. That would have been to criticize a friend. He preferred just to edge away. This was one characteristic at least he did not share with his wife. I was to learn later how fiery and direct her nature could be—she was capable of attacking anyone, except of course the Presidential Candidate himself. I had many quarrels with her in the course of time, she suspected that I laughed a little at her husband, but she never knew how I envied them. I have never known in Europe a married couple with that kind of loyalty.

I said, "You were talking about your mission just now."

"Was I? You must excuse me, talking about myself like that. Mission is too big a word."

"I'm interested."

"Call it a hope. But I guess a man in your profession wouldn't find it very sympathetic."

"You mean it's got something to do with vegetarianism?"

"Yes."

"I'm not unsympathetic. My job is to please my guests. If my guests are vegetarian . . ."

"Vegetarianism isn't only a question of diet, Mr. Brown. It

touches life at many points. If we really eliminated acidity from the human body we would eliminate passion."

"Then the world would stop."

He reproved me gently, "I didn't say love," and I felt a curious sense of shame. Cynicism is cheap—you can buy it at any Monoprix store—it's built into all poor-quality goods.

"Anyway you're on the way to a vegetarian country," I said.

"How do you mean, Mr. Brown?"

"Ninety-five per cent of the people can't afford meat or fish or eggs."

"But hasn't it occurred to you, Mr. Brown, that it isn't the poor who make the trouble in the world? Wars are made by politicians, by capitalists, by intellectuals, by bureaucrats, by Wall Street bosses or Communist bosses—they are none of them made by the poor."

"And the rich and powerful aren't vegetarian, I suppose?"

"No sir. Not usually." Again I felt ashamed of my cynicism. I could believe for a moment, as I looked at those pale blue eyes, unflinching and undoubting, that perhaps he had a point. A steward stood at my elbow. I said, "I don't want soup."

"It's not time for soup yet, sah. The captain asks you kindly to have a word with him, sah."

The captain was in his cabin—an apartment as bare and as scrubbed as himself, with nothing personal anywhere except for one cabinet-sized photograph of a middle-aged woman who looked as if she had emerged that instant from her hairdresser's, where even her character had been capped under the drying helmet. "Sit down, Mr. Brown. Will you take a cigar?"

"No, no thank you."

The captain said, "I wish to come quickly to the point. I have to ask your cooperation. It is very embarrassing."

"Yes?"

He said in a tone heavy with gloom, "If there is one thing I do not like on a voyage it is the unexpected."

"I thought at sea . . . always . . . storms . . ."

"Naturally I am not talking of the sea. The sea presents no problem." He altered the position of an ash-tray, of a cigarbox, and then he moved a centimetre closer to him the photograph of the blank-faced woman whose hair seemed set in grey cement. Perhaps she gave him confidence: she would have given me a paralysis of the will. He said, "You have met this passenger Major Jones. He calls himself Major Jones."

"I've spoken to him."

"What are your impressions?"

"I hardly know . . . I hadn't thought . . ."

"I have just received a cable from my office in Philadelphia. They wish me to reply by cable when and where he lands."

"Surely you know from his ticket . . ."

"They wish to be sure that he does not alter his plans. We go on to Santo Domingo. . . . You have yourself explained to me that you have booked to Santo Domingo, in case at Port-au-Prince . . . He may have the same intention."

"Is it a police question?"

"It may be—it is my conjecture only—that the police are interested. I want you to understand that I have nothing against Major Jones. This is very possibly a routine enquiry set on foot because some filing-clerk . . . But I thought . . . you are a fellow Englishman, you live in Port-au-Prince, on my side a word of warning, and on yours . . ."

I was irritated by his absolute discretion, absolute correctness, absolute rectitude. Had the captain never slipped up once, in his youth or in his cups, in the absence of that well-coiffured wife of his? I said, "You make him sound like a card-sharper. I assure you that he hasn't once suggested a game."

"I never said . . ."

"You want me to keep my eyes open, my ears open?"

"Exactly. No more. If it were anything serious they would surely have asked me to detain him. Perhaps he has run away from his debtors. Who knows? Or some woman business," he added with distaste, meeting the gaze of the hard woman with the stony hair.

18

"Captain, with all respect, I'm not trained to be an informer."

"I am not asking anything like that, Mr. Brown. I cannot very well demand of an old man like Mr. Smith . . . in the case of Major Jones . . ." Again I was aware of the three names, interchangeable like comic masks in a farce. I said, "If I see anything that merits a report—I'm not going to look for it, mind." The captain gave a little sigh of self-commiseration. "As if there were not enough responsibilities for one man on this run . . ."

He began to tell me a long anecdote about something which had occurred two years before in the port we were coming to. At one in the morning there had been the sound of shots and half an hour later an officer and two policemen had appeared at the gangway: they wanted to search his ship. Naturally he had refused permission. This was sovereign territory of the Royal Netherlands Steamship Company. There had been a lot of argument. He had complete belief in his night-watchman— wrongly, as it turned out, for the man had been asleep at his post. Then on his way to speak to the officer of the watch the captain had noticed a trail of blood-spots. It led him to one of the boats and there he had discovered the fugitive.

"What did you do?" I asked.

"He was attended by the ship's doctor and then of course I handed him over to the proper authorities."

"Perhaps he was seeking political asylum."

"I do not know what he was seeking. How could I? He was quite illiterate, and in any case he had no money for his passage."

4

When I saw Jones again, after the interview with the captain, I felt a prejudice in his favour. If he had asked me to play poker at that moment I would have consented without hesitation and gladly have lost to him, for an exhibition of trust might have removed the bad taste which remained in my mouth. I took the port-side route around the deck to avoid Mr. Smith and was slapped with spray; before I could dive down to the cabin I met Mr. Jones face to face. I felt guilty, as though I had already betrayed his secret, when he stopped his walk to offer me a drink.

"It's a bit early," I said.

"Opening time in London." I looked at my watch—it read five minutes to eleven—and felt as though I were checking his credentials. While he went in search of the steward I picked up the book he had left behind him in the saloon. It was an American paperback with the picture of a naked girl sprawled face down upon a luxurious bed and the title was *No Time Like the Present*. Inside the cover in pencil was scrawled his signature— H. J. Jones. Was he establishing his identity or reserving this particular book for his personal library? I opened it at random. " 'Trust?' Geoff's voice struck her like a whiplash . . ." And then Jones came back carrying two lagers. I put the book down and said with unnecessary embarrassment, "*Sortes Virgilianae*."

"*Sortes* what?" Jones raised his glass and turning the pages of his mental dictionary and perhaps rejecting "mud in your eye" as obsolete brought out a more modern term, "Cheers." He added after a swallow, "I saw you talking to the captain just now."

"Yes?"

"An unapproachable old bastard. He'll talk only to the toffs." The word had an antique flavour: this time his dictionary had certainly failed him.

"I wouldn't call myself a toff."

"You mustn't mind me saying that. Toff has a special sense for me. I divide the world into two parts—the toffs and the tarts. The toffs can do without the tarts, but the tarts can't do without the toffs. I'm a tart."

"What exactly is your idea of a tart? It seems to be a bit special too."

"The toffs have a settled job or a good income. They have a stake somewhere like you have in your hotel. The tarts—well, we pick a living here and there—in saloon-bars. We keep our ears open and our eyes skinned."

"You live on your wits, is that it?"

"Or we die of them often enough."

"And the toffs—haven't they any wits?"

"They don't need wits. They have reason, intelligence, character. We tarts—we sometimes go too fast for our own good."

"And the other passengers—are they tarts or toffs?"

"I can't make out Mr. Fernandez. He might be either. And the chemist chap, he's given us no opportunity to judge. But Mr. Smith—he's a real toff if ever there was one."

"You sound as though you admire the toffs?"

"We'd all like to be toffs, and aren't there moments—admit it, old man—when you envy the tarts? Sometimes when you don't want to sit down with your accountant and see too far ahead?"

"Yes, I suppose there are moments like that."

"You think to yourself, 'We have the responsibility, but they have all the fun.'"

"I hope you'll find some fun where you are going. It's a country of tarts all right—from the President downwards."

"That's one danger the more for me. A tart can spot a tart. Perhaps I'll have to play a toff to put them off their guard. I ought to study Mr. Smith."

"Have you often had to play a toff?"

"Not too often, thank the Lord. It's the hardest part of all for me. I find myself laughing at the wrong moment. What, me, Jones, in *that* company, saying that? I get scared sometimes too. I lose the way. It's frightening to be lost, isn't it, in a strange city, but when you get lost inside yourself . . . Have another lager."

"This one's mine."

"I'm not sure I'm right about you. Seeing you there . . . with the captain . . . I looked through the window as I went by . . . you didn't look exactly at your ease . . . you aren't a tart by any chance pretending to be a toff?"

"Does one always know oneself?" The steward came in and

began to distribute the ash-trays. "Two more lagers," I told him.

"Would you mind," Jones said, "if I made it a Bols this time. I get blown up and sort of windy with too much lager."

"Two Bols," I said.

"Do you ever play at cards?" he asked, and I thought that after all the moment *had* come to purge my guilt; all the same I replied with caution, "Poker?"

He was too frank to be true. Why had he talked to me so openly about the toffs and the tarts? I got the impression that he guessed what the captain had said to me and was testing my reaction, dropping his candour into the current of my thoughts to see if it changed colour like a piece of litmus-paper. Perhaps he thought that my allegiance in the last event would not necessarily be to the toffs. Or perhaps my name Brown had sounded to him as phoney as his own.

"I don't play poker," he retorted and twinkled his black eyes at me as much as to say, "I've caught you there." He said, "I always give away too much. In friendly company. I haven't got the knack of hiding what I feel. Gin-rummy's my only game." He pronounced the title as though it were a nursery-game—a mark of innocence. "You play it?"

"I've played it once or twice," I said.

"I'm not pressing you. I just thought it might pass the time till lunch."

"Why not?"

"Steward, the cards." He gave me a little smile as much as to say, "You see, I don't carry my own marked packs."

It really was, in its way, a game of innocence. There was no easy means of cheating. He asked, "What shall we play? Ten cents a hundred?"

Jones brought to the game his own special quality. He noticed first, he told me later, in what part of his hand an inexperienced opponent kept his discards and by that means he judged how near he was to a gin. He knew by the way his opponent arranged his cards, by the length of his hesitation before playing, whether they were good, bad, or indifferent, and if the hand were obviously good he would often propose fresh cards in the certainty of refusal. This gave his opponent a sense of superiority and of security, so that he would be inclined to take risks, to play on too long in the hope of a grand gin. Even the speed with which his opponent took a card and threw one down told him much. "Psychology will always beat mere mathematics," he said to me once, and it was certain that he beat me nearly always. I had to have a hand ready-made to win.

He was six dollars up when the gong went for lunch. That was about the measure of the success he wanted, a modest win, so that no opponent ever refused him the chance to play again. Sixty dollars a week is not a big income, but he told me that he could depend on it, and it kept him in cigarettes and drink. And of course there were the occasional *coups*: sometimes an opponent despised so childlike a game and insisted on fifty cents a point. Once in Port-au-Prince I was to see that happen. If Jones had lost I doubt whether he could have paid, but fortune even in the twentieth century does sometimes favour the brave. The man was *capot* in two columns and Jones rose from the table two thousand dollars the richer. Even then he was moderate in victory. He offered his opponent his revenge and lost five hundred and a few odd dollars. "There's another thing," he once revealed to me. "Women as a rule won't play you at poker. Their husbands don't like it—it has a loose and dangerous air. But gin-rummy at ten cents a hundred—it's only pin-money. And of course it increases one's range of players quite a lot." Even Mrs. Smith, who would have turned away, I am sure, with disapproval from a game of poker, sometimes came and watched our contests.

That day at lunch—I don't know how the conversation arose —we got on to the subject of war. I think it was the pharmaceutical traveller who began it; he had been, he said, a warden in civil defence and he had an urge to recount the usual bomb-stories, as obsessive and boring as other men's dreams. Mr. Smith sat with a fixed mask of polite attention and Mrs. Smith fidgeted with her fork, while the chemist went on and on about the bombing of a Jewish girls' hostel in Store Street ("We were so busy that night no one noticed it had gone") until Jones broke brutally in with, "I lost a whole platoon myself once."

"How did that happen?" I asked, glad to encourage Jones.

"I never knew," he said. "No one came back to tell the tale."

The poor chemist sat with his mouth a little open. He was only half way through his own story and he had no audience left: he resembled a sea-lion who has dropped his fish. Mr. Fernandez took another helping of smoked herring. He was the only one who showed no interest in Jones's story. Even Mr. Smith was intrigued enough to say, "Tell us a little more, Mr. Jones." I noticed that we were all reluctant to give him a military title.

"It was in Burma," Jones said. "We had been dropped behind the Jap lines to make a diversion. This particular platoon lost touch with my H.Q. There was a youngster in command— he wasn't properly trained in jungle-fighting. Of course in those conditions it's always *sauve qui peut*. Strangely enough I didn't have a single other casualty—just that one complete platoon, nipped off our strength like that." He broke off a portion of bread and swallowed it. "No prisoners ever came back."

"Were you one of Wingate's men?" I asked.

"The same kind of outfit," he replied with his recurrent ambiguity.

"You spent a lot of time in the jungle?" the purser asked.

"Oh well, I had a kind of knack for it," Jones said. He added with modesty, "I'd have been no good in the desert. I had a reputation, you know, for being able to smell water like a native."

"That might have been useful in the desert too," I said, and he gave me a look across the table dark with reproach.

"It's a terrible thing," Mr. Smith said, pushing away what was left of his cutlet—a nut-cutlet, of course, specially prepared, "that so much courage and skill can be spent in killing our fellow-men."

"As Presidential candidate," Mrs. Smith said, "my husband had the support of conscientious objectors throughout the state."

"Were none of them meat-eaters?" I asked, and it was the turn now of Mrs. Smith to regard me with disappointment.

"No laughing matter," she said.

"It's a fair question, dear," Mr. Smith gently reproved her. "But it isn't so strange, Mr. Brown, when you think of it, that vegetarianism and conscientious objection should go together. I was telling you the other day about acidity and what effect it has on the passions. Eliminate acidity and you give a kind of elbow-room to the conscience. And the conscience, well it wants to grow and grow and grow. So one day you refuse to have an innocent animal butchered for your pleasure, and the next—it takes you by surprise, perhaps, but you turn away in horror from killing a fellow-man. And then comes the colour question and Cuba . . . I can tell you I had the support of many theosophist groups as well."

"The Anti-Blood Sports League too," Mrs. Smith said. "Not officially, of course, as a League. But many members voted for Mr. Smith."

"With so much support . . ." I began, "I'm surprised . . ."

"The progressives will always be in a minority," Mrs. Smith said, "in our lifetime, but at least we made our protest."

And then of course the usual wearisome wrangle began. The traveller in pharmaceutical products started it—I would like to give him capital initials like those of the Presidential Candidate, for he seemed truly representative, but in his case of a baser world. As a former air-raid warden he regarded himself as a combatant. Besides he had a grievance; his bomb-reminiscences had been interrupted. "I can't understand pacifists," he said, "they consent to be protected by men like us . . ."

"You do not consult us," Mr. Smith gently corrected him.

"It's hard for most of us to distinguish between a conscientious objector and a shirker."

"At least they do not shirk prison," Mr. Smith said.

Jones came unexpectedly to his support. "Many served very gallantly in the Red Cross," he said. "Some of us owe our lives to them."

"You won't find many pacifists where you are going," the purser said.

The chemist persisted, his voice high with personal grievance. "And what if someone attacks your wife, what then?"

The Presidential Candidate stared down the length of the table at the stout pale unhealthy traveller and addressed him as though he were a heckler at a political meeting, with weight and gravity. "I have never claimed, sir, that with removal of acidity we remove all passion. If Mrs. Smith were attacked and I had a weapon in my hand, I cannot promise that I would not use it. We have standards to which we do not always rise."

"Bravo, Mr. Smith," Jones cried.

"But I would deplore my passion, sir. I would deplore it."

5

That evening I went to the purser's cabin before dinner, I forget on what errand. I found him seated at his desk. He was blowing up a French letter till it was the size of a policeman's truncheon. He tied the end up with ribbon and removed it from his mouth. His desk was littered with great swollen phalluses. It was like a massacre of pigs.

"Tomorrow is the ship's concert," he explained to me, "and we have no balloons. It was Mr. Jones's idea that we should use these." I saw that he had decorated some of the sheaths with comic faces in coloured ink. "We have only one lady on board," he said, "and I do not think she will realize the nature . . ."

"You forget she is a progressive."

"In that case she will not mind. These are surely the symbols of progress."

"Suffering as we do from acidity, at least we need not pass it on to our children."

26

He giggled and set to work with a coloured crayon on one of his monstrous faces. The texture of the skin whined under his fingers.

"What time, do you think, we'll arrive on Wednesday?"

"The captain expects to tie up by the early evening."

"I hope we get in before the lights go out. I suppose they still go out?"

"Yes. You will find nothing has changed for the better. Only for the worse. It is impossible to leave the city now without a police-permit. There are barricades on every road out of Port-au-Prince. I doubt if you will be able to reach your hotel without being searched. We have warned the crew that they leave the harbour only at their own risk. Of course they will go just the same. Mère Catherine will always stay open."

"Any news of the Baron?" It was the name some gave to the President as an alternative to Papa Doc—we dignified his shambling shabby figure with the title of Baron Samedi, who in the Voodoo mythology haunts the cemeteries in his top-hat and tails, smoking his big cigar.

"They say he hasn't been seen for three months. He doesn't even come to a window of the palace to watch the band. He might be dead for all anyone knows. If he can die without a silver bullet. We've had to cancel our call at Cap Haïtien the last two trips. The town is under martial law. It's too close to the Dominican border, and we aren't allowed in." He drew a deep breath and began to inflate another French letter. The teat stood out like a tumour on the skull, and a hospital-smell of rubber filled the cabin. He said, "What makes you go back?"

"One can't just leave a hotel one owns . . ."

"But you did leave it."

I wasn't going to confide my reasons to the purser. They were too personal and too serious, if one can describe as serious the confused comedy of our private lives. He blew up another *capote anglaise,* and I thought: "Surely there must be a power which always arranges things to happen in the most humiliating circumstances." When I was a boy I had faith in the Christian

27

God. Life under his shadow was a very serious affair; I saw Him incarnated in every tragedy. He belonged to the *lacrimae rerum* like a gigantic figure looming through a Scottish mist. Now that I approached the end of life it was only my sense of humour that enabled me sometimes to believe in Him. Life was a comedy, not the tragedy for which I had been prepared, and it seemed to me that we were all, on this boat with a Greek name (why should a Dutch line name its boats in Greek?), driven by an authoritative practical joker towards the extreme point of comedy. How often, in the crowd on Shaftesbury Avenue or Broadway, after the theatres closed, have I heard the phrase— "I laughed till the tears came."

"What do you think of Mr. Jones?" the purser asked.

"Major Jones? I leave such questions to you and the captain." It was obvious that he had been consulted as well as I. Perhaps the fact that my name was Brown made me more sensitive to the comedy of Jones.

I picked up one of the great sausages of fish-skin and said, "Do you ever put one of these to a proper use?"

The purser sighed. "Alas, no. I have reached an age . . . Inevitably I get a *crise de foie*. Whenever my emotions are upset."

The purser had admitted me to an intimacy and now he required an intimacy in return, or perhaps the captain had demanded information on me too and the purser saw an opportunity of providing it. He asked me, "How did a man like you ever come to settle in Port-au-Prince? How did you ever become an *hôtelier*? You don't look like an *hôtelier*. You look like— like . . ." But his imagination failed him.

I laughed. He had asked the pertinent question all right, but the answer was one I preferred to keep to myself.

6

The captain honoured us the next night with his presence at dinner, and so did the chief engineer. I suppose there must always be a rivalry between captain and chief, as their responsibilities are equal. So long as the captain had taken his meals alone the chief had done the same. Now, one at the head of the table and the other at the foot, they sat with equality under the dubious balloons. There was an extra course in honour of our last night at sea, and, with the exception of the Smiths, the passengers drank champagne.

The purser was unusually restrained in the presence of his superior officers (I think he would have liked to join the first officer on the bridge in the freedom of the windy dark), the captain and chief were a little bowed under the sense of occasion, like priests serving at a major feast. Mrs. Smith sat on the captain's right and I on his left, and the mere presence of Jones precluded easy conversation. Even the menu was an added difficulty, for on this occasion the Dutch feeling for heavy meat-dishes was given full rein and Mrs. Smith's plate too often reproached us with its bareness. The Smiths, however, had carried with them from the States a number of cartons and bottles which like buoys always marked their places, and perhaps because they felt they had surrendered their principles in drinking something as doubtful in its ingredients as Coca-Cola, they mixed their own beverages tonight with the aid of hot water.

"I understand," the captain said gloomily, "that after dinner there is to be an entertainment."

"We're only a small company," the purser said, "but Major Jones and I felt that something must be done on our last night together. There is the kitchen-orchestra, of course, and Mr. Baxter is going to give us something very special . . ." I exchanged a puzzled glance with Mrs. Smith. Neither of us knew who Mr. Baxter could be. Had we a stowaway on board?

"I have asked Mr. Fernandez to help us in his own way, and he has gladly consented," the purser went happily on. "We shall end by singing 'Auld Lang Syne' for the sake of our Anglo-Saxon passengers." The duck went past a second time, and the Smiths, to keep us company, helped themselves from their packets and bottles.

"Excuse me, Mrs. Smith," the captain said, "but what is that you are drinking?"

"A little Barmene with hot water," Mrs. Smith told him. "My husband prefers Yeastrol in the evening. Or sometimes Vecon. Barmene, he thinks, excites him."

The captain gave a scared look at Mrs. Smith's plate and cut himself a wedge of duck. I said, "And what are you eating, Mrs. Smith?" I wanted the captain to taste the full extravagance of the situation.

"I don't know why *you* should ask, Mr. Brown. You have seen me eat it every evening at the same hour. Slippery Elm Food," she explained to the captain. He put down his knife and fork, pushed away his plate and sat with his head bowed. I thought at first that he was saying a grace, but I think in fact he had been overcome with a feeling of nausea.

"I shall finish up with some Nuttoline," Mrs. Smith said, "if you cannot supply yoghourt."

The captain cleared his throat harshly and looked away from her down the table, flinched a little at the sight of Mr. Smith, who was shovelling some dry brown grains across his plate, and fixed his eyes on harmless Mr. Fernandez, as though he might be in some way responsible. Then he announced in a duty-voice, "Tomorrow afternoon we arrive, I hope, by four o'clock. I would advise you to be prompt at the customs as the lights in the town generally go out around six-thirty."

"Why?" Mrs. Smith demanded. "It must be very inconvenient for everyone."

"For economy," the captain said. He added, "The news on the radio tonight is not good. Rebels are said to have attacked across the Dominican border. The government claims that all is quiet in Port-au-Prince, but I would advise those of you who are stopping there to keep in close touch with your consulates. I have received orders to land passengers promptly and proceed at once to Santo Domingo. I am not to delay for cargo."

"We seem to be hitting a spot of trouble, dear," Mr. Smith

said from his end of the table and he took another spoonful of what I took to be Froment—a dish he had explained to me at lunch.

"Not for the first time," Mrs. Smith replied with grim satisfaction.

A sailor came in, bringing a message for the captain, and as he opened the door a breeze set the French letters asway; they whined where they touched. The captain said, "You must excuse me. My duty. I have to go now. I wish you all a convivial evening," but I wondered whether the message had been pre-arranged—he was not a sociable man and he had found Mrs. Smith hard to accept. The chief rose too, as though he feared to leave the ship alone in the captain's hands.

Now that the officers had gone, the purser became his old self again, and he egged us on to eat more and drink more. (Even the Smiths after a good deal of hesitation—"I am not a true gourmand," Mrs. Smith said—gave themselves a second helping of Nuttoline.) A sweet liqueur was served which the purser explained was "on" the company, and the thought of a free liqueur mesmerized us all—except, of course, the Smiths—into further drinking, even the pharmaceutical traveller, though he looked at his glass with apprehension as though green was the colour for danger. When eventually we reached the saloon a programme was lying on every chair.

The purser said gaily, "Chins up," and began to beat his hands softly on his plump knees as the orchestra entered, led by the cook, a cadaverous young man, with cheeks flushed by the heat of stoves, wearing his chef's hat. His companions carried pots, pans, knives, spoons: a mincer was there to add a grinding note, and the chef held a toasting-fork as a baton. In the programme the piece they played first was called "Nocturne," and it was followed by a "Chanson d'Amour," sung by the chef himself, sweetly and uncertainly. *Automne, tendresse, feuilles mortes*, I could catch only a few of the melancholy words between the hollow crash of spoon on pot. Mr. and Mrs. Smith sat hand-in-hand on the couch, the rug spread over

31

her knees, and the traveller in pharmaceutical products leant earnestly forward, watching the thin singer; perhaps with a professional eye he was considering whether any of his drugs might be of use. As for Mr. Fernandez he sat apart, every now and then writing something down in a notebook. Jones hovered behind the purser's chair, occasionally leaning down and whispering in his ear. He seemed in the throes of a private enjoyment, as if the whole affair were his own invention, and when he applauded it was with a self-congratulatory glee. He looked at me and winked as much as to say, "Just you wait. My imagination doesn't stop here. There are better things yet to come."

I had meant to go to my cabin when the song was over, but Jones's manner awoke my curiosity. The pharmaceutical traveller had already disappeared, but I remembered it was past his usual bedtime. Jones now called the leader of the orchestra into conference: the chief drummer joined them with his big copper saucepan under his arm. I looked at my programme and saw that the next item was a Dramatic Monologue by Mr. J. Baxter. "That was a very interesting performance," Mr. Smith said. "Didn't you find it so, my dear?"

"The pots were serving a better purpose than cooking an unfortunate duck," Mrs. Smith replied. Her passions had not been perceptibly weakened by the removal of acidity.

"Very nicely sung, wasn't it, Mr. Fernandez?"

"Yes," said Mr. Fernandez and sucked the end of his pencil.

The pharmaceutical traveller entered wearing a steel helmet—he had not gone to bed, but had changed into a pair of blue jeans and had a whistle clenched between his teeth.

"So that's Mr. Baxter," Mrs. Smith said in a tone of relief. I think she disliked mysteries; she wanted all ingredients of the human comedy marked as precisely as one of Mr. Baxter's drugs or the label on the bottle of Barmene. The pharmaceutical traveller could easily have borrowed the blue jeans from a member of the crew, but I wondered how he had obtained his steel helmet.

Now he gave a blast of his whistle to silence us, though only

Mrs. Smith had spoken, and announced: "A Dramatic Monologue entitled 'The Warden's Patrol.'" To his obvious dismay a member of the orchestra reproduced an air-raid siren.

"Bravo," Jones said.

"You should have warned me," Mr. Baxter said. "Now I'm off my cue."

He was interrupted again by a roll of distant gunfire produced on the bottom of a frying pan.

"What's that supposed to be?" Mr. Baxter demanded angrily.

"The guns in the estuary."

"You are interfering with my script, Mr. Jones."

"Proceed," Jones said. "The overture is over. The atmosphere is set. London 1940." Mr. Baxter gave him a sad hurt look and announced again, "A Dramatic Monologue entitled 'The Warden's Patrol' composed by Post Warden X." Holding his palm over his eyes, as though to ward off falling glass, he began to recite.

> "The flares came down over Euston, St. Pancras,
> And dear old Tottenham Road,
> And the warden walking his lonely beat
> Saw his shadow like a cloud.

> "Guns in Hyde Park were blasting away
> When the cry of the first bomb came,
> And the warden shook his fist at the sky
> As he mocked at Hitler's fame.

> "London will stand, Saint Paul's will stand,
> And for every death we have here,
> A curse will arise from a German heart
> Against their devilish Führer.

> "Maples is hit, Gower Street's a ghost,
> Piccadilly's alight—but all's well.
> We'll use our ration of bread for toast,
> For the blitzkrieg's dead in Pall Mall."

Mr. Baxter gave a blast on his whistle, came sharply to attention, and said, "The all-clear has sounded."

"And none too soon," Mrs. Smith replied.

Mr. Fernandez cried excitedly, "No, no. Oh no, sir," and I think with the exception of Mrs. Smith there was general agreement that anything coming afterwards would be in the nature of an anticlimax.

"That calls for more champagne," Jones said. "Steward!"

The orchestra went back to the kitchen except for the conductor, who stayed at Jones's request. "The champagne's on me," Jones said. "You deserve a glass if any man did."

Mr. Baxter sat down suddenly beside me and began to tremble all over. His hand beat nervously on the table. "Don't mind me," he said, "it's always been this way. I get my stage-fright afterwards. Would you say that I was well received?"

"Very," I said. "Where did you find the steel helmet?"

"It's just one of those things I carry around in the bottom of my trunk. Somehow I've never parted with it. I expect it's the same with you—there are things you keep . . ."

It was true enough: they were more portable objects than a steel helmet, but they were just as useless—photographs, an old postcard, a membership-receipt long out of date for a night club off Regent Street, an entrance-ticket for one day to the casino at Monte Carlo. I was sure I could find half a dozen such if I turned out my pocketbook. "The blue jeans I borrowed from the second officer—but they have a foreign cut."

"Let me pour you out a glass. Your hand is still trembling."

"You really liked the poem?"

"It was very vivid."

"Then I'll tell you what I've never told anyone before. I was post warden X. I wrote it myself. After the May blitz in '41."

"Have you written much else?" I asked.

"Nothing, sir. Oh, except once—about the funeral of a child."

"And now, gentlemen," the purser announced, "if you will look at our programme you will see that we have come to a very special turn promised us by Mr. Fernandez."

And a very special turn it proved to be, for Mr. Fernandez broke as suddenly into tears as Mr. Baxter had broken into the trembles. Had he drunk too much champagne? Or had he been moved genuinely by Mr. Baxter's recitation? I doubted that, for he seemed to have no words of English except his yes and no. But now he wept, sitting straight upright in his chair; he wept with great dignity, and I thought: "I have never seen a coloured man weep before." I had seen them laughing, angry, frightened, but never overcome like this man with inexplicable grief. We sat silent and watched him; there was nothing any of us could do, we couldn't communicate. His body shook slightly, just as the saloon shook with the vibration of the ship's engines, and I thought that this, after all, was a more suitable way than music and songs to approach the dark republic. There was plenty for all of us to weep for where we were going.

Then I saw the Smiths for the first time at their best. I had disliked the quick rap Mrs. Smith had given poor Baxter—I suppose that any poem about war was offensive to her; but she was the only one of us now to move to Mr. Fernandez' help. She sat down beside him, saying not a word, and took his hand in hers; with the other she stroked his pink palm. She might have been a mother comforting her child among strangers. Mr. Smith followed her and sat down on Mr. Fernandez' other side, so that they formed a little group apart. Mrs. Smith made small clucking noises as she might have done to her child, and, as suddenly as he had begun, Mr. Fernandez ceased to weep. He stood up, lifted Mrs. Smith's old horny hand to his lips, and strode out of the saloon.

"Well," Baxter exclaimed, "what on earth do you suppose . . . ?"

"Very strange," the purser said. "Very strange indeed."

"A bit of a damper," Jones said. He held up the champagne-bottle, but it was empty and he put it down again. The conductor picked up his toasting-fork and returned to the kitchen.

"The poor man has troubles," Mrs. Smith said; it was all the explanation needed, and she looked at her hand as though she expected to see on the skin the impress of Mr. Fernandez' full lips.

"A real damper," Jones repeated.

Mr. Smith said, "If I may make a suggestion, perhaps we should bring the entertainment to a close now with Auld Lang Syne. Midnight is not far off. I wouldn't like Mr. Fernandez, all alone down there, to think that we continued—skylarking." It was hardly the word I would have used to describe our celebrations so far, but I agreed with the principle. We had no orchestra now to accompany us, but Mr. Jones sat down at the piano and picked out a fair rendering of the awful tune. Rather self-consciously we joined hands and sang. Without the cook and Jones and Mr. Fernandez we made a very small circle. We had hardly yet experienced "Old Acquaintance," and yet our cups were already exhausted.

7

It was well after midnight when Jones rapped on my cabin door. I was going through some papers with the idea of destroying anything which might be unfavourably interpreted by the authorities—for instance there had been an exchange of letters concerning the possible sale of my hotel and in some of them there were dangerous references to the political situation. I was sunk in my thoughts and I responded nervously to his knock, as though I were already back in the republic and a Tonton Macoute might be at the door.

"I'm not keeping you awake?" he asked.

"I haven't started undressing."

"I was sorry about tonight—it didn't go as well as I wished. Of course the material was limited. You know I have a kind of thing about a last night on board—one may never see each other again. It's like New Year's Eve, when you want the old codger to go out well. Isn't there something they call a good death? I didn't like that black fellow crying that way. It was as though he saw things. In the future. Of course I'm not a religious man." He looked at me shrewdly. "You neither I would say."

I had the impression he had come to my cabin for a purpose —not merely to express his disappointment at the entertainment, but perhaps to make a request or to ask a question. If he had been in a position to threaten me, I would even have suspected he had come for that. He wore his ambiguity like a loud suit and he seemed proud of it, like a man who says "you must take me as you find me." He continued, "The purser says you really own that hotel . . ."

"Did you doubt it?"

"Not exactly. But you didn't seem the type. We don't always put the right descriptions on our passports," he explained in a tone sweetly reasonable.

"What have you got on yours?"

"Company director. And that's quite true—in a way," he admitted.

"Anyway it's vague enough," I said.

"And what's on yours?"

"Business-man."

"That's even vaguer," he exclaimed triumphantly.

Interrogation, partly concealed, was to be the basis of our relationship in the short time it lasted: we would snatch at small clues, though in great matters we would usually pretend to accept the other's story. I suppose those of us who spend a large part of our lives in dissembling, whether to a woman, to a partner, even to our own selves, begin to smell each other out. Jones and I learnt a lot about one another before the end, for one uses a little truth whenever one can. It is a form of economy.

He said, "You've lived in Port-au-Prince. You must know some of the big boys there?"

"They come and go."

"In the army for example?"

"They've all gone. Papa Doc doesn't trust the army. The chief-of-staff, I believe, is hiding in the Venezuelan embassy. The general's safe in Santo Domingo. There are some colonels

37

left in the Dominican embassy, and there are three colonels and two majors in prison—if they are alive. Did you have introductions to any of them?"

"Not exactly," he said, but he looked uneasy.

"It is well not to present introductions till you are sure your man is still alive."

"I have a chit from the Haitian consul-general in New York recommending me . . ."

"We've been at sea three days, remember. A lot can happen in that time. The consul-general may have sought asylum . . ."

He said as the purser had done, "I wonder what brings *you* back, conditions being what they are."

The truth was less fatiguing than invention and the hour was late. "I found I missed the place," I said. "Security can get on the nerves just as much as danger."

He said, "Yes, I thought I had had my fill of danger in the war."

"What unit were you in?"

He grinned at me; I had played a card too obviously. "Oh, I was a bit of a drifter even in those days," he said. "I moved around. Tell me, what kind of a chap's our ambassador?"

"We haven't got one. He was expelled more than a year ago."

"The chargé then."

"He does what he can. When he can."

"We seem to be sailing towards a strange country."

He went to the porthole as though he expected to be able to see the land across the last two hundred miles of sea, but there was nothing to be observed except the light of the cabin lying on the surface of the dark swell like yellow oil. "Not exactly a tourist-paradise any longer?"

"No. It never really was."

"But perhaps a few opportunities for a man of imagination?"

"It depends."

"On what?"

"The kind of scruples you have."

"Scruples?" He looked out onto the rolling night and he

seemed to be weighing the question with some care. "Oh, well . . . scruples cost a lot . . . Why did you suppose that nigger really wept?"

"I've no idea."

"It was an odd evening. I hope we do better next time."

"Next time?"

"I was thinking of when this year ends. Wherever we may be." He came away from the porthole and said, "Oh well, it's time for shut-eye, isn't it? And Smith, what do you suppose *he's* up to?"

"Why should he be up to anything?"

"You may be right. Don't mind me. I'm going now. The trip's over. No getting out of it now." He added with his hand on the door, "I tried to cheer things up, but it wasn't much of a success. Shut-eye's the answer to all, isn't it? Or that's how I see it."

Chapter Two

I was returning without much hope to a country of fear and frustration, and yet every familiar feature as the *Medea* drew in gave me a kind of happiness. The huge mass of Kenscoff leaning over the town was as usual half in deep shadow; there was a glassy sparkle of late sun off the new buildings near the port which had been built for an international exhibition in so-called modern style. A stone Columbus watched us coming in—it was there Martha and I used to rendezvous at night until the curfew closed us in separate prisons, I in my hotel, she in her embassy, without even a telephone which worked to communicate by. She would sit in her husband's car in the dark and flash her headlights on at the sound of my Humber. I wondered whether in the last month, now that the curfew was over, she had chosen a different rendezvous, and I wondered with whom. That she had found a substitute I had no doubt. No one banks on fidelity nowadays.

I was lost in too many difficult thoughts to remember my fellow-passengers. There was no message waiting for me from the British embassy, so I assumed that at the moment all was well. At immigration and customs there was the habitual confusion. We were the only boat, and yet the shed was full: porters, taxi-drivers who hadn't had a fare in weeks, police, and the occasional Tonton Macoute in his black glasses and his soft hat, and beggars, beggars everywhere. They seeped through every chink like water in the rainy season. A man without legs sat under the customs-counter like a rabbit in a hutch, miming in silence.

A familiar figure forced his way towards me. As a rule, he haunted the airfield, and I had not expected to see him here. He was a journalist known to everyone as Petit Pierre—a *métis* in a country where the half-castes are the aristocrats waiting for the tumbrils to roll. He was believed by some to have connections with the Tonton, for how otherwise had he escaped a beating up or worse? and yet there were occasionally passages in his gossip-column that showed an odd satirical courage—perhaps he depended on the police not to read between the lines.

He seized me by the hands as if we were the oldest of friends and addressed me in English, "Why, Mr. Brown, Mr. Brown."

"How are you, Petit Pierre?"

He giggled up at me, standing on his pointed toe-caps, for he was a tiny figure of a man. He was just as I had remembered him, hilarious. Even the time of day was humorous to him. He had the quick movements of a monkey, and he seemed to swing from wall to wall on ropes of laughter. I had always thought that, when the time came, and surely it must one day come in his precarious defiant livelihood, he would laugh at his executioner, as a Chinaman is supposed to do.

"It's good to see you, Mr. Brown. How are the bright lights of Broadway? Marilyn Monroe, lots of good bourbon, speakeasies . . . ?" He was a little out of date, for he had not been further than Kingston, Jamaica, in thirty years. "Give me your passport, Mr. Brown. Where are your luggage tickets?" He waved them above his head, pushing through the mob, arranging everything, for he knew everyone. Even the customs-man allowed my baggage to pass unopened. He exchanged some words with a Tonton Macoute at the door and by the time I emerged he had found me a taxi. "Sit down, sit down, Mr. Brown. Your luggage is just coming."

"How are things here?" I asked.

"All as usual. All quiet."

"No curfew?"

"Why should there be a curfew, Mr. Brown?"

"The papers reported rebels in the north."

"The papers? American papers? You don't believe what the American papers say, do you?" He leant his head in at the taxi-door and said with his odd hilarity, "You can't think how happy I am, Mr. Brown, to see you back." I almost believed him.

"Why not? Don't I belong here?"

"Of course you belong here, Mr. Brown. You are a true friend of Haiti." He giggled again. "All the same many true friends have left us recently." He lowered his voice just a tone. "The government has been forced to take over some empty hotels."

"Thanks for the warning."

"It would have been wrong to let the properties deteriorate."

"A kindly thought. Who lives in them now?"

He giggled. "Guests of the government."

"Do they run to guests now?"

"There was a Polish mission, but they went away rather soon. Here comes your luggage, Mr. Brown."

"Shall I get to the Trianon before the lights go out?"

"Yes—if you go direct."

"Where else should I go?"

Petit Pierre chuckled and said, "Let me come with you, Mr. Brown. There are road-blocks now between Port-au-Prince and Pétionville."

"All right. Get in. Anything to avoid trouble," I said.

"What were you doing in New York, Mr. Brown?"

I replied truthfully, "I was trying to find someone to buy my hotel."

"You had no luck?"

"No luck at all."

"No enterprise in such a great country?"

"You expelled their military mission. You had the ambassador recalled. You can't expect much confidence there, can you? My God, I completely forgot. There's a Presidential candidate on board the boat."

"A Presidential candidate? I should have been warned."

"Not a very successful one."

"All the same. A Presidential candidate. What does he come here for?"

"He has an introduction to the Secretary for Social Welfare."

"Doctor Philipot? But Doctor Philipot . . ."

"Anything wrong?"

"You know what politics are. It's the same in all countries."

"Doctor Philipot is out?"

"He has not been seen for a week. He is said to be on holiday." Petit Pierre touched the taxi-driver's shoulder. "Stop, *mon ami.*" We hadn't got as far yet as the Columbus statue, and the dark was rapidly falling. He said, "Mr. Brown, I think that I had better go back and find him. You know how it is in your own country—one must avoid giving a false impression. It would not do for me to come to England carrying an introduction to Mr. Macmillan." He waved to me as he went away. "I will come up presently for a whisky. I am so glad, so glad, to see you back, Mr. Brown," and he departed with that air of euphoria, based on nothing at all.

We drove on. I asked the driver—he was probably a Tonton agent, "Shall we get to the Trianon before the lights go out?" He shrugged his shoulders. It was not his job to give away information. The lights were still burning in the exhibition building used by the Secretary of State, and there was a Peugeot parked by the Columbus statue. Of course there were a lot of Peugeots in Port-au-Prince, and I couldn't believe that she would be cruel enough or tasteless enough to choose the same rendezvous. All the same I said to the driver, "I'll get out here. Take my luggage up to the Trianon. Joseph will pay you." I could hardly have been less prudent. The colonel in charge of the Tontons Macoute would certainly know next morning exactly where I had left the taxi. The only precaution I took was to see that the man really drove away. I watched the tail-lights until they were out of sight. Then I made my way towards Columbus and the parked car. I came up behind it and saw the C.D. number plate. It was Martha's car and she was alone.

I watched her for a little while without being seen. It occurred to me that I could wait there, a few yards away, until I saw the man who came to meet her. Then she turned her head and stared in my direction; she knew that someone was watching her. She lowered the window half an inch and said sharply in French, as though I might be one of the innumerable beggars of the port, "Who are you? What do you want?" Then she turned on her headlights. "Oh God," she said, "so you've come back," in the kind of tone she might have used for a recurrent fever.

She opened the door and I got in beside her. I could feel uncertainty and fear in her kiss. "Why have you come back?" she asked.

"I suppose I missed you."

"Did you have to run away to discover that?"

"I hoped that things might change if I went away."

"Nothing has changed."

"What are you doing here?"

"It's a better place than most to miss you in."

"You weren't waiting for anyone?"

"No." She took one of my fingers and twisted it till it hurt. "I can be *sage*, you know, for a few months. Except in dreams. I've been unfaithful in dreams."

"I've been faithful too—in my way."

"You needn't tell me now," she said, "what your way is. Just be quiet. Be here."

I obeyed her. I was half happy, half miserable, because it was only too evident one thing hadn't changed, except that now without my car she would have to drive me back and run the risk of being seen near the Trianon: we wouldn't say good night beside Columbus. Even while I made love to her I tested her. Surely she wouldn't have the nerve to take me if she were expecting another man at the rendezvous, and then I told myself that it wasn't a fair test—she had nerve for anything. It was no lack of nerve that tied her to her husband. She gave a cry which I remembered and stuck her hand over her mouth. Her body lost its tenseness, she was like a tired child resting on my knees. She said, "I forgot to close the window."

"We'd better get up to the Trianon before the lights go out."

"Have you found someone to buy the place?"

"No."

"I'm glad."

In the public park the musical fountain stood black, water-less, unplaying. Electric globes winked out the nocturnal message, *"Je suis le drapeau Haïtien, Uni et Indivisible. François Duvalier."*

We passed the blackened beams of the house the Tontons had destroyed and mounted the hill towards Pétionville. Half way up there was a road-block. A man in a torn shirt and a grey pair of trousers and an old soft hat which someone must have discarded in a dustbin came trailing his rifle by its muzzle to the door. He told us to get out and be searched. "I'll get out," I said, "but this lady belongs to the diplomatic corps."

"Darling, don't make a fuss," she said. "There are no such things as privileges now." She led the way to the roadside, putting her hands above her head and giving the militia-man a smile I hated.

I said to him, "Don't you see the C.D. on the car?"

"And can't you see," she said, "that he can't read?" He felt my hips and ran his hands up between my legs. Then he opened the boot of the car. It was not a very practised search and it was soon over. He cleared a passage through the barrier and let us go by. "I don't like you driving back alone," I said. "I'll lend you a boy—if I've got one left," and then after I had driven half a mile further I went back in my mind to the old suspicion. If a husband is notoriously blind to infidelity, I suppose a lover has the opposite fault—he sees it everywhere. "Tell me what you were really doing, waiting by the statue?"

"Don't be a fool tonight," she said. "I'm happy."

"I never wrote to you that I was coming back."

"It was a place to remember you in, that was all."

45

"It seems a coincidence that just tonight . . ."

"Do you suppose this was the only night I bothered to remember you?" She added, "Luis asked me once why I had stopped going out in the evening for gin-rummy now the curfew had lifted. So next night I took the car as usual. I had no one to see and nothing to do, so I drove to the statue."

"And Luis is content?"

"He's always content."

Suddenly, around us, above us and below us, the lights went out. Only a glow remained around the harbour and the government buildings.

"I hope Joseph has kept a bit of oil for my return," I said. "I hope he's wise as well as virgin."

"Is he virgin?"

"Well, he's chaste. Since the Tontons Macoute kicked him around."

We entered the steep drive lined with palm-trees and bougainvillaea. I always wondered why the original owner had called the hotel the Trianon. No name could have been less suitable. The architecture of the hotel was neither classical in the eighteenth-century manner nor luxurious in the twentieth-century fashion. With its towers and balconies and wooden fretwork decorations it had the air at night of a Charles Addams house in a number of *The New Yorker*. You expected a witch to open the door to you or a maniac butler, with a bat dangling from the chandelier behind him. But in the sunlight, or when the lights went on among the palms, it seemed fragile and period and pretty and absurd, an illustration from a book of fairytales. I had grown to love the place, and I was glad in a way that I had found no purchaser. I believed that if I could own it for a few more years I would feel I had a home. Time was needed for a home as time was needed to turn a mistress into a wife. Even the violent death of my partner had not seriously disturbed my possessive love. I would have remarked, with Frère Laurent in the French version of *Romeo and Juliet*, a sentence that I had reason to remember:

The remedy had been in the success which owed nothing to my partner: in the voices calling from the bathing-pool, in the rattle of ice from the bar where Joseph made his famous rum-punches, in the arrival of taxis from the town, in the hubbub of lunch on the verandah, and at night the drummer and the dancers, with Baron Samedi, a grotesque figure in a ballet, stepping it delicately in his top-hat under the lighted palms. I had known for a short time all of this.

We drew up in the darkness, and I kissed Martha again: it was still an interrogation. I could not believe in a fidelity that lasted for three months of solitude. Perhaps—it was a less disagreeable speculation than another—she had turned to her husband again. I held her against me and said, "How is Luis?"

"The same," she said, "always the same." And yet I thought she must have loved him once. This is one of the pains of illicit love: even your mistress's most extreme embrace is a proof the more that love doesn't last. I had met Luis for the second time when I was among the thirty guests at an embassy cocktail-party. It seemed to me impossible that the ambassador—that stout man in the late forties whose hair gleamed like a polished shoe—did not remark how often our eyes met across the crowded room, the surreptitious touch she gave me with her hand as we passed. But Luis kept his appearance of established superiority: this was his embassy, this was his wife, these were his guests. The books of matches were stamped with his initials, even the bands round his cigars. I remember him raising a cocktail glass to the light and showing me the delicate engraving of a bull's mask. He said, "I had them specially designed for me in Paris." He had a great sense of possession, but perhaps he didn't mind lending what he possessed.

"Has Luis comforted you while I was away?"

"No," she said, and I cursed myself for my cowardice in so phrasing the question that her answer remained ambiguous. She added, "No one has comforted me," and at once I began to think of all the meanings of comfort from which she might choose one to satisfy her sense of truth. For she had a sense of truth.

"You've got a different scent."

"Luis gave me this for my birthday. I'd finished yours."

"Your birthday. I forgot . . ."

"It doesn't matter."

"Joseph is a long time," I said. "He must have heard the car."

She said, "Luis is kind to me. You are the only one who kicks me around. Like the Tontons Macoute with Joseph."

"What do you mean?"

Everything was just as before. After ten minutes we had made love, and after half an hour we had begun to quarrel. I left the car and walked up the steps in the dark. At the top I nearly stumbled on my suitcases, which the driver must have deposited there, and I called "Joseph, Joseph" and no one replied. The verandah stretched on either side of me, but no table was laid for dinner. Through the open door of the hotel I could see the bar by the light of a tiny oil-lamp like the ones you place beside a child's bed or the bed of someone sick. This was my luxury-hotel—a circle of light which barely touched a half-empty bottle of rum, two stools, a syphon of soda crouched in the shadow like a bird with a long beak. I called again, "Joseph, Joseph," and again nobody answered. I went back down the steps to the car and said to Martha, "Stay a moment."

"Is something wrong?"

"I can't find Joseph."

"I ought to be getting back."

"You can't go alone. Don't be in such a hurry. Luis can wait a moment."

I mounted the steps again to the Hotel Trianon. "A centre of Haitian intellectual life. A luxury-hotel which caters equally for the connoisseur of good food and the lover of local customs. Try the special drinks made from the finest Haitian rum, bathe in the luxurious swimming-pool, listen to the music of the Haitian drum and watch the Haitian dancers. Mingle with the *élite* of Haitian intellectual life, the musicians, the poets, the painters who find at the Hotel Trianon a social centre . . ." The tourist-brochure had been nearly true once.

I felt under the bar and found an electric torch. I went through the lounge to my office, the desk covered with old bills and receipts. I had not expected a client, but even Joseph was not there. What a homecoming, I thought, what a home-coming. Below the office was the bathing-pool. About this hour the cocktail-guests should have been arriving from other hotels in the town. Few in the good days drank anywhere else but the Trianon except for those who were booked on round-tours and chalked everything up. The Americans always drank dry Martinis. By midnight some of them would be swimming around in the pool naked. Once I had looked out of my window at two in the morning. There was a great yellow moon and a girl was making love in the pool. She had her breasts pressed against the side and I couldn't see the man behind her. She didn't notice me watching her; she didn't notice anything. That night I thought before I slept, "I have arrived."

I heard steps in the garden coming up from the direction of the swimming-pool, the broken steps of a man limping. Joseph had always limped since his encounter with the Tontons Macoute. I was about to go out onto the verandah to meet him when I looked again at my desk. There was something missing. All the bills were there which had accumulated in my absence, but where was the small brass paper-weight shaped like a coffin, marked with the letters R.I.P., that I bought for myself one Christmas in Miami? It had no value, it had cost me two dollars and seventy-five cents, but it was mine and it amused me and it was no longer there. Why should things change in our ab-sence? Even Martha had changed her scent. The more unstable life is the less one likes the small details to alter.

I went out on to the verandah to meet Joseph. I could see his light as it corkscrewed along the curving path from the pool.

"Is it you, Monsieur Brown?" he called up nervously.

"Of course it's me. Why weren't you here when I arrived? Why have you left my suitcases . . . ?"

He stood below me looking up with a sick expression on his black face.

"Madame Pineda gave me a lift. I want you to drive back with her into the town. You can return on the bus. Is the gardener here?"

"He go away."

"The cook?"

"He go away."

"My paper-weight? What's happened to my paper-weight?"

He looked at me as though he didn't understand.

"Have there been no guests at all since I left?"

"No, monsieur. Only . . ."

"Only what?"

"Four nights ago Doctor Philipot he come here. He say tell nobody."

"What did he want?"

"I tell him he no stay here. I tell him the Tontons Macoute look for him here."

"What did he do?"

"He stay all the same. Then the cook go away and the gardener go away. They say they come back when he go. He very sick man. That's why he stay. I say go to the mountain, but he say no walk, no walk. His feet they swell bad. I tell him he go before you come back."

"It's the hell of a mess for me to come back to," I said. "I'll talk to him. Which room is he in?"

"When I hear the car, I call to him—Tontons, get out quick. He very tired. He not want to go. He say, 'I old man.' I tell him Monsieur Brown he ruined if they find you here along. All same for you, I say, if Tontons find you in the road, but Monsieur Brown he ruined if they catch you here. I tell him I go and talk to them. He go out then quick quick. But it was only that stupid taxi-man with the luggage . . . So I run tell him."

50

"What are we going to do with him, Joseph?" Doctor Philipot was not a bad man as government officials go. He had even during his first year of office made some attempt to improve the conditions of the shanty-town along the waterfront; they had built a water-pump, with his name on a stamped cast-iron label, at the bottom of the Rue Desaix, but the pipes had never been connected because the contractors had not received a proper rake-off.

"When I go in his room he not there any more."

"Do you think he's made for the mountain?"

"No, Monsieur Brown, not the mountain," Joseph said. He stood below me with his head bowed. "I think he gone done a very wicked thing." He added in a low voice the inscription on my paper-weight, "*Requiescat in pace,*" for Joseph was a good Catholic as well as a good Voodooist. "Please, Monsieur Brown, come with me."

I followed him down the path to the bathing-pool in which I had seen the pretty girl making love, once, in another epoch, in the golden age. It was empty of water now. My torch lit the shallows and a litter of leaves.

"Other end," Joseph told me, standing quite still, not going any nearer. Doctor Philipot must have walked up to the narrow cave of shadow made by the diving-plank, and now he lay in a crouched position below it with his knees drawn towards his chin, a middle-aged foetus ready dressed for burial in his neat grey suit. He had cut his wrists first and then his throat to make sure. Above the head was the dark circle of the pipe. We had only to turn on the water to wash the blood away; he had been as considerate as possible. He could not have been dead for more than a few minutes. My first thoughts were selfish ones: you cannot be blamed if a man kills himself in your swimming-pool. There was easy access to it direct from the road without passing the house. Beggars used to come here to try to sell trumpery wooden carvings to the guests swimming in the pool.

I asked Joseph, "Is Doctor Magiot still in town?" He nodded.

"Go to Madame Pineda in the car outside and ask her to

drive you to his house on the way to the embassy. Don't tell her the reason. Bring him back—if he'll come." He was the only doctor in town, I thought, with the courage to attend even a stone-dead enemy of the Baron. But before Joseph could start up the path there was a clatter of footsteps and I heard the unmistakable voice of Mrs. Smith. "The New York customs could learn a thing or two from the men here. They were very polite to us both. You never find such courtesy among white people as you do with coloured."

"Look out, my dear, there's a hole in the path."

"I can see well enough. There's nothing like raw carrots for the sight, Mrs. . . ."

"Pineda."

"Mrs. Pineda."

Martha brought up the rear carrying an electric torch. Mr. Smith said, "We found this good lady in the car outside. There seemed no one around."

"I'm sorry. I'd quite forgotten you were going to stay here."

"I thought Mr. Jones was coming here too, but we left him with a police-officer. I hope he's not in trouble."

"Joseph, get the John Barrymore suite ready. See that there are plenty of lamps for Mr. and Mrs. Smith. I must apologize for the lights. They will come on any moment now."

"We like it," Mr. Smith said. "It feels like an adventure."

If a spirit hovers, as some believe, for an hour or two over the cadaver it has abandoned, what banalities it is doomed to hear, while it waits in a despairing hope that some serious thought will be uttered, some expression which will lend dignity to the life it has left. I said to Mrs. Smith, "Tonight would you mind having only eggs? Tomorrow I'll have everything organized to suit you. Unfortunately the cook went off yesterday."

"Don't bother about the eggs," Mr. Smith said. "To tell you the truth we are a little dogmatic about eggs. But we've got our own Yeastrol."

"And I have my Barmene," Mrs. Smith said.

"Just a little hot water," Mr. Smith said. "Mrs. Smith and I are very mobile. You don't have to worry about us. You've got a fine pool here." To show them the extent of the pool Martha began to move the ray of her lamp towards the diving-board and the deep end. I took it quickly from her and turned it up towards the fretted tower and a balcony which leant over the palms. A light already glowed up there where Joseph was preparing the room. "There's your suite," I said. "The John Barrymore suite. You can see all over Port-au-Prince from there, the harbour, the palace, the cathedral."

"Did John Barrymore really stay here?" Mr. Smith asked. "In that room?"

"It was before my time, but I can show you his liquor-bills."

"A great talent ruined," he remarked sadly.

I couldn't forget that presently the light-rationing would be over and the lamps would go on all over Port-au-Prince. Sometimes the light was out for close on three hours, sometimes for less than one—there was no certainty. I had told Joseph that during my absence "business" was to be as usual, for who could tell whether a couple of journalists might not stop for a few days to write a report on what they would undoubtedly call "The Nightmare Republic"? Perhaps for Joseph "business as usual" meant lights as usual in the palm-trees, lights around the pool. I didn't want the Presidential Candidate to see a corpse coiled up under the diving-board—not on his first night. It was not my idea of hospitality. And hadn't he said something about a letter of introduction he carried to the Secretary for Social Welfare?

Joseph appeared at the head of the path. I told him to show the Smiths to their room and afterwards to drive down town with Mrs. Pineda.

"Our luggage is on the verandah," Mrs. Smith said.

"You'll find it in your room by now. It won't stay dark much longer, I promise. You must excuse us. We are a very poor country."

"When I think of all that waste on Broadway," Mrs. Smith said, and to my relief they began to mount the path, Joseph lighting the way. I stayed at the shallow end of the pool, but now that my eyes were accustomed to the dark I thought I could detect the body like a hump of earth.

Martha said, "Is something wrong?" and flashed her light up towards my face.

"I haven't had time to see yet. Lend me that torch a moment."

"What was keeping you down here?"

I let the torch play on the palm-trees well away from the pool as though I were inspecting the light-installations. "Talking to Joseph. Let's go up now, shall we?"

"And run into the Smiths? I'd rather stay here. It's funny to think I've never been here before. In your home."

"No, we've always been very prudent."

"You haven't asked after Angel."

"I'm sorry."

Angel was her son, the unbearable child who helped to keep us apart. He was too fat for his age, he had his father's eyes like brown buttons, he sucked bon bons, he noticed things, and he made claims—claims all the time on his mother's exclusive attention. He seemed to draw the tenderness out of our relationship as he drew the liquid centre from a sweet, with a long sucking breath. He was the subject of half our conversations. "I must go now. I promised Angel to read to him." "I can't see you tonight. Angel wants to go to the cinema." "My darling, I'm so tired this evening—Angel had six friends to tea."

"How *is* Angel?"

"He was ill while you were away. With the *grippe.*"

"But he's quite better now?"

"Oh yes, he's better."

"Let's go."

"Luis doesn't expect me as early as this. Nor Angel. I'm here. We may as well be hanged for a sheep."

I looked at the dial of my watch. It was nearly eight-thirty. I said, "The Smiths . . ."

"They are busy with their luggage. What's worrying you, darling?"

I said feebly, "I've lost a paper-weight."

"A very precious paper-weight?"

"No—but if a paper-weight's gone, what else has gone?"

Suddenly all around us the lights flashed on. I took her arm and wrenched her round and moved her up the path. Mr. Smith came out on to his balcony and called to us, "Do you think Mrs. Smith could have another blanket on the bed, just in case it turns chilly?"

"I'll have one sent up, but it won't turn chilly."

"It certainly is a fine view from up here."

"I'll turn out the lights in the garden and then you'll see better."

The controlling switch was in my office and we had almost reached it when Mr. Smith's voice came again. "Mr. Brown, there's someone asleep in your pool."

"I expect it's a beggar."

Mrs. Smith must have joined him, for it was her voice I heard now. "Where, dear?"

"Down there."

"The poor man. I've a good mind to take him down some money."

I was tempted to call up, "Take him your letter of introduction. It's the Secretary for Social Welfare."

"I wouldn't do that, dear. You'll only wake the poor fellow up."

"It's a funny place to choose."

"I expect it's for the sake of the coolness."

I reached the office-door and turned out the lights in the garden. I heard Mr. Smith say, "Look there, dear. That white house with the dome. That must be the palace."

Martha said, "A beggar asleep in the pool?"

"It does happen."

"I never noticed him. What are you looking for?"

"My paper-weight. Why should anyone take my paper-weight?"

"What did it look like?"

"A little coffin with R.I.P. stamped on it. I used it for non-urgent mail."

She laughed and held me still and kissed me. I responded as well as I could, but the corpse in the pool seemed to turn our preoccupations into comedy. The corpse of Doctor Philipot belonged to a more tragic theme; we were only a sub-plot affording a little light relief. I heard Joseph move in the bar and called to him, "What are you doing?" Apparently Mrs. Smith had explained their needs to him: two cups, two spoons, a bottle of hot water. "Add a blanket," I said, "and then get moving to the town."

"When shall I see you again?" Martha asked.

"The same place, the same time."

"Nothing has changed, has it?" she asked me with anxiety.

"No, nothing," but my tone had an edge to it, which she noticed.

"I'm sorry, but all the same you've come back."

When at last she drove away with Joseph I went back to the pool and sat on its edge in the dark. I was afraid the Smiths might come downstairs and make conversation, but I had been waiting only a few minutes by the pool when I saw the lights go out in the John Barrymore suite. They must have taken the Yeastrol and the Barmene and they had now lain down to their untroubled sleep. Last night the festivities had kept them up late, and it had been a long day. I wondered what had happened to Jones. He had expressed his intention of staying in the Trianon. I thought too of Mr. Fernandez and his mysterious tears. Anything rather than think of the Secretary for Social Welfare coiled up under the diving-board.

Far up in the mountains beyond Kenscoff a drum beat, marking the spot of a Voodoo *tonelle*. It was not often one heard the drums now under Papa Doc's rule. Something padded through the dark, and when I turned on my torch I saw a thin starved dog poised by the diving-board. It looked at me with dripping eyes and wagged a hopeless tail, as though it were asking my permission to jump down and lick the blood. I shooed it away. A few years ago I had employed three gardeners, two cooks, Joseph, an extra barman, four boys, two girls, a chauffeur, and in the season—it was not yet the end of the season—I would have taken on extra help. Tonight by the pool there would have been a cabaret, and in the intervals of the music I would have heard the perpetual murmur of the distant streets, like a busy hive. Now, even though the curfew had been lifted, there was not a sound, and without a moon not even a dog barked. It was as though my success had gone out of earshot too. I had not known it for very long but I could hardly complain. There were two guests in the Hotel Trianon, I had found my mistress again, and unlike Monsieur le Ministre I was still alive. I settled myself as comfortably as I could on the edge of the pool and began my long wait for Doctor Magiot.

Chapter Three

From time to time in my life I had found it necessary to provide a *curriculum vitae*. It usually began something like this. Born 1906 at Monte Carlo of British parents. Educated at the Jesuit College of the Visitation. Many prizes for Latin verse and Latin prose composition. Embarked early on a business career ... Of course I varied the details of that career according to the recipient of the curriculum.

What a lot too was left out or was of doubtful truth in even those opening statements. My mother was certainly not British, and to this day I am uncertain whether she was French—perhaps she was a rare Monegasque. The man she had chosen for my father left Monte Carlo before my birth. Perhaps his name was Brown. There is a ring of truth in the name Brown—she wasn't usually so modest in her choice. The last time I saw her, when she was dying in Port-au-Prince, she bore the name of the Comtesse de Lascot-Villiers. She had left Monte Carlo (and incidentally her son) hurriedly, soon after the Armistice of 1918, with my bills at the college unsettled. But the Society of Jesus is used to unsettled bills, it works assiduously on the fringe of the aristocracy where returned cheques are almost as common as adulteries, and so the college continued to support me. I was a prize-pupil, and it was half expected that I would prove in time to have a vocation. I even believed it myself; the sense of vocation hung around me like the *grippe*, a miasma of unreality, at a temperature below normal in the cool rational morning but a fever-heat at night. As other boys fought with the demon of masturbation, I fought with faith. I find it strange to think now of my Latin verses and compositions—all that knowledge has vanished as completely as my father. Only one line has obstinately stuck in my head—a memory of the old dreams and ambitions: "*Exegi monumentum aere perennius . . .*" I said it to myself nearly forty years later when I stood, on the day of my mother's death, by the bathing-pool of the Hotel Trianon in Pétionville and looked up at the fantastic tracery of woodwork against the palms and the inky storm clouds blowing over Kenscoff. I more than half owned the place and knew that soon I would own it all. I was already in possession, a man of property. I remember thinking, "I am going to make this the most popular tourist-hotel in the Caribbean," and perhaps I might have succeeded if a mad doctor had not come to power and filled our nights with the discords of violence instead of jazz.

The career of an *hôtelier* was not, as I have indicated, the one which the Jesuits had expected me to follow. That had been finally wrecked by a college performance of *Romeo and Juliet* in its very staid French translation. I was given the part of the aged Friar Lawrence, and some of the lines I had to learn have remained with me to this day, I don't know why. They hardly have the ring of poetry. "*Accorde-moi de discuter sur ton état.*" Frère Laurent had the power of making even the tragedy of the star-crossed lovers prosaic. "*J'apprends que tu dois, et rien ne peut le reculer, Etre mariée à ce comte jeudi prochain.*"

The part must have seemed to the good fathers a suitable one under the circumstances and not too exciting or exacting, but I think my vocational *grippe* was already very nearly over, and the interminable rehearsals, the continual presence of the lovers and the sensuality of their passion, however muted by the French translator, led me to my breakout. I looked a good deal older than my age, and the dramatic director, if he could not make me an actor, had at least taught me adequately enough the secrets of make-up. I "borrowed" the passport of a young lay-professor of English literature and bluffed my way one afternoon into the Casino. There, in the surprising space of forty-five minutes, due to an unlikely run of nineteens and zeros, I gained the equivalent of three hundred pounds, and only an hour later I was losing my virginity, inexpertly and unexpectedly, in a bedroom of the Hôtel de Paris.

My instructress was at least fifteen years older than myself, but in my mind she has remained always the same age, and it is I who have grown older. We met in the Casino, where, seeing that I was pursued by good fortune—I had been making the bets over her shoulder—she began to lay her tokens alongside mine. If I gained that afternoon more than three hundred pounds, perhaps she gained nearly a hundred, and at that point she stopped me, counselling prudence. I am certain there was no thought of seduction in her mind. It is true that she invited me to have tea with her at the hotel, but she had seen through my disguise better than the officials of the Casino, and on the steps she turned to me like a fellow-conspirator and whispered, "How did you get in?" I was no more to her, I am sure, at that moment than an adventurous child who had amused her.

I didn't even pretend. I showed her my false passport, and in the bathroom of her suite she helped me to rub out the traces of make-up which on a winter's afternoon, in the light of the lamps, had passed for genuine lines. I saw Frère Laurent disappear wrinkle by wrinkle in the mirror above the shelf where lay her lotions, her eyebrow-pencils, her pots of pomade. We might have been two actors sharing a dressing-room.

Tea at the college was served on long tables with an urn at the end of each. Long *baguettes* of bread, three to a table, were set out with meagre portions of butter and jam; the china was coarse to withstand the schoolboy clutch and the tea strong. At the Hôtel de Paris I was astonished at the fragility of the cups, the silver tea-pot, the little triangular savoury sandwiches, the éclairs stuffed with cream. I lost my shyness. I spoke of my mother, of my Latin compositions, of *Romeo and Juliet*. Perhaps without evil intention, I quoted Catullus to show off my learning.

I cannot remember now the gradation of events which led to the first long adult kiss upon the sofa. She was married, I remember she told me, to a director of the Banque de l'Indochine, and I had visions of a man ladling coins into a drawer with a brass scoop. He was at the moment on a visit to Saigon, where she suspected him of supporting a Cochinese mistress. It was not a long conversation; I was soon back at the beginning of my studies, learning a first lesson in love on a big white bed with carved pineapple bed-posts, in a small white room. What a lot of details I can still remember of those hours after more than forty years. For writers it is always said that the first twenty years of life contain the whole of experience—the rest is observation, but I think it is equally true of us all.

An odd thing happened as we lay on the bed. She was finding me shy, frightened, difficult. Her fingers had no success, even her lips had failed their office, when into the room suddenly, from the port below the hill, flew a seagull. For a moment the room seemed spanned by the length of the white wings. She gave an exclamation of dismay and retreated: it was she who was scared now. I put out a hand to reassure her. The bird came to rest on a chest below a gold-framed looking-glass and stood there regarding us on its long stiltlike legs. It seemed as completely at home in the room as a cat and at any moment I expected it to begin to clean its plumage. My new friend trembled a little with her fear, and suddenly I found myself as firm as a man and I took her with such ease and confidence it was as though we had been lovers for a long time. Neither of us during those minutes saw the seagull go, although I shall always think that I felt the current of its wings on my back as the bird sailed out again towards the port and the bay.

That was all there was, the victory in the Casino and in the white and gold room a few further triumphant minutes—the only love-affair I have ever had which ended without pain or regret. For she was not even the cause of my departure from the college; that was the result of my own indiscretion in dropping into the collection-bag at mass a roulette-token for five francs which I had failed to cash. I thought I was showing generosity, for my usual contribution was twenty sous, but someone spotted me and reported me to the Dean of Studies. In the interview which followed the last vestige of my vocation was blown away. I parted from the fathers with politeness on both sides; if they felt disappointment I think they also felt a grudging respect— my exploit was not unworthy of the college. I had successfully concealed my small fortune under my mattress, and when they were assured that an uncle, on my father's side, had sent me my fare to England with promises of future support and a position in his firm, they relinquished me without regret. I told them that I would repay my mother's debt as soon as I had earned enough (a promise they accepted with a little embarrassment because they obviously doubted whether it would ever be ful-filled), and I assured them too that I would certainly get in touch with a certain Father Thomas Capriole S.J. at Farm Street, an old friend of the Rector's (a promise which they believed I might keep). As for the notional uncle's letter, it had been a very easy one to compose. If I could deceive the Casino authorities I had no fear of failing with the fathers of the Visi-tation, and not one of them thought of demanding to see the envelope. I set out to England by the international express which halts at the little station below the Casino. It was my last sight of the baroque towers that had dominated my child-hood—a vision of grown-up life, the palace of chance, where anything at all might happen as I had well enough proved.

2

I would lose the proper proportions of my subject if I were to recount every stage of my progress from the casino in Monte Carlo to another casino in Port-au-Prince, where I found myself again in possession of money and in love with a woman, a coin-cidence no more unlikely than the encounter on the Atlantic between three people called Smith, Brown, and Jones.

In the long interval I had led a hand-to-mouth existence,

except for a period of peace and respectability which came with the war, and not all my occupations were of the kind to find a place in my *curriculum vitae*. The first job I obtained, thanks to my good knowledge of French (my Latin was singularly unhelpful), was at a small restaurant in Soho, where I served for six months as a waiter. I never mentioned that, nor my graduation to the Trocadero, thanks to a forged reference from Fouquet's in Paris. After some years at the Trocadero I rose to being adviser to a small firm of educational publishers who were launching a series of French classics with notes of a scrupulously cleansing nature. That did find a place in my curriculum. Others that followed did not. Indeed I was a little spoilt by the security of my employment during the war, when I served in the Political Intelligence Department of the Foreign Office, supervising the style of our propaganda to Vichy territory, and even had a lady-novelist as my secretary. When the war was over I wanted something better than my old life of hand-to-mouth, though nevertheless for some years I returned to that way of life, until at last an idea came to me south of Piccadilly, outside one of those galleries where you are likely to see a less than pedigree work by an obscure seventeenth-century Dutch painter, or perhaps it was outside a gallery a degree lower in the trade where a taste for jovial cardinals enjoying their Friday salmon was mysteriously catered for. A middle-aged man wearing a double-breasted waistcoat and a watch-chain, a man remote, I would have said, from artistic interests, stood gazing at the pictures and suddenly I thought I knew exactly what was passing in his mind. "At Sotheby's last month a picture fetched a hundred thousand pounds. A picture can represent a fortune —if one knew enough or even took a chance," and he stared very hard at some cows in a meadow, as though he were watching a little ivory-ball running round a groove. It was surely the cows in the meadow at which he gazed and not the cardinals. No one could possibly envisage the cardinals in a Sotheby sale.

A week after that vision south of Piccadilly I gambled most of what I had accumulated during more than thirty years and

invested in a trailer-caravan and about twenty inexpensive prints
—there was an Henri Rousseau at one end of the scale and a
Jackson Pollock at the other. I hung these on one side of my
van with a record of the sums which they had fetched at auc-
tion and the date of the sales. Then I procured a young art-
student able to turn me out rapidly a number of rough pastiches
which he signed each time with a different name—I would
often sit with him while he worked and try out signatures on a
piece of paper. In spite of the example of Pollock and Moore,
which proved that even an Anglo-Saxon name could have value,
most of the names were foreign. I remember Msloz only because his work obstinately refused to sell, and in the end we had
to paint out his signature and substitute Weill. I had come to
realize that the purchaser wanted, as his minimum satisfaction,
to be able to pronounce a name—"I got a new Weill the other
day," and the nearest that even I could get to Msloz sounded
like Sludge, a name which may have caused unconscious
purchaser-resistance.

I would drive from one provincial city to another dragging
my trailer, and come to rest in a well-to-do suburb of an indus-
trial city. I soon realized that scientists and women were of little
use to me: scientists know too much, and few housewives love
to gamble without the sight of ready cash that Bingo provides.
I needed gamblers, for the point of my exhibition was really
this: "Here on one side of the gallery you can see the pictures
which have fetched the highest prices in the last ten years.
Would you have guessed that these 'Cyclists' by Léger, this
'Station-Master' by Rousseau were worth a fortune? Here, on
the other, you have a chance to spot their successors and win a
fortune too. If you lose, at least you have something on your
walls to talk about to your neighbours, you gain the reputation
of being an advanced art-patron, and it won't cost you more
than ——" My price varied from twenty to fifty pounds according to the neighbourhood and the customer; I even once sold
a two-headed woman a long way after Picasso for a hundred.

As my young man became more skilful at his job he would

turn me out an assorted half-dozen paintings in a morning and I paid him two pounds ten for each. I was robbing nobody; with fifteen pounds for a morning's work he was well satisfied; I was even helping young promise, and I am sure that many a dinner-party in the provinces went better because of some outrageous challenge to good taste upon the walls. I once sold an imitation Pollock to a man who had Walt Disney dwarfs planted in his garden, around the sun-dial and on either side the crazy paving. Did I harm him? He could afford the money. He had an air of complete invulnerability, though God knows for what aberration in his sexual or business life Dopey and the other dwarfs may have compensated.

It was soon after my success with Dopey's owner that I received my mother's appeal—if you could call it an appeal. It came in the shape of a picture-postcard which showed the ruined citadel of the Emperor Christophe at Cap Haïtien. She wrote on the back of it her name, which was new to me, her address, and two sentences. "Feel a bit of a ruin myself. Nice to see you if you come this way." In brackets after "Maman"— not recognizing her hand I read it first not unsuitably as "Manon"—she had added Comtesse de Lascot-Villiers." It had taken many months to find me.

I hadn't seen my mother since one occasion in Paris in 1934, and I had not heard from her during the war. I daresay I would not have answered her invitation but for two things—it was the nearest she had ever approached to a maternal appeal, and it was really time for me to finish with the travelling art-gallery, for a Sunday paper was trying to find out the source of my paintings. I had more than a thousand pounds in the bank. I sold the caravan, the stock, and the reproductions to a man who never read the *People* for five hundred pounds, and I flew out to Kingston, where I looked around unsuccessfully for business opportunities before taking another plane to Port-au-Prince.

3

Port-au-Prince was a very different place a few years ago. It was, I suppose, just as corrupt; it was even dirtier; it contained as many beggars, but at least the beggars had some hope, for the tourists were there. Now when a man says to you, "I am starving," you believe him. I wondered what my mother was doing at the Hotel Trianon, whether she was existing there on a pension from the count, if there had ever been a count, or whether perhaps she was working as a housekeeper. She had been employed when I saw her last in 1934 as a *vendeuse* in one of the minor *couturiers*. It was regarded in that pre-war period as a rather smart thing to employ an Englishwoman, so she had called herself Maggie Brown (perhaps her married name really was Brown).

For the sake of prudence I took my bags to the El Rancho, a luxurious Americanized hotel. I wanted to be comfortable so long as my money lasted, and nobody at the airport could tell me anything about the Trianon. As I drove up between the palm-trees it looked bedraggled enough: the bougainvillaea needed cutting back and there was more grass than gravel on the drive. A few people were drinking on the balcony, among them Petit Pierre, though I was to learn soon enough that he paid for his drinks only with his pen. A young well-dressed Negro met me on the steps and asked me whether I needed a room. I said I had come to see "Madame la Comtesse"—I couldn't keep the double-barrelled name in mind and I had left the postcard in my hotel-room.

"I am afraid she is sick. Is she expecting you?"

A very young American couple in bath-robes came up from the pool. The man had his arm around the girl's shoulder. "Hi, Marcel," he said, "a couple of your specials."

"Joseph," the Negro called. "Two rum-punches for Mr. Nelson." He turned back to me with his enquiry.

"Tell her," I said, "that Mr. Brown is here."

"Mr. Brown?"

"Yes."

"I will see if she is awake." He hesitated. He said, "You have come from England?"

"Yes."

Joseph came out of the bar carrying the rum-punches. He had no limp in those days.

"Mr. Brown from England?" Marcel asked again.

"Yes, Mr. Brown from England." He went upstairs reluctantly. The strangers on the balcony were watching me with curiosity, except for the young couple—they exchanged cherries intensely with their lips. The sun was about to set behind the great hump of Kenscoff.

Petit Pierre asked, "You have come from England?"

"Yes."

"From London?"

"Yes."

"London was very cold?"

It was like an interrogation by the secret police, but in those days there were no secret police.

"It was raining when I left."

"How do you like it here, Mr. Brown?"

"I have only been here two hours." The next day I had the explanation of his interest: there was a paragraph about me in the social column of the local paper.

"You're coming on fine with your backstroke," the young man said to the girl.

"Oh Chick, do you really mean it?"

"I mean it, honey."

A Negro came halfway up the steps and held out two hideous pieces of wood-carving. Nobody paid him any attention and he stood there, holding them out, saying nothing. I never even noticed when he went away.

"Joseph, what's for dinner?" the girl called.

A man walked round the balcony carrying a guitar. He sat

down at a table near the couple and began to play. Nobody paid him any attention either. I began to feel a little awkward. I had expected a warmer welcome in my mother's home.

A tall elderly Negro with a Roman face blackened by the soot of cities and with hair dusted by stone came down the stairs, followed by Marcel. He said, "Mr. Brown?"

"Yes."

"I am Doctor Magiot. Will you come into the bar for a moment?"

We went into the bar. Joseph was mixing some more rum-punches for Petit Pierre and his party. A cook wearing a high white hat pushed his head through the door and retreated again when he saw Doctor Magiot. A very pretty half-caste maid stopped talking to Joseph and went out on to the balcony carrying linen cloths to cover the tables.

Doctor Magiot said, "You are the son of Madame la Comtesse?"

"Yes." It seemed to me that I had done nothing but answer questions since I arrived.

"Of course your mother is anxious to see you, but I wanted first to tell you certain facts. Excitement is dangerous for her. Please when you see her be very gentle. Undemonstrative."

I smiled. "We have never been demonstrative. What's wrong, doctor?"

"She has had a second *crise cardiaque*. I am surprised that she is alive. She is a very remarkable woman."

"Oughtn't we to call in . . . perhaps . . ."

"You need not be afraid, Mr. Brown. The heart is my speciality. You will not find anyone more competent than I am nearer than New York. I doubt whether you will find one there." He was not boasting; he was just explaining, for he was used to being doubted by white people. "I was trained," he said, "under Chardin in Paris."

"No hope?"

"She can hardly survive another attack. Good night, Mr. Brown. Don't stay with her too long. I am glad you were able to come. I was afraid she might have no one to send for."

"She didn't exactly send for me."

"Perhaps one night you and I might have dinner together. I have known your mother many years. I have a great respect . . ." He gave me the kind of bow with which a Roman emperor might have brought an audience to an end. He was in no way condescending. He knew his exact value. "Good night, Marcel." To Marcel he gave no bow at all. I noticed that even Petit Pierre let him go by without greeting or question. I was ashamed at the thought that I had suggested to a man of his quality a second opinion.

Marcel said, "Will you come upstairs, Mr. Brown?"

I followed him. The walls were hung with pictures by Haitian artists: forms caught in wooden gestures among bright and heavy colours—a cock-fight, a Voodoo ceremony, black clouds over Kenscoff, banana-trees of stormy green, the blue spears of the sugar-cane, golden maize. Marcel opened the door and I went in to the shock of my mother's hair spread over the pillow, a Haitian red which had never existed in nature. It flowed abundantly on either side of her across the great double-bed.

"My dear," she said, as though I had come to see her from the other side of town, "how nice of you to look in." I kissed her wide brow like a whitewashed wall and a little of the white came off on my lips. I was aware of Marcel watching. "And how is England?" she asked as though she were enquiring after a distant daughter-in-law, for whom she did not greatly care.

"It was raining when I left."

"Your father could never stand his own climate," she remarked.

She might have passed anywhere for a woman in her late forties, and I could see nothing of an invalid about her except a tension of the skin around her mouth which I noticed years later in the case of the pharmaceutical traveller.

"Marcel, a chair for my son." He reluctantly drew one from the wall, but, when I sat in it, I was as far from her as ever because of the width of the bed. It was a shameless bed built for one purpose only, with a gilt curlicued footboard more suitable to a courtesan in a historical romance than to an old woman dying.

I asked her, "And is there really a count, Mother?"

She gave me a knowing smile. "He belongs to a distant past," she said, and I could not be certain whether she intended the phrase to be his epitaph or not. "Marcel," she added, "silly boy, you can safely leave us alone. I told you. He is my son." When the door closed, she said with complacency, "He is absurdly jealous."

"Who is he?"

"He helps me to manage the hotel."

"He isn't the count by any chance?"

"*Méchant*," she replied mechanically. She had really caught from the bed—or was it from the count?—an easy enlightened eighteenth-century air.

"Why should he be jealous then?"

"Perhaps he thinks you're not really my son."

"You mean he is your lover?" I wondered what my unknown father, whose name—or so I understood—was Brown, would have thought of his Negro successor.

"Why are you smiling, my dear?"

"You are a wonderful woman, Mother."

"A little luck has come my way at the end."

"You mean Marcel?"

"Oh no. He's a good boy—that's all. I meant the hotel. It is the first real property I have ever possessed. I own it completely. There is no mortgage. Even the furniture is paid for."

"And the pictures?"

"They are for sale, of course. I take a commission."

"Was it alimony from the count which allowed you . . . ?"

"Oh no, nothing like that. I gained nothing from the count except his title, and I have never checked in the Almanac de Gotha to see whether it exists. No, this was a little piece of pure good fortune. A certain Monsieur Dechaux who lived in Port-au-Prince was anxious about his taxes, and as I was working for him at the time in a secretarial capacity I allowed him to put this hotel under my name. Of course I left him the place in my will and as I was over sixty and he was thirty-five the arrangement seemed to him quite a secure one."

"He trusted you?"

"He was quite right to trust me, my dear. But he was wrong in trying to drive a Mercedes sports-car on the roads that we have here. It was a lucky chance he killed only himself."

"And so you took over?"

"He would have been very happy to know of it. My dear, you can't imagine how much he detested his wife. A big fat Negress without education. She could never have run the place properly. Of course after his death I had to alter my will—your father, if he is still alive, might have been next of kin. By the way I have left the fathers of the Visitation my rosary and my missal. I was never quite happy about the manner in which I treated them, but I was very pressed for money at the time. Your father was a bit of a swine, God rest his soul."

"Then he *is* dead?"

"I have every reason to believe it, but no proof. People live so long nowadays. Poor man."

"I've been talking to your doctor."

"Doctor Magiot? I wish I had met him when he was younger. He's quite a man, isn't he?"

"He says if you keep quiet . . ."

"Here I am lying flat in bed," she exclaimed with a knowing and pleading smile. "I can do no more to please him, can I? Do you know the dear man asked me if I would like to see a priest? I said to him, 'But surely, doctor, a long confession would be a little too exciting for me now—with such memories to recall?' Would you mind going to the door, dear, and opening it a little way?"

I obeyed her. The passage was empty. From below came a chink of cutlery and a voice saying, "Oh Chick, do you really think I *could*?"

"Thank you, dear. I just wanted to be quite certain . . .

While you are up, would you give me my brush? Thank you again. So much. How nice it is for an old woman to have a son around . . ." She paused. I think she expected me courteously, like a gigolo, to contradict the fact of her age. "I wanted to speak to you about my will," she went on in a tone of slight disappointment, as she brushed and brushed her improbable and abundant hair.

"Oughtn't you to rest now? The doctor told me not to stay long."

"They have given you a nice room, I hope? Some of the rooms remain a little bare. For want of ready cash."

"I left my bags at El Rancho."

"Oh, but you must stay here, my dear. El Rancho—it wouldn't do—to advertise that joint." She used the American expression. "After all—it was what I had to tell you—this hotel will be yours one day. Only I wanted to explain—the law is so complicated, one must take precautions—that it's in the form of shares, and I have left to Marcel a third interest. He will be very useful if you treat him right, and I had to do something for the boy, hadn't I? He has been rather more than a mere manager. You understand? You are my son, so of course you understand."

"I understand."

"I'm so glad you are here. I didn't want any little slip . . . Never underestimate a Haitian lawyer, when it comes to a testament . . . I'll tell Marcel that you'll take over the actual direction immediately. Only be tactful, that's a good boy. Marcel is very sensitive."

"And you, Mother, rest quiet. If you can, don't think any more about business. Try to sleep."

"They say that to be dead is about as quiet as you can get. I don't see any point in my anticipating death. It lasts a long time."

I put my lips again against the whitewashed wall. She closed her eyes in an artificial gesture of love, and I tip-toed away from her to the door. When I opened it very softly so as not to disturb her I heard a giggle from the bed. "You really are a son of mine," she said. "What part are you playing now?" Those were the last words she ever said to me, and I am not sure to this day what exactly she meant by them.

I took a taxi to El Rancho and stayed there for dinner. The place was crowded, a buffet of Haitian food carefully adapted to American tastes was laid by the swimming-pool, a bony man in a conical hat performed lightning-taps upon a Haitian drum, and it was then, on my first evening, I think, that the ambition was born in me to make the Trianon successful. For the moment it was too obviously a hotel of the second class. I could imagine the small tourists' agents who included it in their round-trip programmes. I doubted whether the profits could possibly satisfy both Marcel and myself. I was determined to succeed, in the biggest possible way; I would have the delight one day of sending the surplus guests uphill to El Rancho with my recommendation. And the strange thing was that my dream did come true for a short time. In three seasons I was able to transform the shabby place into the bizarre high spot of Port-au-Prince, and through three seasons I watched it die again, until now there were only the Smiths upstairs in the John Barrymore suite and Monsieur le Ministre dead in the bathing-pool.

I paid my bill and took a taxi back down the hill and entered what I had already begun to regard as my sole property. To-morrow I would go through the accounts with Marcel, I would interview the staff, I would take control. I was already planning how best to buy Marcel out, but that would have to wait until my mother had gone on to her further destiny. They had given me a big room on the same landing as hers. The furniture, she said, had all been paid for, but the floorboards needed renewal, they bent and creaked under my feet, and the only thing of value in the room was the bed, a fine large Victorian bed—my mother had an eye for beds—with big brass knobs. It was the first time I could remember that I had lain down to sleep in a bed I had not paid for with breakfast included—or had not been in debt for, as was the case at the College of the Visitation. The sensation was an oddly luxurious one and I slept well—until a jangling hysterical old-fashioned bell woke me, while I was dreaming—God knows why—of the Boxer rebellion.

It rang and rang, and now I was reminded of a fire-alarm. I put on my dressing-gown and opened my door. Another door opened at the same moment from the same landing and I saw Marcel emerge, with a half-asleep look on his wide flat Negro face. He wore a pair of bright scarlet silk pyjamas and he hesitated just long enough for me to see the monogram over the pocket: an M interlaced with a Y. I wondered what the Y stood for, until I remembered that my mother's Christian name was Yvette. Were the pyjamas a sentimental gift? I doubted that. More likely the monogram was an act of defiance on my mother's part. She had very good taste, and Marcel had a fine figure to swathe in scarlet silk, and she wasn't petty enough to mind what her second-rate tourists thought.

He saw me watching him and he said in a tone of apology, "She wants me." Then he went slowly, with what seemed reluctance, to her door. I noticed that he didn't knock before he went in.

I had an odd dream when I got back to sleep—odder than the Boxer rebellion. I was walking by the side of a lake in the moonlight and I was dressed like an altar-boy—I felt the magnetism of the still quiet water, so that every step I took was nearer to the verge, until the uppers of my black boots were submerged. Then a wind blew and the surge rose over the lake, like a small tidal wave, but instead of coming towards me, it went in the opposite direction, raising the water in a long retreat, so that I found I walked on dry pebbles and that the lake existed only as a gleam on the far horizon of the desert of small stones, which wounded me through a hole in my boots. I woke to an agitation that shook the stairs and floors throughout the hotel. Madame la Comtesse, my mother, was dead.

I was travelling light, my European suit was too hot to wear, and I had only a choice of gaudy sports-shirts to put on for the chamber of death. The one which I chose I had bought in Jamaica; it was scarlet and covered with print taken from an eighteenth-century book on the economy of the islands. They had tidied my mother up by that time, and she lay on her back in a pink diaphanous night-dress wearing an ambiguous smile of secret or even sensual satisfaction. But her powder had caked a little in the heat, and I couldn't bring myself to kiss the hard flakes. Marcel stood by the bed, dressed correctly in black, and his face dripped with tears like a black roof in a storm. I had thought of him simply as my mother's last extravagance, but it was no gigolo who said to me in a tone of anguish, "It was not my fault, sir. I said to her again and again, 'No, you're not strong enough. Wait just a little. It will be all the better if you wait.'"

"What did she say?"

"Nothing. She just took off the sheets. And when I see her like that it is always the same." He started to leave the room, shaking his head as though to get the rain out of his eyes, and then he came hurriedly back, went down on his knees by the bed, and thrust his mouth against the sheet where it was rounded by her stomach. He knelt there in his black suit looking like some Negro priest at an obscene rite. It was I, not he, who left the room, and it was I who went to the kitchen and set the servants to work again for the guests' breakfast (even the cook was partly incapacitated by tears), and it was I who telephoned to Doctor Magiot. (The telephone frequently worked in those days.)

"She was a great woman," Doctor Magiot said to me later, and "I hardly knew her" was all I could say in my stupefaction.

The next day I went through her papers to find her will. She had not been very tidy: the drawers of her desk were given up indiscriminately to bills and receipts in no order that I could detect; there was a confusion even in the years. Sometimes among a pile of laundry-receipts I came on what used to be called a *billet-doux*. One in English, written in pencil on the back of a hotel-menu, said, "Yvette, come to me tonight. I am dying slowly. I long for the *coup-de-grâce*." Was it from a hotel-guest? I wondered whether she had kept it for the sake of the menu or of the message, for the menu was a very special one for some July 14 celebration.

In another drawer, which otherwise contained mainly tubes of glue, drawing-pins, hair-slides, fountain-pen refills, and paper-clips was a china pig-bank. The pig was light, but it rattled all the same. I didn't want to break it open, but it seemed foolish to throw it away like that, unexamined, on the growing pile of lumber. When I cracked it apart I found a Monte Carlo roulette-token for five francs like the one I had put in the chapel-collection many decades ago and a tarnishing medal, attached to a ribbon. I couldn't make out what it was, but when I showed it to Doctor Magiot he recognized it. "A medal of the resistance," he said, and it was then that he added, "She was a great woman."

A medal of the resistance . . . I had had no communication with my mother during the years of the occupation. Had she earned it or had she filched it or had it been given her as a love-token? Doctor Magiot had no doubt at all, but I had difficulty in thinking of my mother as a heroine, though I had no doubt at all that she could have played the part, as she could have played the *grand amoureuse* with the English tourist. She had convinced the fathers of the Visitation of her moral rectitude, even against the dubious background of Monte Carlo. I knew very little of her, but enough to recognize an accomplished comedian.

However, though her bills were untidy, there was nothing un-tidy about her will. It was clear and precise, signed by the Comtesse de Lascot-Villiers and witnessed by Doctor Magiot. She had turned her hotel into a limited company and assigned a nominal share to Marcel, another to Doctor Magiot, and one to her lawyer, who was called Alexandre Dubois. She possessed the ninety-seven other shares, as well as the three transfers which were neatly pinned to the document. The company owned everything to the last spoon and fork and I was allotted sixty-five shares and Marcel thirty-three. I was to all intents the owner of the Trianon. I could begin at once to realize the dream of the night before—or only with such delay as the quick burial of my mother, a quickness entailed by the climate, presented.

In these arrangements Doctor Magiot proved invaluable; she was transported that very afternoon to the small cemetery in the mountain village of Kenscoff, where she was dug in with due Catholic rites among the small tombs and Marcel wept unashamedly by the grave, which looked like a hole dug for drains in a town street, for all around were the little houses the Haitians constructed for their dead; in them on the Feast of All Souls they would leave their bread and wine. While the ceremonial trowels of earth were deposited on the coffin, I wondered how best I could dispose of Marcel. We had been standing in the gloom of the ink-black clouds which always assembled over the mountain at that hour and now they broke on us with a dash and fury, and we ran for our taxis, the priest in the lead and the gravediggers bringing up the rear. I didn't know it then, but I know now that the diggers would not have returned before the morning to cover up my mother's coffin, for no one will work in a cemetery at night, unless it is a zombie who has left his grave at the command of an *houngan* to labour during the dark hours.

Doctor Magiot gave me dinner that night at his own home, and in addition he gave me a great deal of good advice which I was unwise enough to discount because I thought he might perhaps have an idea of obtaining the hotel for another client. It was the one share he possessed in my mother's company which made me suspicious even though I held the signed transfer.

He lived on the lower slopes of Pétionville in a house of three storeys like a miniature version of my own hotel with its tower and its lace-work balconies. In the garden grew a dry spiky Norfolk pine, like an illustration in a Victorian novel, and the only modern object in the room, where we sat after dinner, was the telephone. It was like an oversight in a museum-arrangement. The heavy drape of the scarlet curtains, the woollen cloths on the occasional tables with bobbles at each corner, the china objects on the chimney-piece that included two dogs with the same gentle gaze as Doctor Magiot's, the portraits of the doctor's parents (coloured photographs mounted on mauve silk in oval frames), the pleated screen in the unnecessary fireplace, spoke of another age; the literary works in a glass-fronted bookcase (Doctor Magiot kept his professional works in his consulting-room) were bound in old-fashioned calf. I examined them while he was out "washing his hands," as he put it in polite English. There were *Les Misérables* in three volumes, *Les Mystères de Paris* with the last volume missing, several of Gaboriau's *romans policiers*, Renan's *Vie de Jésus*, and rather surprisingly among its companions Marx's *Capital* rebound in exactly the same calf so that it was indistinguishable at a distance from *Les Misérables*. The lamp at Doctor Magiot's elbow had a pink glass shade, and quite wisely, for even in those days the electric-current was erratic, it was oil-burning.

"You really intend," Doctor Magiot asked me, "to take over the hotel?"

"Why not? I have a little experience of restaurant-work. I can see great possibilities of improvement. My mother was not catering for the luxury-trade."

"The luxury-trade?" Doctor Magiot repeated. "I think you can hardly depend on that here."

"Some hotels do."

"The good years will not always continue. Not very long now and there will be the elections . . ."

"It doesn't make much difference, does it, who wins?"

"Not to the poor. But to the tourist perhaps." He put a flowered saucer upon the table beside me—an ash-tray would have been out of period in this room where no one had ever smoked in the old days. He handled the saucer carefully, as though it were of precious porcelain. He was very big and very black, but he possessed great gentleness—he would never illtreat, I felt sure, even an inanimate object, such as a recalcitrant chair. Nothing can be more inconsiderate to a man of Doctor Magiot's profession than a telephone. But when it rang once during our conversation he lifted the receiver as gently as he would have raised a patient's wrist.

"You have heard," Doctor Magiot said, "of the Emperor Christophe?"

"Of course."

"Those days could return very easily. More cruelly perhaps and certainly more ignobly. God save us from a little Christophe."

"Nobody could afford to frighten away the American tourists. You need the dollars."

"When you know us better, you will realize that we don't live on money here, we live on debts. You can always afford to kill a creditor, but no one ever kills a debtor."

"Whom do you fear?"

"I fear a small country doctor. His name would mean nothing to you now. I only hope you don't see it one day stuck up in electric-lights over the city. If that day comes I promise you I shall run to cover." It was Doctor Magiot's first mistaken prophecy. He underrated his own stubbornness or his own courage. Otherwise I would not have been waiting for him later beside the dry swimming-pool where the ex-Minister lay still as a hunk of beef in a butcher's shop.

"And Marcel?" he asked me. "What do you propose to do with Marcel?"

"I haven't decided. Tomorrow I must have a word with him. You know he owns a third of the hotel?"

"You forget—I witnessed the will."

"It occurred to me that he might be ready to sell his shares. I have no cash, but I could probably borrow from the bank."

Doctor Magiot put his great pink palms on the knees of his black formal suit and leant towards me as though he had a secret to convey. He said, "I would advise you to do the opposite. Let him buy your shares. Make it easy for him and let him buy them cheap. He is a Haitian. He can live on very little. He can survive." But there again Doctor Magiot proved to be a false prophet. He saw the future of his country clearer than the fate of the individuals who composed it.

I said with a smile, "Oh no, I've taken a fancy to the Trianon. You'll see—I shall stay and I shall survive."

I waited two days more before I spoke to Marcel, but in the interval I had a word with the bank-manager. The last two seasons in Port-au-Prince had been good ones. I outlined my plans for the hotel, and the manager, who was a European, made no difficulty in advancing me the money I needed. The only point on which he proved difficult was the rate of repayment. "You are virtually asking me to repay in three years?"

"Yes."

"Why?"

"Well, you see, before that there are the elections."

I had hardly seen Marcel since the funeral. Joseph, the barman, came to me for orders, the cook and the gardener came to me, Marcel had abdicated without a fight, but I noticed when I passed him on the stairs that he smelt strongly of rum, so I had a glass of it ready for him when we came together at last to talk. He listened without a word and he accepted what I had to say without dispute. What I offered him was a lot of money in Haitian terms, and I offered it in dollars and not gourdes, even though it represented half the nominal value of his shares. For psychological effect I had the money on me in hundred-dollar bills. "You had better count them," I told him, but he put the money in his pocket without checking it. "And now," I said, "if you will sign here," and he signed without reading what he signed. It was as easy as that. No scene at all.

"I'll need your room," I said, "from tomorrow." Was I harsh to him? What partly influenced me was the embarrassment of dealing with my mother's lover, and it must have been awkward for him too to meet her son, a man much older than himself. Just before he left the room he spoke of her. "I pretended not to hear the bell," he said, "but she rang again and again. I thought she might need something."

"But she only needed you?"

He said, "I am ashamed."

I could hardly have discussed with him the powerful influence of my mother's sexual desires. I said, "You haven't finished your rum." He drained the glass. He said, "When she was angry with me or when she loved me she called me 'You big black beast.' That is what I feel now, a big black beast." He went out of the room, one buttock heavily swollen with hundred-dollar bills, and an hour later I watched him going down the drive, carrying an old cardboard suitcase. He had abandoned in his room the scarlet silk pyjamas with the monogram YM.

For a week after that I heard nothing from him. I was very busy at the hotel. The only one who really knew his job was Joseph (I made him famous later for his rum-punches), and I could only suppose that our guests were so used to eating badly at home, they accepted the cook's dishes as just an inseparable feature of human life. He served over-cooked steaks and ice-cream. I found myself living almost entirely on the grapefruit, which he found it hard to spoil. The season was nearly at an end and I longed for the last guest to go, so that I could give the cook his quietus. Not that I knew where to find his successor—good cooks were not easy to find in Port-au-Prince.

One night I felt a strong need to forget the hotel, so I took myself to the casino. In those days, before Doctor Duvalier came to power, there were enough tourists to keep three roulette tables busy. You could hear the music from the night-club below, and occasionally a woman in evening-dress, tired of dancing, would bring her partner to the tables. Haitian women are the most beautiful in the world, I think, and there were faces and figures there which would have made a fortune for their owners in a western capital. And always for me in a casino was the sense that anything might happen. "Man has but one virginity to lose," and I had lost mine that winter afternoon in Monte Carlo.

I had been playing for several minutes before I saw that Marcel was sitting at the same table. I would have shifted, but

I had already won once *en plein*. I have a superstition that only a single table each night is lucky and tonight I had found my lucky table, for in twenty minutes I was already a hundred and fifty dollars to the good. I caught the eye of a young European woman across the table. She smiled and began to follow my stakes, saying a word to her companion, a fat man with an enormous cigar, who fed her with tokens and never played himself. But the table which was so lucky for me was unlucky for Marcel. Sometimes we placed our stakes on the same square and then I lost. I began to wait until he had laid his tokens before I placed my bet, and the girl, who saw what I was at, followed suit. It was as though we were dancing in step—as in a Malayan ron-ron without touching. I was content because she was pretty and because I remembered Monte Carlo. As for the fat man, I could deal with that trouble later. Perhaps he too belonged to the Banque de l'Indochine.

Marcel was following a mad system. It was as though he were bored with the game and the quicker he lost the quicker he could leave the table. Then he saw me and, shovelling together the remainder of his tokens, he laid them all on zero, which had not come up for more than thirty turns. He lost, of course, as one always loses with a desperate throw, and he pushed back his chair. I leant across to him with a ten dollar token. "Have a bit of my luck," I said.

Was I trying to humiliate him, to remind him that he had been my mother's paid lover? I don't remember now, but if that was my motive, I certainly failed. He took the token and replied with great courtesy in his careful French, "*Tout ce que j'ai eu de chance dans ma vie m'est venue de votre famille.*" He bet again on zero and zero came up—I hadn't followed him. He returned me my token and said, "Excuse me. I must go away now. I have a great need to sleep." I watched him leave the *salle*. He had over three hundred dollars to change now. He was off my conscience. And though he was certainly very black and very big, it was unfair, I thought, to have called him, as my mother had done, a beast.

Somehow all the seriousness was drained out of the *salle* when he left. We were all small-timers now, playing for fun, risking nothing and gaining nothing but the price of a few drinks. I raised my winnings to three hundred and fifty dollars and dropped them to two hundred only for the pleasure of see- ing the man with the cigar lose a little too. Then I stopped. Exchanging my tokens, I asked the cashier who the girl was.

"Madame Pineda," he said, "a German lady."

"I don't like Germans," I said with disappointment.

"Nor do I."

"Who is the fat man?"

"Her husband—the ambassador." He named some small South American state, but I forgot it the next moment. I used to be able to distinguish one South American republic from another by the postage-stamps, but I had left my collection behind at the College of the Visitation, as a gift to the boy whom I considered my greatest friend (I have long forgotten his name).

"I don't like ambassadors much either," I told the cashier.

"They are a necessary evil," he replied, counting out my dollar notes.

"You believe that evil is necessary? Then you're a Manichean like myself." Our theological discussion could go no further, for he had not been educated at the College of the Visitation, and in any case the girl's voice interrupted us. "Husbands too."

"What about husbands?"

"A necessary evil," she said, putting down her tokens on the cashier's desk.

We admire the qualities which are beyond our reach; so I admired loyalty, and at that moment I nearly walked away from her forever. I don't know what restrained me. Perhaps I de- tected in her voice another quality which I find admirable—the quality of desperation. Desperation and truth are closely akin— the desperate confession can usually be trusted, and just as it is not given to everyone to make a deathbed confession, so the capacity for desperation is granted to very few, and I was not one of them. But she had it and it excused her in my eyes. I would have done better to have followed my first thought and walked away, for I would have walked away from a lot of unhappiness. Instead I waited for her at the door of the *salle* while she picked up her winnings.

She was the same age as the woman I had known in Monte Carlo, but time had reversed our ages. The first woman had been old enough to be my mother, and now I was old enough to be this stranger's father. She was very dark and small and nervous—I would never have taken her for a German. She came towards me counting her dollars, to hide her timidity. She had made a desperate cast, and now she didn't know what to do with the bite at the end of her line.

I asked, "Where's your husband?"

"In the car," she said and looking out I noticed for the first time the Peugeot car with the C.D. plates. In the front seat beside the wheel the big man sat smoking his long cigar. His shoulders were wide and flat. You could have hung a poster on them. They looked like a wall closing a cul-de-sac.

"When can I see you again?"

"Here. Outside in the car-park. I can't come to your hotel."

"You know who I am?"

"I ask questions too," she said.

"Tomorrow night?"

"At ten. I must be back at one."

"And now—will he want to know what's kept you?"

"He has infinite patience," she said. "It is a diplomatic quality. He waits to speak till the political situation is ripe."

"Then why must you be back at one?"

"I have a child. He always wakes around one and calls for me. It's a habit—a bad habit. He has nightmares. About a robber in the house."

"Your only child?"

"Yes."

She touched my arm and at that moment the ambassador in the car put out his right hand and sounded the horn, twice but not too impatiently. He didn't even turn his head or he would have seen us.

"You're summoned back," I said, and with my first claim on her the shadow of other claims fell on me.

"I suppose it's nearly one." She added quickly, "I knew your mother. I liked her. She was real." She went out to the car. Her husband opened the door for her without turning, and she got behind the wheel: the end of his cigar glowed beside her cheek, like a warning lamp at the edge of a road under repair.

I went back to the hotel and Joseph met me on the steps. He said that Marcel had come back half an hour before and asked for a room for the night.

"Only for tonight?"

"He say he go tomorrow."

He had paid in advance, putting down the sum which he knew to be correct, he had ordered two bottles of rum to be sent up, and he asked if he might have the room of Madame la Comtesse.

"He could have had his old room." But then I remembered that the new guest—an American professor—was there.

I wasn't unduly troubled. In a way I was touched. I was glad that my mother had been so liked by her lover, and by the woman in the casino whose first name I had forgotten to ask. I would have liked her myself perhaps if she had given me half a chance. Perhaps I had in mind the hope that her likeability might have been passed on to me—a great advantage in business —as well as two-thirds of her hotel.

4

I was nearly half an hour late when I found the car with the C.D. sign outside the casino. There had been a great deal to keep me, and I was not really in the humour to come at all. I couldn't pretend to myself that I was in love with Madame Pineda. A bit of lust and a bit of curiosity was all I thought I felt, and driving into town I remembered everything in the

85

register against her, that she was a German, that she had made the first move, that she was an ambassador's wife. (I would certainly hear the chandeliers and the cocktail glasses tinkle in her conversation.)

She opened the car-door for me. "I nearly gave you up," she said.

"I'm sorry. A lot of things have happened."

"Now you are here, we had better drive away. Our colleagues begin to arrive after eleven when the official dinners are over."

She backed the car out. "Where are we going?" I asked.

"I don't know."

"What made you speak to me last night?"

"I don't know."

"You followed my luck?"

"Yes. I suppose I was curious to see what your mother's son was like. Nothing new ever happens here."

Ahead of us the port lay in a wash of temporary floodlights. Two cargo-ships were being unloaded. There was a long procession of bowed figures under sacks. She swung the car round in a half-circle and brought it into a deep patch of shadow close to the white statue of Columbus. "None of our kind come here at night," she said, "and so no beggars come either."

"What about the police?"

"The C.D. plate has some value."

I wondered which of us was using the other. I had not made love to a woman for some months and she—she had obviously reached the dead-end of most marriages. But I was crippled by the events of the day and I wished I had not come and I couldn't help remembering she was German, even though she was too young to bear any guilt herself. There was only one reason for us both to be here and yet we did nothing. We sat and stared at the statue which stared at America.

To escape from the absurdity I put my hand on her knee. The skin felt cold; she wore no stockings. I said, "What's your name?'

86

"Martha." She turned as she answered and I kissed her clumsily and missed her mouth.

She said, "We needn't, you know. We're grown-up people," and suddenly I was back in the Hôtel de Paris and powerless, and no bird came to save me on white wings.

"I only want to talk," she lied to me gently.

"I would have thought you had plenty to talk about at the embassy."

"Last night—would it have been all right, if I could have come to your hotel?"

"Thank God, you didn't," I said. "There was trouble enough there."

"What kind of trouble?"

"Don't let's talk about it now." Again, to disguise my lack of feeling, I acted crudely. I pulled her body out from under the wheel and thrust her across my thighs, scraping her leg on the radio-set, so that she exclaimed with pain.

"I'm sorry."

"It was nothing."

She settled herself more easily, she put her lips against my neck, but I felt nothing: nothing moved in me, and I wondered how long she would put up with her disappointment, if she were disappointed. Then for a long moment I forgot all about her. I was back in the midday heat knocking at the door of what had been my mother's room and getting no response. I knocked and knocked, thinking that Marcel was in a drunken sleep.

"Tell me about the trouble," she said. Suddenly I began to talk. I told her how the room-boy became anxious and then Joseph, and how finally, when there was no reply to my knocking, I used the pass-key and found that the door was bolted. I had to tear down the partition between two balconies and scramble from one to the other—luckily the guests were away swimming on the reef. I found Marcel hanging from his own belt from the centre-light: he must have had great resolution, for he had only to swing a few inches to land his toes on the curlicued ends of my mother's great bed. The rum had all been drunk except a little in the second bottle, and in an envelope addressed to me he had put what was left of the three hundred dollars. "You can imagine," I said, "how I've been occupied since. What with the police—and the guests too. The American professor was reasonable, but there was an English couple who said they were going to report it to their travel-agent. Apparently a suicide places a hotel in a lower price-bracket. It's not an auspicious beginning."

"It was a horrible shock," she said.

"I didn't know him or care about him, but it was a shock, yes, it really was a shock. Apparently I shall have to have the room purified by a priest or an *houngan*. I'm not sure which. And the lamp has to be destroyed. The servants insist on that."

It proved a relief to talk and with words desire came. The back of her neck was against my mouth and one leg spread-eagled across the radio. She shivered and her hand shot out and by bad chance fell on the rim of the wheel and set the klaxon crying. It went on wailing like a wounded animal or a ship lost in fog until the shiver stopped.

We sat in silence in the same cramped position, like two pieces of machinery which an engineer has just failed to fit. It was the moment to say goodbye and go: the longer we stayed the greater demands the future would hold for us. In silence trust begins, contentment grows. I realized I had slept a moment, woken, and found her sleeping. Sleep shared was a bond too many. I looked at my watch. It was long before midnight. The cranes ground over the cargo-ships and the long procession of workers passed from boat to warehouse, bent under their cowls of sacks like capuchin monks. One leg hurt me. I shifted it and woke her.

She struggled away and said sharply, "What's the time?"

"Twenty to twelve."

"I dreamt the car had broken down and it was one in the morning," she said.

I felt put in the place where I belonged, between the hours of ten and one. It was a daunting thought how quickly jealousy grows—I had barely known her for twenty-four hours and already I resented the demands of others.

"What's the matter?" she asked.

"I was wondering when we shall see each other again."

"At the same time tomorrow. Here. This is as good as any other place, isn't it. Take a different taxi-driver, that's all."

"It wasn't exactly an ideal bed."

"We'll get in the back of the car. It will be all right there," she said with a precision that depressed me.

So it was our affair began and so it continued with minor differences: for example a year later she changed her Peugeot for a newer model. There were occasions—once her husband was recalled for consultation—when we escaped the car; once with the help of a woman-friend we passed two days together at Cap Haïtien, but then the friend went home. It sometimes seemed to me that we were less lovers than fellow-conspirators tied together in the commission of a crime. And like conspirators we were well aware of the detectives on our track. One of them was the child.

I went over to a cocktail-party at the embassy. There was no reason why I should not have been invited, for within six months of our meeting I had become an accepted member of the foreign community. My hotel was a modest success—though I was not content with modesty, and I still dreamt of that first-class cook. I had met the ambassador first when he drove one of my guests —a fellow-countryman—back to the hotel after a dinner at the embassy. He accepted and praised one of Joseph's drinks, and the shadow of his long cigar lay for a while across my verandah. I have never heard a man use the word "my" more frequently. "Have one of my cigars." "Please let my chauffeur have a drink." We spoke of the coming elections. "My opinion is the doctor will succeed. He has American support. That is my information." He invited me "to my next cocktail-party."

Why did I resent him? I was not in love with his wife. I had "made" her, that was all. Or so I believed at the time. Was it that in the course of our conversation he had discovered I had been educated by the fathers of the Visitation and claimed a kind of kinship—"I was at the College of Saint Ignatius"—in Paraguay, Uruguay—who cares?

I learnt later that the cocktail-party to which in due course I was invited belonged to the second-class order, the first-class, where caviar was served, being purely diplomatic—ambassadors, ministers, first secretaries—while the third-class was purely "duty." It was a compliment to be included in the second, which was supposed to contain elements of "fun." There were a number of rich Haitians there with wives of a rare beauty. The time had not yet come for them to flee the country or to remain shut in their houses at night for fear of what might happen to them in the dark curfewed streets.

The ambassador introduced me to "my wife"—"my" again, and she led me to the bar to find me a drink. "Tomorrow night?" I asked, and she frowned at me and pursed her lips to indicate I was not to speak—that we were under observation. But it was not her husband whom she feared. He was busy showing "my" collection of Hyppolite's paintings to one of his guests, moving from picture to picture, explaining each one, as though the subjects too belonged to him.

"Your husband can't hear in all this din."

"Can't you see," she said, "that he is listening to every word?" But the "he" was not her husband. A small creature, not much more than three feet high, with dark concentrated eyes, was forcing his way towards us with the arrogance of a midget, thrusting aside the knees of guests as though they were the undergrowth of a wood which belonged to him. I saw he had his eyes on her mouth, as though he were lip-reading.

"My son Angel," she introduced him, and always I thought of him after that in the English pronunciation of the name, like a kind of blasphemy.

Once he had regained her side he hardly left it, though he never spoke at all—he was too busy listening, while his small steely hand grasped hers, like one half of a handcuff. I had met my real rival. She told me when we next met that he had asked a great many questions about me.

"He smells something wrong?"

"How could he at his age? He's barely five."

A year passed, and we found ways of outwitting him, but his claims on her remained. I discovered she was indispensable to me, but when I pressed her to leave her husband, the child blocked her escape. She could do nothing to endanger his happiness. She would leave her husband tomorrow, but how could she survive if he took Angel from her? And it seemed to me that month by month the son grew more to resemble the father. He had a way now of saying "my" mother, and once I saw him with a long chocolate-cigar in his mouth; he was putting on weight rapidly. It was as though the father had incarnated his own demon to ensure that our affair did not go too far, beyond the bounds of prudence.

There was a time when we took a room for meeting above a Syrian store. The store-keeper, whose name was Hamit, was completely reliable—it was just after the doctor came to power, and the shadow of the future was there for anyone to see, black as the cloud on Kenscoff. Any kind of connection with a foreign embassy had value for a stateless man, for who could tell at what hour he might not have to take political asylum? Unfortunately, though we had both closely examined the store, we did not realize that, in a corner behind the pharmaceutical products, there were a few shelves given up to toys of better quality than could be found elsewhere, and among the groceries, for the luxury trade had not yet entirely ceased, a tin of bourbon biscuits could occasionally be found, a favourite provender of Angel between meals. This led to our first big quarrel.

We had already met three times in the Syrian room, which contained a brass bed under a mauve-silk counterpane and four hard upright chairs lined along the wall and a number of hand-tinted photographs of family-groups. I think it was the guest-room, kept immaculate for some important visitor from Lebanon who never came and never would come. The fourth time I waited for two hours and Martha did not appear at all. I went out through the store and the Syrian spoke to me discreetly. "You have missed Madame Pineda," he said. "She was here with her little boy."

"Her little boy?"

"They bought a miniature car and a box of bourbon biscuits."

Later that evening she rang me up. She sounded breathless and afraid and she spoke very rapidly. "I am at the Post Office," she said. "I've left Angel in the car."

"Eating bourbon biscuits?"

"Bourbon biscuits? How did you know? Darling, I couldn't come to you. When I got to the shop I found Angel there with his nurse. I had to pretend I'd come to buy him something as a reward for being good."

"Has he been good?"

"Not particularly. His nurse said they saw me come out last week—it was a good thing we never leave together—and he wanted to see where I'd been and that's how he discovered the biscuits he liked."

"The bourbon biscuits."

"Yes. Oh, he's coming into the Post Office now to find me. Tonight. Same place." The telephone went dead.

So we met again by the Columbus statue in the Peugeot car. That time we didn't make love. We quarrelled. I told her Angel was a spoilt child, and she admitted it, but when I said that he spied on her, she was angry, and when I said he was getting as fat as his father, she tried to slap my face. I caught her wrist and she accused me of striking her. Then we laughed nervously, but the quarrel simmered on, like stock for tomorrow's soup.

I said very reasonably, "You would do better to make a break one way or the other. This kind of life can't go on indefinitely."

"Do you want me to leave you then?"

"Of course not."

"But I can't live without Angel. It's not his fault if I've spoilt him. He needs me. I can't ruin his happiness."

"In ten years he won't need you at all. He'll be slinking off to Mère Catherine or sleeping with one of your maids. Except that you won't be here—you'll be in Brussels or Luxembourg, but there are brothels for him there too."

"Ten years is a long time."

"And you'll be middle-aged and I'll be old—too old to care. You'll live on with two fat men . . . And a good conscience of course. You'll have salvaged that."

"And you? Don't tell me you won't have been comforted by all sorts of women in all sorts of ways."

Our voices rose higher and higher in the darkness under the statue. Like all such quarrels it led to nothing except a wound which easily heals. There are places for so many different wounds before we find ourselves breaking an old scab. I got out of her car and walked across to mine. I sat down at the wheel and began to back the car. I told myself it was the end—the game wasn't worth the candle—let her stay with the beastly child—there were many more attractive women to be found at Mère Catherine's—she was a German anyway. I called, "Goodbye, Frau Pineda," viciously out of the window as I came parallel to her car, and then I saw her bent over the wheel crying. I suppose it was necessary to say goodbye to her once before I realized that I could not do without her.

When I got back beside her, she was already in control. "It's no good," she said, "tonight."

"No."

"Shall we see each other tomorrow?"

"Of course."

"Here. As usual?"

"Yes."

She said, "There is something I meant to tell you. A surprise for you. Something you badly want."

For a moment I thought she was going to surrender to me and promise to leave her husband and her child. I put my arm round her to support her in the great decision and she said, "You need a good cook, don't you?"

"Oh—yes. Yes. I suppose I do."

"We've got a wonderful cook and he's leaving us. I engineered a row on purpose and sacked him. He's yours if you want him." I think she was hurt again by my silence. "Now don't you believe I love you? My husband will be furious. He said that André was the only cook in Port-au-Prince who could make a proper soufflé." I stopped myself just in time from saying, "And Angel? He likes his food too."

"You've made my fortune," I said. And what I said was nearly true—the Trianon soufflé au Grand Marnier was famous for a time, until the terror started and the American Mission left, and the British ambassador was expelled, and the Nuncio never returned from Rome, and the curfew put a barrier between us worse than any quarrel, until at last I too flew out on the last Delta plane to New Orleans. Joseph had only just escaped with his life from his interrogation by the Tontons Macoute and I was scared. They were after me, I felt certain. Perhaps Fat Gracia, the head of the Tontons, wanted my hotel. Even Petit Pierre no longer looked in for a free drink. For weeks I was alone with the injured Joseph, the cook, the maid, and the gardener. The hotel had need of paint and repairs, but what good was there in spending the labour without the hope of guests? Only the John Barrymore suite I kept in good order like a grave.

There was little in our love-affair now to balance the fear and the boredom. The telephone had ceased to work: it stood there on my desk like a relic of better times. With the curfew it was no longer possible for us to meet at night, while in the day there was always Angel. I thought I was escaping from love as well as politics when at last I received my exit-visa at the police-station after ten hours wait, with the heavy smell of urine in the air and policemen returning with a smile of satisfaction from the cells. I remember a priest who sat all day in a white soutane and his stony attitude of long and undisturbed patience as he read his breviary. His name was never called. Pinned behind his head on the liver-coloured wall were the snapshots of Barbot, the dead defector, and his broken companions who had been machine-gunned in a hut on the edge of the capital a month before. When the police-sergeant gave me my visa at last, shoving it across the counter like a crust of bread to a beggar, someone told the priest that the police-station was closed for the night. I suppose he came back next day. It was as good a place as any other for him to read his breviary, for none of the transients dared to speak to him, now that the Archbishop was in exile and the President excommunicated.

What a wonderful place the city had been to leave, as I looked down at it through the free and lucid air, the plane pitching in the thunder-storm which loomed as usual over Kenscoff. The port seemed tiny compared with the vast wrinkled wasteland behind, the dry uninhabited mountains, like the broken backbone of an ancient beast excavated from the clay, stretching into the haze towards Cap Haïtien and the Dominican border. I would find some gambler, I told myself, to buy my hotel, and I would then be as unencumbered as on the day I drove up to Pétionville and found my mother stretched in her great brothelly bed. I was happy to leave, I whispered it to the black mountain wheeling round below, I showed it in my smile to the trim American stewardess bringing me a highball of bourbon and to the pilot who came to report progress. It was four weeks before I woke to misery in my air-conditioned New York room in West 44th street after dreaming of a tangle of limbs in a Peugeot car and a statue staring at the sea. I knew then that sooner or later I would return, when my obstinacy was exhausted, my business-deal written off, and half a loaf eaten in fear would seem so much better than no bread.

Chapter Four

1

Doctor Magiot crouched a long time above the body of the ex-Minister. In the shadow cast by my torch he looked like a sorcerer exorcizing death. I hesitated to interrupt his rites, but I was afraid the Smiths might wake in their tower-suite, so at last I spoke and broke his thoughts. "They can't make it out to be anything but suicide," I said.

"They can make it out to be whatever suits them," he replied. "Do not deceive yourself." He began to empty the contents of the Minister's left pocket, which was exposed by the position of the body. He said, "He was one of the better ones," and looked with care at each scrap of paper like a bank-clerk checking notes for forgery, holding them close to his eyes and his big globular spectacles which he wore for reading only. "We took our anatomy course together in Paris. But in those days even Papa Doc was a good enough man. I remember Duvalier in the typhoid outbreak in the twenties . . ."

"What are you looking for?"

"Anything which could identify him with you. In this island the Catholic prayer is very apt—'The devil is like a roaring lion seeking whom he may devour.' "

"He hasn't devoured you."

"Give him time." He put a notebook in his pocket. "We haven't the leisure to go through all this now." Then he turned the body over. It was heavy to move even for Doctor Magiot. "I'm glad your mother died when she did. She had borne enough. One Hitler is sufficient experience for one lifetime."

We talked in whispers for fear of disturbing the Smiths. "A rabbit's foot," he said, "for luck." He put the object back. "And here is something heavy." He took out my brass paperweight in the shape of a coffin marked R.I.P. "I never knew he had a sense of humour."

"That's mine. He must have taken it from my office."

"Put it back in the same place."

"Shall I send Joseph for the police?"

"No, no. We can't leave the body here."

"They can hardly blame me for a suicide."

"They can blame you because he chose this house to hide in."

"Why did he? I never knew him. I met him once at a reception. That's all."

"The embassies are closely guarded. I suppose he believed in your English phrase, 'An Englishman's home is his castle.' He had so little hope he sought safety in a catch-word."

"It's the hell of a thing to find on my first night home."

"Yes, I suppose it is. Chekhov wrote, 'Suicide is an undesirable phenomenon.'"

Doctor Magiot stood up and looked down at the body. A coloured man has a great sense of occasion—it isn't ruined by Western education: education only changes the form of its expression. Doctor Magiot's great-grandfather might have wailed in the slave-compound to the unanswering stars: Doctor Magiot pronounced a short carefully phrased discourse over the dead. "However great a man's fear of life," Doctor Magiot said, "suicide remains the courageous act, the clear-headed act of a mathematician. The suicide has judged by the laws of chance —so many odds against one that to live will be more miserable than to die. His sense of mathematics is greater than his sense of survival. But think how a sense of survival must clamour to be heard at the last moment, what excuses it must present of a totally unscientific nature."

"I thought that as a Catholic you would have utterly condemned . . ."

"I am not a practising Catholic, and in any case you are thinking of theological despair. In this despair there was nothing theological. Poor fellow, he was breaking a rule. He was eating meat on Friday. In his case the sense of survival did not put forward a commandment of God as an excuse for inaction." He said, "You must come down and take the legs. We have to remove him from here." The lecture was finished, the funeral oration spoken.

It was a comfort to feel myself in the large square hands of Doctor Magiot. I was like a patient who accepts without question the strict régime required for a cure. We lifted the Secretary for Social Welfare out of the bathing-pool and carried him towards the drive, where Doctor Magiot's car stood without lights. "When you get back," Doctor Magiot said, "you must turn on the water and wash away the blood."

"I'll turn it on all right, but whether the water will come . . ."

We propped him on the back-seat. In detective stories a corpse is always so easily made to look like a drunken man, but this dead thing was unmistakably dead—the blood had ceased to flow, but one glance into the car would note the monstrous wound. Luckily no one dared move on the roads at night; it was the hour when only zombies worked or else the Tontons Macoute. As for the Tontons they were certainly abroad: we heard the approach of their car—no other car would be out so late—before we reached the end of the drive. We switched our headlights off and waited. The car was being driven slowly uphill from the capital; we could hear the voices of the occupants arguing above the grind of the third gear. I had the impression of an old car which would never make the grade up the long slope to Pétionville. What would we do if it gave up the ghost at the entrance of the drive? The men would certainly come to the hotel for help and some free drinks, whatever the hour. We seemed to wait a long time before the sound of the engine passed the drive and receded.

I asked Doctor Magiot, "Where do we take him?"

"We can't go far either up or down," he said, "without

reaching a block. This is the road to the north and the militia daren't sleep for fear of inspection. That's probably what the Tontons are doing now. They'll go as far as the police-post at Kenscoff if the car doesn't break down."

"You had to pass a road-block to get here. How did you explain . . . ?"

"I said there was a woman sick after a child-birth. It's too common a case for the man to report, if I am lucky."

"And if he does report?"

"I shall say I could not find the hut."

We drove out on to the main road. Doctor Magiot put on the headlights again. "If anyone should be out and see us," he said, "he will take us for the Tontons."

Our choice of terrain was severely limited by the barrier up the road and the barrier down. We drove two hundred yards uphill—"That will show that he passed the Trianon: he was not on the way there"—and turned into the second lane on the left. It was an area of small houses and abandoned gardens. Here had lived in the old days the vain and the insufficiently successful; they were on the road to Pétionville, but they had not quite arrived there: the advocate who picked up the unconsidered cases, the failed astrologer and the doctor who preferred his rum to his patients. Doctor Magiot knew exactly which of them still occupied his house, and which had fled to escape the forced levies that the Tontons Macoute collected at night for the construction of the new city, Duvalierville. I had contributed a hundred gourdes myself. To me the houses and gardens seemed all equally unlived in and uncared for.

"In here," Doctor Magiot directed. He drove the car a few yards off the road. We had to keep the headlights burning, for we had no hand free to hold a torch. They shone on a broken board, which now announced only " . . . pont. Your Future by . . ."

"So he's gone," I said.

"He died."

"A natural death?"

"Violent deaths are natural deaths here. He died of his environment."

We got the body of Doctor Philipot out of the car and dragged it behind an overgrown bougainvillaea where it could not be seen from the road. Doctor Magiot twisted a handkerchief round his right hand and took from the dead man's pocket a small kitchen knife for cutting steaks. His eye had been sharper than mine at the pool. He laid it a few inches from the Minister's left hand. He said, "Doctor Philipot was left-handed."

"You seem to know everything."

"You forget we took anatomy together. You must remember to buy another steak-knife."

"Has he a family?"

"A wife and a boy of six. I suppose he thought that suicide was safer for them."

We got back into the car and reversed into the road. At the entrance of my drive I got out. "All depends now on the servants," I said.

"They'll be afraid to talk," Doctor Magiot said. "A witness here can suffer just as much as the accused."

2

Mr. and Mrs. Smith came down to breakfast on the verandah. It was almost the first time I had seen him without a rug over his arm. They had slept well and they ate with appetite the grapefruit, the toast, and the marmalade: I was afraid they might require some strange beverage with a name chosen by a public-relations firm, but they accepted coffee and even praised its quality.

"I woke up only once," Mr. Smith said, "and I thought that I heard voices. Perhaps Mr. Jones has arrived?"

"No."

"Odd. The last thing he said to me in the customs was 'We'll meet tonight at Mr. Brown's.'"

"He was probably shanghaied to another hotel."

"I had hoped to take a dip before breakfast," Mrs. Smith said, "but I found Joseph was cleaning the pool. He seems to be a man of all work."

"Yes. He's invaluable. I'm sure the pool will be ready for you before lunch."

"And the beggar?" Mr. Smith asked.

"Oh, he went away before morning."

"Not with an empty stomach, I hope?" He gave me a smile as much as to say: I'm only joking, I know you are a man of goodwill.

"Joseph would certainly have seen to that."

Mr. Smith took another piece of toast. He said, "I thought that this morning Mrs. Smith and I would write our names in the embassy book."

"It would be wise."

"I only thought it would be courteous. Afterwards perhaps I could present my letter of introduction to the Secretary for Social Welfare."

"If I were you I would ask at the embassy whether there has been any change. That is, if the letter is addressed to someone personally."

"A Doctor Philipot, I think."

"I would certainly ask then. Changes happen very quickly here."

"But his successor, I suppose, would receive me? What I have come here to propose would be of great interest to any minister concerned with health."

"I don't think you ever told me what you were planning . . ."

"I come here as a representative," Mr. Smith said.

"Of the vegetarians of America," Mrs. Smith added. "The true vegetarians."

"Are there false vegetarians?"

"Of course. There are even some who eat fertilized eggs."

"Heretics and schismatics have splintered every great movement," Mr. Smith said sadly, "in human history."

"And what do the vegetarians propose to do here?"

"Apart from the distribution of free literature—translated, of course, into French—we plan to open a centre of vegetarian cooking in the heart of the capital."

"The heart of the capital is a shanty-town."

"In a suitable site then. We want the President and some of his ministers to attend the gala opening and take the first vegetarian meal. As an example to the people."

"But he's afraid to leave the palace."

Mr. Smith laughed politely at what he considered my picturesque exaggeration. Mrs. Smith said, "You can hardly expect much encouragement from Mr. Brown. He is not one of us."

"Now, now, my dear, Mr. Brown was only having a little joke with us. Perhaps after breakfast, I could ring up my embassy."

"The telephone doesn't work. But I could send Joseph with a note."

"No, in that case we'll take a taxi. If you'll get us a taxi."

"I'll send Joseph to find one."

"He surely is a man of all work," Mrs. Smith said to me harshly, as though I were a southern plantation-owner. I saw Petit Pierre walking up the drive and I left them.

"Ah, Mr. Brown," Petit Pierre cried, "a very very good morning." He waved a copy of the local paper and said, "You'll see what I have written about you. How are your guests? They have slept well, I hope." He mounted the steps, bowed to the Smiths at their table, and breathed in the sweet flowery smell of Port-au-Prince as though he were a stranger to the place. "What a view," he said, "the trees, the flowers, the bay, the palace." He giggled. "Distance lends enchantment to the view. Mr. William Wordsworth."

Petit Pierre had not come for the view, I was certain, and at this hour he would hardly have come for a free glass of rum. Presumably he wanted to receive information, unless perhaps he wished to impart it. His gay manner did not necessarily mean good news, for Petit Pierre was always gay. It was as though he had tossed a coin to decide between the only two possible attitudes in Port-au-Prince, the rational and the irrational, misery or gaiety; Papa Doc's head had fallen earthwards and he had plumped for the gaiety of despair.

"Let me see what you've written," I said.

I opened the paper at his gossip-column—which always appeared on page four—and read how, among the many distinguished visitors who had arrived yesterday in the *Medea*, was the Honourable Mr. Smith who had been narrowly defeated in the American Presidential elections of 1948 by Mr. Truman. He was accompanied by his elegant and amiable wife, who, under happier circumstances, would have been America's First Lady, an adornment to the White House. Among the many other passengers was the well-loved patron of that intellectual centre, the Hotel Trianon, who was returning from a business visit to New York . . . I looked afterwards at the principal news-page. The Secretary for Education was announcing a six-year plan to eliminate illiteracy in the north—why the north in particular? No details were given. Perhaps he was depending on a satisfactory hurricane. Hurricane Hazel in '54 had eliminated a great deal of illiteracy in the interior—the extent of the death-roll had never been disclosed. There was a small paragraph about a party of rebels who had crossed the Dominican frontier: they had been driven back, and two prisoners had been taken carrying American arms. If the President had not quarrelled with the American Mission, the arms would probably have been described as Czech or Cuban.

I said, "There are rumours about a new Secretary for Social Welfare."

"You can never trust rumours," Petit Pierre said.

"Mr. Smith has brought an introduction to Doctor Philipot. I don't want him to make a mistake."

"Perhaps he ought to wait a few days. I hear that Doctor Philipot is in Cap Haïtien—or somewhere in the north."

"Where the fighting is?"

"I do not believe there is really much fighting."

"What kind of a man is Doctor Philipot?" I felt an itch of

curiosity to know more of someone who had become a kind of distant relative by dying in my pool.

"A man," Petit Pierre said, "who suffers very much from his nerves."

I closed the paper and handed it back to him. "I see you don't mention the arrival of our friend Jones."

"Ah yes, Jones. Who exactly is Major Jones?" I was sure then that he had come with the purpose of receiving rather than giving information.

"A fellow passenger. That's all I know."

"He claims to be a friend of Mr. Smith's."

"In that case, I suppose he must be."

Petit Pierre imperceptibly moved me away down the verandah until we turned the corner out of sight of the Smiths. His white cuffs fell a long way out of his sleeves on to his black hands. "If you would be frank with me," he said, "I might perhaps be of a little help."

"Frank about what?"

"About Major Jones."

"I wish you wouldn't call him Major. Somehow it doesn't suit him."

"You think perhaps he is not . . . ?"

"I know nothing about him. Nothing at all."

"He was going to stay at your hotel."

"He seems to have found a lodging elsewhere."

"Yes. At the police station."

"Why on earth . . . ?"

"I think they found something incriminating in his baggage. I don't know what."

"Does the British embassy know?"

"No. But I do not think they can help very much. These things have to take their course. They are not ill-treating him as yet."

"What would you advise, Petit Pierre?"

"It is probably a misunderstanding—but then there is always

the question of *amour-propre*. The chief of police suffers a great deal from *amour-propre*. Perhaps if Mr. Smith spoke to Doctor Philipot, Doctor Philipot might speak to the Secretary for the Interior. Major Jones could then be fined for a merely technical offence."

"But what is his offence?"

"That question is in itself a technicality," he said.

"But you have just told me Doctor Philipot is in the north."

"True. Perhaps Mr. Smith ought rather to see the Secretary of State." He waved the papers proudly. "He will know how important Mr. Smith is, for he will undoubtedly have read my article."

"I shall go at once and see our chargé."

"It is the wrong method," Petit Pierre said. "It is far easier to satisfy the *amour-propre* of the chief of police than to satisfy national pride. The Haitian government does not accept protests from foreigners."

It was much the same advice at the chargé gave me later that morning. He was a hollow-chested man with sensitive features which reminded me the first time I met him of Robert Louis Stevenson. He spoke with many hesitations and an amused air of defeat—it was the conditions of life in the capital that had defeated him, not the inroads of tuberculosis. He had the courage and the humour of the defeated. For example, he carried a pair of black glasses in his pocket which he always put on when he saw a member of the Tontons Macoute, who wore them as a uniform, to terrify. He collected books on Caribbean flora, but he had sent all but the most common of them home, just as he had sent his children, for there was always the risk of sudden fire aided by a tin of gasoline.

He listened to me without interruption or impatience while I told him of Jones's predicament and Petit Pierre's advice. I felt sure he would have shown no more surprise if I had told him of the Secretary for Social Welfare dead in my bathing-pool and the way in which I had disposed of the body, but

I think he would have been secretly grateful to me that I had not called him in. When I finished my story, he said, "I had a cable from London about Jones."

"So did the captain of the *Medea*. His cable came from the owners in Philadelphia. It wasn't very specific."

"Mine you might say was cautionary. I was not to be unduly helpful. I suspect some consulate somewhere has been taken for a ride."

"All the same a British subject in prison . . . ?"

"Oh, I agree that is a little too steep. Only we have to remember, don't we, that even these bastards may have acted with good reason. Officially I shall proceed with caution— as the cable suggests. A formal enquiry to begin with." He made a movement with his hand across the desk and laughed. "I shall never lose the habit of picking up a telephone."

He was the perfect spectator—the spectator of whom every actor must sometimes dream, intelligent, watchful, amused, and critical in just the right way, a lesson he had learnt from having seen so many performances good and bad in indifferent plays. For some reason I thought of my mother's words to me, when I saw her for the last time, "What part are you playing now?" I suppose I *was* playing a part—the part of an English-man concerned over the fate of a fellow-countryman, of a responsible business-man who saw his duty clearly and who came to consult the representative of his Sovereign. I tempo-rarily forgot the tangle of legs in the Peugeot. I am quite sure that the chargé would have disapproved of my cuckolding a member of the diplomatic corps. The act belonged too closely to the theatre of farce.

He said, "I doubt if my enquiries will do much good. I shall be told by the Secretary for the Interior that the affair is in the hands of the police. He will probably give me a lecture on the separation of the judicial and executive functions. Did I ever tell you about my cook? It happened while you were away. I was giving a dinner for my colleagues and my cook simply disappeared. No marketing had been done. He had been picked up in the street on the way to market. My wife had to open the tins we keep for an emergency. Your Señor Pineda did not appreciate a soufflé of tinned salmon." Why did he say *my* Señor Pineda? "Later I heard that he was in a police-cell. They released him the next day when it was too late. He had been questioned about what guests I entertained. I protested, of course, to the Secretary for the Interior. I said I should have been told, and I would have arranged for him to go to the police-station at a convenient hour. The Minister simply said that he was a Haitian and he could do what he liked with a Haitian."

"But Jones is English."

"I assume so, but I doubt all the same whether our Government in these days will send a frigate. Of course, I'm anxious to help to the best of my ability, but I think Petit Pierre's advice is quite sound. Try other means first. If you get nowhere, of course I'll protest—tomorrow morning. I have a feeling that this is not the first police-cell Major Jones has known. We mustn't exaggerate the situation." I felt a little like the player-king rebuked by Hamlet for exaggerating his part.

When I got back to the hotel the swimming-pool was full, the gardener was pretending to occupy himself by raking a few leaves off the surface of the water, I heard the voice of the cook in the kitchen, everything was near to normal again. I even had guests, for there in the pool, avoiding the gardener's rake, swam Mr. Smith, wearing a pair of dark grey nylon bathing-pants which billowed out behind him in the water, giving him the huge hind-quarters of some prehistoric beast. He swam slowly up and down using the breast-stroke and grunting rhythmically. When he saw me he stood up in the water like a myth. His breasts were covered with long strands of white hair.

I sat down by the pool and called out to Joseph to bring a rum-punch and a Coca-Cola. I was uneasy when Mr. Smith trundled to the deep end before he emerged—he was passing so close to the spot where the Secretary for Social Welfare had died. I thought of Holyrood and the indelible mark of Rizzio's blood. Mr. Smith shook himself and sat down beside me. Mrs. Smith appeared on the balcony of the John Barrymore suite and called down to him, "Dry yourself, dear, or you might catch cold."

"The sun will dry me quickly enough, dear," Mr. Smith called back.

"Put the towel round your shoulders or you'll burn."

Mr. Smith obeyed her. I said, "Mr. Jones has been arrested by the police."

"My goodness. You don't say. What has he done?"

"He hasn't necessarily done anything."

"Has he seen a lawyer?"

"That's not possible here. The police wouldn't allow it."

Mr. Smith gave me an obstinate look. "The police are the same everywhere. It happens often enough at home," he said, "in the South. Coloured men shut up in jail, refused a lawyer. But two wrongs don't make a right."

"I've been to the embassy. They don't think they can do much."

"Now that *is* scandalous," Mr. Smith said. He was referring to the attitude of the embassy rather than to the conditions of Jones's arrest.

"Petit Pierre thinks that the best thing at the moment would be for you to intervene, to see the Secretary of State perhaps."

"I'll do anything I can for Mr. Jones. There's obviously been a mistake. But why does he suppose I would have any influence?"

"You were a Presidential candidate," I said, as Joseph brought the glasses.

"I'll do anything I can," Mr. Smith repeated, brooding into his Coca-Cola. "I very much took to Mr. Jones. (I don't know why it is I can't get round to calling him Major—after all there are some good men in all armies.) He seemed to me the best type of Britisher. There must have been a foolish mistake somewhere."

"I don't want to get you into any trouble with the authorities."

"I'm not afraid of trouble," Mr. Smith said, "with any authorities."

3

The Secretary's office was in one of the exhibition buildings near the port and the Columbus statue. We passed the musical fountain that never played now, the public park with its Bourbon pronouncement: "*Je suis le drapeau Haïtien, Uni et Indivisible. François Duvalier,*" and came at last to the long modern building of cement and glass, the wide staircase, the great lounge with many comfortable armchairs lined with the murals of Haitian artists. It bore as little relation to the beggars of the post-office square and the shanty-town as Christophe's palace of Sans Souci, but it would make a much less picturesque ruin.

The lounge contained more than a dozen middle-class people, fat and prosperous. The women in their best dresses of electric blues and acid greens chattered happily to each other as though they were taking their morning coffee, looking sharply up at every newcomer. Even a suppliant in this lounge bore himself with importance in an air filled with the slow tap of typewriters. Ten minutes after we arrived Señor Pineda walked heavily through with the certitude of diplomatic privilege. He smoked a cigar and looked at no one and without asking a by-your-leave passed through one of the doors which opened on to an inner balcony.

"The Secretary's private office," I explained. "The South American ambassadors are still *persona grata*. Especially Pineda. He hasn't any political refugees in his embassy. Not yet."

We waited for three-quarters of an hour, but Mr. Smith showed no impatience. "It seems very well organized," he said once, when the suppliants were reduced by two after a brief conference with a clerk. "A minister has to be protected."

At last Pineda passed out through the lounge, still smoking a cigar—it was a fresh one. The band was on it: he never removed his bands because they were stamped with his monogram. This time he gave me a bow of recognition—for a moment I thought he was going to pause and speak to me; his bow must have attracted the attention of the young man who accompanied him to the head of the stairs, for he returned and asked us with courtesy what we wanted.

"The Secretary of State," I said.

"He is very busy with the foreign ambassadors. There is a great deal to discuss. You see tomorrow he is leaving for the United Nations."

"Then I think he should see Mr. Smith at once."

"Mr. Smith?"

"You haven't read today's paper?"

"We have been very busy."

"Mr. Smith arrived yesterday. He is the Presidential Candidate."

"The Presidential Candidate?" the young man said with incredulity. "In Haiti?"

"He has business in Haiti—but that is a matter for your President. Now he would like to see the Secretary before he leaves for New York."

"Please wait here a moment." He passed into one of the offices on the inner court and came out, hurriedly, a minute later carrying a newspaper. He knocked on the Secretary's door and went in.

"You know, Mr. Brown, that I'm no longer a Presidential candidate. We made our gesture once and for all."

"There's no need to explain that here, Mr. Smith. After all you belong to history." I could see in those pale blue honest eyes that perhaps I had gone a little too far. I added, "A gesture like yours is there for everyone to read"—I could not specify where. "It belongs to this year as much as to the past."

The young man stood beside us—he had left the newspaper behind. "If you would come with me . . ."

The Secretary of State flashed his teeth at us with great amiability. I saw the newspaper lying at the corner of his desk. The palm he held out to us was large, square, pink, and humid. He told us in excellent English how interested he had been to read of Mr. Smith's arrival and how he had hardly hoped to have the honour, since he was leaving for New York tomorrow . . . There had been no word from the American embassy, or else of course he would have arranged a time . . .

Since the President of the United States, I said, had seen fit to recall his ambassador, Mr. Smith thought it better to make his visit unofficially.

The Secretary said he saw my point. He added to Mr. Smith, "I understand you are seeing the President . . ."

"Mr. Smith has not yet asked for an audience. He was anxious to see you first—before you land in New York."

"I have to make my protest before the United Nations," the Minister explained with pride. "Will you have a cigar, Mr. Smith?" He offered his leather case and Mr. Smith took one. I noticed that the band bore the monogram of Señor Pineda.

"Protest?" Mr. Smith asked.

"The raids from the Dominican Republic. The rebels are being supplied with American arms. We have evidence."

"What evidence?"

"Two men were captured carrying revolvers manufactured in the United States."

"I'm afraid you can buy such things anywhere in the world."

"I have been promised the support of Ghana. And I hope other Afro-Asian countries . . ."

"Mr. Smith has come about quite a different matter," I interrupted them. "A great friend of his who was travelling with him was arrested yesterday by the police."

"An American?"

"An Englishman called Jones."

"Has the British embassy made enquiries? This is really a matter concerning the Secretary for the Interior."

"But a word from you, your excellency . . ."

"I cannot interfere with another department. I'm sorry. Mr. Smith will understand."

Mr. Smith pushed his way into our dialogue with a roughness I had not known him to possess. "You can find out what the charge is, can't you?"

"Charge?"

"Charge."

"Oh—charge."

"Exactly," Mr. Smith said. "Charge."

"There will not necessarily be a charge. You are anticipating the worst."

"Then why keep him in prison?"

"I know nothing about the case. I suppose there is something to be investigated."

"Then he ought to be brought before a magistrate and put on bail. I will stand bail for any reasonable amount."

"Bail?" the Minister said, "bail?" He turned to me with a gesture of appeal from his cigar. "What is bail?"

"A kind of gift to the state if a prisoner should not return for trial. It can be quite a substantial amount," I added.

"You've heard of Habeas Corpus, I suppose," Mr. Smith said.

"Yes. Yes. Of course. But I have forgotten so much of my Latin. Virgil. Homer. I regret that I no longer have time to study."

I said to Mr. Smith, "The basis of the law here is supposed to be the Code Napoléon."

"The Code Napoléon?"

"There are certain differences from the Anglo-Saxon law. Habeas Corpus is one of them."

"A man has to be charged surely."

"Yes. Eventually." I spoke rapidly to the Minister in French. Mr. Smith understood little French, even though Mrs. Smith had reached the fourth lesson in Hugo's. I said, "I think a political mistake has been made. The Presidential Candidate is a personal friend of this man Jones. You ought not to alienate

him just before your visit to New York. You know the importance in democratic countries of being friendly with the opposi-
tion. Unless the affair is of really great importance, I think you
should let Mr. Smith see his friend. Otherwise he will undoubtedly believe that he has been—perhaps—ill-treated."

"Does Mr. Smith speak French?"

"No."

"You see, there is always the possibility that the police may
have exceeded their instructions. I wouldn't want Mr. Smith
to get a bad impression of our police procedure."

"Couldn't you send in a reliable doctor first—to tidy up?"

"Of course there would be nothing really to conceal. It is
only that sometimes a prisoner misbehaves. I am sure even in
your own country . . ."

"Then we can rely on you to have a word with your colleague? What I would suggest is that Mr. Smith should leave
with you a little compensation—in dollars, of course, not
gourdes—for any damage Mr. Jones may have inflicted on a
policeman."

"I will do what I can. So long as the President is not involved. In that case there is nothing that any of us can do."

"No."

Above his head hung the portrait of Papa Doc—the portrait
of Baron Samedi. Clothed in the heavy black tail-suit of
graveyards he peered out at us through the thick lenses of his
spectacles with myopic and expressionless eyes. He was rumoured
sometimes to watch personally the slow death of a Tonton
victim. The eyes would not change. Presumably his interest in
the death was medical.

"Give me two hundred dollars," I said to Mr. Smith. He
picked out two hundred-dollar notes from his case. In the other
pocket I saw that he had the photograph of his wife wrapped
in her rug. I laid the notes on the Minister's desk; I thought
he looked at them with an air of disparagement, but I
couldn't believe that Mr. Jones was worth much more than that.
At the door I turned. "And Doctor Philipot," I asked, "is he

here at the moment? There was something about the hotel I wanted to discuss with him—a drainage plan."

"I believe that he is in the south at Les Cayes about a new hospital project." Haiti was a great country for projects. Projects always mean money to the projectors so long as they are not begun.

"We'll hear from you then?"

"Of course. Of course. But I promise nothing." He was now a little brusque. I have often noticed that a bribe (though, of course, this was not, strictly speaking, a bribe) has that effect— it changes a relation. The man who offers a bribe gives away a little of his own importance; the bribe once accepted he becomes the inferior, like a man who has paid for a woman. Perhaps I had made a mistake. Perhaps I should have left Mr. Smith as an undefined menace. The blackmailer retains his superiority.

4

All the same the Minister proved himself to be a man of his word; we were allowed in due course to see the prisoner.

At the police-station the next afternoon the sergeant was the most important figure, far more important than the Minister's secretary, who accompanied us there. He tried in vain to catch the eye of the great man, but he had to wait his turn at the counter with all the other suppliants. Mr. Smith and I sat under the snapshots of the dead rebel, which were still wilting on the wall after all these months. Mr. Smith looked at them and hastily looked away. In a little room opposite us sat a tall Negro in a natty civilian suit; he had his feet up on his desk and he stared at us continually through dark glasses. Perhaps it was only my nerves that lent him an expression of repulsive cruelty.

"He'll remember us again," Mr. Smith said with a smile.

The man knew that we had spoken of him. He rang a bell on his desk and a policeman came. Without moving his feet or turning his gaze away from us he asked a question, and the policeman glanced at us and replied and the long stare went on. I turned my head, but inevitably after a little I looked back into the two black circular lenses. They were like binoculars through which he was observing the habits of two insignificant animals.

"An ugly customer," I said uneasily. Then I noticed that Mr. Smith was returning the stare. One couldn't see how often the man blinked because of the dark glasses; he might easily have closed his eyes and rested them and we would not have known, yet it was Mr. Smith's blue relentless gaze which won the day. The man got up and closed the door of his office. "Bravo," I said.

"I shall remember him too," Mr. Smith said.

"He probably suffers from acidity."

"It's highly possible, Mr. Brown."

We must have been there more than half an hour before the Foreign Minister's secretary got any attention. In a dictatorship ministers come and go; in Port-au-Prince only the chief of police, the head of the Tontons Macoute, and the commander of the palace-guard had any permanence—they alone could offer security to their employees. The Minister's secretary was dismissed by the sergeant like a small boy who has run an errand and a corporal led us down the long corridor of cells that smelt like a zoo.

Jones sat on an upturned bucket beside a straw-mattress. His face was criss-crossed with pieces of plaster and his right arm was bandaged to his side. He had been tidied up as well as could be, but his left eye could have done with a raw steak. His double-breasted waistcoat looked more conspicious than ever with a small rusty stain of blood. "Well well," he greeted us with a happy smile. "Look who's here."

"You seem to have been resisting arrest," I said.

"That's their story," he said brightly. "Got a cigarette?"

I gave him one.

"You haven't a filter-tip?"

"No."

"Ah well, mustn't look a gift-horse . . . I felt this morning things had taken a turn for the better. They gave me some beans at midday, and a doctor chap came and worked on me."

"What are you charged with?" Mr. Smith asked.

"Charged?" He seemed as puzzled at the word as the Secretary of State had been.

"What do they say you've done, Mr. Jones?"

"I haven't had much of an opportunity to *do* anything. I didn't even get through the Customs."

"There must be some reason? A mistaken identity perhaps?"

"They haven't explained things very clearly to me yet." He touched his eye with caution. "I look a bit the worse for wear, I expect."

"Is that all you have for a bed?" Mr. Smith asked with indignation.

"I've slept in worse places."

"Where? It's hard to imagine—"

He said vaguely and unconvincingly, "Oh, in the war, you know." He added, "I think the trouble is I had the wrong introduction. I know you warned me, but I thought you were exaggerating, like the purser."

"Where did you get your introduction?" I asked.

"Someone I met in Leopoldville."

"What were you doing in Leopoldville?"

"It was more than a year ago. I do a lot of travelling." I had the impression that to him the cell was unremarkable, like one of the innumerable airports on a long route.

"We've got to get you out of here," Mr. Smith said. "Mr. Brown has told your chargé. We've both seen the Secretary of State. We've stood bail."

"Bail?" He had a better sense of reality than Mr. Smith. He said, "I tell you what you *can* do for me, if you wouldn't mind. Of course I'll pay you back later. Give twenty dollars to the sergeant as you go out."

"Of course," Mr. Smith said, "if you think it will do any good."

"Oh, it will do good all right. There's another thing—I have to get that business of the introduction straight. Have you a bit of paper and a pen?"

Mr. Smith provided them and Jones began to write. "You haven't an envelope?"

"I'm afraid not."

"Then I'd better phrase it a bit differently." He hesitated a moment and then he asked me, "What's the French for factory?"

"*Usine?*"

"I was never very good at languages, but I've picked up a bit of French."

"In Leopoldville?"

"Give that to the sergeant and ask him to pass it on."

"Can he read?"

"I think so." He stood up as he returned the pen and said in the polite tone of dismissal, "It was good of you chaps to call."

"You've got another appointment?" I asked him ironically.

"To tell you the truth those beans are beginning to work. I've an appointment with the bucket. If either of you can spare a little more paper . . ."

We collected between us three old envelopes, a receipted bill, a page or two from Mr. Smith's engagement book, and a letter to me which I thought I had destroyed from a New York real-estate agent regretting that at the moment he had no clients interested in the purchase of hotel properties in Port-au-Prince.

"The spirit of the man," Mr. Smith exclaimed in the passage outside. "It's what brought you people safely through the blitz. I'll get him out of there if I have to go to the President himself."

I looked at the fold of paper in my hand. I recognized the name written there. It was that of an officer in the Tontons

Macoute. I said, "I wonder if we ought to involve ourselves any further."

"We *are* involved," Mr. Smith said with pride, and I knew that he was thinking in the big terms I could not recognize, like Mankind, Justice, the Pursuit of Happiness. It was not for nothing that he had been a Presidential candidate.

Chapter Five

1

Next day a number of things distracted me from the fate of Jones, but I do not believe that Mr. Smith for one moment forgot him. I saw him in the bathing-pool at seven in the morning, lumbering up and down, but that slow motion—from the deep to the shallow end and back—probably aided him to think. After breakfast he wrote a number of notes, which Mrs. Smith typed for him on a portable Corona, using two fingers, and he despatched them through Joseph by taxi—one note was to his embassy, another to the new Secretary for Social Welfare, whose appointment had been announced that morning in Petit Pierre's paper. He had enormous energy for a man of his age, and I am sure he was never for a moment distracted from the thought of Jones sitting on the bucket in his prison-cell while he remembered the vegetarian centre which one day would remove acidity and passion from the Haitian character. Simultaneously he was planning an article on his travels which he had promised to write for his home-town journal—a journal needless to say Democratic and antisegregationist and sympathetic towards vegetarianism. He had asked me the day before to look his manuscript over for errors of fact. "The opinions of course are my own," he added with the wry smile of a pioneer.

My first distraction came early, before I had got up, when Joseph knocked on my door to tell me that against all probability the body of Doctor Philipot had already been discovered;

as a consequence several people had left their homes and taken refuge in the Venezuelan embassy, including a local police-chief, an assistant-postmaster, and a schoolteacher (no one knew what their connections had been with the ex-minister). It was said that Doctor Philipot had killed himself, but of course no one knew how the authorities would describe his death—as a political assassination, perhaps, engineered from the Dominican Republic? It was believed the President was in a state of fury. He had badly wanted to get his hands on Doctor Philipot, who one night recently under the influence of rum was said to have laughed at Papa Doc's medical qualifications. I sent Joseph to the market to gather all the information he could.

My second distraction was the news that the child Angel was ill with mumps—in great pain, Martha wrote to me (and I couldn't help wishing him another turn of the screw). She was afraid to leave the embassy in case he asked for her, so it was impossible for her to meet me that night as we had arranged by the Columbus statue. But there was no reason, she wrote, why, after my long absence, I should not call in at the embassy—it would seem natural enough. A lot of people made a point of dropping in now that the curfew had been raised, if they could avoid the eye of the policeman at the gate, and he usually took a ration of rum in the kitchen at nine. She supposed they were preparing the ground in case a time came when they wanted to claim political asylum in a hurry. She added at the end of her note: "Luis will be pleased. He thinks a lot of you"—a phrase which could be interpreted two ways.

Joseph came to my office after breakfast, when I was reading Mr. Smith's article, to tell me the whole story of the discovery of Doctor Philipot's body as it was now known to the stall-holders in the market, if not yet to the police. It was one chance in a thousand which had led the police to the corpse that Doctor Magiot and I had expected to lie concealed for weeks in the ex-astrologer's garden: a bizarre chance, and the story made it hard for me to pay much attention to Mr. Smith's manuscript. One of the militiamen on the road-block below the hotel had taken a fancy to a peasant-woman who was on her way up to the big market at Kenscoff early that morning. He wouldn't let her pass, for he claimed she was carrying something concealed underneath her layers of petticoat. She offered to show him what she had there, and they went off together down the side-road and into the astrologer's deserted garden. She was in a hurry to complete the long road to Kenscoff, so she went quickly down upon her knees, flung up her petticoats, rested her head on the ground, and found herself staring into the wide glazed eyes of the ex-Minister for Social Welfare. She recognized him, for in the days before he came to political office he had attended her daughter in a difficult *accouchement*.

The gardener was outside the window, so I tried not to show undue interest in Joseph's narrative. Instead I turned a page of Mr. Smith's article, "Mrs. Smith and I," he had written, "left Philadelphia with much regret after we had been entertained by the Henry S. Ochses, whom many readers will remember for their hospitable New Year parties at the time they occupied 2041 DeLancey Place, but the sorrow of leaving our good friends was soon lost in the pleasure of making new ones on the S.S. *Medea* . . ."

"Why did they go to the police?" I asked. The natural thing for the couple to have done after the discovery was to slip away and say nothing.

"She scream so loud the other militiaman he come."

I skipped a page or two of Mrs. Smith's typewriting and came to the arrival of the *Medea* at Port-au-Prince. "A black republic —and a black republic with a history, an art, and a literature. It was as if I were watching the future of all the new African republics, with their teething troubles over." (He had no intention, I am sure, of appearing pessimistic.) "Of course a great deal remains to be done even here. Haiti has experienced monarchy, democracy, and dictatorship, but we must not judge a coloured dictatorship as we judge a white one. History in Haiti is a matter of a few centuries, and if we still make mistakes, after two thousand years, how much more right have these people to make similar mistakes and to learn from them perhaps better than we have done? There is poverty here, there are beggars in the streets, there is some evidence of police authoritarianism" (he had not forgotten Mr. Jones in his cell), "but I wonder whether a coloured man landing for the first time in New York would have received the courtesy and friendly help which Mrs. Smith and I enjoyed at the immigration office of Port-au-Prince." I seemed to be reading about a different country.

I said to Joseph, "What are they doing with the body?"

The police wanted to keep it, he said, but the ice-plant at the mortuary was not working.

"Does Madame Philipot know?"

"Oh yes, she has him in Monsieur Hercule Dupont's funeral parlour. I think they bury him, double-quick."

I couldn't help a feeling of responsibility for Doctor Philipot's last rites—he had died in my hotel. "Let me know what the arrangements are," I said to Joseph and turned back to Mr. Smith's travelogue.

"For an unknown stranger like myself to be given an interview by the Secretary of State on my first day in Port-au-Prince was another example of the astonishing courtesy which I have met everywhere here. The Secretary of State was about to leave for New York to attend the conference of the United Nations; nonetheless he gave me half an hour of his precious time and enabled me, through his personal intervention with the Secretary for the Interior, to visit an Englishman in prison, a fellow-passenger on the *Medea* who had unfortunately —through some bureaucratic mistake liable to happen in much older countries than Haiti—fallen foul of the authorities. I am following the case up, but I have small fear of the result. Two qualities which I have always found strongly implanted in my coloured friends—whether living in the relative freedom of

New York or the undisguised tyranny of Mississippi—are a regard for justice and a sense of human dignity." In reading Churchill's prose-works one is aware of an orator addressing a historic chamber, and in reading Mr. Smith I was conscious of a lecturer in the hall of a provincial town. I felt surrounded by well-meaning middle-aged women in hats who had paid five dollars to a good cause.

"I look forward," Mr. Smith continued, "to meeting the new Secretary for Social Welfare and discussing with him the subject which readers of this paper will have long regarded as my King Charles's head—the establishment of a vegetarian centre. Unfortunately Doctor Philipot, the former Minister to whom I carried a personal introduction from a Haitian diplomat attached to the United Nations, is not at the moment in Port-au-Prince, but I can assure my readers that my enthusiasm will carry me through all obstacles, if necessary to the President himself. From him I can expect a sympathetic hearing, for before he went into politics he won golden opinions as a doctor during the great typhoid epidemic some years ago. Like Mr. Kenyatta, the Prime Minister of Kenya, he has also made his mark as an anthropologist" ("mark" was an understatement —I thought of Joseph's crippled legs).

Later that morning Mr. Smith came shyly in to hear what I thought of his article. "It should please the authorities," I said.

"They'll never read it. The paper has no circulation outside Wisconsin."

"I wouldn't bank on their not reading it. Not many letters leave here nowadays. It's easy enough to censor them if they want to."

"You mean they'd open it?" he asked with incredulity, but he added quickly, "Oh well, it's been known to happen even in the U.S.A."

"If I were you—just in case—I'd leave out all reference to Doctor Philipot."

"But I've said nothing wrong."

"They may be sensitive about him at the moment. You see he's killed himself."

"Oh the poor man, the poor man," Mr. Smith exclaimed. "What on earth could have driven him to that?"

"Fear."

"Had he done something wrong?"

"Who hasn't? He had spoken ill of the President."

The old blue eyes turned away. He was determined to show no doubt to a stranger—a fellow white man, one of the slaver's race. He said, "I would like to see his widow—there might be something I could do. At least Mrs. Smith and I ought to send flowers." However much he loved the blacks, it was in a white world he lived; he knew no other.

"I wouldn't if I were you."

"Why not?"

I despaired of explaining, and at that moment as bad luck would have it, Joseph entered. The body had already left Monsieur Dupont's funeral-parlour; they were taking the coffin up to Pétionville for burial and were halted now at the road-block below the hotel.

"They seem in a hurry."

"They very worried," Joseph explained.

"There's nothing to fear now surely," Mr. Smith said.

"Except the heat," I added.

"I shall join the cortège," Mr. Smith said.

"Don't you dream of it."

Suddenly I was aware of the anger those blue eyes were capable of showing. "Mr. Brown, you are not my keeper. I am going to call Mrs. Smith and we shall both . . ."

"At least leave her behind. Don't you really understand the danger . . . ?" And it was on that dangerous word "danger" that Mrs. Smith entered.

"What danger?" she demanded.

"My dear, that poor Doctor Philipot to whom we had an introduction has killed himself."

"Why?"

"The reasons seem obscure. They are taking him for burial to Pétionville. I think we should join the cortège. Joseph, please, s'il vous plaît, taxi . . ."

"What danger were you talking about?" Mrs. Smith demanded.

"Do neither of you realize the kind of country this is? Anything can happen."

"Mr. Brown, dear, was saying he thought I ought to go alone."

"I don't think either of you should go," I said. "It would be madness."

"But—Mr. Smith told you—we had a letter of introduction to Doctor Philipot. He is a friend of a friend."

"It will be taken as a political gesture."

"Mr. Smith and I have never been afraid of political gestures. Dear, I have a dark dress . . . Give me two minutes."

"He can't give you even one," I said. "Listen." Even from my office we could hear the sound of voices on the hill, but it didn't sound to me like a normal funeral. There was not the wild music of peasant pompes funèbres, nor the sobriety of a bourgeois interment. Voices didn't wail: they argued, they shouted. A woman's cry rose above the din. Before I could attempt to stop them Mr. and Mrs. Smith were running down the drive. The Presidential Candidate had a slight lead. Perhaps he maintained it more by protocol than effort, for Mrs. Smith certainly had the better gait. I followed them more slowly, and with reluctance.

The Hotel Trianon had sheltered Doctor Philipot both alive and dead, and we were still not rid of him: at the very entrance of the drive I saw the hearse. It had apparently backed in so as to turn away from Pétionville, in retreat towards the city. One of the hungry unowned cats which haunted that end of the drive had leapt, in fear of the intrusion, on to the top of the hearse and it stood there arched and shivering like something struck by lightning. No one attempted to drive it away—the Haitians may well have believed it to contain the soul of the ex-Minister himself.

Madame Philipot, whom I had met once at some embassy reception, stood in front of the hearse and defied the driver to turn. She was a beautiful woman—not yet forty—with an olive skin, and she stood with her arms out like a bad patriotic monument to a forgotten war. Mr. Smith repeated over and over again, "What's the matter?" The driver of the hearse, which was black and expensive and encrusted with the emblems of death, sounded his horn—I had not realized before that hearses possessed horns. Two men in black suits argued with him one on either side; they had got out of a tumbledown taxi which was also parked in my drive, and in the road stood another taxi pointing up the hill to Pétionville. It contained a small boy whose face was pressed to the window. That was all the cortège amounted to.

"What's going on here?" Mr. Smith cried again in his distress and the cat spat at him from the glass roof.

Madame Philpot shouted *"Salaud"* at the driver and *"Cochon,"* then she flung her eyes like dark flowers at Mr. Smith. She had understood English. *"Vous êtes américain?"*

Mr. Smith, expanding his knowledge of French nearly to its outer limit, said, *"Oui."*

"This *cochon*, this *salaud*," Madam Philipot said, still barring the way to the hearse, "wants to drive back into the city."

"But why?"

"The militia at the barrier up the road will not let us pass."

"But why, why?" Mr. Smith repeated with bewilderment and two men, leaving their taxi in the drive, began to walk down the hill towards the city with an air of purpose. They had put on top-hats.

"They murdered him," Madame Philipot said, "and now they will not even allow him to be buried in our own plot of ground."

"There must be some mistake," Mr. Smith said, "surely."

"I told that *salaud* to drive on through the barrier. Let them shoot. Let them kill his wife and child." She added with illogical contempt, "They probably have no bullets in any case for their rifles."

"*Maman, maman,*" the child cried from the taxi.

"*Chéri?*"

"*Tu m'as promis une glace à la vanille.*"

"*Attends un petit peu, chéri.*"

I said, "Then you got through the first road-block without being questioned?"

"Yes, yes. You understand—with a little payment."

"They wouldn't accept payment up the road?"

She said, "Oh he had orders. He was afraid."

"There must be a mistake," I said, repeating Mr. Smith, but unlike him I was thinking of the bribe which had been refused.

"You live here. Do you really believe that?" She turned on the driver and said, "Drive on. Up the road. *Salaud,*" and the cat, as though it took the insult to itself, leapt at the nearest tree: its claws scrabbled in the bark and held. It spat once more over its shoulder, at all of us, with hungry hatred and dropped into the bougainvillaea.

The two men in black returned slowly up the hill. They had an intimidated air. I had time to look at the coffin—it was a luxurious one, worthy of the hearse, but it bore only a single wreath of flowers and a single card; the ex-Minister was doomed to have an interment almost as lonely as his death. The two men who had now rejoined us were almost indistinguishable one from the other, except that one was a centimetre or so the taller—or perhaps it was his hat. The taller one explained, "We have been to the lower road-block, Madame Philpot. They say we cannot return with the coffin. Not without the authorization of the authorities."

"What authorities?" I asked.

"The Secretary for Social Welfare."

We all with one accord looked at the handsome coffin with its gleaming brass handles.

"*There* is the Secretary for Social Welfare," I said.

"Not since this morning."

"Are you Monsieur Hercule Dupont?"

"I am Monsieur Clement Dupont. This is Monsieur Hercule." Monsieur Hercule removed his top hat and bowed from the hips.

"What's happening?" Mr. Smith asked. I told him.

"But that's absurd," Mrs. Smith interrupted me. "Does the coffin have to wait here till some fool mistake has been cleared up?"

"I'm beginning to fear it was no mistake."

"What else could it be?"

"Revenge. They failed to catch him alive." I said to Madame Philipot, "They will arrive soon. That's certain. Better go to the hotel with the child."

"And leave my husband stranded by the road? No."

"At least tell your child to go and Joseph will give him a vanilla ice."

The sun was almost vertically above us now: splinters of light darted here and there from the glass of the hearse and the bright brass-work of the coffin. The driver turned off his engine and we could hear the sudden silence extending a long long way to where a dog whined on the fringes of the capital.

Madame Philipot opened the taxi-door and lifted the little boy out. He was blacker than she was and the whites of his eyes were enormous, like eggs. She told him to find Joseph and his ice, but he didn't want to go. He clung to her dress.

"Mrs. Smith," I said, "take him to the hotel."

She hesitated. She said, "If there's going to be trouble, I think I ought to stay here with Madame Phili—Phili—you take him, dear."

"And leave you, dear?" Mr. Smith said. "No."

I hadn't noticed the taxi-drivers where they sat motionless in the shadow of the trees. Now, as though they had been exchanging signals with each other while we talked, they started simultaneously to life. One swung his taxi out of the drive, the other reversed and turned. With a grinding of gears they skidded together like decrepit racing-motorists down the hills towards Port-au-Prince. We heard the taxis halt at the road-block and then start off again and fade into the silence.

Monsieur Hercule Dupont cleared his throat. He said, "You are quite right. I and Monsieur Clement will take the child . . ." Each seized a hand, but the little boy dragged to get away.

"Go, chéri," his mother said, 'and find a vanilla ice."

"Avec de la crème au chocolat?"

"Oui, oui, bien sûr, avec de la crème au chocolat."

They made an odd procession, the three of them going up the drive under the palms, between the bougainvillaeas, two top-hatted middle-aged twins with the child between. The Hotel Trianon was not an embassy, but I suppose that the brothers Dupont considered it was perhaps the next best thing—a for-eigner's property. The driver of the hearse too—we had for-gotten him—abruptly climbed down and ran to catch them up. Madame Philipot, the Smiths and I were alone with the hearse and the coffin, and we listened in silence to the other silence on the road.

"What happens next?" Mr. Smith asked after a while.

"It's not in our hands. We wait. That's all."

"For what?"

"For them."

Our situation reminded me of that nightmare of childhood when something in a cupboard prepares to come out. None of us was anxious to look at another and see the private nightmare reflected, so we looked instead through the glass wall of the hearse at the new shining coffin with the brass handles which was the cause of all the trouble. Far away, in the land where the barking dog belonged, a car was taking the first gradients of the long hill. "They're coming," I said. Madame Philipot leant her forehead against the glass of the hearse, and the car climbed slowly up towards us.

"I wish you'd go in," I said to her. "It would be better for all of us if we all went in."

"I don't understand," Mr. Smith said. He put out his hand and gripped his wife's wrist.

The car had halted at the barrier down the road—we could hear the engine running; then it came slowly on in bottom gear, and now it was in view, a big Cadillac dating from the days of American aid for the poor of Haiti. It drew alongside us and four men got out. They wore soft hats and very dark sun-glasses; they carried guns on their hips, but only one of them bothered to draw, and he didn't draw his gun against us. He went to the side of the hearse and began to smash the glass with it, methodically. Madame Philipot didn't move or speak, and there was nothing I could do. One cannot argue with four guns. We were witnesses, but there was no court which would ever hear our testimony. The glass side of the hearse was smashed now, but the leader continued to chip the jagged edges with his gun. There was no hurry and he didn't want anyone to scratch his hands.

Mrs. Smith suddenly darted forward and seized the Tonton Macoute's shoulder. He turned his head and I recognized him. It was the man whom Mr. Smith had outstared in the police-station. He shook himself free from her grip and, putting his gloved hand firmly and deliberately against her face, he sent her reeling back into the bushes of bougainvillaea. I had to put my arms round Mr. Smith and hold him.

"They can't do that to my wife," he shouted over my shoulder.

"Oh yes, they can."

"Let me go," he shouted, struggling to be free. I've never seen a man so suddenly transformed. "Swine," he yelled. It was the worst expression he could find, but the Tonton Macoute spoke no English. Mr. Smith twisted and nearly got free from me. He was a strong old man.

"It won't do any good to anyone if you get shot," I said. Mrs. Smith sat among the bushes; for once in her life she looked bewildered.

They lifted the coffin out of the hearse and carried it to

the car. They wedged it into the boot, but it stuck several feet out, so they tied it securely with a piece of rope, taking their time. There was no need to hurry; they were secure; they were the law. Madame Philipot with a humility which shamed us— but there was no choice between humility and violence and only Mrs. Smith had essayed violence—went over to the Cadillac and pleaded with them to take her too. Her gestures told me that; her voice was too low for me to hear what she said. Perhaps she was offering them money for her dead: in a dictatorship one owns nothing, not even a dead husband. They slammed the door in her face and drove up the road, the coffin poking out of the boot, like a box of fruit on the way to market. Then they found a place to turn and came back. Mrs. Smith was on her feet now; we stood in a little group and we looked guilty. An innocent victim nearly always looks guilty, like the scapegoat in the desert. They stopped the car and the officer—I assumed he was an officer, for the black glasses and the soft hats and the revolvers were all the uniform they wore —swung the car-door open and beckoned to me. I am no hero. I obeyed and crossed the road to him.

"You own this hotel, don't you?"

"Yes."

"Next time you see me don't stare at me. I don't like to be stared at. Who is the old man?"

"The Presidential Candidate," I said.

"What do you mean? Presidential candidate for where?"

"For the United States of America."

"Don't joke with me."

"I'm not joking. You can't have read the papers."

"Why has he come here?"

"How would I know? He saw the Secretary of State yesterday. Perhaps he told *him* the reason. He expects to see the President."

"There's no election now in the United States. I know that much."

"They don't have a President for life like you do here. They have elections every four years."

"What was he doing with this—box of offal?"

"He was attending the funeral of his friend, Doctor Philipot."

"I'm acting under orders," he said with a hint of weakness. I could understand why it was these men wore dark glasses—they were human, but they mustn't show fear: it might be the end of terror in others. The Tontons Macoute in the car stared back at me as expressionless as golliwogs.

I said, "In Europe we hanged a lot of men who acted under orders. At Nuremberg."

"I don't like the way you speak to me," he said. "You are not open. You have a mean way of talking. You've got a servant called Joseph, haven't you?"

"Yes."

"I remember him well. I interviewed him once." He let that fact sink in. "This is your hotel. You make a living here."

"No longer."

"That old man will be leaving soon, but you will stay on."

"It was a mistake you made to hit his wife," I said. "It's the kind of thing he's likely to remember." He slammed the door shut again and they drove the Cadillac back down the hill; we could see the end of the coffin pointing out at us until they turned the corner. Again there was a pause and we heard them at the barrier; then the car put on speed, racing down towards Port-au-Prince. To where in Port-au-Prince? What use to anyone was the body of an ex-Minister? A corpse couldn't even suffer. But unreason can be more terrifying than reason.

"Outrageous. It's outrageous," Mr. Smith said at last. "I'll telephone to the President. I'll get that man . . ."

"The telephone doesn't work."

"He struck my wife."

"It's not the first time, dear," she said, "and he only pushed me. Remember at Nashville. It was worse at Nashville."

"It was different at Nashville," he replied and there were tears in his voice. He had loved people for their colour and he

132

had been betrayed more deeply than are those who hate. He added, "I'm sorry, dear, if I used expressions . . ." He took her arm and Madame Philipot and I followed them up the drive. The Duponts were sitting on the verandah with the little boy, and all three were eating vanilla ices with chocolate sauce. Their top-hats stood beside them like expensive ash-trays.

I told them, "The hearse is safe. They only broke the glass."

"Vandals," Monsieur Hercule said, and Monsieur Clement touched him with a soothing undertaker's hand. Madame Philipot was quite calm now and without tears. She sat down by her child and aided him with the ice-cream. The past was past, and here beside her was the future. I had the feeling that when the time came, in however many years, he would not be allowed to forget. She spoke only once before she left in the taxi which Joseph fetched for her. "One day someone will find a silver bullet."

The Duponts, for want of a taxi, left in their own hearse, and I was alone with Joseph. Mr. Smith had taken Mrs. Smith to the John Barrymore suite to lie down. He fussed over her and she let him have his way. I said to Joseph, "What good to them is a dead man in a coffin? Were they afraid that people might have laid flowers on his grave? It seemed unlikely. He wasn't a bad man, but he wasn't all that good either. The water-pumps for the shanty-town were never finished—I suppose some of the money went into his pocket."

"The people they very frightened," Joseph said, "when they know. They are frightened the President take their bodies too when they die."

"Why care? There's nothing left as it is but skin and bone, and why would the President need dead bodies anyway?"

"The people very ignorant," Joseph said. "They think the President keep Doctor Philipot in the cellar in the palace and make him work all night. The President is big Voodoo man."

"Baron Samedi?"

"Ignorant people say yes."

"So nobody will attack him at night with all the zombies there to protect him? They are better than guards, better than the Tontons Macoute."

"Tontons Macoute they zombies too. So ignorant people say."

"But what do you believe, Joseph?"

"I ignorant man, sir," Joseph said.

I went upstairs to the John Barrymore suite, and I wondered while I climbed where they would dump the body—there were plenty of unfinished diggings and no one would notice one smell the more in Port-au-Prince. I knocked on the door, and Mrs. Smith said, "Come in."

Mr. Smith had lit a small portable paraffin-stove on the chest-of-drawers and was boiling some water. Beside it was a cup and saucer and a cardboard carton marked Yeastrol. He said, "I have persuaded Mrs. Smith for once not to take her Barmene. Yeastrol is more soothing." There was a large photograph of John Barrymore on the wall looking down his nose with more than his usual phoney aristocratic disdain. Mrs. Smith lay on the bed.

"How are you, Mrs. Smith?"

"Perfectly all right," she said with decision.

"Her face is quite unmarked," Mr. Smith told me with relief.

"I keep on telling you he only pushed me."

"One doesn't push a woman."

"I don't think he even realized I was a woman. I was well—sort of assaulting him, I must admit."

"You are a brave woman, Mrs. Smith," I said.

"Nonsense. I can see through a pair of cheap sun-glasses."

"She has the heart of a tigress when roused," Mr. Smith said, stirring the Yeastrol.

"How are you going to deal with the incident in your article?" I asked him.

"I have been considering very carefully," Mr. Smith said. He took a spoonful of Yeastrol to see whether it was the right temperature. "I think one more minute, dear. It's a little too hot still. Oh yes, the article. It would be dishonest, I think, to omit the incident altogether, and yet we can hardly expect readers to see the affair in a proper perspective. Mrs. Smith is much loved and respected in Wisconsin, but even there you will find people who are prepared to use a story like this to inflame passions over the colour-question."

"They would never mention the white police-officer in Nashville," Mrs. Smith said. "*He* gave me a black eye."

"So taking all things into consideration," Mr. Smith said, "I decided to tear the article up. People at home will just have to wait for news of us—that's all. Perhaps later, in a lecture, I might mention the incident when Mrs. Smith is safely by my side to prove that it wasn't very serious." He took another spoonful of Yeastrol. "It's cool enough now, dear, I think."

2

I went reluctantly to the embassy that evening. I would have much preferred to know nothing of Martha's normal surroundings. Then, when she was not with me, she would have disappeared into a void where I could forget her. Now I knew exactly where she went when her car left the Columbus statue. I knew the hall which she passed through with the chained book where visitors wrote their names, the drawing-room that she entered next with the deep chairs and sofas and the glitter of chandeliers and the big photograph of General so-and-so, their relatively benevolent president, who seemed to make every caller an official caller, even myself. I was glad at least that I had not seen her bedroom.

When I arrived at half past nine the ambassador was alone—I had never seen him alone before: he seemed a different man. He sat on the sofa and thumbed through *Paris-Match* like a man in a dentist's waiting-room. I thought of sitting down silently myself and taking *Jours de France*, but he anticipated me with his greeting. He pressed me at once to take a drink, a cigar . . . Perhaps he was a lonely man. What did he do when there was no official party and his wife was out meeting me?

Martha had said that he liked me—the idea helped me to see him as a human being. He seemed tired and out of spirits. He carried his weight of flesh slowly, like a heavy load, between the drink-table and the sofa. He said, "My wife's upstairs reading to my boy. She'll be down presently. She told me you might call."

"I hesitated to come—you must be glad of an evening sometimes to yourselves."

"I'm always glad to see my friends," he said and lapsed into silence. I wondered whether he suspected our relationship or whether indeed he knew.

"I was sorry to hear that your boy had caught mumps."

"Yes. It is still at the painful stage. It's terrible, isn't it, to watch a child suffering."

"I suppose so. I've never had a child."

"Ah."

I looked at the portrait of the general. I felt that at least I should have been here on a cultural mission. He wore a row of medals and he had his hand on his sword-hilt.

"How did you find New York?" the ambassador asked.

"Much as usual."

"I would like to see New York. I know only the airport."

"Perhaps one day you'll be posted to Washington." It was an ill-considered compliment; there was little chance of such a posting if at his age—which I judged to be near fifty—he had stuck so long in Port-au-Prince.

"Oh no," he said seriously, "I can never go there. You see my wife is German."

"I know that—but surely now . . ."

He said, as though it were a natural occurrence in our kind of world, "Her father was hanged in the American zone. During the occupation."

"I see."

"Her mother brought her to South America. They had relations. She was only a child, of course."

"But she knows?"

"Oh yes, she knows. There's no secret about it. She remembers him with tenderness, but the authorities had good reason . . ."

I wondered whether the world would ever again sail with such serenity through space as it seemed to do a hundred years ago. Then the Victorians kept skeletons in cupboards—but who cares about a mere skeleton now? Haiti was not an exception in a sane world: it was a small slice of everyday taken at random. Baron Samedi walked in all our graveyards. I remembered the hanged man in the Tarot pack. It must feel a little odd, I thought, to have a son called Angel whose grandfather had been hanged, and then I wondered how I might feel . . . We were never very careful about taking precautions, it could easily happen that my child . . . A grandchild too of a Tarot card.

"After all, the children are innocent," he said. "Martin Bormann's son is a priest now in the Congo."

But why, I wondered, tell me this fact about Martha? Sooner or later one always feels the need of a weapon against a mistress: he had slipped a knife up my sleeve to use against his wife when the moment of anger came.

The man-servant opened the door and ushered in another visitor. I didn't catch the name, but as he padded across the carpet I recognized the Syrian from whom a year ago we had rented a room. He gave me a smile of complicity and said, "Of course I know Mr. Brown well. I did not know you had returned. And how did you find New York?"

"Any news in town, Hamit?" the ambassador asked.

"The Venezuelan embassy has another refugee."

"They will all be coming to me one day, I suppose," the ambassador said, "but misery likes company."

"A terrible thing happened this morning, excellency. They stopped Doctor Philipot's funeral and stole the coffin."

"I heard rumours. I didn't believe them."

"They are true enough," I said. "I was there. I saw the whole . . ."

"Monsieur Henri Philipot," the man-servant announced, and

a young man advanced towards us through the silence with a slight polio limp. I recognized him. He was the nephew of the ex-Minister, and I had met him once before in happier days, one of a little group of writers and artists who used to gather at the Trianon. I remembered him reading aloud some poems of his own—well-phrased, melodious, a little decadent and *vieux jeu*, with echoes of Baudelaire. How far away those times seemed now. All that was left to recall them were the rum-punches of Joseph.

"Your first refugee, excellency," Hamit said. "I was half expecting you, Monsieur Philipot."

"Oh no," the young man said, "not that. Not yet. I understand when you claim asylum you have to make a promise not to indulge in political action."

"What political action are you proposing to take?" I asked.

"I am melting down some old family silver."

"I don't understand," the ambassador said. "Have one of my cigars, Henri. They are real Havana."

"My dear and beautiful aunt talks about a silver bullet. But one bullet might go astray. I think we need quite a number of them. Besides we have to deal with three devils not one. Papa Doc, the head of the Tontons Macoute, and the colonel of the palace-guard."

"It's a good thing," the ambassador said, "that they bought arms and not microphones with American aid."

"Where were you this morning?" I asked.

"I arrived from Cap Haïtien too late for the funeral. Perhaps it was a lucky thing. I was stopped at every barrier on the road. I think they thought my land-rover was the first tank of an invading army."

"How is everything up there?"

"Only too quiet. The place swarms with the Tontons Macoute. Judging by the sun-glasses you might be in Beverley Hills."

Martha came in while he spoke and I was angry when she looked first at him, though I knew it was prudent to ignore me.

She greeted him a shade too warmly, it seemed to me. "Henri," she said. "I'm so glad you're here. I was afraid for you. Stay with us for a few days."

"I must stay with my aunt, Martha."

"Bring her too. And the child."

"The time hasn't come for that."

"Don't leave it too late." She turned to me with a pretty meaningless smile which she kept in store for second secretaries and said, "We are a third-rate embassy, aren't we, until we have a few refugees of our own."

"How is your boy?" I asked. I meant the question to be as meaningless as her smile.

"The pain is better now. He wants very much to see you."

"Why should he want that?"

"He always likes to see our friends. Otherwise he feels left out."

Henri Philipot said, "If only we had white mercenaries as Tshombe had. We Haitians haven't fought for forty years except with knives and broken bottles. We need a few men of guerrilla experience. We have mountains just as high as those in Cuba."

"But not the forests," I said, "to hide in. Your peasants have destroyed those."

"We held out a long time against the American marines all the same." He added bitterly, "I say 'we,' but I belong to a later generation. In my generation we have learnt to paint—you know they buy Benoit's pictures now for the Museum of Modern Art (of course they cost far less than a European primitive). Our novelists are published in Paris—and now they live there too."

"And your poems?"

"They were quite melodious, weren't they, but they sang the Doctor into power. All our negatives made that one great black positive. I even voted for him. Do you know that I haven't an idea how to use a Bren? Do you know how to use a Bren?"

"It's an easy weapon. You could learn in five minutes."

"Then teach me with diagrams and empty match-boxes, and perhaps one day I'll find the Bren."

"I know someone better equipped than I am as a teacher, but he's in prison at the moment." I told him about "Major" Jones.

"So they beat him up?" he asked with satisfaction.

"Yes."

"That's good. White men react badly to a beating-up."

"He seemed to take it very easily. I almost had the impression he was used to it."

"You think he has some real experience?"

"He told me he had fought in Burma, but I've only got his word for that."

"And you don't believe it?"

"There's something about him I don't believe, not altogether. I was reminded, when I talked to him, of a time when I was young and I persuaded a London restaurant to take me on because I could talk French—I said I'd been a waiter at Fouquet's. I was expecting all the time that someone would call my bluff, but no one did. I made a quick sale of myself, like a reject with the price-label stuck over the flaw. And again, not so long ago, I sold myself just as successfully as an art-expert—no one called my bluff then either. I wonder sometimes whether Jones isn't playing the same game. I remember looking at him one night on the boat from America—it was after the ship's concert —and wondering, are you and I both comedians?"

"They can say that of most of us. Wasn't I a comedian with my verses smelling of Les Fleurs du Mal, published on hand-made paper at my own expense? I posted them to the leading French reviews. That was a mistake. My bluff was called. I never read a single criticism—except by Petit Pierre. The same money would have bought me a Bren perhaps." (It was a magic word to him—Bren.)

The ambassador said, "Come on, cheer up, let us all be comedians together. Take one of my cigars. Help yourself at the bar. My Scotch is good. Perhaps even Papa Doc is a comedian."

"Oh no," Philipot said. "He is real. Horror is always real."

The ambassador said, "We mustn't complain too much of being comedians—it's an honourable profession. If only we could be good ones the world might gain at least a sense of style. We have failed—that's all. We are bad comedians, we aren't bad men."

"For Christ's sake," Martha said in English, as though she were addressing me directly, "I'm no comedian." We had forgotten her. She beat with her hands on the back of the sofa and cried to them in French now, "You talk so much. Such rubbish. My child vomited just now. You can smell it still on my hands. He was crying with pain. You talk about acting parts. I'm not acting any part. I do something. I fetch a basin. I fetch aspirin. I wipe his mouth. I take him into my bed."

She began to weep standing behind the sofa. "My dear," the ambassador said with embarrassment. I couldn't even go to her or look at her too closely: Hamit watched me, ironic and comprehending. I remembered the stains we had left on his sheets, and I wondered whether he had changed them himself. He knew as many intimate things as a prostitute's dog.

"You put us all to shame," Philipot said.

She turned and left us, but her heel came off on the edge of the carpet and she stumbled and nearly fell in the doorway. I followed her and put my hand under her elbow. I knew that Hamit was watching me, but the ambassador, if he noticed anything, covered up well. "Tell Angel I'll be up in half an hour to say good night." I closed the door behind me. She had taken off her shoe and was struggling to fasten the heel. I took it from her.

"There's nothing we can do," I said. "Haven't you another pair?"

"I've twenty other pairs. Does he know, do you think?"

"Perhaps. I don't know."

"Will that make it any easier?"

"I don't know."

"Perhaps we won't have to be comedians any more."

"You said you were no comedian."

"I exaggerated, didn't I? But all that talk irritated me. It made every one of us seem cheap and useless and self-pitying. Perhaps we are, but we needn't revel in it. At least I do things, don't I, even if they are bad things. I didn't pretend not to want you. I didn't pretend I loved you that first evening.

"Do you love me?"

"I love Angel," she said defensively, walking up the wide Victorian staircase in her stockinged feet. We came to a long passage lined with numbered rooms.

"You've got plenty of rooms for refugees."

"Yes."

"Find a room for us now."

"It's too risky."

"It's as safe as the car. And what does it matter, if he knows . . . ?"

" 'In my own house,' he would say, just as you would say 'in our Peugeot.' Men always measure betrayal in degrees. You wouldn't mind so much, would you, if it were someone else's Cadillac?"

"We're wasting time. He gave us half an hour."

"You said you'd see Angel."

"Then afterwards . . . ?"

"Perhaps—I don't know. Let me think."

She opened the third door down, and I found myself where I never wanted to be, in the bedroom she shared with her husband. The two beds were both double-beds: their rose-coloured sheets seemed to fill the room like a carpet. There was a tall pier-glass in which he could watch her prepare for bed. Now I had begun to feel a liking for the man I saw no reason why Martha should not like him too. He was fat, but there are women who love fat men, as they love hunchbacks or the one-legged. He was possessive, but there are women who enjoy slavery.

Angel sat upright against two pink pillows; the mumps had not noticeably increased the fatness of his face. I said, "Hi!" I

don't know how to talk to children. He had brown expressionless Latin eyes like his father—not the blue Saxon eyes of the
hanged man. Martha had those.

"I am ill," he said in a tone of moral superiority.

"So I see."

"I sleep here with my mother. My father sleeps in the dressing-
room. Until the fever has gone. I have a temperature of . . ."

"I said, "What's that you're playing with?""

"A puzzle." He said to Martha, "Is there no one else downstairs?"

"Monsieur Hamit is there and Henri."

"I would like them to come and see me too."

"Perhaps they have never had mumps. They might be afraid
of catching it."

"Has Monsieur Brown had mumps?"

Martha hesitated, and he took note of her hesitation like a
cross-examining counsel. I said, "Yes."

"Does Monsieur Brown play cards?" he asked with apparent
irrelevance.

"No. That is—I don't know," she said as though she feared
a trap.

"I don't like cards," I said.

"My mother used to. She went out nearly every night playing
cards—before you went away."

"We have to go now," Martha said. "Papa will be up in half
an hour to say good night."

He held out the puzzle to me and said, "Do this." It was one
of those little rectangular boxes with glass sides that contain a
picture of a clown and two sockets where his eyes should be
and two little beads of steel which have to be shaken into
the holes. I turned it this way and that way; I would get one
bead in place and then in trying to fix the other I would dis-
lodge the first. The child watched me with scorn and dislike.

"I'm sorry. I'm no good at this sort of thing. I can't do it."

"You aren't properly trying," he said. "Go on." I could feel
the time I had left to be alone with Martha disappearing like

sand in an egg-timer, and I could almost believe that he could see it too. The devilish beads chased each other round the edge of the box and ran across the eye-sockets without falling in; they took dives into corners. I would get them moving slowly downhill towards the sockets on a low gradient and then with the slightest tilt to guide them they plunged to the bottom of the box. All had to be begun again—I hardly moved the box at all now except by a quiver of my nerves.

"I've got one in."

"That's not enough," he said implacably.

I flung the box back at him. "All right. You show me."

He gave me a treacherous unfriendly grin. He picked the box up and holding it over his left hand he hardly seemed to move it at all. One bead even mounted against the slope, tarried on the edge of a socket and fell in.

"One," he said.

The other bead moved straight for the other eye, shaved the socket, turned and dropped into the hole. "Two," he said.

"What's in your left hand?"

"Nothing."

"Then show me nothing."

He opened his fist and showed a small magnet concealed there. "Promise you won't tell," he said.

"And what if I won't?"

We might have been adults quarreling over a trick at cards. He said, "I can keep secrets if you can." His brown eyes gave nothing away.

"I promise," I said.

Martha kissed him and smoothed his pillows and laid him flat and turned on a small night-lamp beside his bed. "Will you come to bed soon?" he asked.

"When my guests have gone."

"When will that be?"

"How can I tell?"

"You can always say that I am ill. I may vomit again. The aspirin isn't working. I'm in pain."

144

"Just lie still. Close your eyes. Papa will be up soon. Then I expect they will all go away and I will come to bed."

"You haven't said good night," he accused me.

"Good night." I put a false friendly hand on his head and ruffled his tough dry hair. My hand smelt afterwards like a mouse.

In the corridor I said to Martha, "Even he seems to know."

"How can he possibly?"

"It's a game all children play." But how difficult it was to consider him a child.

She said, "He has suffered a great deal of pain. Don't you think he's behaving very well?"

"Yes. Of course. Very well."

"Quite like a grown-up?"

"Oh yes. I thought that myself."

I took her wrist and drew her down the corridor. "Who sleeps in this room?"

"No one."

I opened the door and pulled her in. Martha said, "No. Can't you see it's impossible?"

"I've been away three months and we've made love only once since then."

"I didn't make you go away to New York. Can't you feel I'm not in the mood, not tonight?"

"You asked me to come tonight."

"I wanted to see you. That's all. Not to make love."

"You don't love me, do you?"

"You shouldn't ask questions like that."

"Why?"

"Because I might ask you the same."

I recognized the justness of her retort and it angered me, and the anger drove away the desire.

"How many 'adventures' have you had in your life?"

"Four," she said with no hesitation at all.

"And I'm the fourth?"

"Yes. If you want to call yourself an adventure."

Many months later when the affair was over, I realized and appreciated her directness. She played no part. She answered exactly what I asked. She never claimed to like a thing that she disliked or to love something to which she was indifferent. If I had failed to understand her, it was because I failed to ask her the right questions, that was all. It was true that she was no comedian. She had kept the virtue of innocence, and I know now why I loved her. In the end the only quality but beauty which attracts me in a woman is that vague thing, "goodness." The woman in Monte Carlo had betrayed her husband with a schoolboy, but her motive had been generous. Martha too had betrayed her husband, but it was not Martha's love for me which held me, if she did love, it was her blind unselfish attachment to her child. With goodness one can feel secure, why wasn't I satisfied with goodness, why did I always ask her the wrong questions?

"Why not one adventure to last?" I asked as I released her.

"How can I tell?"

I remembered the only real letter which I had ever received from her, apart from notes for rendezvous made ambiguous in case they fell into the wrong hands. It was while I was waiting in New York, and I must have written to her grudgingly, suspiciously, jealously. (I had found a call-girl on East 56th Street, and so I assumed, of course, that she had found an equivalent resource to fill the empty months.) She wrote back to me with tenderness, without rancour. Perhaps having one's father hanged for monstrous crimes puts all our petty grievances into proportion. She wrote of Angel and his cleverness in mathematics, she wrote a great deal about Angel and the nightmares he was having—"I stay in with him nearly every night now," and at once I began to wonder what she did when she did *not* stay in, with whom she passed the evening hours. It was useless to tell myself that she was with her husband, or at the casino where I had first met her.

And suddenly, as though she knew how my thoughts would turn, she wrote—or words to that effect: "Perhaps the sexual life is the great test. If we can survive it with charity to those we love and with affection to those we have betrayed, we needn't worry so much about the good and the bad in us. But jealousy, distrust, cruelty, revenge, recrimination . . . then we fail. The wrong is in that failure even if we are the victims and not the executioners. Virtue is no excuse."

At that moment I found in what she wrote a pretentiousness, a lack of sincerity. I was angry with myself, and so I was angry with her. I tore the letter up in spite of its tenderness, in spite of the fact that it was the only one I had. I thought she was preaching at me because I had spent two hours that afternoon in the apartment on East 56th Street, though how could she possibly have known? That is the reason why of all my jack-daw relics—the paper-weight from Miami, an entrance ticket from Monte Carlo—I have no scrap of her writing with me now. And yet I can remember her writing very clearly, rounded and childish, though I can't remember the tones of her voice.

"Well," I said, "we may as well go downstairs." The room we stood in was cold and unoccupied; the pictures on the wall were probably chosen by an office of works.

"You go. I don't want to see those people."

"The Columbus statue when he's better?"

"The Columbus statue."

Just as I was expecting nothing she put her arms round me. She said, "Poor darling. What a home-coming."

"It's not your fault."

She said, "Let's do it. Let's do it quickly." She lay on the edge of the bed and pulled me towards her, and I heard the voice of Angel down the passage calling "Papa. Papa."

"Don't listen," she said. She had drawn up her knees and I was reminded of Doctor Philipot's body under the diving-board: birth, love and death in their positions closely resemble each other. I found I could do nothing, nothing at all, no white-bird flew in to save my pride. Instead there were the footsteps of the ambassador mounting the stairs.

"Don't worry," she said. "He won't come here," but it wasn't the ambassador who had chilled me. I stood up and she said, "It doesn't matter. It was a bad idea of mine, that's all."

"The Columbus statue?"

"No. I'll find something better. I swear I will."

She went out of the room in front of me and called, "Luis."

"Yes, dear?" He came to the door of their room carrying Angel's puzzle.

"I'm just showing Mr. Brown the rooms up here. He says we could do with a few refugees." There was not a false note in her voice; she was perfectly at ease, and I thought of her anger when we talked of comedians, although now she proved to be the best comedian of us all. I played my part less well; there was a dryness in my voice which betrayed anxiety and I said, "I must go."

"Why? It's still quite early," Martha said. "We haven't seen you for a long time, have we, Luis?"

"There's a rendezvous I have to keep," I told her without knowing that I spoke the truth.

3

The long long day was not yet over: midnight was an hour or an age away. I took my car and drove along the edge of the sea, the road pitted with holes. There were very few people about; perhaps they had not realized the curfew was raised or they feared a trap. On my right hand were a line of wooden huts in little fenced saucers of earth where a few palm-trees grew and slithers of water gleamed between, like scrap-iron on a dump. An occasional candle burned over a little group bowed above their rum like mourners over a coffin. Sometimes there were furtive sounds of music. An old man danced in the middle of the road—I had to brake my car to a standstill. He came and giggled at me through the glass—at least there was one man in Port-au-Prince that night who was not afraid. I couldn't make out the meaning of his *patois* and I drove on. It was two years or more since I had been to Mère Catherine's, but tonight I needed her services. My impotence lay in my body like a curse which it needed a witch to raise. I thought of the girl on East 56th Street, and when reluctantly I thought of Martha I whipped up my anger. If she had made love to me when I had wanted her, this would not be happening.

Just before Mère Catherine's the road branched—the tarmac, if you could call it tarmac, came to an abrupt end (money had run out or someone hadn't received his cut). To the left was the main southern highway, almost impassable except by jeep. I was surprised to find a road-block there, for no one expected invasion from the south. I stood, while they searched me more carefully than usual, under a great placard which announced "U.S.A.-Haitian Joint Five Year Plan. Great Southern Highway," but the Americans had left and nothing remained of all the five-year plan but the notice-board, over the stagnant pools, the channels in the road, the rocks, and the carcass of a dredger which nobody had bothered to rescue from the mud.

After they let me go I took the right fork and arrived at Mère Catherine's compound. All was so quiet I wondered whether it was worth my while to leave the car. A long low hut like a stable divided into stalls were the quarters here for love. I could see a light burning in the main building where Mère Catherine received her guests and served them drinks, but there was no sound of music and dancing. For a moment fidelity became a temptation and I wanted to drive away. But I had carried my malady too far along the rough road to be put off now, and I moved cautiously across the dark compound towards the light, hating myself all the way. I had foolishly turned the car against the wall of the hut, so that I was in darkness, and almost at once I stumbled against a jeep, standing lightless; a man slept at the wheel. Again I nearly turned and went, for there were few jeeps in Port-au-Prince which were not owned by the Tontons Macoute, and if the Tontons Macoute were making a night of it with Mère Catherine's girls, there would be no room for outside custom.

But I was obstinate in my self-hatred, and I went on. Mère Catherine heard me stumbling and came to meet me on the threshold, holding up an oil-lamp. She had the face of a kind nanny in a film of the deep South, and a tiny delicate body which must once have been beautiful. Her face didn't belie her nature, for she was the kindest woman I knew in Port-au-Prince. She pretended that her girls came from good families, that she was only helping them to earn a little pin-money, and you could almost believe her, for she had taught them perfect manners in public. Till they reached the stalls her customers too had to behave with decorum, and to watch the couples dance you would almost have believed it to be an end-of-term celebration at a convent-school. On one occasion three years before I had seen her go in to rescue a girl from some brutality. I was drinking a glass of rum and I heard a scream from what we called the stable, but before I could decide what to do Mère Catherine had taken a hatchet from the kitchen and sailed out like the little *Revenge* prepared to take on a fleet. Her opponent was armed with a knife, he was twice her size, and he was drunk with rum. (He must have had a flask in his hip-pocket, for Mère Catherine would never have allowed him to go outside with a girl in that condition.) He turned and fled at her approach, and later when I left, I saw her through the window of the kitchen, with the girl upon her knee, crooning to her as though she were a child, in a *patois* which I couldn't understand, and the girl slept against the little bony shoulder.

Mère Catherine whispered a warning to me, "The Tontons are here."

"All the girls taken?"

"No, but the girl you like is busy."

I hadn't been here for two years, but she remembered, and what was even more remarkable the girl was with her still—she would be close on eighteen by now. I hadn't expected to find her, and yet I was disappointed. In age one prefers old friends, even in a *bordel*.

"Are they in a dangerous mood?" I asked her.

"I don't think so. They are looking after someone important. He's out with Tin Tin now."

I nearly went away, but my grudge against Martha worked like an infection.

"I'll come in," I said. "I'm thirsty. Give me a rum and Coke."

"There's no more Coke." I had forgotten that American aid was over.

"Rum and soda then."

"I have a few bottles of Seven-up left."

"All right. Seven-up."

At the door of the *salle* a Tonton Macoute was alseep on a chair; his sun-glasses had fallen into his lap and he looked quite harmless. The flies of his grey flannel trousers gaped from a lost button. Inside there was complete silence. Through the open door I saw a group of four girls dressed in white muslin with balloon-skirts. They were sucking orangeade through straws, not speaking. One of them took her empty glass and moved away, walking beautifully, the muslin swaying, like a little bronze by Degas.

"No customers at all?"

"They all left when the Tontons Macoute came."

I went in, and there at a table by the wall with his eyes fixed on me as though I had never once escaped from them was the Tonton Macoute I had seen in the police-station, who had smashed the windows of the hearse to get out the coffin of the *ancien ministre*. His soft hat lay on a chair, and he wore a striped bow-tie. I bowed to him and started towards another table. I was scared of him, and I wondered whom it could be— more important than this arrogant officer—that Tin Tin was consoling now. I hoped for her sake he was not a worse man as well.

The officer said, "I seem to see you everywhere."

"I try to be inconspicuous."

"What do you want here tonight?"

"A rum and Seven-up."

He said to Mère Catherine, who was bringing in my drink upon a tray, "You said you had no Seven-up left." I noticed that there was an empty soda-water bottle on the tray beside my glass. The Tonton Macoute took my drink and tasted it. "Seven-up it is. You can bring this man a rum and soda. We need all the Seven-up you have left for my friend when he returns."

"It's so dark in the bar. The bottles must have got mixed."

"You must learn to distinguish between your important customers and," he hesitated and decided to be reasonably polite, "the less important. You can sit down," he said to me.

I turned away.

"You can sit down here. Sit down."

I obeyed. He said, "You were stopped at the cross-roads and searched?"

"Yes."

"And at the door here? You were stopped at the door?"

"By Mère Catherine, yes."

"By one of my men?"

"He was asleep."

"Asleep?"

"Yes."

I had no hesitation in telling tales. Let the Tontons Macoute destroy themselves. I was surprised when he said nothing and made no move towards the door. He only stared blankly through me with his black opaque lenses. He had decided something, but he would not let me know his decision. Mère Catherine brought me in my drink. I tasted it. The rum was still mixed with Seven-up. She was a brave woman.

I said, "You seem to be taking a lot of precautions tonight."

"I am in charge of a very important foreigner. I have to take precautions for his security. He asked to come here."

"Is he safe with little Tin Tin? Or do you keep a guard in the bedroom, captain? Or is it commandant?"

"My name is Captain Concasseur. You have a sense of humour. I appreciate humour. I am in favour of jokes. They have political value. Jokes are a release for the cowardly and the impotent."

"You said an important foreigner, captain? This morning I had the impression that you didn't like foreigners."

"My personal view of every white man is very low. I admit I am offended by the colour, which reminds me of turd. But we accept some of you—if you are useful to the State."

"You mean to the Doctor?"

With a very small inflexion of irony he quoted, "*Je suis le drapeau Haïtien, Uni et Indivisible.*" He took a drink of rum. "Of course some white men are more tolerable than others. At least the French have a common culture with us. I admire the General. The President has written to him offering to join *la Communauté Européene.*"

"Has he received a reply?"

"These things take time. There are conditions which we have to discuss. We understand diplomacy. We don't blunder like the Americans—and the British."

I was haunted by the name Concasseur. Somewhere I had heard it before. The first syllable suited him well, and perhaps the whole name, with its suggestion of destructive power, had been adopted like that of Stalin or Hitler.

"Haiti belongs by right to any Third Force," Captain Concasseur said. "We are the true bastion against the Communists. No Castro can succeed here. We have a loyal peasantry."

"Or a terrified one." I took a long drink of rum; drink helped to make his pretensions more supportable. "Your important visitor is taking his time."

"He told me he had been away from women for a long time." He barked at Mère Catherine, "I want service. Service," and stamped the floor. "Why is no one dancing?"

"A bastion of the free world," I said.

The four girls rose from their table, and one put on the gramophone. They began to dance together in a graceful slow old-fashioned style. Their balloon skirts swung like silver censers and showed their slender legs the colour of young deer; they smiled gently at each other and held one another a little apart. They were beautiful and undifferentiated, like birds of the same plumage. It was impossible to believe they were for sale. Like everyone else.

"Of course the free world pays better," I said, "and in dollars."

Captain Concasseur saw where I was looking; he missed nothing through those black glasses. He said, "I will treat you to a woman. That small girl there, with a flower in her hair, Louise. She doesn't look at us. She is shy because she thinks I might be jealous. Jealous of a *putain*! What absurdity! She will serve you very well if I give her the word."

"I don't want a woman." I could see through his apparent generosity. One flings a *putain* to a white man as one flings a bone to a dog.

"Then why are you here?"

He had a right to ask the question. I could only say, "I've changed my mind," as I watched the girls revolve, worthy of a better setting than the wooden shed, the rum-bar, and the old advertisements for Coca-Cola.

I said, "Are you never afraid of the Communists?"

"Oh, there's no danger from them. The Americans would land Marines if they ever became a danger. Of course we have a few Communists in Port-au-Prince. Their names are known. They are not dangerous. They meet in little study-groups and read Marx. Are you a Communist?"

"How could I be? I own the Hotel Trianon. I depend on American tourists. I am a capitalist."

"Then you count as one of us," he said with the nearest he ever came to courtesy, "except for your colour, of course."

"Don't insult me too far."

"Oh, you cannot help your colour," he said.

"I meant, don't say I'm one of you. When a capitalist state gets too repulsive, it is in danger of losing the loyalty even of the capitalists."

"A capitalist will always be loyal if he is allowed a cut of twenty-five per cent."

"A little humanity is necessary too."

"You speak like a Catholic."

"Yes. Perhaps. A Catholic who has lost his faith. But isn't there a danger that your capitalists may lose their faith too?"

"They lose their lives but never their faith. Their money is their faith. They guard it to the end and leave it to their children."

"And this important man of yours—is he a loyal capitalist or a right-wing politician?" While he chinked the ice in his glass I thought I remembered where I had heard the name Captain Concasseur before. It was Petit Pierre who had spoken of him, with some degree of awe. He had withdrawn all the dredges and pumps belonging to an American water-company, after the employees had been evacuated and the Americans had withdrawn their ambassador, and he had sent them to work on a wild project of his own, at the mountain-village of Kenscoff. He hadn't got very far, for the labourers had left him at the end of a month because they were unpaid; it was said too that he hadn't cleared himself satisfactorily with the chief of the Tontons Macoute, who would have expected his proper cut. So Concasseur's folly stood on the slopes of Kenscoff— four cement columns and a cement floor already racking in the heat and the rains. Perhaps the important man now playing with Tin Tin in the stables was a financier who was going to help him out? But what financier in his senses would think of lending money in this country, from which all the tourists had fled, in order to build an ice-skating rink on the slopes of Kenscoff?

"We need technicians, even white technicians," Concasseur said.

"The Emperor Christophe did without them."

"We're more modern than Christophe."

"An ice-skating rink instead of a castle?"

"I think I have borne with you nearly enough," Captain

Concasseur said, and I knew I had gone too far. I had touched his raw wound and I was a little scared. If I had made love to Martha what a different night this would have been; I would have been sleeping deeply in my own bed at the hotel, unconcerned with politics and the corruption of power. The captain took the revolver out of his holster and laid it on the table, beside his empty glass. His chin dropped against his shirt of white and blue stripes. He sat in a lugubrious silence as though he were weighing carefully the advantages and the disadvantages of a quick shot between the eyes. I could see no disadvantages so far as he was concerned.

Mère Catherine came and stood behind me and deposited two glasses of rum. She said, "Your friend has been more than half an hour with Tin Tin. It is time . . ."

"He must be allowed," the captain said, "whatever time he wants. He is an important man. A very important man." Small bubbles of spittle gathered at the corners of his lips like venom. He touched the revolver with the tips of his fingers. He said, "An ice-rink is very modern." His fingers played between the rum and the revolver. I was glad when he picked up the glass. He said, "An ice-rink is chic. It is snob."

Mère Catherine said, "Your payment was for half an hour."

"My watch keeps a different time," the captain said. "You lose nothing. There are no other customers."

"There is Monsieur Brown."

"Not tonight," I said. "I wouldn't know how to follow such an important guest."

"Then why are you staying here?" the captain asked.

"I'm thirsty. And curious. It's not often in Haiti we have important visitors. Is he financing your ice-rink?" The captain looked at his revolver, but the moment of spontaneity, which was the moment of real danger, had passed. Only signs of it remained like traces of old sickness: the streak of blood across the yellow eye-balls, the striped tie which had somehow gone vertically askew. I said, "You wouldn't like your important foreign guest to come in and find a white corpse. It would be bad for business."

"That can always be arranged later . . ." he said with sombre truth, and then an extraordinary smile opened his face like a crack in the cement of his own ice-rink, a smile of civility, even of humility. He stood up and, hearing the door of the *salle* close behind me, I turned and saw Tin Tin all in white, smiling too, modestly, like a bride at a churchdoor. But Concasseur and she were not smiling at each other, both their smiles were directed at the guest of great importance on whose arm she had entered. It was Mr. Jones.

4

"Jones," I exclaimed. There were still the relics of battle on his face, but they were neatly covered now with pieces of sticking-plaster.

"Why, if it isn't Brown," he said. He came and shook my hand with great warmth. "It's good to see one of the old lot," he said as though we were veterans at some regimental reunion who had not met since the last war but one.

"You saw me yesterday," I said, and I detected a slight embarrassment—when an unpleasantness was over Jones forgot it as quickly as possible. He explained to Captain Concasseur, "Mr. Brown and I were shipmates on the *Medea*. And how is Mr. Smith?"

"Much as he was yesterday when he visited you. He has been anxious about you."

"About me? But why?" He said, "Forgive me. I haven't introduced my young friend here."

"Tin Tin and I know each other well."

"That's fine, fine. Sit down, dear, and we'll all have a snifter." He pulled out a chair for her and then took my arm and led me a little aside. He said in a low voice, "You know all that business is past history now."

157

"I'm glad to see you safely out."

He explained vaguely. "My note did it. I thought it would. I was never really worried. Mistakes on both sides. I wouldn't want the girls to know about it though."

"You would find them very sympathetic. But doesn't *he* know?"

"Oh yes, but he's bound to secrecy. I would have told you tomorrow how things had gone, but tonight I badly needed a roll in the hay. So you know Tin Tin?"

"Yes."

"She's a sweet girl. I'm glad I chose her. The captain wanted me to take that girl with the flower."

"I don't suppose you'd have noticed the difference. Mère Catherine caters for a sweet tooth. What are you doing with *him?*"

"We're in a bit of business together."

"Not an ice-rink?"

"No. Why an ice-rink?"

"Be careful, Jones. He's dangerous."

"Don't worry about me," Jones said. "I know the world." Mère Catherine passed: her tray was loaded with rum and what was probably the last of the Seven-ups and Jones grabbed a glass. "Tomorrow they are finding me transport. I'll come and see you when I've got my car." He waved to Tin Tin; to the captain he called "*Salut.*" "I like it here," he said. "I've landed on my feet."

I left the *salle,* my mouth cloyed with too much Seven-up, and shook the sentry by the shoulder as I passed—I might as well do someone a good turn. I felt my way past the jeep to my own car, and heard footsteps behind me and dodged sideways. It might be the captain come to preserve the honour of his ice-rink, but it was only Tin Tin.

She said, "I told them I go *faire pipi.*"

"How are you, Tin Tin?"

"Very well and you . . ."

"*Ça marche.*"

"Why not stay a little while in your car? *They* will go soon. The Englishman is *tout à fait épuisé*."

"I don't doubt it, but I'm tired. I've got to go. Tin Tin, did he behave all right to you?"

"Oh yes. I liked him. I liked him a lot."

"What did you like so much?"

"He made me laugh," she said. It was a sentence which was to be repeated to me disquietingly in other circumstances. I had learnt in a disorganized life many tricks, but not the trick of laughter.

Part Two

Chapter One

1

Jones fell from view for a while as completely as the body of the Secretary for Social Welfare. No one ever learnt what was done with *his* corpse, though the Presidential Candidate made more than one attempt to discover. He penetrated to the bureau of the new Secretary where he was received with celerity and politeness. Petit Pierre had done his best to spread his fame as "Truman's opponent," and the Minister had heard of Truman.

He was a small fat man who wore, for some reason, a fraternity pin, and his teeth were very big and white and separate, like tombstones designed for a much larger cemetery. A curious smell crossed his desk as though one grave had stayed open. I accompanied Mr. Smith in case a translator were needed, but the new Minister spoke good English with a slight twang which went some way to support the fraternity pin (I learnt later that he had served for a while as "the small boy" at the American Embassy. It might have been a rare example of merit rising if he had not served an interim period in the Tontons Macoute, where he had been a special assistant to Colonel Gracia—known as Fat Gracia).

Mr. Smith excused the fact that his letter of introduction was addressed to Doctor Philipot.

"Poor Philipot," the Minister said, and I wondered whether at last we were to receive the official version of his end.

"What happened to him?" Mr. Smith asked with admirable directness.

"We will probably never know. He was a strange moody man, and I must confess to you, Professor, his accounts were not in good order. There was the matter of a water-pump in Desaix Street."

"Are you suggesting he killed himself?" I had underrated Mr. Smith. In a good cause he could show cunning and now he played his cards close to his chest.

"Perhaps, or perhaps he has been the victim of the peoples' vengeance. We Haitians have a tradition of removing a tyrant in our own way, Professor."

"Was Doctor Philipot a tyrant?"

"The people in Desaix Street were sadly deceived about their water."

"So the pump will be set working now?" I asked.

"It will be one of my first projects"—he waved his hand at the files on the shelves behind him—"but as you see I have many cares." I noticed that the steel grips on many of his "cares" had been rusted by a long succession of rainy seasons: a "care" was not soon disposed of.

Mr. Smith came smartly back at him. "So Doctor Philipot is still missing?"

"As your war-communiqués used to put it, 'missing believed killed.' "

"But I attended his funeral," Mr. Smith said.

"His what?"

"His funeral."

I watched the Minister. He showed no embarrassment. He gave a short bark, which was meant to be a laugh (I was reminded of a French bull-dog), and said, "There was no funeral."

"It was interrupted."

"You cannot imagine, Professor, the unscrupulous propaganda put about by our opponents."

"I am not a professor and I saw the coffin with my own eyes."

"That coffin was filled with stones, Professor—I am sorry, Mr. Smith."

"Stones?"

"Bricks to be exact, brought from Duvalierville, where we are constructing our beautiful new city. Stolen bricks. I would like to show you Duvalierville one morning when you are free. It is our answer to Brasilia."

"But his wife was there."

"Poor woman, she was used, I hope innocently, by unscrupulous men. The morticians have been arrested."

I gave him full marks for readiness and imagination. Mr. Smith was temporarily silenced.

"When are they to be tried?" I asked.

"The enquiries will take some time. The plot has many ramifications."

"Then it's not true what the people think—that the body of Doctor Philipot is in the palace working as a zombie?"

"All that is Voodoo stuff, Mr. Brown. Luckily our President has rid the country of Voodoo."

"Then he has done more than the Jesuits could do."

Mr. Smith broke in with impatience. He had done his best in the cause of Doctor Philipot and now it was his mission which demanded full attention. He was anxious not to antagonize the Minister with such irrelevancies as zombies and Voodoo. The Minister listened to him with great courtesy, doodling at the same time with a pencil. Perhaps it was not a sign of inattention, for I noticed the doodle took the form of innumerable percentage marks and crosses—so far as I could see there were no minus signs.

Mr. Smith spoke of a building which would contain a restaurant, kitchen, a library and a lecture-hall. If possible there should be enough room for extensions. Even a theatre and cinema might be possible, one day; already his organization could supply documentary films, and he hoped that soon —given the opportunities for production—there might arise a school of vegetarian dramatists. "In the meanwhile," he said, "we can always fall back on Bernard Shaw."

"It is a great project," the Minister said.

Mr. Smith had been in the republic a week now. He had seen the kidnapping of Docotor Philipot's body; I had driven him through the worst of the shanty-town. That morning he had insisted against my advice in going to the Post-Office himself to buy stamps. I had lost him momentarily in the crowd, and when I found him again he had not been able to approach a foot towards the *guichet*. Two one-armed men and three one-legged men hemmed him round. Two were trying to sell him dirty old envelopes containing out-of-date Haitian postage-stamps: the others were more frankly begging. A man without legs at all had installed himself between his knees and removed his shoe-laces preparatory to cleaning his shoes. Others seeing a crowd collected were fighting to join it. A young fellow, with a hole where his nose should have been, lowered his head and tried to ram his way through towards the attraction at the centre. A man with no hands raised his pink polished stumps over the heads of the crowd to exhibit his infirmity to the foreigner. It was a typical scene in the Post-Office except that foreigners were rare nowadays. I had to fight my way to reach him, and once my hand encountered a stiff inhuman stump, like a piece of hard rubber. I forced it on one side, and I felt revolted by myself, as though I were rejecting misery. The thought even came to me, "What would the Fathers of the Visitation have said to me?" So deeply embedded are the disciplines and myths of childhood. It took me five minutes to get Mr. Smith clear, and he had lost his shoe-laces. We had to replace them at Hamit's before we called on the Secretary for Social Welfare.

Mr. Smith said to the Minister, "The centre, of course, would not be run at a profit, but I calculate we ought to give employment to a librarian, secretary, accountant, cook, waiters —and eventually of course the cinema usherettes . . . At least twenty people. The film-shows would be educational and free of charge. As for the theatre—well, we mustn't look too far ahead. All vegetarian products would be supplied at cost-price, and the literature for the library would be gratis."

I listened to him with astonishment. The dream was intact. Reality could not touch him. Even the scene in the Post-Office had not sullied his vision. The Haitians, freed from acidity, poverty, and passion, would soon be bent happily over their nut-cutlets.

"This new city of yours, Duvalierville," Mr. Smith said, "might provide an admirable situation. I'm not an opponent of modern architecture—not at all. New ideas need new shapes, and what I want to bring to your republic is a new idea."

"It might be arranged," the Minister said. "There are sites available." He was making a whole row of little crosses on his sheet, all plus signs. "You have plenty of funds, I am sure."

"I thought a mutual project with the Government . . ."

"Of course you realize, Mr. Smith, we are not a socialist state. We believe in free enterprise. The building would have to be put up to tender."

"Fair enough."

"Of course the government would make the final decision between the tenders. It is not a mere matter of the lowest bid. There are the amenities of Duvalierville to be considered. And of course questions of sanitation are of first importance. For that reason I think the project might well come in the first place under the Ministry for Social Welfare."

"Fine," Mr. Smith said. "Then I would be dealing with you."

"Later of course we would have to have discussions with the Treasury. And the Customs. Imports, of course, are the responsibility of the Customs."

"Surely there are no duties here on food?"

"Films . . ."

"Educational films?"

"Oh well, let us talk about all that later. There is first the question of the site. And its cost."

"Don't you think the Government might be inclined to contribute the site? In view of our investment in labour. I guess land here doesn't fetch a high price anyway."

"The land belongs to the people, not the Government, Mr.

Smith," the Minister said with gentle reproof. "All the same you will find nothing is impossible in modern Haiti. I would myself suggest, if my opinion is asked, a contribution for the site equivalent to the cost of construction ..."

"But that's absurd," Mr. Smith said, "the two costs bear no relation."

"Returnable, of course, on completion of the work."

"So you mean the site would be free?"

"Quite free."

"Then I don't see the point of the contribution."

"To protect the workers, Mr. Smith. Many foreign projects have come suddenly to an end, and the worker on pay-day has found nothing in his envelope. A tragic thing for a poor family. We still have many poor families in Haiti."

"Perhaps a bank-guarantee ..."

"Cash is a better notion, Mr. Smith. The gourde has remained stable for a generation, but there are pressures on the dollar."

"I would have to write home to my committee. I doubt ..."

"Write home, Mr. Smith, and say that the Government welcomes all progressive projects and will do all it can." He rose from behind his desk to signify that the interview was at an end, and his wide toothy smile showed that he expected it to be beneficial to all parties. He even put his arm around Mr. Smith's shoulders to demonstrate that they were partners in the great work of progress.

"And the site?"

"You will have a great choice of sites, Mr. Smith. Perhaps close to the cathedral? Or the college? Or the theatre? Anything which does not conflict with the amenities of Duvalierville. Such a beautiful city. You will see. I will show it to you myself. Tomorrow I am very busy. So many deputations. You know how it is in a democracy, but Thursday ..."

In the car Mr. Smith said, "He seemed interested all right."

"I would be careful about that contribution."

"It's returnable."

168

"Only when the building's completed."

"His story about the bricks in the coffin. Do you suppose there's something in that?"

"No."

"After all," Mr. Smith said, "none of us have actually seen Doctor Philipot's body. One mustn't judge hastily."

2

For some days after my visit to the embassy I heard nothing from Martha, and I was worried. I played the scene over and over again in my mind, trying to judge whether any irrevocable words had been spoken, but I remembered none. I was relieved, but angered too, by her short untender note when it came at last: Angel was better, the pain was over, she could meet me, if I wished, by the statue. I went to the rendezvous and found nothing changed.

But even in the lack of change and in her tenderness, I found cause for resentment. Oh yes, she was ready to make love now in her own good time . . . I said, "We can't live in a car."

She said, "I've been thinking a lot about that too. We shall ruin ourselves with secrecy. I will come to the Trianon—if we can avoid your guests."

"The Smiths will be in bed by this time."

"We'd better take both cars in case . . . I can say I've brought you a message from my husband. An invitation. Something of the sort. You go first. I'll give you five minutes." I had expected a night of argument, and then suddenly the door which I had pushed against so often before flew open. I walked through and found only disappointment. I thought, "She thinks quicker than I do. She knows the ropes."

The Smiths surprised me when I reached the hotel by their audible presence. There was a clatter of spoons and the clinking of tins and a gentle punctuation of voices. They had taken over the verandah tonight for their evening Yeastrol and Bar-

mene. I had wondered sometimes what they spoke about together when they were alone. Did they refight old campaigns?
I parked the car and stood awhile and listened before I mounted
the steps. I heard Mr. Smith say, "You've put in two spoonfuls
already, dear."

"Oh no. I'm sure I haven't."

"Just try it first and you'll see."

From the silence that followed I gathered he was right.

"I have often wondered," Mr. Smith said, "what happened
to that poor man who was alseep in the pool. Our first night.
Do you remember, dear?"

"Of course I remember. And I wish I had gone down as I
wanted to at the time," Mrs. Smith said. "I asked Joseph next
day, but I think he lied to me."

"Not lied, dear. He didn't understand."

I walked up the stairs and they greeted me. "Not in bed
yet?" I asked rather stupidly.

"Mr. Smith had to catch up with his mail."

I wondered how I could shift them from the verandah before
Martha arrived. I said, "You mustn't be too late. The Secretary
is taking us to Duvalierville tomorrow. We start early."

"That's all right," Mr. Smith said. "My wife will stay behind.
I don't want her bumped along the roads in the sun."

"I can stand it quite as well as you can."

"I *have* to stand it, dear. For you there's no necessity. It
will give you a chance to catch up on your lessons in Hugo."

"But you need your sleep too," I said.

"I can do with very little, Mr. Brown. You remember, dear,
that second night in Nashville . . ."

I had noticed how Nashville came back often to their common memory: perhaps because it was the most glorious of their
campaigns.

"Do you know whom I saw in town today?" Mr. Smith
asked.

"No."

"Mr. Jones. He was coming out the palace with a very fat

man in uniform. The guard saluted. Of course I don't suppose they were saluting Mr. Jones."

"He seems to be doing pretty well," I said. "From prison to palace. It's almost better than log-cabin to White House."

"I have always felt that Mr. Jones has great character. I'm very glad he's prospering."

"If it's not at someone else's expense."

At even that hint of criticism Mr. Smith's expression slammed shut (he stirred his Yeastrol nervously to and fro) and I was seriously tempted to tell him of the telegram sent to the captain of the *Medea*. Wasn't it possibly a flaw in character to believe so passionately in the integrity of all the world?

I was saved by the sound of a car, and a moment later Martha came up the steps.

"Why, it's that charming Mrs. Pineda," Mr. Smith exclaimed with relief. He rose and busied himself arranging a seat. Martha looked at me with despair and said, "It's late. I can't stop. I've just brought a message from my husband . . ." She produced an evelope from her bag and pushed it into my hand.

"Have a whisky while you are here," I said.

"No, no. I really must get home."

Mrs. Smith remarked, a little stiffly. I thought, but perhaps it was in my imagination, "Don't hurry away, Mrs. Pineda, because of us. Mr. Smith and I are just off to bed. Come along, dear."

"I have to go in any case. My son has mumps, you see." She was explaining too much.

"Mumps?" Mrs. Smith said, "I'm so sorry to hear it, Mrs. Pineda. In that case you will certainly want to be at home."

"I'll see you to your car," I said and got her away. We drove to the end of the drive and stopped.

"What went wrong?" Martha asked.

"You shouldn't have given me a letter addressed to you in my handwriting."

"I wasn't prepared. It was the only one I had in my bag. She couldn't have seen."

"She sees an awful lot. Unlike her husband."

"I'm sorry. What shall we do?"

"We can wait until they are in bed."

"And then creep by and see the door open suddenly and Mrs. Smith ..."

"They're not on my floor."

"Then we'll meet her for certain at the corner of the stairs. I can't."

"Another meeting spoilt," I said.

"Darling, that first night when you returned, by the pool ... I wanted so much ..."

"They still have the John Barrymore suite just overhead."

"We can get under the trees. And the lights are out now. It's dark. Even Mrs. Smith can't see in the dark."

I felt an inexplicable reluctance. I said, "The mosquitoes ..." trying to account for it.

"Damn the mosquitoes."

The last time we had been together we quarrelled because of her unwillingness. Now it was my turn. I thought angrily: If her house must not be defiled, why should my house be any less sacred? And then I wondered, sacred to what? A dead body in a bathing-pool?

We left the car and went as softly as we could towards the pool. A light was on in the Barrymore suite and the shadow of a Smith passed across the mosquito-netting. We lay down in a shallow declivity under the palms like bodies given a common burial, and I remembered another death, Marcel hanging from the chandeliers. Neither of us would ever die for love. We would grieve and separate and find another. We belonged to the world of comedy and not of tragedy. The fire-flies moved among the trees and lit intermittently a world in which we had no part. We—the uncoloured—were all of us too far away from home. I lay as inert as Monsieur le Ministre.

"What's the matter, darling? Are you angry about something?"

"No."

She said humbly, "You don't want me."

"Not here. Not now."

"I angered you last time. But I wanted to make it up."

I said, "I never told you what happened that night. Why I sent you away with Joseph."

"I thought you were protecting me from the Smiths."

"Doctor Philipot was lying dead in the pool, just over there. You see that patch of moonlight . . ."

"Killed?"

"He had cut his own throat. To escape the Tontons Macoute."

She moved a little away. "I understand. Oh God, it's terrible, the things that happen. They are like nightmares."

"Only the nightmares are real in this place. More real than Mr. Smith and his vegetarian centre. More real than ourselves."

We lay quietly side by side in our grave, and I loved her as I had never done in the Peugeot or the bedroom above Hamit's store. We approached one another by words more nearly than we had ever approached by touch. She said, "I envy you and Luis. You believe in something. You have explanations."

"Have I? Do you think I still believe?"

She said, "My father believed too." (It was the first time she had ever mentioned him to me.)

"In what?" I asked.

"In the God of the Reformation," she said. "He was a Lutheran. A pious Lutheran."

"He was lucky to believe in anything."

"And people in Germany too cut their throats to escape his justice."

"Yes. The situation isn't abnormal. It belongs to human life. Cruelty's like a searchlight. It sweeps from one spot to another. We can only escape it for a time. We are trying to hide now under the palm trees."

"Instead of doing anything?"

"Instead of doing anything."

She said, "I almost prefer my father."

"No."

"You know about him?"

"Your husband told me."

"At least he wasn't a diplomat."

"Or a hotel-keeper who depends on the tourist trade?"

"There's nothing wrong in that."

"A capitalist waiting for the dollars to return."

"You speak like a Communist."

"Sometimes I wish I were."

"But you are Catholics, you and Luis—"

"Yes, we were both brought up by the Jesuits," I said. "They taught us to reason, so at least we know the kind of part we play now."

"Now?"

We lay there, holding each other, for a long while. Sometimes I wonder whether it was not the happiest moment we ever knew together. For the first time we had trusted each other with something more than a caress.

3

We drove out next day to Duvalierville, Mr. Smith and I and the Minister with a Tonton Macoute for a driver; perhaps he was there to protect us, perhaps to observe us, perhaps just to help us pass the road-blocks, for this was the road to the north along which, as most people in the city hoped, the tanks from Santo Domingo would one day come. I wondered what good the three shabby militiamen at the road-block would be then.

Hundreds of women were flocking into the capital for market, riding side-saddle on their *bourriques*; they stared at the fields on either side and paid us no attention: we didn't exist in their world. Buses went by, painted in stripes of red and yellow and blue. There might be little food in the land, but there was always colour. The deep blue shadows sat permanently on the mountain-slopes, the sea was peacock green. Green was everywhere in all its varieties, the poison-bottle green of sisal slashed with black, the pale green of banana-trees beginning to turn yellow at the tip to match the sand at the edge of the flat green sea. The land was stormy with colour. A big American car went by with reckless speed on the bad road and covered us with dust, and only the dust lacked colour. The Minister brought out a bright scarlet handkerchief and dabbed his eyes.

"*Salauds!*" he exclaimed.

Mr. Smith put his mouth close to my ear and whispered, "Did you see who those people were?"

"No."

"I do believe one of them was Mr. Jones. I may have been mistaken. They went very fast."

"It seems unlikely," I said.

On the flat shoddy plain between the hills and the sea a few white one-room boxes had been constructed, a cement playground, and an immense cockpit which among the small houses looked almost as impressive as the Coliseum. They stood together in a bowl of dust which, when we left the car, whirled around us in the wind of the approaching thunderstorm: by night it would have turned to mud again. I wondered, in the wilderness of cement, where the notional bricks had come from for Doctor Philipot's coffin.

"Is that a Greek theatre?" Mr. Smith asked with interest.

"No. It's where they kill cocks."

His mouth twitched, but he put the pain away from him: to feel pain was a kind of criticism. He said, "I don't see many folk around here."

The Secretary for Social Welfare said proudly, "There were several hundred on this very spot. Living in miserable mud-huts. We had to clear the ground. It was quite a major operation."

"Where did they go?"

"I suppose some went into town. Some into the hills. To relatives."

"Will they come back when the city's built?"

"Oh well, you know, we are planning for a better class of people here."

Beyond the cockpit there were four houses built with tilted wings like wrecked butterflies; they resembled some of the houses of Brasilia seen through the wrong end of a telescope.

"And who will live in these?" Mr. Smith asked.

"These are for tourists."

"Tourists?" Mr. Smith asked.

Even the sea had receded out of sight; there was nothing anywhere but the great cockpit, the cement field, the dust, the road, and the stony hillside. Outside one of the white boxes a Negro with white hair sat on a hard chair under a sign that showed him to be a justice of the peace. He was the only human being in sight—he must have had a lot of influence to be installed so soon. There was no sign of men working, though a bulldozer stood on the cement playground with one wheel detached.

"The visitors who come to see Duvalierville." He led us nearer to one of the houses: it was no different from the other boxes except for the useless wings, which I could imagine dropping off in the hard rains. "Now one of these—they are designed by our finest architect—might do for your centre. You wouldn't have to begin then on a bare site."

"I had thought of something larger."

"You could take over the whole group."

"What would happen to your tourists then?" I asked.

"We would build some more over there," he said, waving his hand at the dry insignificant plain.

"It seems a bit out of the world," Mr. Smith said gently.

"We are going to house five thousand people here. For a start."

"Where will they work?"

"We shall bring industries to them. The Government believes in decentralization."

"And the cathedral?"

"It will be over there, beyond the bulldozer."

Around the corner of the great cockpit came seesawing one other human being. The justice of peace was not after all the sole inhabitant of the new city. It already had its beggar too. He must have been sleeping in the sun, until he was woken by our voices. Perhaps he thought that the architect's dream had come true and there really were tourists in Duvalierville. He had very long arms and no legs and he moved imperceptibly nearer like a rocking-horse. Then he saw our driver and his dark glasses and his gun, and he stopped. Instead he set up a crooning murmur, and from under his torn cobweb of a shirt he drew a small wooden statuette which he held out towards us.

I said, "You have your beggars then."

"He is no beggar," the Minister explained. "He is an artist."

He spoke to the Tonton Macoute, who went and fetched the statuette; it was the figure of a half-naked girl indistinguishable from dozens in the Syrian stores that waited for gullible tourists who never came now.

"Let me make you a present," the Minister said, handing the statuette to Mr. Smith, who took it with embarrassment. "An example of Haitian art."

"I must pay the man," Mr. Smith said.

"No need. The Government looks after him." The Minister began to lead the way back to the car, his hand on Mr. Smith's elbow to guide him over the broken ground. The beggar rocked to and fro, making sounds of melancholy and desperation. No words were distinguishable; I think he had no roof to his mouth.

"What is he saying?" Mr. Smith asked.

The Minister ignored the question. "Later," he said, "we will have a proper art-centre here where the artists can live and relax and get their inspiration from nature. Haitian art is famous. Our pictures are collected by many Americans, and there are examples in the Museum of Modern Art in New York."

Mr. Smith said, "I don't care what you say. I'm going to pay that man." He shook off the protecting hand of the Secretary for Social Welfare and ran back towards the cripple. He pulled out a bunch of dollar-bills and held them out. The cripple looked at him with incredulity and fear. Our driver made a motion to interfere, but I blocked his way. Mr. Smith bent down and pressed the money into the cripple's hand. The cripple with an enormous effort began to rock back towards the cockpit. Perhaps he had a hole there in which he could hide the money . . . There was an expression of rage and disgust on the driver's face as though he had been robbed. I think he contemplated drawing his gun (his fingers went to his belt) and putting an end to at least one artist, but Mr. Smith was coming back along his line of fire. "He's made a sale all right," Mr. Smith said with a satisfied smile.

The justice of the peace had risen to watch the transaction outside his box beyond the playground—standing he was an enormous man. He put his hand over his eyes to see better in the hard sunlight. We took our places in the car, and there was a momentary silence. Then the Secretary said, "Where would you like to go now?"

"Home," said Mr. Smith laconically.

"I could show you the site we have chosen for the college."

"I've seen enough," Mr. Smith said. "I'd rather go home if you don't mind."

I looked back. The justice of the peace was running fast on long loping legs across the cement playground, and the cripple was rocking back with desperation towards the cockpit; he reminded me of a sand-crab scuttling to its hole. He had only another twenty yards to go, but he hadn't a chance. When I looked round a minute later Duvalierville was hidden by the dust-cloud of our car. I said nothing to Mr. Smith, for he was smiling happily at a good action accomplished; I think he was already rehearsing the story he would tell to Mrs. Smith, a story which would enable her to share his sense of happiness.

After we had gone a few miles the Minister said, "Of course the tourist-site is partly the responsibility of the Secretary for Public Works, and the Secretary for Tourism would also have to be consulted, but he is a personal friend of mine. If you cared to make the necessary arrangements with me, I would see that the others were satisfied."

"Satisfied?" Mr. Smith asked. He was not wholly guileless; though he had been unshaken by the beggars in the Post-Office, I believe the city of Duvalierville had opened his eyes.

"I mean," the Minister said—he produced a box of cigars from the back of the car, "you will not want to be involved in endless discussions. I will represent your views to my colleagues. Take a couple of cigars, Professor."

"No, thank you. I don't smoke." The driver did. He saw what was going on in his mirror, and leaning back he abstracted two cigars. One he lit and one he put in his shirt-pocket.

"My views?" Mr. Smith said. "If you want them, you shall have them. I don't see your Duvalierville being exactly a centre of progress. It's too remote."

"You would prefer a site in the capital?"

"I'm beginning to reconsider the whole project," Mr. Smith said in a voice so final that even the Minister relapsed into uneasy silence.

4

And yet Mr. Smith lingered on. Perhaps when he went over the events of the day with Mrs. Smith, the aid he had given the cripple re-established his sense of hope, hope that he could do something for the human race. Perhaps she strengthened his faith and fought his doubts (she was more a fighter than he). Already by the time we arrived at the Hotel Trianon, after more than an hour of gloomy silence, he had begun to revise his severest criticisms. The thought that he might possibly have been unfair haunted him. He had said goodbye with distant courtesy to the Secretary for Social Welfare and thanked him "for a very interesting excursion," but suddenly on the steps of the verandah he halted and turned to me. He said, "That word 'satisfy'—I guess I took him up too hard. It made me sore, but then English isn't his native tongue. Maybe he didn't intend . . ."

"He intended it all right, but he hadn't meant to say it so openly to you."

"I wasn't very favourably impressed by that project, I'll allow, but you know even Brasilia . . . and they have all the technicians they need . . . it's something to want a thing even if you fail."

"I don't think they are quite ripe for vegetarianism."

"I was thinking the same, but perhaps . . ."

"Perhaps you must have enough cash to be carnivorous first."

He gave me a quick look of reproach and said, "I'll talk it all over with Mrs. Smith." Then he left me alone—at least I thought I was alone until I entered my office and found the British chargé there. Joseph had furnished him, I saw, with his special rum-punch. "A lovely colour," the chargé said, holding it up to the light when I entered.

"It's the grenadine."

"I'm going on leave," he said, "next week. And so I'm saying my adieux."

"You won't be sorry to be out of here."

"Oh, it's interesting," he said, "interesting. There are worse places."

"The Congo perhaps? But people die quicker there."

"At least I'm glad," the chargé said, "that I'm not leaving a fellow-countryman in gaol. Mr. Smith's intervention proved successful."

"I wonder if it was Mr. Smith. I got the impression Jones would have got out anyway, on his own steam."

"I wish I knew what makes the steam. I won't pretend to you I haven't had enquiries . . ."

"Like Mr. Smith he carried a letter of introduction, but like Mr. Smith I suspect it was to the wrong man. That was why they arrested him, I imagine, when they took it off him at the airport. I have a suspicion his letter was to one of the army-officers."

"He came to see me the night before last," the chargé said. "I wasn't expecting him. He was very late. I was just going to bed."

"I haven't seen him since the night he was released. I think his friend Captain Concasseur doesn't regard me as sufficiently reliable. I was there, you see, when Concasseur broke up Philipot's funeral."

"Jones gave me the impression he was engaged on some sort of project for the Government."

"Where's he staying?"

"They've put him up at the Villa Créole. You know the Government took the place over? They lodged the Polish mission there after the Americans left. The only guests they've had up till now. And the Poles departed very quickly. Jones has a car and a driver. Of course the driver may be his gaoler too. He's a Tonton Macoute. You haven't any idea what the project could be?"

"Not a clue. He ought to be careful. To sup with the Baron you need a very long spoon."

"That's more or less what I told him. But I think he knows well enough—he's not a stupid man. Were you aware that he had been in Leopoldville?"

"I think he did say once . . ."

"It came out quite accidentally. He was there at the time of Lumumba. I checked up with London. Apparently he was helped out of Leopoldville by our consul. That doesn't mean much—a lot of people have been helped out of the Congo. The consul gave him his ticket to London, but he got off in Brussels. That's nothing against him either, of course . . . I think what he really wanted with me was to check up whether the British embassy had the right of asylum. In case of difficulties. I had to tell him no. No legal right."

"Is he in trouble already?"

"No. But he's sort of surveying his ground. Like Robinson Crusoe climbing the highest tree. But I didn't much fancy his Man Friday."

"Who do you mean?"

"His driver. A man as fat as Gracia with a lot of gold teeth. I think he must collect gold teeth. He probably has good opportunities. I wish your friend Magiot would take that big gold molar out and put it in his safe. A gold tooth always attracts greed." He drank the last of his rum.

This was a noonday for visitors. I had got into my bathing-trunks and dived into the pool only a little before the next comer arrived. I found I had to conquer some repugnance at bathing there, and the repugnance returned when I saw young Philipot looking down at me from the margin of the pool, standing just above the spot at the deep end where his uncle had bled to death. I had been swimming underwater, and I had not heard his approach. I was startled when his voice came through the skin of water. "Monsieur Brown."

"Why, Philipot, I didn't know you were here."

"I did what you advised, Monsieur Brown. I went and saw Jones."

I had quite forgotten our conversation. "Why?"

"Surely you remember—the Bren?"

Perhaps I had not taken him seriously enough. I had thought of the Bren as a new poetic symbol of his, like the pylons in the poems of my youth: after all those poets never joined the Electricity Board.

"He's staying up at the Villa Créole with Captain Concasseur. I waited last night until I saw Concasseur go out, but there was still Jones's driver sitting at the foot of the stairs. The one with the gold teeth. The man who ruined Joseph."

"He did that? How do you know?"

"Some of us keep a record. We have a lot of names on it

now. My uncle, I am ashamed to say, was on the same list. Because of the pump in the Rue Desaix."

"I don't think it was altogether his fault."

"Nor do I. Now I have persuaded them his name belongs to the other list. The list of victims."

"I hope you keep your files in a very safe place."

"At least they have copies of them across the border."

"How did you get to see Jones?"

"I climbed into the kitchen through a window and then I went up the service-stairs. I knocked on his door. I pretended to have a message from Concasseur. He was in bed."

"He must have been a bit startled."

"Monsieur Brown, do you know what those two are up to?"

"No. Do you?"

"I am not sure. I think so, but I am not sure."

"What did you say to him?"

"I asked him to help us. I told him the raiders across the border could do nothing to shift the Doctor. They kill a few Tontons Macoute and then they get killed themselves. They have no training. They have no Brens. I told him how seven men once captured the army-barracks because they had tommy-guns. 'Why are you telling this to me?' he asked. 'You are not an *agent provocateur*, are you?' I said no; I said if we hadn't been prudent so long, Papa Doc wouldn't be there in the palace. Then Jones said, 'I've seen the President.'"

"Jones has seen Papa Doc?" I asked incredulously.

"He told me so, and I believe him. He's up to something, he and Captain Concasseur. He told me Papa Doc was as interested in weapons and training as I was. 'The army's gone,' Jones said, 'not that it was any good to anyone, and what the Tontons Macoute have left of the American arms is all rusting away for want of proper care. So you see it's no good coming to me—unless you have a better proposition than the President's named already.'"

"But he didn't say what proposition?"

"I tried to see the papers on his desk—they looked like the plans of a building, but he said to me 'Leave those alone. They mean a lot to me.' Then he offered me a drink to show he had nothing personally against me. He said to me, 'One has to earn a living the best way one can. What do you do?' I said, 'I used to write verses. Now I want a Bren gun. And training. Training too.' He asked me, 'Are there many of you,' and I told him that numbers were not so important. If the seven men had had seven Brens . . .'"

I said, "The Brens are not magical, Philipot. Sometimes they stick. Just as a silver bullet can miss. You are going back to Voodoo, Philipot."

"And why not? Perhaps the gods from Dahomey are what we need now."

"You are a Catholic. You believe in reason."

"The Voodooists are Catholic too, and we don't live in a world of reason. Perhaps only Ogoun Ferraille can teach us to fight."

"Was that all Jones said to you?"

"No. He said, 'Come on. Have a Scotch, old man,' but I wouldn't take the drink. I went down the front stairs, so that the driver could see me. I wanted him to see me."

"Not very safe for you if they question Jones."

"Without a Bren, the only weapon I have is distrust. I thought that if they began to distrust Jones something might happen . . ." There were tears in his voice; a poet's tears for a lost world or a child's tears for the Bren that no one would give him? I swam away to the shallow end that I mightn't see him weep. My lost world was the naked girl in the pool, and what was his? I remembered the evening when he read his derivative verses to me and to Petit Pierre and to the young beat-novelist who wanted to be the Kerouac of Haiti; there was an ageing painter too who drove a *camion* during the day and worked at night with his callused fingers at the American art-centre, where they gave him paints and canvases. Propped against the verandah was his latest picture—cows in a field, but not the kind of cows they sold south of Piccadilly, and a pig with his head stuck through a hoop, among green banana leaves darkened by the perpetual storm coming down the mountain. It had something which my art-student failed to find.

I rejoined him by the end of the pool when I had given him time enough to check the tears. "Do you remember," I asked him, "that young man who wrote a novel called *La Route du Sud?*"

"He is in San Francisco where he always wanted to be. He escaped after the massacre in Jacmel."

"I was thinking of the evening when you read to us . . ."

"I don't regret those days. They were not real. The tourists and the dancing and the man dressed up as Baron Samedi. Baron Samedi is not an entertainment for visitors."

"They brought money to the island."

"Who saw the money? At least Papa Doc has taught us to live without money."

"Come to dinner on Saturday, Philipot, and meet the only tourists here."

"No, I have something to do that night."

"Be careful at any rate. I wish you'd start writing poems again."

He flashed white teeth at me in a malicious smile. "The poem about Haiti has already been written once and for all. You know it, Monsieur Brown," and he began to recite to me,

> "*Quelle est cette île triste et noire?—C'est Cythère,*
> *Nous dit-on, un pays fameux dans les chansons,*
> *Eldorado banal de tous les vieux garçons.*
> *Regardez, après tout, c'est une pauvre terre.*"

A door opened overhead and one of *les vieux garçons* stepped out on to the balcony of the John Barrymore suite. Mr. Smith picked his bathing-pants off the rail and looked down into the garden. "Mr. Brown," he called.

"Yes?"

"I've been talking to Mrs. Smith. She thinks perhaps I was a bit hasty in my judgment. She thinks we ought to give the Minister the benefit of the doubt."

"Yes?"

"So we shall stay on a while and try again."

5

I had asked Doctor Magiot to dine that Saturday in order to meet the Smiths. I wanted the Smiths to know that all Haitians were not either politicians or torturers. Besides I had not seen the doctor since the night when we disposed of the body and I did not wish him to feel I had kept away from cowardice. He arrived just after the electricity had been cut, and Joseph was on the point of lighting the oil-lamps. He turned the wick of one too high and the flames shooting up the chimney made the shadow of Doctor Magiot unroll down the verandah like a black carpet. He and the Smiths greeted each other with old-fashioned courtesy, and it seemed for a moment that we were back in the nineteenth century, when oil-lamps shone softer than electric-globes, and our passions—or so one believed—were gentler too.

"I am an admirer," Doctor Magiot said, "of Mr. Truman for some of his internal policies, but you will forgive me if I cannot pretend to be his supporter over the Korean war. I am honoured in any case to meet his opponent."

"Not a very important opponent," Mr. Smith said. "The Korean War was not an issue in the 1948 campaign—though it goes without saying I'm against all wars, whatever excuses politicians may find for them. It was for the sake of vegetarianism I ran against him."

"I had not realized," Doctor Magiot said, "that vegetarianism was an issue in the election."

"I'm afraid it wasn't, except in one state."

"We pulled ten thousand votes," Mrs. Smith said. "My husband's name was printed on the ballot."

She opened her bag and after a little search among the Kleenex pulled out a ballot-paper. Like most Europeans I knew little of the American electoral system: I had a vague idea that there were two or three candidates, at the most, and that all voters everywhere voted for their Presidential choice. I hadn't realized that on the ballots of most states the name of the Presidential candidate was not even shown, only the names of the Presidential electors for whom the votes were actually cast. In the State of Wisconsin, however, the name of Mr. Smith was clearly printed under a big black square containing an emblem, which, I think, must have represented a cabbage. I was surprised at the number of parties: even the socialists were split in two, and there were Liberal and Conservative candidates for minor offices. I could see from Doctor Magiot's expression that he was as lost as myself. If an English election is less complex than an American, a Haitian is simpler than either. In Haiti, if one put any value on one's skin, one stayed at home, even during the relatively peaceful days of Doctor Duvalier's predecessor.

We handed the ballot-paper from one to the other under the eyes of Mrs. Smith, who watched it as closely as a hundred-dollar note.

"Vegetarianism is an interesting idea," Doctor Magiot said. "I am not sure it is suited to all mammals. I doubt for example whether a lion would flourish on green things."

"Mrs. Smith once had a vegetarian bull-dog," Mr. Smith said with pride. "Of course it took some training."

"It took authority," Mrs. Smith said and her eyes challenged Doctor Magiot to deny it.

I told him of the vegetarian centre and of our journey to Duvalierville.

"I had a patient from Duvalierville once," Doctor Magiot said. "He had been working on the site—I think it was on the cockpit, and he was sacked because one of the Tontons Macoute there wanted the job for a member of his family. My patient made a very foolish mistake. He appealed to the Tontons on the grounds of his poverty, and the Tonton shot him once through the stomach and once through the thigh. I saved his life, but he is a paralysed beggar by the Post-Office now. I wouldn't settle in Duvalierville if I were you. It is not the right *ambiance* for vegetarianism."

"Is there no law in this country?" Mrs. Smith demanded.

"The Tontons Macoute are the only law. The words, you know, mean bogey-men."

"Is there no religion?" Mr. Smith asked in his turn.

"Oh yes, we are a very religious people. The State religion is the Catholic Church—the Archbishop's in exile, the Papal Nuncio is in Rome and the President is excommunicated. The popular religion is Voodoo, which has been taxed almost out of existence. The President was a strong Voodooist once, but since he has been excommunicated he can take no part—you have to be a Catholic communicant to take part in Voodoo."

"But it's heathenism," Mrs. Smith said.

"Who am I to say? I believe no more in the Christian God than I do in the gods of Dahomey. The Voodooists believe in both."

"Then what do you believe in, Doctor?"

"I believe in certain economic laws."

"Religion is the opium of the people?" I quoted flippantly at him.

"I don't know where Marx wrote that," Doctor Magiot said with disapproval, "if he ever did, but since you were born a Catholic, as I was, you should be pleased to read in *Das Kapital* what Marx has to say of the Reformation. He approved of the monasteries in that state of society. Religion can be an excellent means of therapy for many states of mind—melancholy, despair, cowardice. Opium, remember, is used in medicine. I'm not against opium. Certainly I am not against Voodoo. How lonely my people would be with Papa Doc as the only power in the land."

"But it's paganism," Mrs. Smith persisted.

"The right therapy for Haitians. The American Marines tried

188

to destroy Voodoo. The Jesuits tried. But the celebrations go on yet when a man can be found rich enough to pay the priest and the tax. I wouldn't advise you to go."

"She's not easily frightened," Mr. Smith replied. "You should have seen her in Nashville."

"I don't question her courage, but there are features that for a vegetarian . . ."

Mrs. Smith asked sternly, "Are you a Communist, Doctor Magiot?"

It was a question I had wanted to ask many times and I wondered how he would answer.

"I believe, madame, in the future of communism."

"I asked if you were a Communist."

"My dear," Mr. Smith said, "we have no right . . ." He tried to distract her. "Let me give you a little more Yeastrol."

"To be a Communist here, madame, is illegal. But since American aid stopped we have been allowed to study communism. Communist *propaganda* is forbidden, but the works of Marx and Lenin are not—a fine distinction. So I may say I believe in the future of communism; that is a philosophical outlook."

I had drunk too much. I said, "As young Philipot believes in the future of the Bren gun."

Doctor Magiot said, "You cannot stop martyrs. You can only try to reduce their number. If I had known a Christian in the days of Nero I would have tried to save him from the lions. I would have said, 'Go on living with your belief, don't die with it.'"

"Surely very timid advice, doctor," Mrs. Smith said.

"I cannot agree, Mrs. Smith. In the western hemisphere, in Haiti and elsewhere, we live under the shadow of your great and prosperous country. Much courage and patience is needed to keep one's head. I admire the Cubans, but I wish I could believe in their heads—and in their final victory."

Chapter Two

I had not told them at dinner that a rich man had been found
and a Voodoo ceremony was to take place that night somewhere on the mountains above Kenscoff. It was Joseph's secret
and he had only confided in me because he needed a lift in my
car. If I had refused I am sure he would have tried to drag his
damaged limb the whole way. The hour was past midnight: we
drove some twelve kilometres and when we left the car on the
road behind Kenscoff we could hear the drums beating very
gently like a labouring pulse. It was as though the hot night lay
there out of breath. Ahead was a thatched hut open to the
winds, a flicker of candles, a splash of white.

This was the first and the last ceremony I was to see. During
the two years of prosperity, I had watched, as a matter of duty,
the Voodoo dances performed for tourists. To me who had
been born a Catholic they seemed as distasteful as the ceremony of the Eucharist would have seemed performed as a ballet on Broadway. I only went now because I owed it to Joseph,
and it is not the Voodoo ceremony I remember with most
vividness but the face of Philipot, on the opposite side of the
tonelle, paler and younger than the Negro faces around him;
with his eyes closed, he listened to the drums which were
beaten softly, clandestinely, insistently, by a choir of girls in
white. Between us stood the pole of the temple, stuck up, like
an aerial, to catch the passage of the gods. A whip hung there
in memory of yesterday's slavery, and, a new legal requirement,

a cabinet-photograph of Papa Doc, a reminder of today's. I remembered how young Philipot has said to me in reply to my accusation, "The gods of Dahomey may be what we need." Governments had failed him, I had failed him, Jones had failed him—he had no Bren gun; he was here, listening to the drums, waiting, for strength, for courage, for a decision. On the earth-floor, around a small brazier, a design had been drawn in ashes, the summons to a god. Was it a summons to Legba, the gay seducer of women, to sweet Erzulie, the virgin of purity and love, to Ogoun Ferraille, the patron of warriors, or to Baron Samedi in his black clothes and his black Tonton glasses, hungry for the dead? The priest knew, and perhaps the man who paid for the ceremony, and I suppose the initiates could read the hieroglyphics of ash.

The ceremony went on for hours before the climax; it was the face of Philipot that kept me awake through the chanting and the drum-beats. Among the prayers were little oases of familiarity, "*Libera nos a malo,*" "*Agnus dei,*" holy banners swayed past inscribed to the saints, "*Panem nostrum quotidianum da nobis hodie.*" Once I looked at the dial of my watch and saw in pale phosphorescence the hands approaching three.

The priest came in from his inner room swinging a censer, but the censer which he swung in our faces was a trussed cock —the small stupid eyes peered into my eyes and the banner of Saint Lucy swayed after it. When he had completed the circle of the *tonelle* the *houngan* put the head of the cock in his mouth and crunched it cleanly off; the wings continued to flap while the head lay on the dirt-floor like part of a broken toy. Then he bent down and squeezed the neck like a tube of toothpaste and added the rusty colour of blood to the ash-grey patterns on the floor. When I looked to see how the delicate Philipot was accepting the religion of his people, I saw he was no longer there. I would have gone too, but I was tied to Joseph and Joseph was tied to the ceremony in the hut.

The drummers became more reckless as the night advanced.

They no longer tried to muffle the beats. Something was happening in the inner room, where the banners were stacked around an altar, and where a cross stood below a poker-work prayer, and presently a procession emerged. They were carrying what I thought at first was a corpse wrapped in a white sheet for burial—the head was covered and a black arm dangled free. The priest knelt beside the fire and blew the embers up into flames. They laid the corpse beside him, and he took the free arm and held it in the flames. As the body flinched I realized it was alive. Perhaps the neophyte screamed—I couldn't hear because of the drums and the chanting women, but I could smell the burning of the skin. The body was carried out and another took its place, and then another. The heat of the flames beat on my face as the night-wind blew through the hut. The last body was surely a child's—it was less than three feet long, and on this occasion the *houngan* held the hand a few inches above the flame—he was not a cruel man. When I looked again across the *tonelle* Philipot was back in his place, and I remembered that one arm which had been held in the flames appeared as light as a mulatto's. I told myself it could not possibly have been Philipot's. Philipot's poems had been published in an elegant limited edition, bound in vellum. He had been educated like myself by the Jesuits; he had attended the Sorbonne; I remembered how he had quoted the lines of Baudelaire to me at the swimming-pool. If Philipot was one of the initiates what a triumph that would represent for Papa Doc as he dragged his country down. The flames lit the photograph nailed on the pillar, the heavy spectacles, the eyes staring at the ground as though at a body ready for dissection. Once he had been a country doctor struggling successfully against typhoid; he had been a founder of the Ethnological Society. With my Jesuit training I could quote Latin as well as the *houngan* who was now praying for the gods of Dahomey to arrive. "*Corruptio optimi . . .*"

It wasn't sweet Erzulie who came to us that night, although

for a moment her spirit seemed to enter the hut and touch a woman who sat near Philipot, for she rose and put her hands over her face and swayed gently this way, gently that. The priest went to her and tore away her hands. She had an expression of great sweetness in the candlelight, but the *houngan* would have none of her. Erzulie was not wanted. We had not assembled tonight to meet the goddess of love. He put his hands on her shoulders and thrust her back on her bench. He had scarcely time to turn before Joseph was in the ring.

Joseph moved in a circle, the pupils of his eyes turned up so high that I saw only the whites, his hand held out as though he were begging. He lurched upon his wounded hip and seemed on the point of falling. The people around me leant forward with grave attention as though they they were watching for some sign to prove that the god was really there. The drums were silent: the singing stopped: only the *houngan* spoke in some language older than Creole, perhaps older than Latin, and Joseph paused and listened, staring up the wooden pillar, past the whip and Papa Doc's face into the thatch where a rat moved, crackling the straw.

Then the *houngan* went to Joseph. He carried a red scarf, and he flung it across Joseph's shoulders. Ogoun Ferraille had been recognized. Someone came forward with a machete and clamped it in Joseph's wooden hand as though he were a statue waiting completion.

The statue began to move. It slowly raised an arm, then swung the machete in a wide arc so that everyone ducked for fear it would fly across the *tonelle*. Joseph began to run, the machete flashing and cutting; those in the front row scrambled back, so that for a moment there was panic. Joseph was no longer Joseph. His face ran with sweat, his eyes looked blind or drunk as he stabbed and swung, and where was his injury now? He ran without a stumble. Once he paused and seized a bottle which had been abandoned on the dirt-floor when the people fled. He drank a long draught and then ran on.

193

I saw Philipot isolated on his bench: all those around him had fallen back. He leant forward watching Joseph, and Joseph ran across the floor towards him, swinging the machete. He took Philipot's hair in his hand, and I thought he was going to strike him down with the machete. Then he forced Philipot's head back and poured the spirit down his throat. Philipot's mouth belched liquid like a drain-pipe. The bottle fell between them, Joseph revolved twice on the floor and fell. The drums beat, the girls chanted, Ogoun Ferraille had come and gone.

Philipot was one of the three men who helped carry Joseph into the room behind the *tonelle*, but as for me I'd had enough. I went out into the hot night and drew a long breath of air, which smelt of wood-fire and rain. I told myself that I hadn't left the Jesuits to be the victim of an African god. The holy banners moved in the *tonelle*, the interminable repetitions went on, I returned to my car, where I sat waiting for Joseph to come back. If he could move so agilely in the hut, he could find his way without my help. After a while the rain came. I closed the windows and sat in stifling heat, while the rain fell like an extinguisher over the *tonelle*. The noise of the rain silenced the drums, and I felt as lonely as a man in a strange hotel after a friend's funeral. I kept a flask of whisky in the car against emergencies and I took a pull from it, and presently I saw the mourners going by, grey shapes in the black rain.

Nobody stopped at the car: they divided and flowed past on either side. Once I thought I heard an engine start—Philipot must have brought his car, but the rain hid it. I should never have gone to this funeral, I should never have come to this country, I was a stranger. My mother had taken a black lover, she had been involved, but somewhere years ago I had forgotten how to be involved in anything. Somehow somewhere I had lost completely the capacity to be concerned. Once I looked out and thought I saw Philipot beckoning to me through the glass. It was an illusion.

Presently when Joseph had not appeared I started the car and drove home alone. It was nearly four o'clock in the morning and too late to sleep, so that I was wide-awake at six when the Tontons Macoute drove up to the verandah steps and shouted to me to come down.

2

Captain Concasseur was the leader of the party and he held me at gun-point on the verandah while his men searched the kitchen and the servants' quarters. I could hear the bang of cupboards and doors and the screech of smashed glass. "What are you looking for?" I asked.

He lay on a wicker *chaise longue* with the gun in his lap pointing at me and at the hard upright chair on which I sat. The sun had not yet risen, but he wore his dark glasses all the same. I wondered whether he could see clearly enough to shoot, but I preferred to take no risks. He made no reply to my question. Why should he? The sky reddened over his shoulder and the palm-trees turned black and distinct. I was sitting on a straight dining-room chair and the mosquitoes bit my ankles.

"Or is it someone you're looking for? We have no refugees here. Your men are making enough noise to wake the dead. And I have guests," I added with reasonable pride.

Captain Concasseur changed the position of his gun as he changed the position of his legs—perhaps he suffered from rheumatism. The gun had been pointing at my stomach; now it pointed at my chest. He yawned, his head went back, and I thought he had fallen asleep, but I couldn't see his eyes through his dark glasses. I made a slight movement to rise and he spoke immediately, "*Asseyez-vous.*"

"I'm stiff. I want to stretch." The gun was now pointing at my head. I said, "What are you and Jones up to?" It was a rhetorical question, and I was surprised when he answered.

"What do you know about Colonel Jones?"

"Very little," I said. I noticed that Jones had risen in rank.

Then came an extra loud crash from the kitchen, and I wondered whether they were dismantling the range. Captain

Concasseur said, "Philipot was here." I kept silent, not knowing whether he meant the dead uncle or the live nephew. He said, "Before coming here he went to see Colonel Jones. What did he want with Colonel Jones?"

"I know nothing. Haven't you asked Jones? He's a friend of yours."

"We use white men when we have to. We don't trust them. Where is Joseph?"

"I don't know."

"Why isn't he here?"

"I don't know."

"You drove out with him last night."

"Yes."

"You returned alone."

"Yes."

"You had a rendezvous with the rebels."

"You're talking nonsense. Nonsense."

"I could shoot you very easily. It would be a pleasure for me. You would have been resisting arrest."

"I don't doubt it. You must have had plenty of practice."

I was frightened, but I was even more frightened of showing my fear—that would unleash him. Like a savage dog he was safer while he barked.

"Why would you have arrested me?" I asked. "The embassy would want to know that."

"At four o'clock this morning a police-station was attacked. One man was killed."

"A policeman?"

"Yes."

"Good."

He said, "Do not pretend that you have courage. You're very frightened. Look at your hand." (I had wiped it once or twice against my pyjama-trousers to get rid of the moisture.)

I gave a bad imitation of a laugh. "The night's hot. My conscience is quite clear. I was in bed by four o'clock. What happened to the other policemen? I suppose they ran away."

"Yes. We shall deal with them in due course. They left their arms behind, when they ran way. That was a bad mistake."

The Tontons Macoute came streaming out of the kitchen-quarters. It was odd to be surrounded by men in sun-glasses in the murk of the early dawn. Captain Concasseur made a sign to one of them and he hit me on the mouth cutting my lip. "Resisting arrest," Captain Concasseur said. "There has to be a struggle. Then, if we are polite, we will show your body to the chargé. What is his name? I forget names easily."

I could feel my nerve going. Courage even in the brave sleeps before breakfast and I was never brave. I found it needed an effort to stay upright in my chair, for I had a horrible desire to fling myself at Captain Concasseur's feet. I knew the move would be fatal. One didn't think twice about shooting trash.

"I will tell you what happened," Captain Concasseur said. "The policeman on duty was strangled. He was probably asleep. A man with a limp took his gun, a *métis* took his revolver, they kicked open the door where the others were sleeping . . ."

"And they let them get away?"

"They would have shot my men. Sometimes they spare the police."

"There must be a lot of men with limps in Port-au-Prince."

"Then where is Joseph? He should be sleeping here. Someone recognized Philipot, and he is not at his home. When did you last see him? Where?"

He signalled to the same man. This time the man kicked me hard on the shin, while another snatched the chair from under me, so that I found myself where I didn't wish to be, at Captain Concasseur's feet. His shoes were a horrible red-brown. I knew that I had to get upright again or I would be finished, but my leg hurt me and I wasn't sure I could stand. I was in an absurd position sitting there on the floor as though at an informal party. Everyone was waiting for me to do my turn. Perhaps when I stood up they would kick me down again. That might be their idea of a party-joke. I remembered Joseph's broken hip. It was safer to stay where I was. But I stood up. My right leg gave a shoot of pain. I leant back for support against the balustrade of the verandah. Captain Concasseur changed the position of his gun to cover me, but without any haste. He had an attitude of great comfort in the *chaise longue*. Indeed he looked as though he owned the place. Perhaps that was his intention.

I said, "What were you saying? Oh yes . . . I went last night with Joseph to a Voodoo ceremony. Philipot was there. But we didn't speak. I left before it was over."

"Why?"

"I was disgusted."

"You were disgusted by the religion of the Haitian people?"

"Every man to his taste."

The men in sun-glasses came a little nearer. The glasses were turned towards Captain Concasseur. If only I could have seen one pair of eyes and the expression . . . I was daunted by the anonymity. Captain Concasseur said, "You are so frightened of me that you have pissed in your *pantalon*." I realized that what he said was true. I could feel the wet and the warmth. I was dripping humiliatingly on the boards. He had got what he wanted, and I would have done better to have stayed on the floor at his feet.

"Hit him again," Captain Concasseur told the man.

"*Dégoutant*," a voice said. "*Tout à fait dégoutant.*"

I was as astonished as they were. The American accent with which the words were spoken had to me all the glow and vigour of Mrs. Julia Ward Howe's "Battle Hymn of the Republic." The grapes of wrath were trampled out in them and there was a flash of the terrible swift sword. They stopped my opponent with his fist raised to strike.

Mrs. Smith had appeared at the opposite end of the verandah behind Captain Concasseur, and he had to lose his attitude of lazy detachment in order to see who it was who spoke, so that the gun no longer covered me and I moved out of reach of the fist. Mrs. Smith was dressed in a kind of old colonial nightgown and her hair was done up in metal rollers which gave her an oddly cubist air. She stood there firmly in the dawn-light and let them have it in sharp fragmented phrases torn out of Hugo's Self-Taught. She told them of the *bruit horrible* which had roused her and her husband from their sleep; she accused them of *lâcheté* in striking an unarmed man; she demanded their warrant to be here at all—warrant and again warrant: but here Hugo's vocabulary failed her—"*Montrez-moi votre warrant*"; "*Votre warrant où est-il?*" The mysterious word menaced them more than the words they understood.

Captain Concasseur began to speak, "Madame," and she turned on him the focus of her fierce short-sighted eyes. "You," she said, "oh, yes, I've seen you before. You are the woman-striker." Hugo's had no word for that—only English could serve her indignation now. She advanced on him, all her hard-won vocabulary forgotten. "How dare you come here flourishing a revolver? Give it to me," and she held out her hand for it as though he were a child with a catapult. Captain Concasseur may not have understood her English, but he understood very well the gesture. As though he were guarding a precious object from an angry mother, he buttoned the gun back inside the holster. "Get out of that chair, you black scum. Stand up when you speak to me." She added, in defence of all her past, as though this echo of Nashville racism had burnt her tongue, "You are a disgrace to your colour."

"Who is this woman?" Captain Concasseur asked me weakly.

"The wife of the Presidential Candidate. You have met her before." I think for the first time he remembered the scene at Philipot's funeral. He had lost his grip: his men stared at him through their dark glasses waiting for orders which didn't come.

Mrs. Smith had recovered her grasp on Hugo's vocabulary. How she must have worked all that long morning when Mr. Smith and I visited Duvalierville. She said in her atrocious accent, "You have searched. You have not found. You can go." Except for the absence of certain nouns the sentences would have been suitable ones for the second lesson. Captain Concasseur hesitated. Too ambitiously she attempted both the subjunctive and the future tense and got them wrong, but he recognized very well what she intended to say, "If you don't go, I will fetch my husband." He capitulated. He led his men out and soon they were going down the drive more noisily than they had come, laughing hollowly in an attempt to heal their wounded pride.

"Who was that?"

"One of Jones's new friends," I said.

"I shall speak to Mr. Jones about it at the first opportunity. You can't touch pitch without . . . Your mouth is bleeding. You had better come upstairs and I will wash it in Listerine. Mr. Smith and I never travel anywhere without a bottle of Listerine."

3

"Does it hurt?" Martha asked me.

"Not much," I said, "now." I could not remember a time when we had been so alone and so at peace. The long hours of the afternoon faded behind the mosquito-netting over the bedroom-window. When I look back on that afternoon it seems to me we had been granted the distant sight of a promised land—we had come to the edge of a desert—the milk and honey awaited us: our spies went by carrying their burden of grapes. To what false gods did we turn then? What else could we have done other than we did?

Never before had Martha come of her own will, unpressed, to the Trianon. We had never slept before in my bed. It was for half-an-hour only, but the sleep was deeper than any I have known since. I woke flinching from her mouth with my wounded gum. I said, "I received a letter of apology from Jones. He told Concasseur that he took it as a personal insult that a friend of his should be treated like that. He threatened to break off relations."

"What relations?"

"God knows. He asked me to have a drink with him tonight. At ten. I shan't go."

We could hardly see each other now in the dusk. Every time she spoke I thought it was to say that she could stay no longer. Luis was back in South America reporting to his Foreign Office, but there was always Angel. I knew that she had invited some friends of his for tea, but tea doesn't last very long. The Smiths were out—another meeting with the Secretary for Social Welfare. This time he had asked them to come alone, and Mrs. Smith had taken the Hugo's Self-Taught with her in case interpretations were required.

Now I thought I heard a door slam, and I said to Martha, "I think the Smiths are back."

"I don't care about the Smiths," she said. She put her hand on my chest and said, "Oh, I'm tired."

"A good tired or a bad tired?"

"A bad tired."

"What's wrong?" It was a stupid question in our position, but I wanted to hear the words I often spoke, on her own tongue.

"I'm tired of not being alone. I'm tired of people. I'm tired of Angel."

I said in amazement, "Angel?"

"Today I gave him a whole box of new puzzles. Enough to occupy him for a week. I wish I could have that week with you."

"A week?"

"I know. It's not long enough, is it? This isn't an adventure any more."

"It stopped being that when I was in New York."

"Yes."

Somewhere from far away in the town came the sound of shots. "Somebody's being killed," I said.

"Haven't you heard?" she asked.

Two more shots came.

"I mean about the executions?"

"No. Petit Pierre hasn't been up for days. Joseph has disappeared. I'm cut off from news."

"As a reprisal for the attack on the police-station, they've taken two men from the prison to shoot them in the cemetery."

"In the dark?"

"It's more impressive. They've rigged up arc-lights with a television-camera. All the school children have to attend. Orders from Papa Doc."

"Then you'd better wait for the audience to disperse," I said.

"Yes. That's all it means to us. We aren't concerned."

"No. We wouldn't make very good rebels, you and I."

"I don't imagine Joseph will either. With that damaged hip."

"Or Philipot without his Bren. I wonder if he's got Baudelaire in his breast-pocket to stop the bullets."

"Don't be too hard on me then," she said, "because I'm German and the Germans did nothing." She moved her hand as she spoke and my desire came back, so that I didn't bother to ask her what she meant. Not with Luis safely away in South America and Angel occupied with his puzzles and the Smiths out of sight and hearing. I could imagine the taste of milk on her breasts and the taste of honey between her thighs and I could imagine for a moment that I was entering the promised land, but the spasm of hope was soon over, and she spoke as though her thoughts had not for a moment left their furrow. She said, "Haven't the French a word for going into the streets?"

"My mother must have gone into the streets, I suppose, unless it was her lover who gave her the resistance medal."

"My father went into the streets too in 1930, but he became a war-criminal. Action is dangerous, isn't it?"

"Yes, we've learnt from their example."

It was time to dress and go downstairs. Every stair down was a stair nearer Port-au-Prince. The Smiths' door stood open and Mrs. Smith looked up as we went by. Mr. Smith sat with his hat in his hands, and she had laid her hand on the back of his neck. After all, they were lovers too.

"Well," I said as we walked to the car, "they've seen us. Afraid?"

"No. Relieved," Martha said.

I went back into the hotel and Mrs. Smith called to me from the first floor. I wondered whether, like one of the old inhabitants of Salem, I was to be denounced for adultery. Would Martha have to wear a scarlet letter? I have no idea why, but I had assumed them to be puritan because they were vegetarian. Yet it was not the passion of love which was caused by acidity, and they were both enemies of hate. I went reluctantly upstairs and found them in the same attitude. Mrs. Smith said with an odd note of defiance as though she had read my thoughts and resented them, "I would have liked to have said good evening to Mrs. Pineda."

I put it as blackly as I knew how, "She had to hurry home to her child," and Mrs. Smith did not so much as wince. She said, "She is a woman I would have liked to know better." Why had I assumed it was only for the coloured races that she felt charity? Was it my guilt which had deciphered disapproval on her face the other night? Or was she the kind of woman who, when she had once tended a man, forgave him everything? I had been shriven perhaps by the Listerine. She took her hand from her husband's neck to lay it on his hair.

I said, "It's not too late. She'll come back another day."

"We go home tomorrow," she said. "Mr. Smith despairs."

"Of a vegetarian centre?"

"Of everything here."

He looked up and there were tears in the old pale eyes. What an absurd fancy it had been for him to pose as a politician. He said, "You heard the shots?"

"Yes."

"We passed the children on the way from school." He said,

"I had never conceived . . . when we were freedom riders, Mrs. Smith and I . . ."

"One can't condemn a colour, dear," she said.

"I know. I know."

"What happened with the Minister?"

"The meeting was a short one. He wanted to attend the ceremony."

"Ceremony?"

"At the cemetery."

"Does he know you are leaving?"

"Oh yes, I had made my decision before—that ceremony. The Minister had been thinking the affair over and he had come to the conclusion that I was not after all a sucker. The alternative was that I was as crooked as himself. I had come here to get money, not to spend it, so he showed me a method—it only meant splitting three ways, instead of two, with someone in charge of public works. As I understood it I would have to pay for some materials but not for many materials, and they would really be bought out of our share of the pickings."

"And how were they going to get the pickings?"

"The government would guarantee wages. We would hire the labour at a much lower wage, and at the end of a month the labourers would be dismissed. Then we'd keep the project idle for two months and afterwards engage a fresh lot of workers. Of course the guaranteed wages during the idle months would go into our own pockets—apart from what we paid out for materials and the commission on these would keep the head of the Public Works Ministry—I think it was the Public Works Ministry—happy. He was very proud of the scheme. He pointed out that in the end there might even possibly be a vegetarian centre."

"The scheme sounds full of holes to me."

"I didn't let him go into the details. I think he would have patched up all the holes as they occurred—patched them up out of the pickings."

Mrs. Smith said with sorrowful tenderness, "Mr. Smith came here with such high hopes."

"You too, dear."

"One lives and learns," Mrs. Smith said. "It is not the end."

"Learning comes easier to the young. Forgive me, Mr. Brown, if I sound kind of dejected, but we didn't want you to misunderstand our leaving your hotel. You have made us very welcome. We have been very happy here under your roof."

"I've been glad to have you. Are you catching the *Medea*? She's due back tomorrow."

"No. We won't wait for her. I've written out our address for you at home. We are going to fly to Santo Domingo tomorrow and we'll stay there a few days at least—Mrs. Smith wants to see Columbus's tomb. I'm expecting some vegetarian literature to arrive here on the next boat. If you will be kind enough to redirect it . . ."

"I'm sorry about the centre. But, you know, Mr. Smith, it would never have done."

"I realize that now. Perhaps we seem rather comic figures to you, Mr. Brown."

"Not comic," I said with sincerity, "heroic."

"Oh, we're not made at all in *that* mould. I'll say good night to you, Mr. Brown, now, if you'll excuse me. I'm feeling kind of exhausted this evening."

"It was very hot and damp in the city," Mrs. Smith explained, and she touched his hair again as though she were touching some tissue of great value.

Chapter Three

1

Next day I saw the Smiths off at the airport. There was no sign of Petit Pierre, and yet surely the departure of a Presidential Candidate rated one paragraph in his column, even though he would have had to omit the final macabre scene which took place outside the Post-Office. Mr. Smith asked me to stop the car in the centre of the square, and I thought he intended to take a photograph. Instead he got out, carrying his wife's hand-bag, and the beggars approached from all directions—there was a low babble of half articulated phrases, and I saw a policeman run down the steps of the Post-Office. Mr. Smith opened the handbag and began to scatter notes—gourdes and dollars indiscriminately. "For God's sake," I said. One or two of the beggars gave high unnerving screams: I saw Hamit standing amazed at the door of his shop. The red light of evening turned the pools and mud the colour of laterite. The last money was scattered, and the police began to close in on their prey. Men with two legs kicked down men with one, men with two arms grasped those who were armless by their torsos and threw them to the ground. As I hustled Mr. Smith back into my car, I saw Jones. He sat in a car behind his Tonton driver and he looked bewildered, worried, for once in his life lost. Mr. Smith said, "Well, my dear, I guess they won't squander that any worse than I would have done."

I saw the Smiths on to their plane, dined alone, and then drove to the Villa Créole—I was curious to see Jones.

The chauffeur was slumped at the bottom of the stairs. He watched me with suspicion, but he let me pass. A voice from the landing above cried angrily, *"la volonté du diable,"* and a Negro, who flashed a gold ring under the light, went by me.

Jones greeted me as though I were an old school-friend whom he had not seen for years, and with a hint of patronage because our relative positions had changed since those days. "Come in, old man. I'm glad to see you. I expected you the other night. Forgive the confusion. Try that chair—you'll find it pretty snug." The chair was certainly warm: it still held the heat of the last angry occupant. Three packs of cards were scattered over the table: the air was blue with cigar-smoke, and an ash-tray had toppled over, leaving some butts on the floor.

"Who's your friend?" I asked.

"Someone in the Treasury Department. A bad loser."

"Gin-rummy?"

"He shouldn't have raised the stakes half way through, when he was well ahead. But you don't argue with someone in the Treasury, do you? In any case at the end the old ace of spades turned up and it was over in a flash. I'm two thousand to the good. But he paid me in gourdes not dollars. What's your poison?"

"Have you a whisky?"

"I have next to everything, old man. You wouldn't fancy a dry Martini?"

I would have preferred a whisky, but he seemed anxious to show off the riches of his store, so, "If it's very dry," I said.

"Ten to one, old man."

He unlocked the cupboard and drew out a leather travelling-case—a half-bottle of gin, a half-bottle of vermouth, four metal beakers, a shaker. It was an elegant expensive set, and he laid it reverently on the tumbled table as though he were an auctioneer showing a prized antique. I couldn't help commenting on it. "Asprey's?" I asked.

"As good as," he replied quickly and began to mix the cocktails.

"It must feel a little odd finding itself here," I said, "so far from W. 1."

"It's used to much stranger places," he said. "I had it with me in Burma during the war."

"It's come out remarkably unscathed."

"I had it furbished up again."

He turned away from me to find a lime, and I took a closer look at the case. Asprey's trade mark was visible inside the lid. He came back with the lime and saw me looking.

"I'm caught, old man. It *is* from Asprey's. I didn't want to seem pretentious, that's all. As a matter of fact there's quite a history around that case."

"Tell me."

"Try the drink first and see if it's to your taste."

"It's fine."

"I got that case as a result of a bet with some other chaps in the outfit. The brigadier had one like it, and I couldn't help envying him. I used to dream of a case like that on patrol—the shaker clinking with the ice. I had two young chaps out with me from London—never been much further than Bond Street before. Well-lined, both of them. They teased me about the brigadier's cocktail-set. Once when we got pretty near to the end of our water they challenged me to find a stream before night. If I did I could have a cocktail-case like that next time anyone went home. I don't know whether I've told you that I can smell water ..."

"Was that the time you lost the whole platoon?" I asked. He looked up at me over his glass and I'm sure he read my thoughts. "That was another occasion," he said and changed the subject abruptly.

"How are Smith and Mrs. Smith?"

"You saw what happened by the Post-Office."

"Yes."

"It was the last instalment of American aid. They left this evening on the plane. They sent their regards to you."

"I wish I'd seen more of them," Jones said. "There's something about him . . ." He added surprisingly, "He reminded me of my father. Not physically, I mean, but . . . well, a sort of goodness."

"Yes I know what you mean. I don't remember my father."

"To tell you the truth my memory's a bit dim too."

"Let's say the father we would have liked to have."

"That's it, old man, exactly. Don't let your Martini get warm. I always felt that Mr. Smith and I had a bit in common. Horses out of the same stable."

I listened with astonishment. What could a saint possibly have in common with a rogue? Jones gently closed the cocktail-case, and then, taking a cloth from the table, he began to stroke the leather, as tenderly as Mrs. Smith had smoothed her husband's hair, and I thought: innocence perhaps.

"I'm sorry," Jones said, "about that affair with Concasseur. I told him if he touched a friend of mine again I was finished with the lot of them."

"Be careful what you say. They're dangerous."

"I have no fear of them. They need me too much, old man. Did you know young Philipot came to see me?"

"Yes."

"Just imagine what I could have done for *him*. They realize that."

"Have you a Bren for sale?"

"I've got myself, old man. That's better than a Bren. All the rebels need is a man who knows the way around. Think of it—on a clear day, you can see Port-au-Prince from the Dominican border."

"The Dominicans will never march."

"They are not needed. Give me fifty Haitians with a month's training and Papa Doc would be on a plane to Kingston. I wasn't in Burma for nothing. I've thought a lot about it. I've studied the map. Those raids near Cap Haïtien were a folly the way they were done. I know exactly where I'd put in my feint and where I'd strike."

"Why didn't you go with Philipot?"

"I was tempted, oh I was tempted all right, but I've got a deal on here which only happens once in a man's life. It means a fortune if I can get away with it."

"Where to?"

"Where to?"

"Get away where to?"

He laughed happily. "Anywhere in the world, old man. Once before I nearly brought it off in Stanleyville, but I was dealing with a lot of savages and they got suspicious."

"And they aren't suspicious here?"

"They are educated. You can always get round the educated."

While he poured out two more Martinis I was wondering what form his swindle took. One thing at least was certain—he was living better than he had done in his prison-cell. He had even put on a little weight. I asked him directly, "What are you up to, Jones?"

"Laying the foundations of a fortune, old man. Why not come in with me? It's not a long-term project. Any moment now I'll have the bird by the tail, but I could do with a partner. That's what I wanted to talk to you about, but you never came. There's a quarter of a million dollars in it. Perhaps more if we keep our nerve."

"And the partner's job?"

"To complete the deal I have to do a spot of travelling, and I want a man I can rely on to watch things here while I'm away."

"You don't trust Concasseur?"

"I don't trust one of them. It's not a question of colour, but think of it, old man, a quarter of a million pure profit. I can't take any chances. I'd have to deduct a little of it for expenses—ten thousand dollars would probably cover that, and then we'd divide the rest. The hotel's not doing too well, is it? And think what you could do with your share. There are islands in the

Caribbean just waiting for development—a beach, an hotel, an air-strip. You'd end a millionaire, old man."

I suppose it was my Jesuit education which reminded me of that moment when, from a high mountain above the desert, the devil displayed all the kingdoms of the world. I wondered whether the devil really had them to offer or whether it was all a gigantic bluff. I looked around the room in the Villa Créole for evidence of the thrones and powers. There was a record-player which Jones must have bought at Hamit's—he would hardly have carried it all the way from America in the *Medea*, for it was a cheap enough machine. Beside it rather suitably lay a disc of Edith Piaf, "*Je ne regrette rien*," and there was little other sign of personal possessions, little sign that he had been enabled to draw much of his wealth in advance for the goods which he had to deliver—what goods?

"Well, old man?"

"You haven't given me a very clear idea of what you want me to do."

"I can't let you into it very well, can I, until I know you are with me?"

"How can I tell whether I'm with you if I know nothing?"

He looked at me across the scattered cards; the lucky ace of spades lay face upwards. "It comes down to a matter of trust, doesn't it?"

"It certainly does."

"If only we'd been in the same outfit during the war, old man. Under those conditions you learn to trust . . ."

I said, "What division were you with?" and he replied without the slightest hesitation "4 Corps." He even elaborated a little, "77 Brigade." He had the answers right. I checked them that night at the Trianon in a history which some client had left behind of the Burma campaign, but even then it occurred to my suspicious mind that it was possible he possessed the same book and had drawn his data from it. But I was unjust to him. He really had been in Imphal.

"What hope have you got for your hotel?"

"Very little."

"You couldn't find a purchaser if you tried. Any day now you'll be dispossessed. They'll say you are not making proper use of your property and take it over."

"It might happen."

"What is it, old man? Woman trouble?"

I suppose my eyes gave me away.

"You're too old for fidelity, old man. Think of what you can get for one hundred and fifty thousand dollars." (I noticed that the reward had increased.) "You can go further than the Caribbean. Do you know Bora-Bora? There's nothing there but an air-strip and a rest-house, but with a little capital . . . and the girls, you've never seen such girls, the mothers had them off the Americans twenty years ago, Mère Catherine can't show you better . . ."

"What will *you* do with your money?"

I would never have thought that Jones's flat brown eyes like copper coins had the capacity to dream, yet they moistened now with some kind of emotion. "Old man, I've one particular spot in mind not far from here: a coral-reef and white sand, real white sand that you could build castles with, and behind are green slopes as smooth as real turf and God-made natural hazards—a perfect spot for a golf-course. I'll build a club-house, bungalow-suites with showers, it will be more exclusive than any other golf-club in the Caribbean. Do you know what I mean to call it? . . . the Sahib House."

"You don't suggest I'm to be your partner there."

"One can't have partners in a dream, old man. Conflicts would arise. I've got the place planned as I want it to the last detail" (I wondered whether those were the blueprints Philipot had seen). "I've gone an awfully long way to get there, but it's in sight now—I can even see exactly where to put the nineteenth hole."

"You're keen on golf?"

"I don't play myself. I've somehow never had the time. It's

the idea that appeals to me. I'm going to get a first-class social hostess. Someone good looking with background. I did think at the beginning of having bunny-girls, but the more I thought about it, the more I realized they would be out of place in a golf-club of class."

"Were you planning all this in Stanleyville?"

"I've been planning it for twenty years, old man, and now the moment's nearly here. Have another Martini?"

"No, I must be going."

"I'm going to have a long bar made of coral called the Desert Island Bar. With a barman trained at the Ritz. I'm going to have chairs made out of driftwood—of course we'll make them comfortable with cushions. Parakeets on the curtains, and a big brass telescope in the window focused on the eighteenth hole."

"We'll talk about it again."

"I've never talked about it to anyone before—anyone who could understand what I have in mind, that is. I used to talk to my boy in Stanleyville when I was thinking out the details, but the poor little bugger hadn't got a clue."

"Thanks for the Martinis."

"I'm glad you liked the case." When I looked back he had taken off the cloth and was polishing it again. He called after me, "We'll have another talk soon. If only you'd agree in principle . . ."

2

I had no wish to return to the Trianon, which was empty now of guests, and I had received no word from Martha all day, so I was drawn back to the casino as the nearest equivalent of a home, but it was a casino much changed since the night when I had met Martha. There were no tourists, and few residents of Port-au-Prince cared to venture out after dark. Only one roulette-table was functioning and only one player was seated there —an Italian engineer whom I knew slightly called Luigi; he worked with the erratic electricity plant. No private company could have kept a casino running under these conditions, and the government had taken it over; now every night they made a loss, but it was a loss in gourdes and the government could always print more.

The croupier sat with a scowl on his face—perhaps he wondered where his pay would come from. Even with two zeros the chances in favor of the bank were too fine. With so few players one or two losses *en plein* and the bank would be down for the night.

"Winning?" I asked Luigi.

"I'm a hundred and fifty gourdes up," he said. "I haven't the heart to leave the poor devil," but on the next run he made another fifteen.

"Do you remember this place in the old days?"

"No. I wasn't here then."

They had tried to economize on the lighting, so we played in a cavernous obscurity. I played without interest, placing my tokens on the first column, and won also. The face of the croupier grew darker. "I've got a good mind," Luigi said, "to put all my winnings on red and give him a chance to recuperate."

"But you might win," I said.

"There's always the bar. They must make a good cut out of the drinks."

We bought whiskies—it seemed too cruel to order rum, though whisky was hardly wise for me on top of the dry Martinis. Already I began to feel . . .

"Why, if it isn't Mr. Jones," a voice called from the end of the *salle*, and I turned to see the purser of the *Medea* advancing on me with a damp and welcoming hand.

"You've got the name wrong," I said. "I'm Brown, not Jones."

"Breaking the bank?" he asked jovially.

"It doesn't need much breaking. I thought you never ventured into town as far as this."

"I don't follow my own advice," he said and winked. "I went first to Mère Catherine's, but the girl has got family trouble— she won't be there till tomorrow."

"Nobody else you fancied?"

"I always like to eat off the same plate. How are Mr. and Mrs. Smith?"

"They flew out today. Disappointed."

"Ah, he should have come with us. Any trouble with the exit-visa?"

"We got it through in three hours. I've never seen the immigration department and the police work faster. They must have wanted to be rid of him."

"Political trouble?"

"I think the Ministry for Social Welfare found his ideas upsetting."

We had a few more drinks and watched Luigi lose a few gourdes for conscience' sake.

"How's the captain?"

"He longs to be off. He cannot endure this place. His temper will not be right until we are at sea again."

"And the man with the tin hat? Did you leave him safely in Santo Domingo?"

I felt an odd nostalgia when I talked of my fellow-passengers, perhaps because it was the last time that I had experienced a sense of security—the last time too I had possessed any real hope; I had been returning to Martha and I had believed that everything might be changed.

"The tin hat?"

"Don't you remember? He recited at our concert."

"Oh yes, poor fellow. We left him safely behind all right—in the cemetery. He had a heart-attack before we landed."

We gave Baxter the tribute of two seconds' silence, while the ball bounced and chinked for Luigi alone. He won a few more gourdes and rose with a gesture of despair.

"And Fernandez?" I asked. "The black man who wept."

"He proved invaluable," the purser said. "He knew all the

ropes. He took charge of everything. You see, it turned out that he was an undertaker. The only thing which worried him was Mr. Baxter's faith. In the end he put him in the Protestant cemetery because he found in his pocket a calendar about the future. Old something . . ."

"Old Moore's Almanack?"

"That was it."

"I wonder what the entry was for Baxter."

"I looked to see. It was not very personal. A hurricane was going to cause great damage. There would be a severe sickness in the Royal family, and the price of steel-shares would rise several points."

"Let's go," I said. "An empty casino is worse than an empty tomb." Luigi was already cashing in his chips, and I did the same. The night outside was heavy with the usual storm.

"Have you got a taxi?" I asked the purser.

"No. He wanted to be paid off."

"They don't like to stay around at night. I'll drive you to the ship."

The lights across the playground flashed on and off and on. "*Je suis le drapeau Haïtien, Uni et Indivisible. François Duvalier.*" The "f" had fused, so it read, "*rançois Duvalier.*") We passed Columbus's statue and came to the port and the *Medea.* A light shone down along the gangplank upon a policeman standing at the foot. There was a light shining too onto the bridge from the captain's cabin. I looked up at the deck where I had sat watching the passengers reel by me on their morning rounds. In port (she was the only ship there) the *Medea* seemed oddly dwarfed. It was the empty sea which gave the little boat her pride and magnitude. Our footsteps ground upon coal-dust, and the taste of grit lodged between our teeth.

"Come on board for a last drink."

"No. If I did I might want to stay. What would you do then?"

"The captain would ask to see your exit-visa."

"That fellow would ask first," I said, looking at the police-man who stood at the foot of the gangplank.

"Oh, he is a good friend of mine."

The purser mimicked the action of a man drinking and pointed towards me. The policeman grinned back. "You see—he has no objection."

"All the same," I said, "I won't come up. I've mixed too many drinks tonight." But I lingered at the plank.

"And Mr. Jones," the purser asked. "What has become of Mr. Jones?"

"He's doing well."

"I liked him," the purser said. For a man of such ambiguity, whom we all trusted so little, Jones had a knack of winning friendship.

"He told me he was Libra—a birthday in October, so I looked him up."

"In Old Moore? What did you find?"

"An artistic temperament. Ambitious. Successful in literary enterprises. But as for the future—I could find only an impor-tant press conference by General de Gaulle and electrical storms in South Wales."

"He tells me he's about to make a fortune of a quarter of a million dollars."

"A literary enterprise?"

"Hardly that. He invited me to be his partner."

"So you will be rich too?"

"No. I refused. I used to have my dreams of making a for-tune. Perhaps I'll be able to tell you one day about the travel-ling art-gallery, it was the most successful dream I ever had, but I had to get out quick, and so I came here and found my hotel. Do you think I'd give up that security?"

"You think the hotel security?"

"It's the nearest I've ever come to it."

"When Mr. Jones is a rich man you will be sorry you did not give up that kind of security."

217

"Perhaps he'll lend me enough to carry on with my hotel until the tourists return."

"Yes. I think he is a generous man in his way. He gave me a very large tip, but it was in Congo currency and the bank wouldn't change it. We shall be here till tomorrow night at least. Bring Mr. Jones to see us."

The lightning began to play over the slopes of Pétionville: sometimes a blade quivered in the ground long enough to carve out of the dark the shape of a palm or the corner of a roof. The air was full of coming rain, and the low sound reminded me of voices chanting the responses at school. We said good night.

Part Three

Part Three

Chapter One

1

I found it hard to sleep. The lightning flashed on and off as regularly as Papa Doc's publicity in the park, and only when the rain ceased for a while did a little air filter through the mosquito-screens. I thought quite a lot about Jones's promised fortune. If I could really share it, would Martha leave her husband? But it was not money which held her, it was Angel. He would be happy enough, I could imagine myself persuading her, if I pensioned him off with a weekly issue of puzzles and bourbon biscuits. I fell asleep and dreamt I was a boy kneeling at the communion-rail in the college chapel in Monte Carlo. The priest came down the row and placed in each mouth a bourbon biscuit, but when he came to me he passed me by. The communicants on either side came and went away, but I knelt obstinately on. Again the priest distributed the biscuits and left me out. I stood up then and walked sullenly away down the aisle, which had become an immense aviary where parrots stood in ranks chained to their crosses. Someone called out sharply behind me, "Brown, Brown," but I was not certain whether that was my name or not, for I didn't turn. "Brown." This time I awoke and a voice came up to me from the verandah below my room.

I got out of bed and went to the window, but I could see nothing through the mosquito-screen. Footsteps shuffled below and a voice further off called urgently, "Brown," under another window. I could hardly hear it through the holy mutter of the rain. I found my torch and went downstairs. In my office I

221

picked up the only weapon handy, the brass coffin marked R.I.P. Then I unlocked the side-door and shone my torch to show that I was there. The light fell on the path leading to the bathing-pool. Presently round the corner of the house and into the circle of the light came Jones.

He was drenched with rain and his face was smeared with dirt. He carried a parcel under his coat to guard it from the rain. He said, "Turn out the light. Let me in quick." He followed me into the office and took the parcel from under his wet jacket. It was the travelling cocktail-case. He laid it gently on my desk like a pet animal and stroked it down. He said, "Everything has gone. Finished. *Capot* in three columns."

I put out a hand to turn on the light. "Don't do that," he said, "they might see the light from the road."

"They can't," I said and pressed the switch.

"Old man, I'd rather if you don't mind . . . I feel better in the dark." He turned out the light again. "What's that in your hand, old man?"

"A coffin."

He was breathing heavily—I could smell the gin. He said, "I've got to get out quick. Somehow."

"What happened?"

"They've begun investigating. At midnight I had a call from Concasseur—I didn't even know the bloody telephone worked. It gave me a shock ringing like that suddenly by my ear. It had never rung before."

"I suppose they fixed up the telephone when they put the Poles in. You're living in a government rest-house for V.I.P.s."

"Very important pooves we called them in Imphal," Jones said with the ghost of a laugh.

"I could give you a drink if you let me put on the light."

"There isn't time, old man. I've got to get out. Concasseur was speaking from Miami. They'd sent him to check up. He wasn't suspicious yet, only puzzled. But in the morning when they find I've skipped . . ."

"Skipped where?"

"Yes, that's the question, old man, that's the sixty-four-thousand-dollar question."

"The *Medea's* in port."

"The very place . . ."

"I'll have to put on some clothes." He followed me like a dog, leaving wet patches in his wake. I missed Mrs. Smith's help and advice, for she had a high opinion of Jones. While I dressed—he had to allow me a little light for that—he ambled nervously from wall to wall, well away from the window.

"I don't know what your game was," I said, "but surely with a quarter of a million dollars at stake you could be certain that one day they'd investigate."

"Oh, I'd thought that one out. I'd have gone over to Miami with the investigator."

"But they'd have kept you here."

"Not if I'd left a partner behind. I hadn't realized time was so short—I thought I had a week or more at least—or I'd have tried to persuade you earlier."

I stopped with one leg in my trousers and asked him with astonishment, "You're telling me just like that, that I was to be the fall-guy?"

"No, no, old man, you exaggerate. You can be dead sure I'd have tipped you off in time for you to get into the British Embassy. If it was ever necessary. But it wouldn't have been. The investigator would have cabled O.K. and taken his cut, and you would have joined us afterwards."

"How big a cut had you planned for *him*? I know it's only of academic interest now."

"I'd allowed for all that. What I offered you, old man, was net not gross. All yours."

"If I survived."

"One always survives, old man." As he dried his confidence returned. "I've had my setbacks before. I was just as near the *grand coup*—and the end—in Stanleyville."

"If your plan had anything to do with arms," I said, "you've made a bad mistake. They've been stung before . . ."

"How do you mean, stung?"

"There was a man here last year who arranged half a million dollars' worth of arms for them, fully paid up in Miami. But the American authorities were tipped off, the arms were seized. The dollars, of course, stayed in the agent's pocket. Nobody knew how many real arms there had ever been. They wouldn't be taken for the same ride twice. You should have done more homework before you came here."

"My scheme was not exactly that. In fact there were no arms at all. I don't look like a man with that much capital, do I?"

"Where did that introduction of yours come from?"

"From a typewriter. Like most introductions. But you are right about the homework. I put the wrong name on the letter. I talked myself out of that one though."

"I'm ready to go." I looked at him where he fidgeted in a corner with a light flex: the brown eyes, the not quite trim officer's moustache: the grey indifferent skin. "I don't know why I'm running this risk for you. A fall-guy again . . ."

I took the car out on the road with the lights off, and we cruised slowly down towards the city. Jones crouched low and whistled to keep his courage up. I think the tune dated from 1940—"The Wednesday after the War." Just before the road-block I switched the lights on. There was a chance the militia-man was asleep, but he wasn't.

"Did you pass here tonight?" I asked.

"No. I made a détour through a couple of gardens."

"Well, there's no avoiding him now."

But he was too sleepy to be troublesome: he limped across the road and raised the barrier. His big toe was bound up in a dirty bandage and his backside showed through a hole in his grey-flannel trousers. He didn't bother to search us for arms. We drove on down, past the turning to Martha's, past the British Embassy. I slowed down there: all seemed quiet enough —the Tontons Macoute would surely have put guards at the gate if they had known of Jones's escape. I said, "What about going in there? You'll be safe enough."

"I'd rather not, old man. I've been a bother to them before, and they won't exactly welcome me."

"You'd have a worse welcome from Papa Doc. This is your great chance."

"There are reasons, old man . . ." He paused, and I thought he was going at last to confide in me, but, "Oh God," he said, "I've forgotten my cocktail-case. I left it in your office. On the desk."

"Is it so important?"

"I love that case, old man. It's been with me everywhere. It's my luck."

"I'll bring it to you tomorrow if it's so important to you. You want to try the *Medea* then?"

"If there's a snag we can always come back here as a last resort." He tried out another tune—I think it was "A Nightingale Sang"—but stuck. "To think after all we've been through together that I'd leave it . . ."

"Is it the only bet you ever won?"

"Bet? What do you mean, bet?"

"You told me you won it in a bet."

"Did I?" He brooded awhile. "Old man, you're running a big risk for me, and I'll be straight with you. That wasn't exactly the truth. I pinched it."

"And Burma—was that not the truth either?"

"Oh, I was in Burma all right. I promise that."

"You pinched it from Asprey's?"

"Not with my hands, of course."

"With your wits again?"

"I was working at the time. Something in the city. I used one of the company's cheques, but I signed my own name. I wasn't going to be sent down for forgery. It was just a temporary loan. You know it was love at first sight when I saw that case and I remembered the brigadier's."

"It wasn't with you in Burma then?"

"I was romancing a bit there. But I did have it with me in the Congo."

I left the car by the Columbus statue—the police must have been accustomed to seeing my car there at night, though not alone—and I went ahead of Jones to reconnoitre. It was easier than I thought. For some reason the policeman was no longer by the gangplank, which had been kept down for latecomers from Mère Catherine's: perhaps he had a beat, perhaps he'd gone behind the wall to urinate. One of the crew was on guard at the top, but seeing our white faces he let us go by.

We went up to the top-deck and Jones's spirits rose—he had hardly uttered a sound since his confession. As he passed the saloon-door he said, "Remember the concert? That was a night, wasn't it? Remember Baxter and his whistle? 'Saint Paul's will stand, London will stand.' He was too good to be true, old man."

"He isn't true any more. He's dead."

"Poor bugger. That makes him sort of respectable, doesn't it?" he added with a kind of yearning.

We climbed the ladder to the captain's cabin. I did not relish the interview, for I remembered his attitude to Jones after he had received the wireless enquiry from Philadelphia. Everything had gone easily up till now, but I had small hope that our luck would last. I rapped on the door and with hardly an interval the captain's voice came hoarse and authoritative, bidding me enter.

At least I had not woken him from sleep. He was propped up in his berth wearing a white cotton nightshirt, and he had put on very thick reading-glasses which made his eyes look like broken chips of quartz. He held a book tilted below the reading-lamp, and I saw it was one of Simenon's novels, and this encouraged me a little—it seemed to be a sign that he had human interests.

"Mr. Brown," he exclaimed in surprise, like an old lady

disturbed in her hotel-room, and like an old lady his left hand went instinctively to the neckline of his nightshirt.

"And Major Jones," Jones added jauntily and moved out from behind me into view.

"Oh, Mr. Jones," the captain said in a tone of distinct displeasure.

"I hope you've room for a passenger?" Jones asked with his unconvincing hilarity. "Not short of schnapps, I hope?"

"Not for a passenger. But are you a passenger? At this hour of the night, I would imagine you lack a ticket . . ."

"I have the money to pay for one, captain."

"And an exit-visa?"

"A formality for a foreigner like myself."

"A formality which is complied with by all except the criminal classes. I think you're in trouble, Mr. Jones."

"Yes. You might say I'm a political refugee."

"Then why have you not gone to the British embassy?"

"I felt I'd be more at home in the dear old *Medea*"—the phrase had a good music-hall ring and perhaps that was why he repeated it. "Dear old *Medea*."

"You were never a welcome guest, Mr. Jones. I had too many enquiries about you."

Jones looked at me, but I could give him little help. "Captain," I said, "you know how they treat prisoners here. Surely you can stretch a rule . . ."

His white nightshirt, embroidered around the neck and cuffs, perhaps by that formidable wife of his, had a horribly judicial air; he looked down at us from the height of his bunk as from a bench.

"Mr. Brown," he said, "I have my career to consider. I must return here every month. Do you think that at my age the company would give me another command, on another route? After an indiscretion such as you propose?"

Jones said, "I'm sorry. I never thought of that," with a gentleness which surprised, I think, the captain as it surprised me, for when the captain spoke again it was almost as though he were offering an excuse.

"I do not know whether you have a family, Mr. Jones. But I certainly have."

"No, I have no one," Jones admitted. "No one at all. Unless you count a bit of tail here and there. You're right, captain, I'm expendable. I'll have to sort this out some other way." He brooded a little, while we watched him, then suddenly suggested, "I could stow away if you'd turn a blind eye."

"In that case I would have to hand you over to the police in Philadelphia. Does that suit you, Mr. Jones? I have an idea there are people in Philadelphia who want to ask you questions."

"It's nothing serious. I owe a little money, that's all."

"Of your own?"

"On second thoughts perhaps it wouldn't suit me all that well."

I admired Jones's calm: he might have been a judge himself, sitting in chambers with two experts in a tricky Chancery case.

"The choice of action seems to be strictly limited," he summed the problem up.

"Then I would suggest again the British embassy," the captain said in the chill voice of one who always knows the correct answer and expects no disagreement.

"You're probably right. I didn't get on with the consul in Leopoldville very well, that's the truth. And they all come out of the same stable—Career out of Diplomatic Bag. I'm afraid they'll have a report on me here too. It's a problem, isn't it? You really would be bound to hand me over to the coppers in Philadelphia?"

"I'd be bound to."

"It's just as short as it's long, isn't it?" He turned to me. "What about some other embassy where there'd be no report . . . ?"

"These things are governed by diplomatic rules," I said. "They couldn't claim a foreigner had the right of asylum.

They'd be stuck with you for keeps, as long as this government lasted."

Steps came rattling up the companionway. A hand knocked on the door. I saw Jones catch his breath. He wasn't nearly so calm as he tried to show.

"Come in."

The second officer entered. He looked at us without surprise as though he expected to find strangers. He spoke to the captain in Dutch, and the captain asked him a question. He replied with his eye on Jones. The captain turned to us. As though he had at last abandoned the hope of Maigret for the night he put his book down. He said, "There's a police-officer at the gangway with three men. They want to come on board."

Jones gave a deep unhappy sigh. Perhaps he was watching Sahib House and the eighteenth hole and the Desert Island Bar disappearing forever.

The captain gave an order in Dutch to the second officer, who left the cabin. He said, "I must get dressed." He balanced shyly on the edge of the bunk like a hausfrau, then heavily descended.

"You're letting them come on board!" Jones exclaimed. "Where's your pride? This is Dutch territory, isn't it?"

"Mr. Jones, if you will please go into the toilet and keep quiet, it will be easier for all of us."

I opened a door at the end of the bunk and pushed Jones through. He went reluctantly. "I'm trapped here," he said, "like a rat," then altered the phrase quickly to "a rabbit, I mean," and gave me a frightened smile. I set him firmly down like a child on the lavatory-seat.

The captain was pulling his trousers on and tucking in his nightshirt. He took a uniform jacket off a peg and put it on— the nightshirt was concealed by the collar.

"You're not going to let them search?" I protested. He had no time to reply or to put on his shoes and socks before the knock came on the door.

I knew the police-officer who entered. He was a real bastard, as bad as any of the Tontons Macoute; a man as big as Doctor Magiot and one who wielded a terrific punch; many broken jaws in Port-au-Prince testified to his strength. His mouth was full of gold teeth, probably not his own: he carried them as an Indian brave used to carry scalps. He looked at us both with insolence, while the second officer, a pimply youth, hovered nervously behind. He said to me, the words like an insult, "I know *you*."

The little thin captain looked very vulnerable in his bare feet, but he replied with spirit, "I don't know you."

"What are you doing on board at this hour?" the policeman said to me.

The captain said in French to the second officer so that his meaning was clear to everyone, "I thought I told you he was to leave his gun behind?"

"He refused, sir. He pushed me on one side."

"Refused? Pushed?" The captain drew himself up and almost reached the Negro's shoulder. "I invited you on board—but only on conditions. I am the only man allowed to carry arms on this ship. You are not in Haiti now."

That phrase spoken with conviction really disconcerted the officer. It was like a magic spell—he felt unsafe. He looked around at all of us, he looked around the cabin, "*Pas à Haiti?*" he exclaimed, and I suppose he saw only the unfamiliar, a framed certificate on the wall for saving life at sea, a photograph of a grim white woman with iron-grey waves in her hair, a stone-bottle of something called Bols, a photograph of the Amsterdam canals ice-bound in winter. He repeated distractedly, "*Pas à Haiti?*"

"*Vous êtes en Hollande,*" the captain said with a masterly laugh as he held out his hand. "Give me your revolver."

"I am under orders," the bully said miserably. "I am doing my duty."

"My officer will return it to you when you leave the ship."

"But I am looking for a criminal."

"Not in my ship."

"He came here in your ship."

"I am not responsible for that. Now give me your revolver."

"I must search."

"You can search all you like on shore but not here. Here I am responsible for law and order. Unless you give me your revolver I shall call the crew to disarm you and afterwards I will have you pitched into the harbour."

The man was beaten. His eye was drawn to the disapproving face of the captain's wife as he unbuttoned his holster and handed over his gun. The captain put it in her charge. "Now," he said, "I am prepared to answer any reasonable questions. What is it you want to know?"

"We want to know if you have a criminal on board. You know him—a man called Jones."

"Here is a passenger-list. If you can read."

"His name will not be on it."

"I have been captain on this line for ten years. I stick to the letter of the law. I will never carry a passenger who is not on that list. Nor a passenger without an exit-visa. Has he an exit-visa?"

"No."

"Then I can promise you, lieutenant, that he will never be a passenger in this ship."

The sound of his rank seemed to mollify the police-officer a little. "He may be hidden," he said, "without your knowledge."

"In the morning before sailing I will have the ship searched, and if he is found, I shall put him ashore."

The man hesitated. "If he is not here," he said, "he must have gone to the British embassy."

"It would be a more natural place," the captain said, "than the Royal Netherlands Steamship Company." He handed the revolver to the second officer. "You will give it him," he said, "at the foot of the gangway." He turned his back and left the officer's black hand floating in mid-air like a catfish in an aquarium.

We waited in silence until the second officer returned and

told the captain that the lieutenant had driven away with his men; then I let Jones out of the lavatory. He was effusively grateful. "You were superb, captain," he said.

The captain regarded him with dislike and contempt. He said, "I told him only the truth. If I had discovered you stowing away I would have put you on shore. I am glad I did not have to lie. I would have found it hard to forgive myself or you. Please leave my ship as soon as it is safe." He removed his jacket, he pulled his white nightshirt out of his trousers so that he could remove them with modesty, we went away.

Outside I leant over the rail and looked at the policeman, who had returned to the foot of the gangway. He was last night's policeman, and there was no sign of the lieutenant or his men. I said, "It's too late now for the British Embassy. It will be well guarded by this time."

"What do we do then?"

"God knows, but we've got to leave the boat. If we are still here in the morning the captain will be as good as his word."

The purser, who woke quite cheerfully from his sleep (he was lying flat on his back when we entered with a lubricious smile on his face), saved the situation. He said, "There is no difficulty about Mr. Brown leaving, the policeman knows him already. But there is only one solution for Mr. Jones. He must leave as a woman."

"But the clothes?" I asked.

"There is an acting box here for the ship's parties. We have the dress of a Spanish señorita and a peasant-costume from Vollendam."

Jones said piteously, "But my moustache."

"You must shave it off."

Neither the Spanish costume, which was designed for a flamenco-dancer, nor the elaborate headgear of the Dutch peasant was inconspicuous. We tried our best to make an unobtrusive mixture of the two, jettisoning the Vollendam headgear and the wooden sabots of the one and the mantilla of the other, as well as a great many underskirts in both cases. Meanwhile Jones gloomily and painfully shaved—there was no hot water. Oddly enough he looked more reliable without his moustache; it was as though before he had been wearing an incorrect uniform. Now I could almost believe in his military career. Odder still, when once the great sacrifice had been made, he entered with a kind of expert enthusiasm into the spirit of the charade.

"You have no rouge or lipstick?" he asked the purser, but the purser had none and Jones had to make do for cosmetics with a stick of Remington pre-shave powder. It gave him, above the black Vollendam skirt and the spangled Spanish blouse, a look of lurid pallor. "At the foot of the gangway," he told the purser, "you must kiss me. It will help to hide my face."

"Why not kiss Mr. Brown?" the purser asked.

"He's taking me home. It wouldn't be natural. You have to imagine that we've passed quite an evening together, all three of us."

"What kind of an evening?"

"An evening of riotous abandonment," Jones said.

"Can you manage your skirt?" I asked.

"Of course, old man." He added mysteriously, "This is not the first time. Under very different circumstances, of course."

He went down the gangway on my arm. The skirts were so long that he had to gather them in one hand like a Victorian lady picking her way across a muddy street. The ship's sentry stared at us agape: he hadn't known there was a woman aboard, and such a woman, too. Jones, as he passed the sentry, gave him an appraising and provocative glance from his brown eyes. I noticed how fine and bold they looked now below his shawl; they had been killed by the moustache. At the foot of the gangway he embraced the purser and left him smudged on both cheeks with pre-shave powder. The policeman watched us with dulled curiosity—it was obvious that Jones was not the first woman to leave the boat in the early hours, and he could hardly have appealed to any man acquainted with the girls at Mère Catherine's.

We walked slowly arm in arm to the place where I had left my car. "You're holding your skirt too high," I warned him.

"I was never a modest woman, old man."

"I mean the *flic* can see your shoes."

"Not in the dark."

I would never have believed our escape could prove so easy. No footsteps followed us, the car was there, unwatched, peace and Columbus reigned over the night. I sat and thought while Jones arranged his skirts. He said, "I played Boadicea once. In a skit. To amuse the fellows. I had royalty in the audience."

"Royalty?"

"Lord Mountbatten. Those were the days. Would you mind lifting your left leg? My skirt's caught."

"Where do we go from here?" I said.

"Search me. The man I wrote the introduction to, he's dossing down in the Venezuelan embassy."

"It's the most heavily guarded of the lot. They have half the general staff there."

"I'd be quite satisfied with something more modest."

"Perhaps you wouldn't be taken in. You aren't exactly a political refugee, are you?"

"Doesn't deceiving Papa Doc count as resistance?"

"Perhaps you wouldn't be welcome as a permanent guest. Have you thought of that?"

"They'd hardly push me out, would they, if I were once safely in?"

"I think one or two of them might even do that."

I started the engine, and we began to drive slowly back into the town. I didn't wish to give the impression of flight. I watched before every turn for the light of another car, but Port-au-Prince was as empty as a cemetery.

"Where are you taking me?"

"To the only place I can think of. The ambassador's away."

I felt relief as we mounted the hill. There would be no road-block on this side of the familiar turning. At the gates a police-man looked briefly into the car. He knew my face and Jones passed easily enough for a woman when the dashboard-light was out. Obviously there had not yet been a general alarm—Jones was only a criminal; he was not a patriot. They had probably warned the road-blocks and put some Tontons Macoute around the British embassy. With the *Medea* covered and probably my hotel, too, they must think they had him cornered.

I told Jones to stay in the car and I rang the bell. Somebody was awake, for I could see a light burning in a window on the ground-floor. Yet I had to ring twice, and I waited with impatience as heavy steps came from a long way back inside, ponderous, unhurried. A dog yapped and whined—I was puz-zled by the noise, for I had never seen a dog in the house. Then a voice—I supposed that it was the night-porter's—asked who was there.

I said, "I want Señora Pineda. Tell her it is Monsieur Brown. Something urgent."

The door was unlocked, unbolted, and then unchained, but the man who threw it open was not the porter. The ambassador himself stood there, peering myopically. He was in his shirt-sleeves, and he wore no tie: I had never before seen him less than immaculate. Beside him, on guard, was a horrible minia-ture dog, all long grey hair, the shape of a centipede. "You want my wife?" he said. "She is asleep." Seeing his tired and wounded eyes, I thought: "He knows. He knows everything."

"Do you want me to wake her?" he asked. "Is it so urgent? She is with my son. They are both asleep."

I said lamely and ambiguously, "I didn't know that you had returned."

"I came in on tonight's plane." He put up his hand to where his tie should have been. "There's a lot of work waiting for me to do. Papers to be read . . . you know how it is." It was as though he were apologizing to me and proffering me humbly his passport—Nationality: human being. Special peculiarities: cuckold.

I said with a sense of shame, "No, please don't wake her. It was really you I wanted to see."

"Me?" I thought for a moment he would give way to a panic impulse, that he would retreat inside and close the door. Perhaps he believed I was about to tell him what he was afraid to hear. "Won't it wait until morning?" he implored me. "So late. So much to do." He felt for a cigar-case which wasn't there. I think he half intended to press a bundle of cigars into my hands as another might have pressed money—to persuade me to go. But there weren't any cigars. He said in miserable surrender, "Come in then if you must."

I said, "The dog doesn't like me."

"Don Juan?" He rapped out an order to the miserable creature, which began to lick his shoe.

I said, "I have a companion," and signalled to Jones.

The ambassador watched with despairing incredulity the appearance of Jones. He must still have thought that I intended to confess all and perhaps demand the break-up of his marriage, and what part, he probably demanded, could "she" play in the affair; was she a witness, a nurse to look after Angel, a substitute wife? In a nightmare anything, however cruel or grotesque, is possible and this to him was certainly a nightmare. First out of the car came the heavy rubber-soled shoes, a pair of socks striped in scarlet and black like a school-tie worn in the wrong place, then fold after fold of blue-black skirt, and last the head and shoulders wrapped in a scarf, the Remington-white face and the provocative brown eyes. Jones shook himself like a sparrow after a dust-bath and advanced rapidly to join us.

"This is Mr. Jones," I said.

"Major Jones," he corrected me. "I'm glad to meet you, your excellency."

"He wants asylum here. The Tontons Macoute are after him. There's not a hope of getting him into the British embassy. It's too well guarded. I thought perhaps . . . although he is not a South American . . . He is in extreme danger."

A look of enormous relief spread over the ambassador's face while I spoke. This was politics. This he could deal with. This was everyday. "Come in, Major Jones, come in. You are very welcome. My house is at your disposition. I will wake my wife at once. One of my rooms shall be prepared." In his relief he threw his possessive articles around like confetti. Then he closed, locked, bolted, and chained the door, and absent-mindedly offered his arm to Jones to escort him into the house. Jones took it and moved magnificently across the hall like a Victorian matron. The horrible grey dog swept the ground beside him with his matted hair, smelling at the fringe of Jones's skirt.

"Luis!" Martha stood on the landing and looked down at us with sleepy amazement.

"My dear," the ambassador said, "let me introduce you—this is Mr. Jones. Our first refugee."

"Mr. Jones!"

"Major Jones," Jones corrected them both, lifting the scarf from his head as though it were a hat.

Martha leant over the banisters and laughed; she laughed till her eyes filled with tears. I could see her breasts through her nightdress and even the shadow of her hair, and so, I thought, could Jones. He smiled up at her and said, "In the woman's army, of course," and I remembered the girl called Tin Tin at Mère Catherine's who, when I asked her why she liked him, had said to me, "He made me laugh."

2

There was not much of the night left for me in which to sleep. As I returned to the Trianon the same police-officer who had boarded the *Medea* stopped me at the entrance to the drive and demanded where I had been. "You know that as well as I do,"

I said, and he searched my car very thoroughly in revenge—a stupid man.

I rummaged in the bar for a drink; but the ice-containers had been left dry, and there was only a bottle of Seven-up remaining on the shelves. I laced it heavily with rum and sat out on the verandah to wait for the sun to rise—the mosquitoes had long ceased to trouble me, I was stale and tainted meat. The hotel behind me seemed emptier than it had ever done before; I missed the limping Joseph as I might have missed a familiar wound, for perhaps unconsciously I had ached a little with him in his halting progress from the bar to the verandah and up and down the stairs. His footstep was at least one I could easily recognize, and I wondered in what waste of mountain it was sounding now, or whether he was dead already among the stony knobs of Haiti's spine. It seemed to me the only sound to which I had ever had the time to become accustomed. I was filled with self-pity, sweet like the bourbon biscuits of Angel. Could I yet separate even the sound of Martha's footsteps, I asked myself, from another woman's? I doubted it, and certainly I had never learnt to know my mother's before she left me behind with the fathers of the Visitation. And my real father? He had deposited not so much as one childish memory. Presumably he was dead, but I wasn't sure—this was a century in which old men lived beyond their time. But I felt no genuine curiosity about him; nor had I any wish to seek him out or find his tombstone, which was possibly, but not certainly, marked with the name Brown.

Yet my lack of curiosity was a hollow where a hollow should not have been. I had not plugged the hollow with a substitute, as a dentist puts in a temporary filling. No priest had come to represent a father to me, and no region of the earth had taken the place of home. I was a citizen of Monaco, that was all.

The palms had begun to detach themselves from the anonymous darkness; they reminded me of the palms outside the casino on that blue artificial coast where even the sand was an importation. A faint breeze stirred the long leaves, which were serrated like the keyboard of a piano; the keys were depressed two or three at a time as though by an invisible player. Why was I here? I was here because of a picture-postcard from my mother which could easily have gone astray—no odds at any casino could have been higher than that. There are those who belong by their birth inextricably to a country, who even when they leave it feel the tie. And there are those who belong to a province, a county, a village, but I could feel no link at all with the hundred or so square kilometres around the gardens and boulevards of Monte Carlo, a city of transients. I felt a greater tie here, in the shabby land of terror, chosen for me by chance.

The first colours touched the garden, deep green and then deep red—transience was my pigmentation; my roots would never go deep enough anywhere to make me a home or make me secure with love.

Chapter Two

1

There were no longer any guests in the hotel; when the Smiths departed, the cook who had made my kitchen famous with his soufflés gave up all hope and moved to the Venezuelan embassy, where at least there were a few refugees to feed. For my meals I would boil myself an egg or open a tin, or share the Haitian food with my last remaining maid and the gardener, or sometimes I would have a meal with the Pinedas, not often, for the presence of Jones irritated me. Angel now went to a school organized by the Spanish ambassador's wife, and in the afternoons Martha would drive quite openly up the Trianon drive and leave her car in my garage. The fear of discovery had left her, or perhaps a complaisant husband now gave us a limited freedom. In my bedroom we would pass the hours making love or talking and only too often quarrelling. We even quarrelled about the ambassador's dog. "It gives me the creeps," I said. "Like a rat wearing a wool-shawl, or a long centipede. What induced him to buy it?"

"I suppose he wanted company," she said.

"He has you."

"You know how little he has of me."

"Have I got to feel sorry for him too?"

"It wouldn't do any of us harm," she said, "to feel sorry for someone."

She was more astute than I at seeing the distant cloud of a quarrel when it was still no bigger than a man's hand, and she would usually take the right avoiding action, for when an embrace was over the quarrel was usually over too—for that occasion at least. Once she spoke of my mother and their friendship. "Strange wasn't it? My father was a war-criminal and she was a heroine of the resistance."

"You really think she was?"

"Yes."

"I found a medal in a piggy-bank, but I thought it might be the memento of a love-affair. There was a holy medal in the pig too, but that meant nothing—she was certainly not a pious woman. When she left me with the Jesuits it was for convenience only. They could afford an unpaid bill."

"You were with the Jesuits?"

"Yes."

"I remember now. I used to think you were—nothing."

"I am nothing."

"Yes, but a Protestant nothing, not a Catholic nothing. I am a Protestant nothing."

I had a sense of coloured balls flying in the air, a different colour for every faith—or even every lack of faith. There was an existentialist ball, a logical-positivist ball. "I even thought you might be a Communist nothing." It was gay, it was fun so long as with great agility one patted the balls around: it was only when a ball fell to the ground one had the sense of an impersonal wound, like a dog dead on an arterial road.

"Doctor Magiot's a Communist," she said.

"I suppose so. I envy him. He's lucky to believe. I left all such absolutes behind me in the chapel of the Visitation. Do you know they even thought once that I had a vocation?"

"Perhaps you are a *prêtre manqué.*"

"Me? You are laughing at me. Put your hand here. This has no theology." I mocked myself while I made love. I flung myself into pleasure like a suicide on to a pavement.

What made us, after that short furious encounter, talk of Jones again? I am confusing together in memory many afternoons, many love-makings, many discussions, many quarrels, all of them a curtain-raiser for the final quarrel of all. For example there was the afternoon when she left early and to my enquiry why she was going—Angel would not be back from school for a long time yet—she replied, "I promised Jones that he could teach me gin-rummy." It was only ten days after I had deposited Jones under her roof, and when she told me that, I felt the premonition of jealousy like the first shiver which announces a fever.

"It must be an exciting game. You prefer it to making love?"

"Darling, we've made love all we can. I don't want to disappoint him. He's a good guest. Angel likes him. He plays a lot with Angel."

And an afternoon much later the quarrel began in another way. She asked me suddenly—it was the first sentence she spoke after our bodies separated—what the word "midge" meant.

"A kind of small mosquito. Why?"

"Jones always calls the dog Midge, and he answers to the name. His real name is Don Juan, but he's never learnt that."

"I suppose you are going to tell me the dog likes Jones too."

"Oh but he does—better than he likes Luis. Luis always feeds him, he won't even allow Angel to do that, and yet Jones has only to call 'Midge' . . ."

"What does Jones call you?"

"How do you mean?"

"You go to him when he calls. You leave early to play gin-rummy."

"That was three weeks ago. I've never done it again."

"We spend half our time now talking about that damned crook."

"You brought the damned crook to our house."

"I didn't know he was going to become such a friend of the family."

242

"Darling, he makes us laugh, that's all." She couldn't have chosen an explanation which worried me more. "There isn't much to laugh about here."

"Here?"

"You're twisting every word. I don't mean here in bed. I mean here in Port-au-Prince."

"Two different languages cause misunderstanding. I should have taken lessons in German. Does Jones speak German?"

"Not even Luis does. Darling, when you want me I'm a woman, but when I hurt you I'm always a German. What a pity Monaco never had a period of power."

"It had. But the English beat the Prince's fleet in the Channel. Like the Luftwaffe."

"I was ten years old when you beat the Luftwaffe."

"I did no beating. I sat in an office translating propaganda against Vichy into French."

"Jones had a more interesting war."

"Oh yes?"

Was it innocence which caused her so often to introduce his name or did she feel a compulsion to have it on her tongue?

"He was in Burma," she said, "fighting the Japs."

"He's told you that?"

"He's very interesting when he talks about guerrilla-fighting."

"The resistance could have done with him here. But he preferred the government to the resistance."

"But he's seen through the government now."

"Or have they seen through him? Did he tell you about the lost platoon?"

"Yes."

"And how he has a nose for water?"

"Yes."

"Sometimes I wonder that he didn't end up at least a brigadier."

"Darling, what's the matter?"

"Othello charmed Desdemona with his stories of adventure. It's an old technique. I ought to tell you how I was hounded by the *People*. It might win your sympathy."

"What people?"

"Never mind."

"A change of subject in an embassy is always something. The first secretary is an authority on turtles. It was interesting for a while in a natural-history way, but it palled all the same. And the second secretary is an admirer of Cervantes, but not of *Don Quixote*, which he says was a bid for easy popularity."

"I suppose the Burmese war too will become stale in time."

"At least he doesn't repeat himself yet like the others."

"Has he told you the history of his cocktail-case?"

"Yes. Indeed he has. Darling, you underrate him. He's a very generous man. You know how our shaker leaks, so he gave Luis his—in spite of all the memories attached. It's a very good one—it came from Asprey's in London. He said it was the only thing he had with which to return our hospitality. We said we'd borrow it—and do you know what he did? He gave money to one of the servants to take it to Hamit's and have it inscribed. So there it is—we can't give it back. Such a quaint inscription, "To Luis and Martha from their grateful guest, Jones." Like that. No christian name. No initials. Like a French actor."

"And *your* first name."

"And Luis's. Darling, it's time I left."

"What a long time we've spent, haven't we, talking about Jones?"

"I expect we'll spend a lot more. Papa Doc won't give him a safe-conduct. Not even as far as the British Embassy. The government makes a formal protest every week. They claim he's a common criminal, but, of course, that's nonsense. He was ready to work with them, but then his eyes were opened— by young Philipot."

"Is that what he claims?"

"He tried to sabotage a supply of arms to the Tontons Macoute."

"An ingenious story."

"So that really does make him a political refugee."

"He lives on his wits, that's all."

"Don't we all to some extent?"

"How quickly you leap to his defence."

Suddenly I had a grotesque vision of the two of them in bed, Martha naked as she was now, and Jones still in his female finery, his face yellow with pre-shave powder, lifting his great black velvet skirt above his thighs.

"Darling, what is it now?"

"It's so stupid. To think that I brought the little crook to live with you. And now there he stays—for life perhaps. Or until someone can get near enough to Papa Doc with a silver bullet. How long has Mindszenty stayed in the American embassy in Budapest? A dozen years? Jones sees you all day long . . ."

"Not in your way."

"Oh, Jones has to have his periodic woman—I know that. I've seen him in action. And as for me I can only see you for dinner, or cocktail-parties of the second order."

"You're not at dinner now."

"He's climbed the wall. He's in the garden itself."

"You should have been a novelist," she said. "Then we would all have been your characters. We couldn't say to you we are not like that at all, we couldn't answer back. Darling, don't you see you are inventing us?"

"I'm glad at least I've invented this bed."

"We can't even talk to you, can we? You won't listen if what we say is out of character—the character you've given us."

"What character? You're a woman I love. That's all."

"Oh yes, I'm classified. A woman you love."

She got out of bed and began very rapidly to dress. She swore—"*Merde!*"—when a suspender failed to snap, she got her dress twisted over her head and had to start again—she was like someone escaping from a fire. She couldn't find the second stocking.

I said, "I'm going to get your guest away soon. Somehow."

"I don't mind if you do or not. As long as he's safe."

"Angel will miss him though."

"Yes."

"And Midge."

"Yes."

"And Luis."

"He amuses Luis."

"And you?"

She thrust her feet into her shoes and didn't answer.

"We'll have peace together when he's gone. You won't be torn in two between us then."

She looked at me a moment as though I had said something that shocked her. Then she came up to the bed and took my hand as though I were a child who didn't understand the meaning of his words but who must be warned all the same not to repeat them. She said, "My darling, be careful. Don't you understand? To you nothing exists except in your own thoughts. Not me, not Jones. We're what you choose to make us. You're a Berkeleyan. My God, what a Berkeleyan. You've turned poor Jones into a seducer and me into a wanton mistress. You can't even believe in your mother's medal, can you? You've written her a different part. My dear, try to believe we exist when you aren't there. We're independent of you. None of us is like you fancy we are. Perhaps it wouldn't matter much if your thoughts were not so dark, always so dark."

I tried to kiss her mood away, but she turned quickly and standing at the door said to the empty passage, "It's a dark Brown world you live in. I'm sorry for you. As I'm sorry for my father."

I lay in bed a long while and wondered what I could possibly have in common with a war-criminal responsible for so many unidentified deaths.

246

The headlights swept up between the palms and settled like a yellow moth over my face. I could see nothing clearly when they were switched off—only something large and black approaching the verandah. I had suffered one beating-up, I didn't want another. I shouted, "Joseph," but of course Joseph wasn't there. I had been sleeping over my glass of rum and I had forgotten.

"Is Joseph back?" It was a relief to hear Doctor Magiot's voice. He came slowly, with his inexplicable dignity, up the broken verandah steps as though they were the marble steps of the senate-house and he was a senator from the outer empire granted Roman citizenship.

"I was asleep. I wasn't thinking. Can I get you something, doctor? I am my own cook now, but I can easily beat you up an omelette."

"No, I'm not hungry. May I put my car away in your garage in case anyone comes?"

"No one ever comes here at night."

"You never know. In case . . ."

When he returned I repeated my offer of food, but he would take nothing. "I wanted company, that's all." He chose a hard straight chair to sit in. "I used often to come and see your mother here—in the happier days. I find it lonely now after the sun sets."

The lightning had begun and the nightly deluge would soon descend. I drew my chair a little further in to the shelter of the verandah. "Do you see nothing of your colleagues?" I asked.

"What colleagues? Oh, there are a few old men left like myself behind their locked doors. In the last ten years three-quarters of the doctors who graduated here preferred to go elsewhere as soon as they could buy an exit-permit. Here one buys an exit-permit not a practice. If you want to consult a Haitian doctor, better go to Ghana." He lapsed into silence. It was company not conversation that he needed. The rain began to fall, tingling in the swimming-pool which was empty again; the night was so dark I couldn't see Doctor Magiot's face, only the tips of his fingers laid out on the arms of his chair, like carved wood.

"The other night," Doctor Magiot said, "I had an absurd dream. The telephone sounded—think of that, the telephone, how many years is it since I heard a telephone? I was summoned to the general hospital for a casualty. When I arrived I saw with satisfaction how clean the ward was, the nurses too were young and spotless (of course you will find they have all left for Africa as well). My colleague advanced to meet me, a young man in whom I had great hopes; he is fulfilling them now in Brazzaville. He told me that the opposition-candidate (how old-fashioned even the words sound today) had been attacked by rowdies at a political meeting. There were complications. His left eye was in danger. I began to examine the eye, but it turned out not to be the eye at all but the cheek, which was cut open to the bone. My colleague returned. He said, 'The chief of police is on the telephone. The assailants have been arrested. The President is anxious to know the result of your examination. The President's wife has sent these flowers . . .'" Doctor Magiot began to laugh softly in the dark. "Even at the best," he said, "even under President Estimé it was never like that. Freud's wish-fulfillment dreams are usually not so obvious."

"Not a very Marxist dream, Doctor Magiot. With an opposition-candidate."

"Perhaps the Marxist dream of a far far future. When the state has withered away and there are only local elections. In the parish of Haiti."

"When I came to your house I was surprised to find *Das Kapital* openly on a shelf. Is that safe?"

"I told you once before. Papa Doc makes a distinction between philosophy and propaganda. He wants to keep his window open towards the east until the Americans give arms to him again."

"They'll never do that."

"I will make you a bet of ten to one that, in a matter of months, relations are healed and the American ambassador returns. You forget—Papa Doc is a bulwark against Communism. There will be no Cuba and no Bay of Pigs here. Of course there are other reasons. Papa Doc's lobbyist in Washington is the lobbyist for certain American-owned mills (they grind grey flour for the people out of imported surplus-wheat— it is astonishing how much money can be made out of the poorest of the poor with a little ingenuity). And then there's the great beef-racket. The poor here can eat meat no more than they can eat cake, so I suppose they don't suffer when all the beef that exists goes to the American market—it doesn't matter to the importers that there are no standards here of cattle-raising —it goes into tins for underdeveloped countries paid for by American aid, of course. It wouldn't affect the Americans if this trade ceased, but it would affect the particular Washington politician who receives one cent for every pound exported."

"Do you despair of any future?"

"No, I don't despair, I don't believe in despair, but our problems won't be solved by the Marines. We have had experience of the Marines. I'm not sure I wouldn't fight for Papa Doc if the Marines came. At least he's Haitian. No, the job has to be done with our own hands. We are an evil slum floating a few miles from Florida, and no American will help us with arms or money or counsel. We learned a few years back what their counsel meant. There was a resistance group here who were in touch with a sympathizer in the American embassy: they were promised all kinds of moral support, but the information went straight back to the C.I.A. and from the C.I.A. by a very direct route to Papa Doc. You can imagine what happened to the group. The State Department didn't want any disturbance in the Caribbean."

"And the Communists?"

"We are better organized and more discreet than the others, but, if we ever tried to take over, you can be certain the Marines would land and Papa Doc would remain in power. In Washington we seem a very stable country—not suitable for tourists, but tourists are a nuisance anyway. Sometimes they see too much and write to their senators. Your Mr. Smith was very disturbed by the executions in the cemetery. By the way Hamit has disappeared."

"What happened?"

"I hope he's gone into hiding, but his car was found abandoned near the port."

"He has a lot of American friends."

"But he is not an American citizen. He is a Haitian. You can do what you like with Haitians. Trujillo murdered twenty thousand of us in time of peace on the River Massacre, peasants who had come to his country for cane-cutting—men, women and children—but do you imagine there was one protest from Washington? He lived nearly twenty years afterwards fat on American aid."

"What do you hope for, Doctor Magiot?"

"Perhaps a palace-revolution. Papa Doc never stirs outside, you can only reach him in the palace. And then, before Fat Gracia settles in his place, a purge by the people."

"No hope from the rebels?"

"Poor souls, they don't know how to fight. They go waving their rifles, if they've got them, at a fortified post. They may be heroes, but they have to learn to live and not to die. Do you think Philipot knows the first thing about guerrilla-fighting? And your poor lame Joseph? They need someone of experience and then perhaps in a year or two . . . we are as brave as the Cubans, but the terrain is very cruel. We have destroyed our forests. You have to live in caves and sleep on stones. And there's the question of water . . ."

Like a comment on his pessimism the deluge fell. We couldn't even hear ourselves speak. The lights of the town were blotted out. I went into the bar and brought out two glasses of rum and set them between the doctor and myself. I had to guide his hand to his glass. We sat in silence till the worst of the storm was over.

"You're an odd man," Doctor Magiot said at last.

"Why odd?"

"You listen to me as though I were an old man speaking of a distant past. You seem so indifferent—and yet you live here."

"I was born in Monaco," I said. "That is almost the same as being a citizen of nowhere."

"If your mother had lived to see these days she would not have been so indifferent; she might well be up in the mountains now."

"Uselessly?"

"Oh, yes uselessly, of course."

"With her lover?"

"He certainly would never have let her go alone."

"Perhaps I take after my father."

"Who was he?"

"I've no idea. Like my country of birth he has no face."

The rain diminished: I could hear the separate sound of the drops now on the trees, on the bushes, on the hard cement of the bathing-pool. I said, "I take things as they come. That's what most of the world does, surely? One has to live."

"What do you want out of life, Brown? I know how your mother would have answered."

"How?"

"She would have laughed at me for not knowing the answer. Fun. But 'fun' for her included almost everything. Even death."

Doctor Magiot got up and stood at the edge of the verandah. "I thought I heard something. Imagination. The nights make us all nervy. I really loved your mother, Brown."

"And her lover—what did you make of him?"

"He made her happy. What do *you* want, Brown?"

"I want to run this hotel—I want to see it as it used to be.

Before Papa Doc came. Joseph busy behind the bar, girls in the bathing-pool, cars coming up the drive, all the stupid noises of enjoyment. Ice in glasses, laughter in the bushes, and of course, oh yes, the rustle of dollar-notes."

"And then?"

"Oh, I suppose a body to love. As my mother had."

"And after that?"

"God knows. Isn't that enough for what's left of a lifetime? I'm nearly sixty now."

"Your mother was a Catholic."

"Not much of one."

"I retain a faith, even if it's only the truth of certain economic laws, but you've lost yours."

"Have I? Perhaps I never had one. Anyway it's a limitation to believe, isn't it?"

We sat in silence for a while with empty glasses. Then Doctor Magiot said, "I had a message from Philipot. He's in the mountains behind Les Cayes, but he plans to move north. He has a dozen men with him, including Joseph. I hope the others aren't cripples. Two lame men are enough. He wants to join with the guerrillas near the Dominican border—there are said to be thirty men there."

"What an army! Forty-two men."

"Castro had twelve."

"But you can't tell me that Philipot is a Castro."

"He thinks he can establish a base near the frontier for training . . . Papa Doc has chased the peasants away for a depth of ten kilometres, so there is a possibility of secrecy, if not of recruits . . . He needs Jones."

"Why Jones?"

"He has a great belief in Jones."

"He would do much better to find himself a Bren."

"Training is more important than weapons at the start. You can always take weapons from the dead, but first you have to learn how to kill."

"How do you know all this, Doctor Magiot?"

"At times they have to trust even one of us."

"One of you?"

"A Communist."

"It's a wonder you survive."

"If there were no Communists—most of our names are on the C.I.A. list—Papa Doc would cease to be a bulwark of the free world. There may be another reason too. I'm a good doctor. The day might arrive . . . he's not immune."

"If only you could convert your stethoscope into something fatal."

"Yes, I've thought of that. But he will probably outlive me."

"French medicine is fond of suppositories and *piqûres*?"

"They would be tested first by someone of no importance."

"And you really think that Jones . . . He's only good to make a woman laugh."

"He had the right experience in Burma. The Japanese were cleverer than the Tontons Macoute."

"Oh yes, he boasts about that time. I hear he holds them spellbound in the embassy. He sings for his supper."

"He can't want to spend his whole life in the embassy."

"He doesn't want to die on the doorstep either."

"There are always means of evasion."

"He'd never risk it."

"He was risking a lot when he tried to swindle Papa Doc. Don't underrate him. Just because he boasts a lot . . . And you can trap a man who boasts. You can call his bluff."

"Oh don't mistake me, Doctor Magiot. I want him out of the embassy every bit as much as Philipot can."

"And yet you put him there."

"I didn't realize."

"What?"

"Oh, that's quite a different matter. I'd do anything . . ."

Somebody was walking up the drive. The footsteps squealed on the wet leaves and the scraps of old coconut-shells. We both sat silent, waiting . . . In Port-au-Prince nobody walked at night.

I wondered whether Doctor Magiot carried a gun. But it wasn't in his character. Somebody halted at the edge of the trees where the drive turned. A voice called, "Mr. Brown."

"Yes?"

"Have you no light?"

"Who is it?"

"Petit Pierre."

I was suddenly aware that Doctor Magiot was no longer with me. It was extraordinary how silently the big man could move when he chose.

"I'll fetch one," I called. "I am alone."

I felt my way back into the bar. I knew where I would find a torch. When I turned it on, I saw that the door into the kitchen-quarters was open. I came back with a lamp and Petit Pierre climbed the steps. It was weeks since I had seen those sharp ambiguous features. His jacket was sopping wet and he hung it on the back of a chair. I helped him to a glass of rum and awaited an explanation—it was unusual to see him after sundown.

"My car broke down," he said. "I waited till the worst rain was over. The lights are late tonight in coming on."

I said mechanically—it was part of the small talk of Port-au-Prince, "Did they search you at the block?"

"Not in this rain," he said. "There are no road-blocks when it rains. You can't expect a militiaman to work in a storm."

"It's a long time since I've seen you, Petit Pierre."

"I've been very busy."

"Surely there's not much for your gossip column?"

He giggled in the dark. "There's always something. Mr. Brown, today is a great day in the history of Petit Pierre."

"Don't tell me you've got married?"

"No, no, no. Guess again."

"You've inherited a fortune?"

"A fortune in Port-au-Prince? Oh no. Mr. Brown, today I have installed a hi-fi stereo."

"Congratulations. Does it work?"

"I haven't bought any discs yet, so I cannot tell. I have ordered discs from Hamit of Juliette Greco, Françoise Hardy, Johnny Halliday . . ."

"I've heard that Hamit isn't with us any more."

"Why? What has happened?"

"He's disappeared."

"For once," Petit Pierre said, "you are ahead of me with the news. Who told you?"

"I guard my sources."

"He went too often to the foreign embassies. It wasn't wise."

Suddenly the lights came on, and for the first time I caught Petit Pierre off guard, brooding, disquieted, before he reacted to the light and said with his habitual gaiety, "I shall have to wait for my discs then."

"I have some records in the office I can lend you. I used to keep them for the guests."

"I was at the airport tonight," Petit Pierre said.

"Did anyone get off?"

"As a matter of fact, yes. I didn't expect to see him. People sometimes stay longer than they have planned in Miami and he has been away a long time, and what with all the trouble . . ."

"Who was it?"

"Captain Concasseur."

I thought I knew now why Petit Pierre had made his friendly call—it was not just to tell me about the purchase of his hi-fi stereo. He had a warning to convey.

"Has he been in trouble?"

"Anyone who touches Major Jones is in trouble," Petit Pierre said. "The Captain is very angry. He was much insulted in Miami—they say he spent two nights in a police-station. Think of it! Captain Concasseur! He wants to rehabilitate him self."

"How?"

"By getting Major Jones somehow."

"Jones is safe in the embassy."

"He should stay there as long as he can. He had better not trust any safe-conduct. But who knows what attitude a new ambassador might take?"

"What new ambassador?"

"There is a rumour that the President has told Señor Pineda's government that he is no longer *persona grata*. Of course there may be no truth in it. May I see your discs please? The rain is over and I must be going."

"Where have you left your car?"

"At the side of the road below the block."

"I will drive you home," I said. I fetched my car from the garage. When I turned on the headlights I could see Doctor Magiot sitting patiently in his car. We didn't speak.

3

After I had left Petit Pierre at the shack which he called his home I drove to the embassy. The guard at the gate stopped my car and peered inside before he let me through the gates. When I rang the bell I could hear the dog barking in the hall and Jones's voice saying with the tone of an owner, "Quiet, Midge, quiet."

They were alone that night, the ambassador, Martha, and Jones, and I had the impression of a family-party. Pineda and Jones were playing gin-rummy—needless to say Jones was well ahead, while Martha sat in an armchair sewing. I had never before seen her with a needle in her fingers; it was as though Jones had brought into the house with him a kind of domesticity. Midge sat down at his feet as though he were the master, and Pineda raised his wounded unwelcoming eyes and said, "You will excuse us if we finish this *partie*."

"Come and see Angel," Martha said; we went up the stairs together, and half way up I heard Jones say, "*J'arrête à deux.*" On the landing we turned left, into the room of our quarrel, and she kissed me freely and happily. I told her of Petit Pierre's rumour. "Oh, no," she said, "no. It can't be true," and then she added, "Luis has been worried about something the last few days."

"But if it should be true . . ."

Martha said, "The new ambassador would have to keep Jones just the same. He couldn't turn him out."

"I wasn't thinking of Jones. I was thinking of ourselves." Could a woman continue to call a man by his surname, I wondered, if she were sleeping with him?

She sat down on the bed and stared at the wall with a look of amazement as though the wall had suddenly come closer. "I don't believe it's true," she said. "I won't believe it."

"It was bound to happen one day."

"I always thought . . . when Angel was old enough to understand . . ."

"How old would I be by then?"

"You've thought about it too," she accused me.

"Yes, I've thought a lot about it. It was one of the reasons why I tried to sell the hotel in New York. I wanted money to go after you wherever you were sent. But nobody will ever buy the hotel now."

She said, "Darling, we'll manage somehow, but Jones—it's life or death for him."

"I suppose if we were still young we'd think it was life or death for us too. But now—'men have died and worms have eaten them, but not for love.' "

Jones called out from below, "The game's finished"; his voice came into the room like a tactless stranger. "We'd better go," Martha said. "Don't say anything, not until we know."

Pineda sat with the awful dog on his knees, stroking it; it accepted his caresses listlessly as though it wanted to be elsewhere, and it watched Jones with bleary devotion where he sat adding up the score. "I'm 1200 up," he said. "I'll send to Hamit's in the morning and buy bourbon biscuits for Angel."

"You spoil him," Martha said. "Buy something for yourself. To remember us by."

"As if I could ever forget," Jones said, and he looked at her, just as the dog on Pineda's knees looked at Jones, with an expression mournful, dewy, and a bit false at the same time.

"Your information service seems to be bad," I said. "Hamit has disappeared."

"I hadn't heard," Pineda said. "Why . . . ?"

"Petit Pierre thinks he has too many foreign friends."

"You must do something," Martha said. "Hamit helped us in so many ways." I remembered one of them, the small room with the brass bedstead and the mauve silk coverlet and the hard eastern chairs ranged against the wall. Those afternoons belonged to our easiest days.

"What can I do?" Pineda said. "The Secretary of the Interior will accept two of my cigars and tell me politely that Hamit is a citizen of Haiti."

"Give me my old company back," Jones said, "and I'd go through the police-station like a dose of salts till I found him."

I couldn't have asked for a quicker or better response: Magiot had said, "You can trap a man who boasts." When Jones spoke he looked at Martha with the expression of a young man seeking approval, and I could imagine all those domestic evenings when he had amused them with his stories of Burma. It was true he wasn't young, but there was nearly ten years between us all the same.

"There are a lot of police," I said.

"If I had fifty of my own men I could take over the country. The Japs outnumbered us, and they knew how to fight . . ."

Martha moved towards the door, but I stopped her. "Please don't go." I needed her as a witness. She stayed, and Jones went on, suspecting nothing at all. "Of course they had us on the run at first in Malaya. We didn't know a thing about guerrilla-war then, but we learnt."

"Wingate," I said encouragingly, for fear he wouldn't go far enough.

258

"He was one of the best, but there are others I could name. I was proud enough of some of my own tricks."

"You could smell water," I reminded him.

"That was something I hadn't got to learn," he said. "It was born in me. Why, as a child . . ."

"What a tragedy it is you are shut up here," I interrupted him. His childhood was too distant for my purpose. "There are men in the mountains now who only need to learn. Of course they've got Philipot."

It was like a duet between the two of us. "Philipot," he exclaimed. "He hasn't a clue old man. Do you know he came to see me? He wanted my help in training . . . He offered . . ."

"Weren't you tempted?" I said.

"I certainly was. One misses the old Burmese days. You can understand that. But, old man, I was in the government service. I hadn't seen through them then. Perhaps I'm innocent, but a man's only got to be straight with me . . . I trusted them . . . If I'd known what I know now . . ."

I wondered what explanation he had given to Martha and Pineda for his flight. He had obviously elaborated a good deal on the story he had told me the night of his escape.

"It's a great pity you didn't go with Philipot," I said.

"A pity for both of us, old man. Of course, I'm not running him down. Philipot's got courage. But I could have turned him, given the opportunity, into a first-rate commando. That attack on the police-station—it was amateurish. He let the most of them escape and the only arms he got . . ."

"If another opportunity arose . . ." No inexperienced mouse could have moved more recklessly towards the smell of cheese. "Oh, I'd go like a shot now," he said.

I said, "If I could arrange for your escape . . . to join Philipot . . ."

He hardly hesitated at all, for Martha's eyes were on him. "Just show me the way, old man," he said. "Just show me the way."

Midge at that moment leapt upon his knee and licked his face, from nose to chin, as though to give the hero a long farewell; he made some obvious joke—for he was unaware then that the trap had really closed—which set Martha laughing, and I comforted myself that the days of laughter were numbered.

"You have to be ready at a moment's warning," I told him.

"I travel light, old man," Jones said. "Not even a cocktail-case now." He could risk that reference; he was so sure of me . . .

Doctor Magiot was sitting in my office, in the dark, although the lights had come on. I said. "I've hooked him. Nothing could have been easier."

"You sound very triumphant," he said. "But what is it after all? One man can't win a war."

"No, I've other reasons for triumph."

Doctor Magiot spread a map out on my desk and we went over in detail the southern road to Les Cayes. If I was to return alone I must appear to have no passenger.

"But if they search the car?"

"We will come to that."

I would need a police-pass for myself and a reason for my journey. "You must get a pass for Monday, the twelfth . . ." he told me. It would take the best part of a week for him to get a reply from Philipot, so the 12th was the earliest date possible— "there's hardly any moon then and that's in your favour. You leave him here by the cemetery before you reach Aquin and drive on to Les Cayes."

"If the Tontons Macoute find him before Philipot . . ."

"You won't get there before midnight, and no one goes into a cemetery after dark. If anyone finds him it will be a bad look out for you," Magiot said. "They'll make him talk."

"I suppose there's no other possible way . . ."

"I would never get a pass to leave Port-au-Prince or I would have offered . . ."

"Don't worry. I have a personal score to settle with Concasseur."

"We all have that. At least there is one thing we can depend on . . ."

"What's that?"

"The weather."

4

There was a Catholic mission and a hospital at Les Cayes and I had thought up some story to tell of a package of theological books and a parcel of medicines which I had promised to deliver there. The story as it happened hardly mattered; the police were only concerned with the dignity of their office. A pass to Les Cayes cost so many hours of waiting, that was all, in the smell of the zoo, under the snapshots of the dead rebels, in the steam of the stovelike day. The door of the office in which Mr. Smith and I had first seen Concasseur was closed. Perhaps he was already in disgrace and my score settled for me.

Just before one o'clock struck, my name was called and I went to a policeman at the desk. He began to fill in the innumerable details, of myself and my car, from my birth in Monte Carlo to the colour of my Humber. A sergeant came and looked over his shoulder. "You are mad," he said.

"Why?"

"You'll never get to Les Cayes without a jeep."

"The great southern highway," I said.

"A hundred and eighty kilometres of mud and pot-holes. Even with a jeep it takes eight hours."

That afternoon Martha came to see me. As we were resting side by side she said to me, "Jones takes you seriously."

"I meant him to."

"You know you wouldn't get past the first road-block."

"Are you so anxious about him?"

"You are such a fool," she said. "I think if I were going away forever, you'd spoil the last moment . . ."

"Are you going away?"

"One day. Of course. It's certain. One always moves on."

"Would you tell me beforehand?"

"I don't know. I mightn't have the courage."

"I'd follow you."

"Would you? What a baggage-train. To arrive in a new capital with a husband and Angel and a lover as well."

"At least you would have left Jones behind."

"Who knows? Perhaps we could smuggle him out in the diplomatic bag. Luis likes him better than he does you. He says he's more honest."

"Honest? Jones?" I gave a good imitation of a laugh, but my throat was dry after love.

As so often before, the dusk came down while we talked of Jones; we didn't make love a second time: the subject was anaphrodisiac.

"It's strange to me," I said, "how easily he makes friends. Luis and you. Even Mr. Smith was fond of him. Perhaps the crooked appeals to the straight or the guilty to the innocent, like blonde appeals to black."

"Am I innocent?"

"Yes."

"And yet you think I sleep with Jones."

"That has nothing to do with innocence."

"Would you really follow me if we went away?"

"Of course. If I could raise the cash. Once I had a hotel. Now I have only you. Are you leaving? Are you keeping something secret?"

"I'm not. But Luis may be."

"Doesn't he tell you everything?"

"Perhaps he's more afraid to make me unhappy than you are. Tenderness is more—tender."

"How often does he make love to you?"

"You think me insatiable, don't you? I need you and Luis and Jones," she said, but she didn't answer my question. The palms and the bougainvillaea had turned black, and the rain began, in single drops like gouts of heavy oil. Between the drops the sultry silence fell and then the lightning struck and the roar of the storm came down the mountain. The rain was hammered into the ground like a prefabricated wall.

I said, "It will be a night like this, when the moon's hidden, that I'll come for Jones."

"How will you get him past the road-blocks?"

I repeated what Petit Pierre had said to me, "There are no road-blocks in a storm."

"But they'll suspect you when they find out . . ."

"I trust you and Luis not to let them find out. You have to close Angel's mouth, and the dog's too. Don't let him go whining round the house looking for lost Jones."

"Are you frightened?"

"I wish I had a jeep, that's all."

"Why are you doing it?"

"I don't like Concasseur and his Tontons Macoute. I don't like Papa Doc. I don't like them feeling my balls in the street to see if I have a gun. That body in the bathing pool—I used to have different memories. They tortured Joseph. They ruined my hotel."

"What difference can Jones make if he's a fake?"

"Perhaps after all he isn't. Philipot believes in him. Perhaps he did fight the Japs."

"If he was a fake he wouldn't want to go, would he?"

"He committed himself too far in front of you."

"I'm not that important to him."

"Then what is? Did he ever speak to you about a golf-club?"

"Yes, but you don't risk death for a golf-club. He wants to."

"Do you believe that?"

"He asked me to lend him back his cocktail-shaker. He said it's a mascot. He always had it with him in Burma. He says he'll return it when the guerrillas enter Port-au-Prince."

"He certainly has his dreams," I said. "Perhaps he's an innocent too."

"Don't be angry," she implored me, "if I go home early. I

promised him a party—of gin-rummy, I mean, before Angel comes back from school. He's so good with Angel. They play commandos and unarmed combat. There may not be time for many more gin-rummies. You do understand, don't you? I want to be kind."

I felt weariness more than anger when she left me, weariness of myself most of all. Was I incapable of trust? But when I poured myself out a whisky and heard the vast inundation of silence flooding round, venom returned; venom was an antidote to fear. I thought, why should I trust a German, the child of a hanged man?

5

A few days later I received a letter from Smith—it had taken more than a week to come from Santo Domingo. They had stopped off, he wrote to me, for a few days to look around and see the tomb of Columbus, and who did I think they had met? I could answer that without even turning the page. Mr. Fernandez, of course. He happened to be at the airport when they arrived. (I wondered whether his profession made him stand by on the airfield like an ambulance.) Mr. Fernandez had shown them so much, so interestingly, that they had decided to stay on longer. Apparently Mr. Fernandez' vocabulary had increased. In the *Medea* he had been suffering from a great grief, and that was the reason he had broken down at the concert; his mother had been seriously ill, but she had recovered. The cancer had proved to be no more than a *fibrome*, and Mrs. Smith had converted her to a vegetarian diet. Mr. Fernandez even thought that there were possibilities for a vegetarian centre in the Dominican Republic. "I must admit," he wrote, "that conditions here are more peaceful, although there is a great deal of poverty. Mrs. Smith has met a friend from Wisconsin." He sent his cordial best wishes to Major Jones and thanked me for all my help and hospitality. He was an old man with beautiful manners, and suddenly I realized how much I missed him. In the school-chapel at Monte Carlo we prayed every Sunday, "*Dona nobis pacem*," but I doubt whether that prayer was answered for many in the life that followed. Mr. Smith had no need to pray for peace. He had been born with peace in his heart instead of the splinter of ice. That afternoon Hamit's body was found in an open sewer on the edge of Port-au-Prince.

I drove out to Mère Catherine's (why not if Martha was at home with Jones?), but none of the girls had ventured out that evening from their homes. The story of Hamit was probably circulating by this time all over town, and they feared that one body was not sufficient to make a feast-day for Baron Samedi. Madame Philipot and her child had joined the other refugees at the Venezuelan embassy, and there was a feeling of uncertainty everywhere. (I noticed, driving by, that two guards were now outside Martha's embassy.) I was stopped at the road-block below the hotel and searched, although the rain had begun. I wondered whether some of the activity was due to Concasseur's return—he had to prove himself loyal.

At the Trianon I found Doctor Magiot's boy waiting with a note—an invitation to dine with him. It was already past the hour of dinner and we drove accompanied by thunder to his house. This time we were not stopped—the rain was falling too heavily now and the militiaman crouched in his shelter of old sacks. The Norfolk pine dripped beside the drive like a broken umbrella, and Doctor Magiot waited for me in his Victorian sitting room with a decanter of port.

"Have you heard about Hamit?" I asked. The two glasses stood on little bead-mats with floral designs to protect a *papier-mâché* table.

"Yes, poor man."

"What had they got against him?"

"He was one of Philipot's post-boxes. And he didn't talk."

"And you are another?"

He poured out the port. I have never learned to enjoy port as an apéritif, but I took it that night without protest; I was in the mood for any drink. He didn't answer my question, so I asked him another. "How do you know he didn't talk?"

He gave me the obvious answer. "I am here." The old woman called Madame Ferry who looked after the house and cooked his meals opened the door and reminded us that dinner was ready. She wore a black dress and had a white cap on her head. It might seem an odd setting for a Marxist, but I remembered hearing of the lace-curtains and the china-cabinets in the early Ilyushin jets. Like her they gave a sense of security.

We had an excellent steak and creamed potatoes with a touch of garlic and as good a claret as could be expected so far away from Bordeaux. Doctor Magiot was not in a humour to talk, but his silence was as monumental as his conversation. When he said, "Another glass?" the phrase was like a simple name carved on a tombstone. When dinner was finished, he said, "The American ambassador is returning."

"Are you sure?"

"And friendly discussions are to be opened with the Dominican Republic. We are abandoned again."

The old lady came in with coffee and he was silent. His face was hidden from me by the glass dome which covered an arrangement of wax-flowers. I felt that after dinner we should have joined other members of the Browning Society for a discussion of the *Sonnets from the Portuguese*. Hamit lay in his drain a very long way from here.

"I have some Curaçao or there is a little Benedictine left if you prefer it."

"Curaçao, please."

"The Curaçao, Madame Ferry," and again silence settled except for the thunder outside. I wondered why he had summoned me and at last when Madame Ferry had come and gone I heard. "I've received a reply from Philipot."

"A good thing it came to you and not to Hamit."

"He says he will be at the rendezvous for three nights running next week. Beginning on Monday."

"The cemetery?"

266

"Yes. On those nights there should be hardly any moon."

"But suppose there's no storm either?"

"Have you ever known three nights without a storm at this time of year?"

"No. But my pass is for one day only—Monday."

"A detail. Few policemen can read. You leave Jones and drive on. If something goes wrong and you are suspected I'll try and warn you at Les Cayes. You might possibly get away by fishing-boat."

"I hope to God nothing does go wrong. I have no wish to be on the run. My life's here."

"You will have to get beyond Petit Goave before the storm is over or they'll search your car there. After Petit Goave there should be no trouble before Aquin and you'll be alone again when you reach Aquin."

"I wish to God I had a jeep."

"So do I."

"What about the guards at the embassy?"

"Don't bother about them. During the storm they will take rum in the kitchen."

"We must warn Jones to be ready. I have an idea he may back out."

Doctor Magiot said, "I don't want you to visit the embassy between now and the night you leave. I shall go there tomorrow —to treat Jones. Mumps is a dangerous disease at his age; it may cause sterility or even impotence. The incubation period after the child's attack might seem curiously long to a doctor, but the servants won't realize that. He will have to be isolated and kept very quiet. You should be back from Les Cayes a long time before anyone knows he's gone."

"And you, doctor?"

"I treated him for as long as was necessary. That period is your alibi. And my car will not leave Port-au-Prince—that is mine."

"I only hope he's worth all the trouble we are taking."

"Oh I assure you, so do I. So do I."

Chapter Three

1

Next day I received a note from Martha that Jones had been taken ill and that Doctor Magiot feared complications. She was nursing him herself and couldn't at the moment leave the embassy. It was a note written for other people to read, a note to leave about, and yet it chilled me. Surely between the lines it would have been possible for her to have indicated some unobtrusive sign of love. The danger was not all Jones's, it was mine as well, but all the comfort of her presence these last days was to belong to him. I pictured her sitting on his bed, while he made her laugh as he had made Tin Tin laugh in the stable at Mère Catherine's. Saturday came and passed, then Sunday began its long course. I was impatient to be finished.

On Sunday afternoon, as I was reading on the verandah, Captain Concasseur drove up in a jeep—I envied him the jeep. The driver who had been assigned to Jones, with the big belly and the gold teeth, sat beside him wearing a fixed grin like an ape being delivered at a zoo. Concasseur didn't get out; they both stared at me through their black glasses, and I stared at them in return, but they had the advantage—I couldn't see them blink.

After a long time Concasseur said, "I hear you're going to Les Cayes."

"Yes."

"Which day?"

"Tomorrow—I hope."

"Your pass is for a short trip only."

"I know that."

"A day to go and a day to return and one night at Les Cayes."

"I know."

"Your business must be very important to take you on such an uncomfortable journey."

"I told my business at the police-station."

"Philipot is in the mountains near Les Cayes and your man Joseph too."

"You know more than I do. But it's your job."

"You are alone here now?"

"Yes."

"No presidential candidate. No Madame Smith. Even your chargé is on leave. You are very isolated here. Are you frightened sometimes at night?"

"I'm getting used to it by now."

"We'll be watching for you along the road, noting your arrival at each post. You will have to account to us for your time." He said something to his chauffeur and the man laughed. "I said to him that he or I will ask you questions if you linger on the road."

"Just as you questioned Joseph?"

"Yes. Exactly in the same way. How is Major Jones?"

"Not well at all. He has caught mumps from the ambassador's son."

"They say there will be a new ambassador soon. The right of asylum ought not to be abused. Major Jones would be well advised to move to the British embassy."

"Shall I tell him that you'll give him a safe-conduct?"

"Yes."

"I'll tell him when he's better. I'm not sure I've had mumps and I don't want to take any risks."

"We can still be friends, Monsieur Brown. I feel certain you do not like Major Jones any more than I do."

"You may be right. Anyway I'll give him the message."

Concasseur backed the jeep into the bougainvillaea, breaking branches with the same pleasure he felt in breaking limbs, turned, and drove away. His visit was the only thing that interrupted the monotony of the long Sunday. For once the lights were turned out exactly on time, and the storm poured down the flanks of Kenscoff as though started by a stop-watch; I tried to read in a paper-back volume of his short stories Henry James's *Great Good Place*, which someone long ago had left behind; I wanted to forget that tomorrow was Monday, but I failed. "The wild waters of our horrible times," James had written, and I wondered what temporary break in the long enviable Victorian peace had so disturbed him. Had his butler given notice? I had built my life around this hotel—it represented stability more profoundly than the God whom the fathers of the Visitation had hoped I would serve; once it had represented success better than my travelling art-gallery with the phoney paintings; it was in a sense a family tomb. I put *The Great Good Place* down and went upstairs with a lamp. I thought it possible—if things went wrong—that this might be the last night I would spend in the Hotel Trianon.

On the stairs most of the paintings had been sold or returned to their owners. My mother had the wisdom in her early days in Haiti to buy a Hyppolite, and I had kept it against all American officers, through the good and the bad years, as an insurance-policy. There remained too a Benoit that represented the great hurricane Hazel of 1954, a grey river in flood carrying down all kinds of strangely chosen objects, a dead pig floating on its back, a chair, the head of a horse, and a bedstead with floral decorations, while a soldier and a priest prayed on the bank and the gale beat the trees all one way. On the first landing there was a picture by Phillippe Auguste of a carnival procession, men, women and children wearing bright masks. Of a morning, when the sunlight shone through the first-floor windows, the harsh colours gave an impression of gaiety, the drummers and the trumpeters seemed about to play a lively air. Only when you came closer you saw how ugly the masks were and how the masquers surrounded a cadaver in grave-clothes; then the primitive colours went flat as though the clouds had come down from Kenscoff and the thunder would soon follow. Wherever that picture hung, I thought, I would feel Haiti close to me. Baron Samedi would be walking in the nearest grave-yard, even though the nearest graveyard was in Tooting Bec.

I went up first to the John Barrymore suite. When I looked out of the window I could see nothing; the city was in darkness, except for a cluster of lights in the palace and a line of lamps which marked the port. I noticed Mr. Smith had left a vege-tarian handbook by the bed. I wondered how many he carried with him for distribution. I opened it and found on the flyleaf a message written in his clear slanting American hand. "Dear Unknown Reader, do not close this Book, but read a little before you sleep. There is Wisdom here. Your Unknown Friend." I envied him his assurance, yes and the purity of his intention too. The capital initials gave the same impression as a Gideon Bible.

On the floor below was my mother's room (I slept there now), and among the closed guest-rooms, which had known no visitors for a long time, were Marcel's room and the one in which I had lain that first night in Port-au-Prince. I remem-bered the clanging bell and the great black figure in the scarlet pyjamas and the monogram on the pocket and how he had said to me sadly and apologetically, "She wants me."

I went into the two rooms in turn: they contained nothing of that remote past. I had changed the furniture, I had painted the walls, I had even altered their shapes, so that bathrooms could be added. Dust lay thick on the porcelain of the bidets and the hot-water taps ran no longer. I went into my room and sat down on the big bed which had been my mother's. I almost expected, even after all the intervening years, to find a thread on the pillows of that impossibly Titian hair. But nothing survived of her except what I had deliberately chosen to keep. On a table by the bed was a *papier mâché* box in which my mother had stored some improbable jewelry. The jewelry I had sold to

Hamit for next to nothing, and the box now contained only that mysterious medal of the resistance and the picture-postcard of the ruined citadel which carried the only writing I had of hers addressed to me—"Nice to see you if you come this way" and the signature that I had taken for Manon and the name she had never had the time to explain to me, "Comtesse de Lascot-Villiers." There was also another message in the box written in her hand but not to me. I had found it in Marcel's pocket when I cut him down. I don't know why I preserved it, or why two or three times I had reread it, for it only deepened my sense of being without parentage. "Marcel, I know I'm an old woman and as you say a bit of an actress. But please go on pretending. As long as we pretend we escape. Pretend that I love you like a mistress. Pretend that you love me like a lover. Pretend that I would die for you and that you would die for me." I read the message again now; I thought it movingly phrased . . . And he had died for her, so perhaps he was no *comédien* after all. Death is a proof of sincerity.

2

Martha greeted me with a glass of whisky in her hand. She was wearing a gold linen dress and her shoulders were bare. She said, "Luis is out. I was taking a drink to Jones."

"I'll take it up for you," I said. "He'll need it."

"You haven't come for him?" she asked.

"Oh yes, I have. The rain is just beginning. We'll have to give it a little while longer until the guards take shelter . . ."

"What earthly use will he be? Out there?"

"A great deal if all he says is true. It only needed one man in Cuba . . ."

"How often I've heard that. It's a parrot-phrase. I'm sick of it. This is not Cuba."

"It will be easier for you and me when he's gone."

"Is that all you think about?"

"Yes. I suppose it is."

She had a small bruise just below the shoulder-bone. Trying to make the question sound like a joke, I said, "What have you been doing to yourself?"

"What do you mean?"

"That bruise." I touched it with my finger.

"Oh that? I don't know. I bruise easily."

"At gin-rummy?"

She put the glass down and turned her back. She said, "Give yourself a drink. You will need it too."

I said, as I poured myself a whisky, "I'll be back on Wednesday by one if I leave Les Cayes at dawn. Will you come up to the hotel? Angel will be at school."

"Perhaps. Let's wait and see."

"We haven't been together for several days." I added, "There'll be no gin-rummy to take you home early." She turned back to me, and I saw she was crying. "What's the matter?" I asked.

"I told you. I bruise easily."

"What have I said?" Fear has strange effects: it releases adrenalin into the blood: it makes a man wet his trousers: in me it injected a desire to hurt. I said, "You seem upset at losing Jones?"

"Why shouldn't I be?" she said. "You think you're lonely up there at the Trianon. Well I'm lonely here. I'm lonely with Luis, silent in a twin bed. I'm lonely with Angel, doing his interminable sums for him when he comes back from school. Yes, I've been happy having Jones here—hearing people laugh at his bad jokes, playing gin-rummy with him. Yes, I'll miss him. I'll miss him till it hurts. How I'll miss him."

"More than you missed me when I went to New York?"

"You were coming back. At least you said you were. I'm not sure now whether you ever did."

I took the two glasses of whisky and went upstairs. On the landing I realized I didn't know which was Jones's room. I called softly, so that the servants shouldn't hear me, "Jones. Jones."

"I'm here."

I pushed a door open and went in. He sat on his bed fully dressed: he had even put on his gumboots. "I heard your voice," he said, "down below. Tonight's the night, old man?"

"Yes. You'd better drink this."

"I can do with it." He gave a sour grimace.

"I've got a bottle in the car."

He said, "I've done my packing. Luis has lent me a kitbag." He ran over the items on his fingers to check them: "Change of shoes, change of pants. Two pairs of socks. Change of shirt. Oh, and the cocktail-shaker. That's for luck. You see it was given me . . ." He stopped abruptly. Perhaps he remembered he had told me the truth of *that* story.

"You don't seem to anticipate a long campaign," I said to help him out.

"I mustn't carry more than my men. Give me time, and I'll have our supplies organized." For the first time he sounded professional, and I wondered whether perhaps I had maligned him. "You can help us there, old man. When I've got a courier-system working properly."

"Let's think of the next few hours. We have to get through them."

"I've a lot to thank you for." Again his words surprised me. "It's a big chance for me, isn't it. Of course I'm scared to hell. There's no denying that."

We sat in silence side by side, drinking our whiskies, listening to the thunder which shook the roof. I had been so certain Jones would resist when the moment came that I felt a little at a loss what to do next, and it was Jones who took command. "We'd better get cracking if we're to be out of here before the storm's over. I'll say goodbye, if you'll excuse me, to my lovely hostess."

When he came back he had a trace of lipstick at the corner of his mouth: an awkward embrace on the mouth or an awkward embrace on the cheek—it was hard to tell which. He said,

"The police are safe in the kitchen drinking rum. We'd better be off."

Martha unbolted the front door for us. "You go first," I said to Jones, trying to re-establish command. "Stoop down below the windscreen if you can."

We were both wet through the moment after we emerged. I turned to say goodbye to Martha, but even then I couldn't resist the question, "Are you still crying?"

"No," she said, "it's the rain," and I could see she spoke the truth. The rain ran down her face as it ran down the wall behind her. "What are you waiting for?"

"Don't I rate a kiss as much as Jones?" I said, and she put her mouth against my cheek: I could feel the listless indifference of the embrace. I said accusingly, "I'm running a bit of danger too."

"But I don't like your motive," she said.

It was as though somebody I hated spoke from my mouth before I could silence him. "Have you slept with Jones?" I regretted the question even before the last word was said. If the heavy peal of thunder which followed had drowned it I would have been content, I would never have repeated it. She stood flat against the door as though she were facing a firing squad, and I thought for some reason of her father before his execution. Had he flung a defiance at his judges from the scaffold? Had he worn an expression of anger and disdain?

"You've been asking me that for weeks," she said, "every time I've seen you. All right then. The answer's yes, yes. That's what you want me to say, isn't it? Yes. I've slept with Jones." The worst thing was I only half believed her.

3

There were no lights in Mère Catherine's as we passed the turning to her brothel and took the southern highway, or else we couldn't see them through the rain. I drove at about twenty miles an hour; I felt like a man blindfolded, and this was the easy part of the road. It had been constructed with the help of American engineers in the much advertised five-year plan, but the Americans had gone home and the metalled road ceased about seven miles out of Port-au-Prince. This was where I expected a road-block, but I was startled when my headlamps picked up an empty jeep outside a militiaman's hut, which meant the Tontons Macoute were there as well. I had little time to accelerate, but no one came from the hut—if the Tontons were inside, they were keeping dry too. I listened for the sound of pursuit, but all I could hear was the drumming of the rain. The great highway had become no more than a country-track: our speed went down to eight miles an hour as we bumped from rock to rock and splashed through standing pools. For more than an hour we drove in silence too shaken about to speak.

A rock crashed under the car and I thought for a moment an axle was broken. Jones said, "Can I find your whisky?"

When he had found it he took a swill and handed the bottle to me. The car because of my momentary inattention skidded sideways and the rear-wheels stuck in wet laterite. It took us twenty minutes' hard labour before we moved again. "Shall we make your rendezvous on time?" Jones asked.

"I doubt it. You may have to keep under cover till tomorrow night. I brought you some sandwiches in case."

He chuckled. "It's the life," he said. "I've often dreamt of something like this."

"I thought it was the life you'd always led."

He fell silent again as though aware of an indiscretion.

Suddenly for no reason at all the road improved. The rain was easing rapidly; I hoped it wouldn't stop altogether before we passed the next police-post. Afterwards there was no problem before the cemetery this side of Aquin. I said, "And Martha? How did you get on with Martha?"

"She's a wonderful girl," he said with caution.

"I got the impression she was fond of you."

It was a bad sign of the weather clearing that sometimes I

276

could detect a streak of sea between the palms like the flash of a match. Jones said, "We got on like a house on fire."

"I sometimes envied you, but perhaps she's not your type." It was like stripping a bandage from a wound: the more slowly I pulled the longer the pain would last, but I lacked the courage to rip the bandage right away, and all the time I had to watch the difficult road.

"Old man," Jones said, "every girl's my type, but she was something special."

"You know she's German?"

"The fräuleins understand a thing or two."

"As well as Tin Tin?" I tried to ask in a casual clinical way.

"Tin Tin was not in the same class, old man." We might have been two medical students boasting of rudimentary experiences. I didn't speak again for a long time.

We were approaching Petit Goave—I knew the place from better days. The police-station, I remembered, was off the highway, and I would be supposed to drive there to report. I hoped the rain was still heavy enough to keep the police in their quarters—they were unlikely to have militia posted here. Dank huts wobbled in the headlights beside the road, the mud and thatch broken and bedraggled in the rain: no lamps burned, there was no human being to be seen, not even a cripple. In the small yards the family-tombs looked more solid than the family-huts. The dead were allotted mansions of a better class than the living—houses of two storeys with window-embrasures where food and lights could be placed on the night of All Souls. I couldn't let my attention wander until we had passed Petit Goave, and I was afraid in any case of my next question—I had reached the door and I could delay no longer—I had to push it open. In a long yard beside the road there were rows of little crosses with what looked like tresses of blonde hair looped between, as though they had been ripped from the skulls of women buried below.

"Good God," Jones said, "what was that?"

"Only sisal drying."

"Drying? In this rain?"

"Who knows what's happened to the owner? Perhaps he's shot. In prison. Fled to the mountains."

"It was a bit eery, old man. Sort of Edgar Allan Poe. It looked more like death than the cemeteries do."

Nobody was about in the main street of Petit Goave. We passed something called the Yo-Yo Club and a big sign for Mère Merlan's Brasseries and a *boulangerie* belonging to someone called Brutus and a garage owned by Cato—so the stubborn memories of this black people preserved the memories of a better republic—and then to my relief we were in the country again, tossing from rock to rock. "We've made it," I said.

"Nearly there?"

"We're nearly half way."

"I think I'll take another drop of whisky, old man."

"Drink what you like. You'll have to make it last a long time, though."

"I'd better finish it before I join the boys. It wouldn't go far with them."

I took another pull myself to give me courage, and yet I postponed the unambiguous question.

"How did you get on with the husband?" I asked him cautiously.

"Fine. I wasn't stealing any greens of his."

"Weren't you?"

"She doesn't sleep with him any more."

"How do you know?"

"I have my reasons," he said, taking the bottle and sucking at it loudly. The road again required all my attention. Our speed was practically reduced to walking-pace now: I had to thread between the rocks like a pony at a gymkhana.

"We ought to have had a jeep," Jones said.

"Where would you find a jeep in Port-au-Prince? Borrowed it from the Tonton?"

The road branched, and we left the sea behind us and turned

inland, climbing into the hills. The track for a while became plain laterite and there was only the mud to clog our passage. It was a change of exercise. We had been going for three hours—it was close to one in the morning.

"Little danger of militia now," I said.

"But the rain's stopped."

"They're afraid of the hills."

"From which cometh our help," Jones quipped. The whisky was loosening him up. I could wait no longer and I pushed the question home. "Was she a good lay?"

"Re-markable," Jones said, and I clung to the wheel to keep my hands off him. It was a long while before I spoke again, but he noticed nothing. He fell asleep with his mouth open, leaning back against the door where Martha had often leant; he slept as peacefully as a child, innocently. Perhaps he was really as innocent as Mr. Smith, and that was the reason they had liked each other. Anger soon left me: the child had broken a dish, that was all—yes, a dish, I thought, is just how he would have described her. Once he woke for a moment and offered to drive, but I felt enough danger in our situation without that.

And then the car gave out altogether; perhaps my attention had wandered, perhaps it was just waiting for one extra heavy lurch to shake its innards out. The wheel whirled in my hands as I tried to recover the road after bouncing off a rock: we struck hard against another boulder and came to rest, the front-axle cracked in two and one headlamp smashed. There was nothing whatever to be done—I couldn't get to Les Cayes, and I couldn't go back to Port-au-Prince. I was tied for that night anyway to Jones.

Jones opened his eyes and said, "I dreamt . . . why have we stopped? Are we there?"

"The front-axle's bust."

"How far are we, do you suppose, from—there?"

I looked at the mileage and said, "A couple of kilometres I'd say, perhaps three."

"Shank's pony," Jones said. He began to haul his kitbag out

of the car. I put the car-keys in my pocket, I didn't know why—I doubted whether there was a garage in Haiti capable of mending the car, and anyway who would trouble to come down this road to fetch it? The roads around Port-au-Prince were littered with abandoned cars and overturned buses; once I had seen a breakdown van with its crane lying sideways in a ditch— it was like a lifeboat broken on the rocks, a contradiction of nature.

We began to walk. I had brought a torch, but it was very rough-going and Jones's gumboots slithered on the wet laterite. It was after two, and the rain had stopped. "If they are following us," Jones said, "they won't have much difficulty now. We're a bloody advertisement for human existence."

"There's no reason why they should be following us."

"I was thinking of that jeep we passed," he said.

"There was nobody in it."

"We don't know who was in the hut watching us go by."

"Anyway we have no choice. We couldn't walk two yards without a light. On this road we'd hear a car coming a couple of miles away."

When I flashed the torch towards either side of the road there was only rock and earth and low wet scrub. I said, "We mustn't miss the cemetery and walk bang into Aquin. There's a military post in Aquin." I could hear Jones breathing heavily, and I offered to take his kitbag for a spell, but he would have none of it. "I'm a bit out of condition," he said, "that's all," and a little further on he said, "I talked a lot of nonsense in the car. I'm not always exactly trustworthy."

It seemed to me an understatement, but I wondered why he made it.

At last my torch picked out what I was looking for: a cemetery on my right, stretching uphill into the dark. It was like a city built by dwarfs, street after street of tiny houses, some nearly big enough to hold ourselves, some too small for a new-born child, all of the same grey stone, from which the plaster had long flaked. I turned my torch to the other side where I had

280

been told there would be a ruined hut, but mistakes are always made in the plan of a rendezvous. The hut should have been opposite the first corner of the cemetery we came to, standing alone, but there was nothing except a slope of earth.

"The wrong cemetery?" Jones asked.

"It can't be. We must be near Aquin now." We went on down the track and opposite the further corner we did find a hut, but it didn't seem ruined so far as I could tell in the torch-light. There was nothing we could do but try it. If anyone lived there, he would be at least as scared as we were.

"I wish I had a gun," Jones said.

"I'm glad you haven't, but what about your unarmed combat?" He muttered something that sounded like "rusty."

But there was nobody inside when the door opened to my push. A patch of paling night-sky showed through a hole in the roof. "We are two hours late," I said. "He's probably come and gone."

Jones sat on his kitbag and panted. "We should have started earlier."

"How could we? We were timed by the storm."

"What do we do now?"

"When it's light I'll go back to the car. There's nothing compromising in a wrecked car on this road. Some time during the day I know there's a local bus between Petit Goave and Aquin, and perhaps I can hitch a ride on from there, or there may be another bus as far as Les Cayes."

"It sounds simple," Jones said with envy. "But what do I do?"

"Hold out until tomorrow night." I added viciously, "You're in your familiar jungle now." I looked out of the doorway: there was nothing to be seen or heard, not even a barking dog. I said, "I don't like staying here. Suppose we fell asleep—some-one might come. The soldiers must sometimes patrol these roads—or a peasant going to work. He'd inform on us. Why shouldn't he? We are white."

Jones said, "We can keep watch in turn."

"There's a better way. We'll sleep in the cemetery. No one will come there except Baron Samedi."

We crossed the so-called road and clambered over a low stone wall and found ourselves in the street of the miniature town, where the houses were only shoulder-high. We climbed the hillside slowly because of Jones's kitbag. I felt safer in the very middle of the cemetery, and there we found a house higher than ourselves. We put the bottle of whisky in one of the window embrasures and sat down with our backs to a wall. "Oh well," Jones said mechanically, "I've been in worse places." I wondered how bad a place would have to be before he forgot his signature-tune.

"If you see a top-hat among the tombs," I said, "it will be the Baron."

"Do you believe in zombies?" Jones asked.

"I don't know. Do you believe in ghosts?"

"Let's not talk about ghosts, old man, let's have another whisky."

I thought I heard a movement and switched on the torch. It shone the whole length of a street of graves into a cat's eyes, which reflected like Franco studs. It leapt upon a roof and was gone.

"Ought we to show a light, old man?"

"If there was anyone about to see it, he would be too scared to come. You couldn't do better than to dig in here tomorrow" —it was not a happily chosen phrase to use in a cemetery. "I doubt if anyone comes here except to bury the dead." Jones sucked in more whisky, and I warned him, "There's only a quarter of a bottle left. You've got all tomorrow before you."

"Martha filled the shaker for me," he said. "I've never known a girl so thoughtful."

"Or such a good lay?" I asked.

There was a spell of silence—I thought perhaps he was remembering with pleasure the occasions. Then Jones said, "Old man, the game's turned serious now."

"What game?"

"Playing at soldiers. I can understand why people want to confess. Death's a bloody serious affair. A man doesn't feel quite worthy of it. Like a decoration."

"Have you such a lot to confess?"

"We all have. I don't mean to a priest or God."

"To whom?"

"To anyone at all. If I had a dog here tonight instead of you, I'd confess to the dog."

I didn't want his confessions, I didn't want to hear how many times he had slept with Martha. I said, "Did you confess to Midge?"

"There wasn't any occasion. The game hadn't turned serious then."

"A dog at least has to keep your secrets."

"I don't care a damn who tells what, but I don't fancy a lot of lies after I'm dead. I've lied enough before."

I heard the cat come scrambling back over the roofs, and again I turned on my torch and lit the eyes. This time it flattened itself upon a stone and began to scrape its nails. Jones opened his kitbag and pulled out a sandwich. He broke it in half and tossed one half towards the cat, which fled, as though the bread were a stone.

"You'd better be careful," I said. "You're on short rations now."

"The poor devil's hungry." He put the half-sandwich back, and we and the cat were silent a long while. It was Jones who broke the silence with his obstinate obsession. "I'm an awful liar, old man."

"I've always assumed that," I said.

"What I said about Martha—there wasn't a word of truth in it. She's only one of fifty women I haven't had the courage to touch."

I wondered if he was telling the truth now or graduating to a more honorable sort of lie. Perhaps he had detected something in my manner which told him all. Perhaps he pitied me. One could hardly sink lower, I thought, than that—to be pitied by

Joncs. He said, "I've always lied about women." He gave an uneasy laugh. "The moment I had Tin Tin, she became a leading member of the Haitian aristocracy. If there had been anyone around to tell about it. Do you know, old man, I haven't had a single woman in my life I haven't paid—or at least promised to pay. Sometimes I've had to welsh when things were bad."

"Martha told me she'd slept with you."

"She can't have told you that. I don't believe you."

"Oh yes. It was almost the last words she said to me."

"I never realized," he said gloomily.

"Realized what?"

"That she was your girl. Another of my lies has found me out. You mustn't believe her. She was angry because you were going away with me."

"Or angry because I was taking you away."

There was a scrabble in the dark where the cat had found the bit of sandwich. I said, "There's quite a jungle-atmosphere here. You'll feel at home."

I heard him take a pull at the whisky and then he said, "Old man, I've never been in a jungle in my life—unless you count the Calcutta Zoo."

"Were you never in Burma?"

"Oh, yes, I was. Or nearly. Anyway I was only fifty miles from the border. I was at Imphal, in charge of entertaining the troops. Well, not exactly in charge. We had Noel Coward once," he added with pride and a sense of relief—it was something true that he could boast about.

"How did the two of you get on?"

"I didn't actually speak to him," Jones said.

"But you were in the army?"

"No. I was rejected. Flat feet. They found I'd managed a cinema in Shillong, so they gave me this job. I had a uniform of a kind but without badges or rank. I was in liaison," he added with that note of odd pride, "with E.N.S.A."

I flashed my torch around the acre of grey tombs. I said, "Why the hell are we here then?"

"I boasted a bit too much, didn't I?"

"You've let yourself into a nasty situation. Aren't you frightened?"

"I'm like a fireman at his first fire," he said.

"Your flat feet won't enjoy these mountain tracks."

"I can manage with supports," Jones said. "You won't tell them, old man? It was a confession."

"They'll soon find out without my telling them. So you can't even use a Bren?"

"They haven't got a Bren."

"You've spoken too late. I can't smuggle you back."

"I don't want to go back. Old man, you don't know what it was like in Imphal. I used to make friends sometimes—I could introduce them to girls, and then they'd go away and never come back. Or they'd come back once or twice for a yarn. There was a man called Charters who could smell water . . ." He broke off abruptly, remembering.

"Another lie," I said, as though I myself were a man of scrupulous rectitude.

"Not exactly a lie," he said. "You see, when he told me that, it was like someone calling me by my real name."

"Which wasn't Jones?"

"Jones was on my birth-certificate," he said; "I've seen it there myself," and brushed the question aside. "When he told me that, I knew I could do the same with a bit of practice. I knew I had it in me. I made my clerk hide glasses of water in the office and then I'd wait till I had a big thirst and sniff. It didn't work very often, but then tap-water is not the same." He added, "I think I'll ease my feet a bit," and I could tell from his movements that he was pulling off his gumboots.

"How did you come to be in Shillong?" I asked.

"I was born in Assam. My father planted tea—or so my mother said."

"You had to take it on trust?"

"Well, he went home before I was born."

"Your mother was Indian?"

"Half-Indian, old man," he said as though he attributed importance to fractions. It was like meeting an unknown brother—Jones and Brown, the names were almost interchangeable, and so was our status. For all we knew we were both bastards, although of course there might have been a ceremony—my mother had always given me that impression. We had both been thrown into the water to sink or swim, and swim we did—we had swum from very far apart to come together in a cemetery in Haiti. "I like you, Jones," I said. "If you don't want that half a sandwich, I could do with it."

"Of course, old man." He fingered in his kitbag and felt for my hand in the dark.

"Tell me more, Jones," I said.

"I came to Europe," he said, "after the war. I got into a lot of scrapes. Somehow I couldn't find what I was intended to do. You know there had been times in Imphal when I almost wished the Japs would reach us. The authorities would have armed even the camp-followers then, like me and the clerks in N.A.A.F.I. and the cooks. After all I had a uniform. A lot of unprofessionals do well in war, don't they? I've learnt a lot, listening, studying maps, watching . . . You can feel a vocation, can't you, even if you can't practice it? And there I was, checking transport and travel-vouchers for third-class entertainers— Mr. Coward was one of the exceptions—and I had to keep an eye on the girls. I called them girls. Old troupers more like. My office smelt like a stage dressing-room."

"The grease-paint drowned the smell of water?" I said.

"You are right. It wasn't a fair test. I only wanted my chance," he added, and I wondered whether perhaps in all his devious life he had been engaged on a secret and hopeless love-affair with virtue, watching virtue from a distance, hoping to be noticed, perhaps, like a child doing wrong in order to attract the attention of virtue.

"And now you have the chance," I said.

"Thanks to you, old man."

"I thought that what you wanted most was a golf-club . . ."

"That's true. It was my second dream. You have to have two, don't you? In case the first goes wrong."

"Yes. I suppose so." Making money had been my dream also. Had there been another? I had no wish to search so far back.

"You'd better try to sleep a while," I said. "It won't be safe to sleep in daylight."

And sleep he did, almost at once, curled up like an embryo below the tomb. That was one quality he shared with Napoleon, and I wondered whether perhaps there might be others. Once he opened his eyes and remarked that this was "a good place" and then slept again. I could see nothing good in it, but in the end I slept as well.

After a couple of hours something woke me. I imagined for a moment it was the noise of a car, but I thought it unlikely that a car would be out on the road so early, and the wreck of a dream stayed with me and accounted for the noise—I had been driving my car across a river on a bed of boulders. I lay still and listened with my eyes watching the grey early sky. I could see the shapes of the tombs standing around. Soon the sun would be up. It was time to get back to the car. When I was sure of the silence I woke Jones.

"You'd better not sleep again now," I said.

"I'll walk a little way with you."

"Oh no, you won't. For my sake. You must keep away from the road until it's dark. The peasants will be going to market soon. They'll report any white man they see."

"Then they'll report you."

"I have my alibi. A smashed car on the road to Les Cayes. You'll have to keep company with the cat till dark. Then go to the hut and wait for Philipot."

Jones insisted on shaking hands. In the reasonable light of day the affection which I had felt for him was leaking rapidly away. I thought again of Martha, and as though he were half-aware of my thoughts, he said, "Give my love to Martha when you see her. Luis and Angel too, of course."

"And Midge?"

"It was good," he said. "It was like being in a family."

I walked down a long street of graves towards the road. I was not born for the *maquis*—I took no precautions. I thought: Martha had no reason to lie, or had she? Opposite the wall of the cemetery stood a jeep, but the sight of it for a moment didn't change the current of my thoughts. Then I stopped and stood waiting. It was too dark yet to see who was at the wheel, but I knew very well what was going to happen next.

The voice of Concasseur whispered, "Stay just there. Quite still. Don't move." He got out of the jeep, followed by the fat chauffeur with the gold teeth. Even in the half light he wore the black spectacles which were his only uniform. A tommy-gun of ancient make was pointed at my chest. "Where is Major Jones?" Concasseur whispered.

"Jones?" I said as loudly as I dared. "How would I know? My car broke down. I have a pass to Les Cayes. As you know."

"Speak quietly. I am taking you and Major Jones back to Port-au-Prince. Alive, I hope. The President would prefer that. I have to make my peace with the President."

"You're being absurd. You must have seen my car by the road. I was on the way . . ."

"Oh yes, I saw it. I was expecting to see it." The tommy-gun twisted in his hands and pointed away somewhere to my left. There was no advantage to me in that—the chauffeur had his gun covering me too. "Come forward," Concasseur said. I made a step forward, and he said, "Not you. Major Jones." I turned and saw Jones was standing there behind me. He held what was left of the whisky in his hand.

I said, "You bloody fool. Why didn't you stay put?"

"I'm sorry. I thought perhaps you might need the whisky waiting."

"Get into the jeep," Concasseur said to me. I obeyed. He went up to Jones and struck him in the face. "You cheat," he said.

"There was enough in it for both of us," Jones said, and Concasseur hit him again. The chauffeur stood and watched. There was enough light to see the wink of his gold teeth as he grinned.

"Get in beside your friend," Concasseur said. While the chauffeur held us covered, he turned and began to walk towards the jeep.

A noise, if it is loud and close enough, almost escapes the hearing: I felt a vibration in my ear-drums rather than heard the explosion. I saw Concasseur knocked backwards as though struck by an invisible fist: the chauffeur pitched upon his face: a scrap of the cemetery wall leapt in the air and dropped, a long time afterwards, with a small ping in the road. Philipot came out of the hut and Joseph limped after him. They carried tommy-guns of the same ancient make. Concasseur's black glasses lay in the road. Philipot ground them to pieces under his heel and the body showed no resentment. Philipot said, "I left the driver for Joseph."

Joseph was bending down over the driver and working on his teeth. "We've got to move quickly," Philipot said. "They'll have heard the shots in Aquin. Where is Major Jones?"

Joseph said, "He went into the cemetery."

"He must be fetching his kitbag," I said.

"Tell him to hurry."

I walked up between the little grey houses to the spot where we had passed the night. Jones was there, kneeling beside the tomb in the attitude of prayer, but the face he turned to me was olive-green with sickness. He had vomited on the ground. He said, "I'm sorry, old man. One of those things. Please don't tell them, but I've never seen a man die before."

Chapter Four

1

I drove along many kilometres of wire-fencing to find a gate. Mr. Fernandez had procured for me in Santo Domingo a small sports car at a cut-rate, perhaps a too flippant car for my errand, and I had a personal introduction from Mr. Smith. I had left Santo Domingo in the afternoon and now it was sunset; there were no road-blocks in those days in the Dominican Republic and all was peace—there was no military junta and the American Marines had not yet landed. For half the distance I followed a wide highway where cars went by me at a hundred miles an hour. The sense of peace was very real after the violence of Haiti, which seemed more than a few hundred kilometres away. Nobody stopped me to examine my papers.

I came to a gate in the fence, which was locked. A Negro in a steel helmet and blue dungarees asked my business from the other side of the wire. I told him I had come to see Mr. Schuyler Wilson.

"Let me see your pass," he demanded, and I felt as though I were back where I had come from.

"He expects me."

The Negro went to a hut and I saw him telephoning (I had almost forgotten that telephones worked). Then he opened the gate and gave me a badge which he said I was to wear so long as I was on the mining-estate. I could drive as far as the next barrier. I drove a good many miles beside the flat blue Caribbean sea. I passed a small landing-ground with a wind-stocking blowing towards Haiti and then a harbour empty of boats. The red bauxite dust lay everywhere. I came to another barrier closing the road and another Negro in a tin hat. He examined my badge and took my name again and my business and telephoned. Then he told me to wait where I was. Someone would come for me. I waited ten minutes.

"Is this the Pentagon," I asked him, "or the headquarters of the C.I.A.?" He wouldn't speak to me. He probably had orders not to speak. I was glad he didn't carry a gun. Then a motorcycle arrived driven by a white man in a tin helmet. He spoke practically no English and I knew no Spanish; he indicated I was to follow his motor-cycle. We drove on for a few kilometres more of red earth and blue sea before we reached the first administrative buildings, rectangular blocks of cement and glass with no one in sight. Further on was a luxurious trailer-park where children played with space-uniforms and space-guns. Women looked out of windows over kitchen-stoves, and there was a smell of cooking. At last before a great glass building we came to a halt. There was a flight of steps wide enough for a parliament and a terrace with lounging-chairs. A large fat man with an anonymous face shaved as smooth as marble stood at the top. He might have been a city mayor waiting to deliver a freedom.

"Mr. Brown?"

"Mr. Schuyler Wilson?"

He looked at me in a surly way. Perhaps I had pronounced his first name wrong. Perhaps he disliked my sports car. He said grudgingly, "Have a Coke," and gestured towards one of the lounging-chairs.

"If you could spare a whisky?"

He said without enthusiasm, "I'll see what we can do," and walked into the great glass building leaving me alone. I felt I had chalked up a black mark. Perhaps only visiting directors or leading politicians got whisky. I was only a potential catering-manager, seeking a job. However he brought the whisky, carrying a Coke in his other hand like a reproach.

"Mr. Smith wrote to you about me," I said. I just stopped myself from saying the Presidential Candidate.

"Yes. Where did you two meet?"

"He stayed at my hotel in Port-au-Prince."

"That's right." It was as though he were double-checking the facts to see if one of us had lied. "You're not a vegetarian?"

"No."

"Because the boys here like their steak and french fries." I drank a little of the whisky, which was drowned in soda. Mr. Schuyler Wilson watched me closely as though he begrudged me every drop. I felt more and more that the job would not come my way.

"What's your experience in catering?"

"Well, I owned this hotel in Haiti until a month ago. I've worked too at the Trocadero in London—" and I added the ancient lie, "Fouquet's in Paris."

"Got any testimonials?"

"I could hardly write my own, could I? I've been my own employer a good many years now."

"Your Mr. Smith's a bit of a crank, isn't he?"

"I like him."

"Did his wife tell you he ran for president once? On the vegetarian ticket." Mr. Schuyler Wilson laughed. It was an angry laugh without amusement, like the menace of a hidden beast.

"I suppose it was a form of propaganda."

"I don't like propaganda. We've had leaflets here pushed under the wire. Trying to get at the men. We pay them well. We feed them well. What made you leave Haiti?"

"Trouble with the authorities. I helped an Englishman to escape from Port-au-Prince. The Tontons Macoute were after him."

"What's the Tontons Macoute?"

We were less than three hundred kilometres from Port-au-Prince; it seemed strange he could ask me that, but I suppose

292

there hadn't been a story for a long time in any newspaper he read.

"The secret police," I said.

"How did *you* get out?"

"His friends helped me across the border." It was a brief enough statement to cover two weeks of fatigue and frustration.

"Who do you mean—his friends?"

"The insurgents."

"You mean the Communists?" He was cross-examining me as though I had applied for a job as agent in the C.I.A. and not as catering-manager for a mining-company. I lost my temper a little. I said, "Insurgents are not always Communists until you make them so."

My irritation amused Mr. Schuyler Wilson. He smiled for the first time; it was a smile of self-satisfaction as though he had uncovered by adroit questioning something I had wanted to keep secret.

"You're quite an expert," he said.

"An expert?"

"I mean owning your own hotel, working at that place you mentioned in Paris. I guess you wouldn't be very happy here. Just plain American cooking is all we need." He got up to show me that the interview was over. I finished my whisky while he watched me with impatience, and then, "Glad to have met you," he said without shaking hands. "Give up your badge at the second gate."

I drove away past the private landing-ground and the private port. I handed over my badge; I was reminded of the entry-permit you leave with immigration at Idlewild.

2

I drove to the Ambassador Hotel on the outskirts of Santo Domingo where Mr. Smith was staying. It wasn't the right set-

293

ting for him, or so it seemed to me. I had become accustomed to the stooping figure, the mild and modest face and the wild white hair, in surroundings of poverty. In this wide glittering hall men sat wearing purses on their belts instead of revolver-holsters, and when they wore dark glasses it was only to save their eyes from the bright light. There was a continuous rattle from the one-armed bandits and you could hear the calls from the croupier in the casino. Everyone had money here, even Mr. Smith. Poverty was out of sight, down in the city. A girl in a bikini wearing a gay bathrobe came in from the swimming-pool. She asked at the desk whether a Mr. Hochstrudel, Junior, had arrived yet. "I mean Mr. Wilbur K. Hochstrudel." The clerk said, "No, but Mr. Hochstrudel is expected."

I sent a message to Mr. Smith that I was below and found myself a seat. At the table nearest me the men were drinking rum-punches and I thought of Joseph's. He made better ones than they served here, and I missed him.

I had stayed only twenty-four hours with Philipot. He was polite enough to me in a restrained way, but he was a changed man from the one I used to know. I had been a good audience in the past for his Baudelairean verses, but I was too old for war. It was Jones he needed now and Jones's company which he sought. He had nine men with him in his hide-out and to hear him talking to Jones you would have imagined he commanded at least a battalion. Jones very wisely listened and didn't speak much, but once I woke, during the night I spent with them, and heard Jones say, "You have to establish yourself. Near enough to the frontier for newspapermen to come over. Then you can demand recognition." Were they really, in this hole among the rocks (and they changed their hole, I learnt, each day) already thinking in terms of a provisional government? They had with them three old tommy-guns from the police-station—which had probably seen service first in the days of Al Capone, a couple of first-war rifles, a shotgun, two revolvers, and one man had nothing better than his machete. Jones added like an old hand, "This kind of war is a bit like a

confidence-trick. There was one way we deceived the Japs . . ."
He hadn't found his golf-course, but I really believe he was
happy. The men clustered close; they couldn't understand a
word he said, but it was as though a leader had come into the
camp.

Next day I was sent off with Joseph as my guide to try to
cross the Dominican frontier. My car and the bodies had been
long discovered by now, and there was no safety for me anywhere in Haiti. They could spare Joseph easily because of his
damaged hip, and he could fulfil at the same time a second
function. Philipot planned that I was to slip over the international road, which divided the two republics for about fifty
kilometres north of Banica. It was true that, every few kilometres on either side of the road, there were Haitian and
Dominican guard-posts, but it was said, with what truth he
wanted to find out, that the posts on the Haitian side were
deserted at night for fear of a guerrilla-attack. All peasants had
been expelled from the border, but there was said to be still that
party of about thirty men operating in the mountains with
which Philipot wanted to make contact. Joseph's information
would be of value if he got back, and he was more expendable
than the others. I suppose, too, his lame walk was considered
slow enough to enable a man of my age to keep up with him.
The last words Jones said to me in private were, "I'm going to
keep it up, old man."

"And the golf-club?"

"The golf-club's for old age. After we've taken Port-au-
Prince."

The journey was slow, rough, and tiring and took us eleven
days, nine days of lying up, of sudden dashes from one point to
another, of doubling on our tracks, and finally two last days of
imprudence because of hunger. I was glad enough when we
came in sight at dusk, from our grey eroded mountain where
nothing grew, of the deep Dominican forest. You could see all
the twists of the frontier by the contrast between our bare rocks
and their vegetation. It was the same mountain range, but the

trees never crossed into the poor dry land of Haiti. Half way down the slope was a Haitian guard-post—a collection of decrepit huts—and across the way a hundred yards from it was a castellated fort, like something from the Spanish Sahara. A little before dusk we saw the Haitian guards straggle out, leaving not one sentinel behind. We watched them go to god knows what hide-out (there were no roads or villages where they could escape the pitiless rock), then I said goodbye to Joseph, making some silly joke about rum-punch, and scrambled down the track of a meagre stream onto the international road—a grand name for a track little better than the great southern highway to Les Cayes. Next morning the Dominicans put me on an army-truck which came daily to the fort with supplies, and I landed in Santo Domingo in torn and dusty clothes, with a hundred unchangeable gourdes in my pocket and fifty American dollars comprised in a single note which I had sewn for safety into the lining of my pants. With the help of that note I took a room and a bath and cleaned myself up and slept for twelve hours before I went to beg for money at the British consulate and for expatriation—to where?

It was Mr. Smith who saved me from that humiliation. He happened to be driving by in Mr. Fernandez' car and he saw me on the street as I tried to ask my way to the consulate from a Negro who only spoke Spanish. I wanted Mr. Smith to drop me at the consulate, but he would have none of it; all such matters, he said, could wait till after lunch, and when lunch was over he told me it was quite out of the question to borrow money from an unsympathetic consul since he, Mr. Smith, was there with plenty of American Express dollars. "Think what I owe you," he said, but I could think of nothing that he owed me. He had paid his bill at the Hotel Trianon. He had even supplied his own Yeastrol. He appealed against me to Mr. Fernandez and Mr. Fernandez said, "Yes," and Mrs. Smith remarked angrily that, if I thought her husband was the kind of man to let a friend down, then I should have been with them that day in Nashville . . . Waiting for him now, I thought what a continent of difference divided him from Mr. Schuyler Wilson.

He was alone when he joined me in the lounge of the Ambassador. He apologized for the absence of Mrs. Smith, who was taking her third lesson in Spanish from Mr. Fernandez. "You should hear the two of them talking away together," he said. "Mrs. Smith has a remarkable talent for languages."

I told him how I had been received by Mr. Schuyler Wilson. "He assumed I was a Communist," I said.

"Why?"

"Because the Tontons were after me. Papa Doc, you remember, is a bulwark against communism. And insurgent, of course, is a dirty word. I wonder how President Johnson would deal now with something like the French resistance. That too was infiltrated (another dirty word) by the Communists. My mother was an insurgent—lucky I didn't tell Mr. Schuyler Wilson that."

"I don't see what harm a Communist could do as a catering-manager." Mr. Smith looked at me with an expression of sadness. He said, "It's not at all pleasant to feel ashamed of a fellow-countryman."

"You must have experienced it often enough in Nashville."

"That was different. There it was a disease, a fever. I could be sorry for them. In my state we still have a tradition of hospitality. When a man knocks on the door we don't ask him about his politics."

"I'd hoped to be able to pay you back your loan."

"I'm not a poor man, Mr. Brown. There's plenty more where that came from. I suggest you take another thousand dollars now."

"How can I? I have no security to offer you."

"If that's what's worrying you, we'll draw up a paper—quite fair and legal, and I'll take a mortgage on your hotel. After all it's a fine property."

"It's not worth a nickel now, Mr. Smith. The government has probably taken it over."

"Things will change one day."

"I've heard of another job in the north. Near Monte Cristi. As canteen-manager for a fruit company."

"You don't have to fall as low as that, Mr. Brown."

"I've fallen a lot lower than that in my time and less respectably. If you don't mind my using your name again . . . This is an American company too."

"Mr. Fernandez was telling me that he needs an Anglo-Saxon partner. It's a fine prosperous little business he has here."

"I've never thought of becoming an undertaker."

"It's a valuable social service, Mr. Brown. And there's security too. No business recessions."

"I'll try the canteen first. I've more experience there. If that fails who knows . . . ?"

"Did you know Mrs. Pineda was in town?"

"Mrs. Pineda?"

"That charming lady who came up to the hotel. Surely you remember her?"

For a moment I really hadn't known whom he meant. "What's she doing in Santo Domingo?"

"Her husband has been transferred to Lima. She's staying a few days here at her embassy with her little boy. I forget his name."

"Angel."

"That's right. A fine boy. Mrs. Smith and I are very fond of children. Perhaps because we never had any of our own. Mrs. Pineda was glad to hear you'd come out of Haiti in one piece, but she was naturally anxious about Major Jones. I thought we might all have a little dinner together tomorrow night and you could tell her the story."

"I'm planning to go north tomorrow early," I said. "Jobs can't wait. I've been hanging around here long enough. Tell her I'll write to her all I know about Jones."

3

I had a jeep to withstand the road on this occasion, arranged for me again at a cut-price by Mr. Fernandez. Nevertheless I was not to reach Monte Cristi and the banana-plantations, and I shall never know whether I would have proved acceptable as a canteen-manager. I set off at six in the morning and reached San Juan by breakfast-time. There was a good road as far as Elias Pinas, but then along the frontier, perhaps because there was no traffic except the daily bus and a few military *camions*, the international road was more suitable for mules and cows. I had reached the military post of Pedro Santana when I was stopped—I didn't understand why. The lieutenant, whom I knew by sight because I had met him a month ago when I came over the frontier, was busy talking to a fat man in city-clothes; he was being shown a lot of glittering junk-jewelry, necklaces, bracelets, watches, rings—the frontier was a happy hunting-ground for smugglers. Money changed hands and the lieutenant came to my jeep.

"What's wrong?" I asked.

"Wrong? Nothing is wrong." He spoke French as well as I did.

"Your men won't let me go on."

"It's for your own safety. There's a lot of firing on the other side of the international road. Wild firing. I've seen you before, haven't I?"

"I came across the road a month ago."

"Yes. I remember now. I daresay we shall be seeing some more people like you presently."

"Do you often get refugees here?"

"We had about twenty guerrillas over just after you came. They are in a camp now in Santo Domingo. I thought there were none left."

He must have meant the band which Philipot had wanted to contact. I remembered Jones and Philipot talking in the night, while the men listened, of the great plans for an established strongpoint, for a provisional government, for visiting journalists.

"I want to get up to Monte Cristi before dark."

"You would do better to go back to Elias Pinas."

"No, I'll wait around if you don't mind."

"You are welcome."

I had a bottle of whisky in my car and I made myself more welcome. The man selling jewelry tried to interest me in some ear-rings which he said were sapphire and diamond. Presently he drove away in the direction of Elias Pinas. He had sold the lieutenant a watch and the sergeant two necklaces.

"For the same woman?" I asked the sergeant.

"For my wife," he said and closed one eye.

It was high noon. I sat on the steps of the guardroom in the shade and considered what I should do if the fruit-company turned me down. There was always Mr. Fernandez' offer; I wondered whether I would have to wear a black suit.

Perhaps there is an advantage in being born in a city like Monte Carlo, without roots, for one accepts more easily what comes. The rootless have experienced, like all the others, the temptation of sharing the security of a religious creed or a political faith, and for some reason we have turned the temptation down. We are the faithless; we admire the dedicated, the Doctor Magiots and the Mr. Smiths, for their courage and their integrity, for their fidelity to a cause, but through timidity, or through lack of sufficient zest, we find ourselves the only ones truly committed—committed to the whole world of evil and of good, to the wise and to the foolish, to the indifferent and to the mistaken. We have chosen nothing except to go on living, "rolled round on Earth's diurnal course, With rocks and stones and trees."

The argument interested me; I daresay it eased the never quiet conscience which had been injected into me without my consent, when I was too young to know, by the fathers of the Visitation. Then the sun came round onto the steps and drove me into the guardhouse with its bunks like stretchers, its pinups and relics of many homes, its heavy airless smell. There the lieutenant came to find me. He said, "You'll be able to go on soon now. They are coming in."

Some Dominican soldiers were plodding up the road to the post, walking in single file so as to keep in the shade of the trees. They bore their rifles slung and carried in their hands the weapons of the men who had emerged from the Haitian hills and who walked a few paces behind them, limp with fatigue, wearing an abashed look on their faces like the expression of children who have broken something of value. I didn't recognize any of the Negroes, but nearly at the tail of the little column I saw Philipot. He was naked to the waist and he had used his shirt to tie his right arm to his side. When he saw me he said defiantly, "We had no ammunition left," but I don't think he recognized me then—he saw only what he thought was an accusing white face. At the very end of the small column two men carried a stretcher. On it lay Joseph. His eyes were open, but he couldn't see the foreign country into which they were carrying him.

One of the men asked, "Do you know him?"

"Yes," I said. "He used to make good rum-punches."

The two men looked at me with disapproval; I realized it was not the kind of speech one should make over the dead, Mr. Fernandez would have done better, and I followed after the stretcher in silence like a mourner.

Somebody had given Philipot a chair inside the guardhouse and a cigarette. The lieutenant was explaining to him that they had no transport until next day and that they had no doctor in the post.

"It's only a broken arm," Philipot said. "I fell coming down the ravine. It's nothing at all. I can wait."

The lieutenant said with kindness, "We have made a comfortable camp for your people near Santo Domingo. In an old lunatic-asylum . . ."

Philipot began to laugh—"A lunatic-asylum! You are right"—and then to cry. He put his hands over his eyes to hide them.

I said, "I have a car here. If the lieutenant permits, you needn't wait."

"Emil is wounded in the foot."

"We can take him with us."

"I don't want to be separated from them now. Who are you? Oh, of course, I know you. My mind's confused."

"The two of you need a doctor. There's no point in waiting here till tomorrow. Are you expecting anyone else to come across?" I was thinking of Jones.

"No, there's no one else."

I tried to remember how many had come up the road. "All the rest are dead?" I asked.

"All dead."

I made the two men as comfortable as I could in the jeep, and the fugitives stood and watched with pieces of bread in their hands. There were six of them, and Joseph lying dead on a stretcher in the shade. They had the dazed look of men who have narrowly escaped from a forest-fire. We drove away, two men waved, the others munched their bread.

I said to Philipot, "And Jones—is he dead?"

"By this time."

"Was he wounded?"

"No, but his feet gave out."

I had to drag the information out of him. I thought at first that he wanted to forget, but he was just preoccupied. I said, "Was he all that you hoped?"

"He was a wonderful man. With him we began to learn, but he didn't have enough time. The men loved him. He made them laugh."

"But he spoke no Creole."

"He did not need words. How many men are there in this lunatic-asylum?"

"About twenty. All those you were looking for."

"When we can get arms again, we will go back."

I said to comfort him, "Of course."

"I would like to find his body. I would like him to have a

proper grave. I'm going to put up a stone where we crossed the frontier, and one day when Papa Doc is dead, we shall put a similar stone at the spot where he died. It will be a place of pilgrimage. I shall get the British ambassador, perhaps a member of the Royal Family ..."

"I hope Papa Doc doesn't outlive us all." We turned out of Elias Pinas on to the good road for San Juan. I said, "So after all he proved that he could do it."

"Do what?"

"Lead a commando."

"He had proved that against the Japanese."

"Yes. I had forgotten."

"He was a cunning man. You know how he deceived Papa Doc?"

"Yes."

"Do you know that he could smell water a long way off?"

"He really could?"

"Of course, but, as it happened, water was not a thing we ever lacked."

"Was he a good shot?"

"Our weapons were so old, so out of date. I had to teach him. He was not a good shot, he went through Burma with a walking stick, he told me, but he knew how to lead."

"On his flat feet. How did the end come?"

"We came up to the border to find the others, and we were ambushed. It was not his fault. Two men were killed. Joseph was badly hurt. There was nothing to do but escape. We could not go fast because of Joseph. He died coming down the last ravine."

"And Jones?"

"He could hardly move because of his feet. He found what he called a good place. He said he'd keep the soldiers off till we had time to reach the road—none of them was anxious to risk himself very close. He said he would follow slowly, but I knew he could never come."

"Why?"

"He told me once that there was no room for him outside of Haiti."

"I wonder what he meant."

"He meant his heart was there."

I thought of the captain's cable from the office in Philadelphia and the message that the chargé had received. There was more in his past than a cocktail-shaker stolen from Asprey's, that was certain.

Philipot said, "I had grown to love him. I would like to write about him to the Queen of England . . ."

4

They held a Mass for Joseph and the other dead men (all three were Catholics), and Jones, whose beliefs were not known, was included out of courtesy. I went to the small Franciscan church in a side-street with Mr. and Mrs. Smith. It was a tiny congregation. One felt surrounded by the indifference of the world outside Haiti. Philipot led in the small company from the lunatic-asylum, and at the last moment Martha entered with Angel at her side. A Haitian refugee-priest said the Mass, and of course Mr. Fernandez was there—he looked professional and accustomed to such occasions.

Angel behaved well, and he seemed to be thinner than I remembered him. I wondered why in the past I had found him so detestable, and I wondered, too, looking at Martha two paces in front, why our semi-attached life had been so important. It seemed to belong now exclusively to Port-au-Prince, to the darkness and the terror of the curfew, to the telephones that didn't work, to the Tontons Macoute in their dark glasses, to violence, injustice, and torture. Like some wines our love could neither mature nor travel.

The priest was a young man of Philipot's age with the light skin of a *métis*. He preached a very short sermon on some words of Saint Thomas the Apostle: "Let us go up to Jerusalem and die with him." He said, "The Church is in the world, it is part of the suffering in the world, and though Christ condemned the disciple who struck off the ear of the high priest's servant, our hearts go out in sympathy to all who are moved to violence by the suffering of others. The Church condemns violence, but it condemn indifference more harshly. Violence can be the expression of love, indifference never. One is an imperfection of charity, the other the perfection of egoism. In the days of fear, doubt, and confusion, the simplicity and loyalty of one apostle advocated a political solution. He was wrong, but I would rather be wrong with Saint Thomas than right with the cold and the craven. Let us go up to Jerusalem and die with him."

Mr. Smith shook his head sorrowfully; it was not a sermon which appealed to him. There was in it too much of the acidity of human passion.

I watched Philipot go up to the altar-rail to receive communion, followed by most of his little band. I wondered whether they had confessed their sins of violence to the priest; I doubted whether he had required of them a firm purpose of amendment. After Mass I found myself standing beside Martha and the child. I noticed that Angel had been crying. "He loved Jones," Martha said. She took me by the hand and led me into a side-chapel: we were alone with a hideous statue of Saint Clare. She said, "I have bad news for you."

"I know already. Luis has been transferred to Lima."

"Is that really such bad news? We had reached an end, hadn't we, you and I?"

"Had we? Jones is dead."

"He mattered more to Angel than to me. You made me angry that last night. If it hadn't been Jones you worried about it would have been someone else. You were looking for a way to finish. I never slept with Jones. You've got to believe that. I loved him—but in quite a different way."

"Yes. I can believe you now."

"But you wouldn't have believed me then."

The fact that after all she had been faithful to me was ironic, but it seemed singularly unimportant now. I almost wished that Jones had had his "fun." "What *is* your bad news?"

"Doctor Magiot is dead."

I never knew the day when my father died, if he had died, so that I experienced for the first time the sense of sudden separation from someone on whom as a last resort I could depend. "How did it happen?"

"The official version is he was killed resisting arrest. They accused him of being an agent of Castro's, a Communist."

"He was a Communist certainly, but I'm pretty sure he was no one's agent."

"The true story is that they sent a peasant to his door asking him to come and help a sick child. He came out on to the path and the Tontons Macoute shot him down from a car. There were witnesses. They killed the peasant too, but that was probably not intended."

"It had to happen. Papa Doc is a bulwark against communism.

"Where are you staying?"

I told her the name of the small hotel in the city. "Shall I come and see you?" she asked. "I can this afternoon. Angel has friends."

"If you really want to."

"I leave for Lima tomorrow."

"If I were you," I told her, "I know that I wouldn't come."

"Will you write and tell me how things go with you?"

"Of course."

I sat in the hotel through the whole afternoon in case she came, but I was glad she stayed away. I remembered how twice before our love-making had been disturbed by the dead—first Marcel and then the *ancien ministre.* Now it was Doctor Magiot who had joined the dignified and disciplined ranks; they rebuked our levity.

In the evening I had dinner with the Smiths and Mr. Fernandez—Mrs. Smith acted as my interpreter, she had learnt enough Spanish for that, but Mr. Fernandez too was able to talk a little. It was agreed I should become a junior partner in the Fernandez business. I was to deal with the French and the Anglo-Saxon bereaved, and we were both promised an interest in Mr. Smith's vegetarian centre when it was established. Mr. Smith thought it only fair, since our business might be adversely affected by the success of vegetarianism. Perhaps the centre would really have been established if violence had not come in turn a few months later to Santo Domingo—violence which brought a measure of prosperity to Mr. Fernandez and myself, though as usual in such cases the dead mainly belonged to Mr. Fernandez' side of the business. Coloured people get killed more easily than Anglo-Saxons.

That night when I went back to my hotel-room I found a letter on my pillow—a letter from the dead. I never learned who had brought it. The clerk could tell me nothing. The letter was not signed, but the writing was unmistakably Doctor Magiot's.

"Dear friend," I read, "I write to you because I loved your mother and in these last hours I want to communicate with her son. My hours are limited: I expect any moment that knock upon the door. They can hardly ring the bell, for the electricity as usual is off. The American ambassador is about to come back and Baron Samedi will surely pay a little tribute in return. It happens like that all over the world. A few Communists can always be found, like Jews and Catholics. Chiang Kai-shek, the heroic defender of Formosa, fed us, you remember, into the boilers of railway-engines. God knows for what medical research Papa Doc may find me useful. I only ask you to remember *ce si gros neg*. Do you remember that evening when Mrs. Smith accused me of being a Marxist? Accused is too strong a word. She is a kind woman who hates injustice. Yet I have grown to dislike the word "Marxist." It is used so often to describe only a particular economic plan. I believe of course in that economic plan—in certain cases and in certain times, here in Haiti, in Cuba, in Vietnam, in India. But Communism, my friend, is more than Marxism, just as Catholicism—remember I was born a Catholic too—is more than the Roman Curia. There is a *mystique* as well as a *politique*. We are humanists, you and I. You won't admit it perhaps, but you are the son of your mother and you once took that dangerous journey which we all have to take before the end. Catholics and Communists have committed great crimes, but at least they have not stood aside, like an established society, and been indifferent. I would rather have blood on my hands than water like Pilate. I know you and love you well, and I am writing this letter with some care because it may be the last chance I have of communicating with you. It may never reach you, but I am sending it by what I believe to be a safe hand—though there is no guarantee of that in the wild world we live in now (I do not mean my poor insignificant little Haiti). I implore you—a knock on the door may not allow me to finish this sentence, so take it as the last request of a dying man—if you have abandoned one faith, do not abandon all faith. There is always an alternative to the faith we lose. Or is it the same faith under another mask?"

I remembered Martha saying, "You are a *prêtre manqué*." How strangely one must appear to other people. I had left involvement behind me, I was certain, in the College of the Visitation: I had dropped it like the roulette-token in the offertory. I had felt myself not merely incapable of love—many are incapable of that—but even of guilt. There were no heights and no abysses in my world—I saw myself on a great plain, walking and walking on the interminable flats. Once I might have taken a different direction, but it was too late now. When I was a boy the fathers of the Visitation had told me that one test of a belief was this: that a man was ready to die for it. So Doctor Magiot thought too, but for what belief did Jones die?

Perhaps, under the circumstances, it was only natural that I dreamt of Jones. He lay among the dry rocks on the flat plain beside me and he said, "Don't ask me to find water. I can't. I'm tired, Brown, tired. After the seven hundredth performance I sometimes dry up on my lines—and I've only two lines."

I said to him, "Why are you dying, Jones?"

"It's in my part, old man, it's in my part. But I've got this comic line—you should hear the whole theatre laugh when I say it. The ladies in particular."

"What is it?"

"That's the trouble. I've forgotten it."

"Jones, you must remember."

"I've got it now. I have to say—just look at these bloody rocks—'This is a good place,' and everyone laughs till the tears come. Then you say, 'To hold the bastards up?' and I reply, 'I didn't mean that.' "

The ringing of the telephone woke me—I had overslept. The call came, so far as I could make out, from Mr. Fernandez, who was summoning me to my first assignment.